GOODBYE BAY

ALSO BY JENNIFER RAHIM

Fiction
Songster
Curfew Chronicles

Poetry
Mothers are not the Only Linguists
Between the Fence and the Forest
Approaching Sabbaths
Ground Level
Sanctuaries of Invention

PUBLISHER'S NOTE

When I did a final reading of this book before going to press, I was struck by the fact that I'd missed so much of the significance of the sequence of allusions to popular calypsos of the period in which *Goodbye Bay* is set, particularly when I did a little research of my own and consulted some real calypso experts. I suspected that non-Trinidadians or even young Trinidadians might also miss out on what was going on – as a consequence of the narrator's declared intention of telling her story but not explaining because that kills a story. I'm sure Jennifer Rahim would have objected to any apparatus of notes within the book, and I would have agreed with her, but as a gesture of respect and admiration, I wrote a short essay that explores these calypso allusions, which can be found on the Peepal Tree website at:
https://www.peepaltreepress.com/blog/whappen/calypsos-allusion-and-not-explaining-jennifer-rahims-goodbye-bay
It can also be found to print at bit.ly/GoodbyeBay

Jeremy Poynting

JENNIFER RAHIM

GOODBYE BAY

PEEPAL TREE

First published in Great Britain in 2023
Peepal Tree Press Ltd
17 King's Avenue
Leeds LS6 1QS
England

© 2023 The estate of Jennifer Rahim

ISBN13: 9781845235390

All rights reserved
No part of this publication may be
reproduced or transmitted in any form
without permission

Macaima and environs are fictional places
imagined to be on the island of Trinidad;
so too are all characters, incidents and references.

CONTENTS

1.	An Arrival	7
2.	A Name. A Place	16
3.	A Shadow on the Trace	21
4.	Looking Around	30
5.	A White Envelope	42
6.	A Case of Fleas	49
7.	Look Trouble	56
8.	Brenda's Battle	64
9.	Bones	71
10.	A Golden Thread	80
11.	Equal Place	87
12.	Same Rider	94
13.	Face the People	99
14.	Writing on the Road	109
15.	A Return	119
16.	Monday's Child	128
17.	Storm Warning	136
18.	Under God Armpit	140
19.	Revelations	144
20.	A Woman in the Room	151
21.	Inside	164
22.	A Certain Kinda Miracle	170
23.	Ritual	176
24.	The Stage Comes Down	184
25.	A Departure	191
26.	… For the Sake of Love	201
27.	No Quiet Revolution	211
28.	Warnings	219
29.	Dog Star	225
30.	To Play-A-Mas	233
31.	A Request	240
32.	Maria's Parang	250
33	Thanksgiving	257
34.	Beginning again…	263

The common end of all narrative, nay of all poems is to convert a series into a whole: to make those events which in real or imagined History move in a strait Line, assume to our Understandings a Circular motion – the snake with its Tail in its Mouth.
— S.T. Coleridge

…every day / something has tried to kill me / and has failed.
— Lucille Clifton

CHAPTER 1 – AN ARRIVAL

I arrived in Macaima in September, 1963. Petit Careme season. The island was one year a nation, free to practice what it meant to have a flag to hoist and an anthem to sing. We had a prime minister, a government sitting inside the Red House; our Governor General became a citizen. That year, too, we had retrenchment in the oil sector and disgruntled sugar workers triggered a series of union-led strikes not seen since the Water Riots. The PM, in an effort to take control, ordered a Commission of Inquiry to sniff out subversion in the ranks of the trade union movement. That September, four girls died in the bombing of a Baptist church in Birmingham, Alabama, and hurricane Flora mashed up Tobago. In October, Mandela went on trial in South Africa; Cuba was in the midst of the missile crisis; nine Vietnamese monks were killed for flying their Buddhist flag; Martin Luther King delivered his *I Have a Dream* speech at the Lincoln Memorial; John F. Kennedy was assassinated; C.L.R. James published *Beyond a Boundary*; the Mighty Sparrow was crowned king of Carnival with "Dan is de Man"; the Beatles and Doris Troy had number one hits with "Love Me Do" and "Just One Look"; Elizabeth Taylor starred in *Cleopatra*; a woman was arrested and released without charge for selling souse and black pudding on a pavement in San Fernando; and a man was murdered on his hospital bed.

It was Sunday, midmorning. The village was deserted. I had no clue what I was coming to, but Macaima was where I had landed the job as temporary postmistress. People from town would be quick to ask: *Macaima, where on earth is that? No place on this island call by that name.* Maybe so, but I was there. See me, Annabelle

Bridgemohan, who had spent all my life in bright-lights Port of Spain, waiting on a junction for a Mr Elton, whom I had never met but who had promised to get me settled in the rental where I would spend the agreed-upon year.

I had done a three-year stint at the Port of Spain head office, though it seemed like an age. I needed more than a change of scenery or pace; whether Macaima would give it I hadn't a clue. *Life is a decision to live* my mother said to me when I told her I had accepted the Macaima post. She collected maxims like that. Maybe she had discovered what they meant. I did not want to live her life. When I landed the job at head office, the first thing I did was to rent a one-bedroom apartment on the edge of the city; small, but it was my space.

Until my arrival on Macaima Junction with nothing but my two suitcases, I hadn't realised that those words were still mine to learn. I was twenty-four and adrift. My relationship with my boyfriend Miles had come to a painful end; he had become increasingly bitter about my decision to end things between us and what he considered my unforgivable crime in choosing not to have our baby; my friend Thea had left the island for graduate school in the States and I could no longer put up with the conspiratorial climate in the office as management tried to fend off unionisation with divide and rule tactics. When I arrived in Macaima, I felt no more real than a ghost left over from another life.

★

Neville, the driver I had hired for the trip, pulled up alongside a shop on the Macaima junction and parked under its eave to escape the sun. He stretched in his seat, pushing against the backrest so much that I had to shift my legs sideways. He glanced back with slight amusement, his arm extended along the backrest.

– Miss, yuh sure is here you suppose to wait for… What he name again?

– Mr Elton. Yes. He said the shop on the junction. So I guess this is it.

– Well it look like he forget. This place deader than midnight grave.

– Give him a few minutes more. He said he would be here.

The repeat was more for my benefit than Neville's. He looked doubtfully at the empty road ahead and then at me.

– Okay, but I have to head back.

I sighed.

– Doh stress. I operate professional. I not going to leave you here stranded. Where is here again?

He didn't wait for an answer and seemed happy to fiddle with his radio. Static crackled. It was not long before he gave up and dozed off. With nothing else to do but wait, I tried to map Macaima's layout from what I could see. The junction was not a full crossroads, but a Y, formed by the arm of the road that broke off from the main road and travelled up into the hills. It was obviously the hub around which everything was arranged: shop, hardware, warden's office, post office, police station, and school – all sporting weather-beaten string pennants in the national colours, leftovers from the Independence Day celebrations. Everything looked, as you'd expect, closed for the day, including *Johnny's Shop and Bar.* The signage was sprawled across wooden, double doors and competed for visibility with all manner of advertisements: Coca-Cola, Guinness, Bata, Nestlé's Sweetened Condensed Milk, Trinidad Orange Juice, Holiday Foods, Solo – so the shop name could only be read when the doors were closed. Maybe it didn't matter. Competition can't have been a concern.

Everywhere burst with the verdant green of the wet season. Dog-bark and cockcrow, a ground dove's mourning call, tree-speak, river and sea-wash produced the sense of being looked at and listened to. I focused on the deserted road ahead, drawn to the point of light at the road's turn, where it disappeared. From the distance of the shop, you couldn't be sure whether the road curved inland and continued on or came to an abrupt end. At that point, the sky brightened so intensely it both attracted and disturbed the eye. The village was coastal and its elevation drew the eyes to the sea's expanse, a borderless zone that gave the illusion that the land was continuous with sky.

I did not see when the man appeared at the junction. He leaned against the dazzle of galvanized sheets that partitioned a gateway at the side of the shop, apparently waiting for something or someone. It was not long before I discovered what: a package passed through a square opening cut into the sheeting. The man put some bills into the hand of whoever had served him and said something as he stuffed what looked like a flask wrapped in newspaper into his back pocket. The exchange awakened Neville, who assessed the scene from his rearview mirror and slapped the dashboard knowingly.

– Big Sunday, but he too thirsty to wait!

Neville turned so that he could face me with that slight glow of amusement on his face I had come to recognise. He tapped his wristwatch. Time was up. The face of the shiny silver Timex with a black band was gently rubbed clean on the sleeve of a cotton shirt, densely populated with colourful parrots. Along with his black slacks, it was no doubt his self-prescribed uniform. I had learnt, on the way in, that he also worked the airport. Money was good driving tourists to and from their hotels for greens.

– Time to head out, Miss. I on the clock.

I looked about the junction. The man who had made the purchase was casually looking our way.

– Is not my business, Miss, but I hope yuh didn't come quite here to take flambeau to see in daylight what already in plain sight.

He grinned sheepishly.

– Why would you say that? You don't know a thing about me.

– Is only joke I joking.

Neville shook his head and focused all his attention on wiping, yet again, the Morris's already immaculate dashboard. I had overreacted, but I didn't want to give him the impression that he could voice his assumptions and opinions without rein. One thing I had learnt from Thea was to draw the line when it came to what she called *protecting the sanctity of your soul case*. And she was right. I second guessed all my gut reactions – a symptom, she joked, of unclear politics. Already I missed her, but the plans she had for her life meant leaving the island to further her studies; and I had been, at the time, committed to my relationship with Miles.

The man who had been at the galvanized gate was now perched dangerously on a broken chair he had propped up against the shop, making himself a brazen spectator of our waiting. Neville was growing restless. The plush crimson fabric of the seat-cover, which had irritated my legs and arms for the entire journey, was fast becoming intolerable. I shifted to the opposite side of the car. Neville noticed and ventured another more cautious question.

– You want me to ask if he know about your concern?

He indicated the man on the chair. I looked at the man, now clouded in exhaled smoke.

– I sure Mr Elton will be here.

Neville checked his watch. I was pushing my luck but I had picked up that Neville was not unreasonable.

– Okay, but five minutes is all I have.

★

Punctuality was important to Neville's service. His newspaper ad had offered in bold type: **Prompt, Reliable Transport. Any Place. Any Time**. As promised, he arrived exactly at ten o'clock and parked his black Morris at the front gate. When I emerged from the house and shut the door behind me, I could see his curiosity piqued as he moved briskly to relieve me of my luggage, making sure that I was well settled into the backseat before taking his place at the wheel. He glanced at the front door expectantly and then back at me.

– Like yuh travelling solo, Miss?

I nodded. He bounced the starter and then turned to fix his gaze on me as if to be sure I was committed to my departure. I focused on the road ahead and he followed my lead, adjusting himself in his seat before manoeuvring the car onto the street. We drove towards the arc of the Queens Park Savannah. Traffic was Sunday morning easy. There were a few joggers and strollers. Most people were probably in their houses, post-church, post-market. Maybe they were reading newspapers, preparing for the midday meal, packing a car for the beach.

We passed the line of mansions, the Botanical Gardens, then the Governor General's house where pennants in the national colours flapped in the breeze. Later that evening crowds would gather for the special independence celebration concert. Maybe Miles, Yolanda, James and the rest of the gang from the office would be there. My stomach had cramped as Neville negotiated the roundabout to the Lady Young Road and climbed the mountain through Morvant after passing the spot called *the lookout*.

Miles had once parked there to show me the city at night. It was breathtaking – the pulsing lights, the silver platter of the Gulf where ships from all over the globe sat waiting their turn to offload at the port. I knew so little of the world, those places that the island was connected to by years and years of trade, and how trade was what began us as a place.

As we travelled south, the realisation that I was shifting worlds sank in. I had left nothing behind but the empty rooms where I had lived for the last three years; all my ghosts were with me. Macaima was the future, or so I tried to reassure myself. Mrs Bailey from Appointments had handled my transfer and provided what she could as a general guide to the village. She had never been there herself but was certain that we would find it with little trouble. The village was on the southern coast, closer to the eastern peninsula, but had to be reached from the western end. On the eastern side, the coastal road through Mayaro and Guaya came to an abrupt end long before it reached Macaima, so the only access by car was from the west. Her help for getting me settled there included making phone contact with this Mr Elton. He was a friend of a friend who would be able to assist me with a decent rental for the year. She was right. Mr Elton, who was the warden in the district, was more than willing to help and had promised to meet me at the junction on the day of my arrival.

The trip to Macaima was a welcome challenge to Neville and, although it was his first time there, he didn't seem to need directions. He drove instinctively, making good time by first heading south towards San Fernando, then cutting through Ste Madeleine and Princes Town, not seeming to mind the winding roads, the potholes and the endless terrain of green, broken only by a few villages and scattered farms. He talked with enthusiasm about cricket, politics, religion; he whistled plaintive songs I could not name – or listened to the radio, upping the volume whenever a calypso aired.

Neville needed no audience. His own enthusiasm was entertainment and affirmation enough. I didn't mind. He kept my thoughts at bay. As we were breezing through deep country, and the road stretched on and on, he adjusted his rearview mirror so that I was in full focus. He had a question:

– Miss, who yuh running from? I go come myself and brace him. No joke!

He posed so playfully and so poignantly that a laugh burst from me. He winked knowingly into his rearview, and with no more than a breath, moved on share that his father used to help prepare the pitch at the Oval, and that he could still get him a free pass to any match.

– I know all-dem fellas: Sobers, Worrell, Kanhai… Nevo is how they call me.

I let him run on as he skipped through anecdotes that included his last daughter, Ria. He told with unrestrained pride how she loved water and that he was teaching her to swim.

– She is a little fish. Smart too bad!

He explained, too, with enough detail to wake up hunger, the correct way to cook curry duck.

– Plenty people make mistake and think coconut milk or chadon beni is my secret ingredient. All dem thing important, but that is not it. Is not even pepper – though scotch bonnet is essential. How to cook a good curry duck is to slow-stew yuh pot. If yuh have to add water, use only spring. Fresh. Nothing else.

He glanced back.

– Guess where I learn that from?

He didn't need a response.

– River lime.

He laughed good-naturedly, enjoying his own narration, and reached into the glove compartment. That was the first appearance of the neatly folded orange dust-cloth, which he slid almost lovingly along the already oiled dashboard.

– I bet you cyah guess why my car so nice-an-shiny?

Before providing his answer, he worked his way with a single, uninterrupted swipe from his side to the passenger's, following the contours of the surface, then folded the cloth and put it away.

– River water. No chlorine to leave spot on yuh vehicle. Now listen to this one. Is good advice. Drink cocoa tea, pure ground when nighttime come. That good for any heart condition and yuh sleep like baby.

His revelations, I felt, was his way of saying his place had taught him what he needed to know.

★

When my five minutes grace was up, Neville again indicated that he was ready to leave. We both knew that his remark about my being forgotten by Mr Elton had unmasked my earlier efforts to sidestep his questions about my move to Macaima. He sighed deeply and scanned the junction once more.

– Miss, I going to have to leave you here.

I got out of the car, perhaps too abruptly. He had been more than generous with his time but I was anxious about being left alone. He went to the rear and removed my luggage from the trunk. The lid held shut after two forceful slams. He noticed that I had jumped at the noise.

– Lock problems.

I managed a smile as he deposited the suitcases close to where I stood.

– I have to make tracks – wedding in Carapichaima. I driving for some aunties and I done get warn not to be late. I drive them maticoor night, too. They not easy. Yuh ever went – maticoor?

– No, I haven't.

He feigned disbelief.

– Nah, Miss. Bacchanal fuh so! Yuh should go one. It guarantee to relax yuh stress – so I hear. Anyway, Miss, I gone. Things go work out.

He cleared his throat.

– Yes, they will, Neville. Safe trip back.

He hopped into the driver's seat.

– Call me whenever yuh ready to leave inside here. I go be on time, and on spot.

To the man seated on the broken chair, he hailed jovially:

– Soldier, watch-out for d-lady. She waiting on somebody.

The man saluted and the radio in the Morris, which had lost and regained the station's signal countless times on the way in, suddenly came alive. Neville upped the volume. The speakers blasted – *Dr. Kitch, dis is terrible...* He howled with delight.

– Oh LAARD! *Dat* is tune!

– Play it Mr Dri-VA. Play I-T.

Neville complied. The request came from a woman who had entered the junction balancing a heavy load on her head. She carried herself with a straight back, her neck long and perfectly aligned, and even in clumsy tall tops she walked with sass, moving easily into a rhythmic chip, waist turning, shoulders moving as she went on her way, but not before her comeback:

– Bring it Dr Kitch. I more than A-ble!

Neville bawled again and made a perfect U-turn along the road that had brought us into the village, leaving me at the junction with the lyrics of "The Needle" playing on.

CHAPTER 2 – A NAME, A PLACE

The strangeness of the place intensified as the car disappeared. I was alone and conscious of being quietly observed by the man seated on the chair. I was wondering what I could do apart from asking this stranger for help, when a question shot at me.
– You Miss Bridgemohan?
– Who wants to know?
– Warden send me.
– Oh, you mean Mr Elton. Why didn't you say so?
– I see you in conversation with yuh mister. I know my manners. Elton busy so I here to settle you.

The mention of Elton's name came as such a relief, I let his presumption pass about my relationship to Neville. In one motion, he sprang to his feet. Released of his weight, the chair landed lopsided.
– Franco is d-name.

His manner was abrupt, though he touched the rim of a fedora that was a sun-bleached shade of sand.
– We going down so to Beach Trace. Not too far from here.

He gestured vaguely in a direction beyond the shop, along the road that disappeared at the bend. With his still-wrapped purchase safely tucked into his back pocket, he eyed my bags.
– Yuh travel light, Miss Bri.
– Call me Miss Bridgemohan, thank you.

His face grew stern. Eyes steeled.
– No problem.

I could see he was assessing me in the pause he allowed himself.
– No offence intend.

I did not miss his tone of exaggerated deference that told me my reaction had amused more than unsettled him.

– None taken.

– OK. Is jus bad habit we have in here. Quick tuh put name on people or shorten what is theirs. Like Franco is not my name. Franklyn is how I christen, but people find I talk my mind straight. Here in Macaima, we not so particular.

– I think names are important. That is all.

– Yuh father must be proud of he name for you to want to hold it up.

– It's my mother's name.

– Oh-ho. Look at that. Then let we go, Miss Bridgemohan.

– Sure. Lead on, Mr Franco.

Without another word he walked east, occupying the middle of the road, my suitcases higher and lower on each side, like unequal scales. I followed disconsolately, disappointed that Mr Elton had not kept his word, or had felt that sending Franco in his stead was as good as keeping it. The hot asphalt sank under my feet with every step.

It was not the best of beginnings, but I consoled myself with the thought that the year would soon be over. I was to replace a Mrs Gomez who had fallen seriously ill and succumbed rather suddenly. The job, though, had come just when I needed it. I had not as yet figured out my path, but the idea of spending my days sidestepping Miles in the office – along with the soured relationship between staff and management – was spur enough to leave. I knew, too, that office gossip travelled quickly. So it was good that the vacancy meant beginning right away. One year was the plan. I would pick up my life after that.

At first Franco wasn't disposed to talk. He seemed blunt, almost indifferent to my questions about where I was to stay and his relationship to the warden. I tried to shift his mood by asking questions about the village. He relaxed enough to point out that Macaima was much more than one village. What I had seen at the junction was merely a gathering point. The hinterlands were more populated because of the cocoa estates. He did admit, but without explanation, that people were leaving the interior, gravitating towards the main road or moving out of the district to pursue different kinds of work. When I asked why, he grunted as though I had asked the obvious. Cocoa was in decline.

The district, he said, comprised Railway, at its entrance on the western end, and Salvador somewhere on the northern face of Macaima's mountains. He pointed out the main buildings, including the post office, which I had already spotted, but added a few interesting details. The modest wooden structure had been a private dwelling, then set up as an independent enterprise, not run from someone's house or shop as in most country towns. It sported the familiar French-style hip-and-gable roof which extended to cover a walkway to a flight of about six steps. The eaves were trimmed with gingerbread lattice work. What used to be an open veranda had been partially enclosed and glass-louvred windows had probably replaced wooden jalousies. It had been, Franco told me, the house of the original owner of the estate, Francisco De Valremy, before his grand manor had been built high up on estate lands.

The district had been a big producer of cocoa, and having a post office of its own was a sign of an importance now lost. The police station I had seen on the way in. The warden's office, a newer building, judging from its utilitarian design – a rectangular wooden structure with a gabled roof – faced the post office. Both buildings sat on the road that climbed gradually uphill. The sign said L'Avenir Road, although Franco called it Mountain Road. It was the main access to the estate which Franco pronounced *Ave-near*. I supposed he meant L'Avenir, the future. The translation came easily, thanks to Miss Allister, the French teacher at the convent school, where my mother had never tired of saying I was lucky to be, thanks to Mr Henderson's generosity. He was my mother's employer, for whom she worked as the live-in maid. We had our own place in the maid's quarters – an annex in their backyard.

I remembered how *ave* was a greeting that doubled as a welcome and a farewell. On the day of Miss Allister's departure, she had included that observation in her farewell speech to the class. She was saying goodbye to us but was herself being welcomed by the nuns. Maybe for her the move seemed a natural transition. We never saw her again but that was not because she had stayed cloistered in the convent that adjoined the school. We heard other things. She was sent on mission somewhere, and left the order to marry a parishioner. It was great gossip during lunchtime when we sat cross-legged on the cool terrazzo eating lunch. None of the sisters mentioned Miss Allister except Sister Thomas who, rather grudgingly, taught us Home Economics, irately thumping our backs for forgetting never to sprinkle cooked eggs, poached or otherwise, with salt and black pepper. For an entire term to Christmas, every mention of Miss Allister was a tangle of wonderment: *Imagine that! The woman get up and get.* We had a good laugh among ourselves that Miss Allister had decided she preferred her eggs garnished.

    I thought about this as I surveyed a building that Franco said was the *church-school*. The boys were housed in the front portion and the girls occupied the back. They all shared a common playground behind the school. On Sundays, the building apparently served as a chapel, a temporary arrangement that had become permanent. On the far side of the school, where the bush thickened as the road ascended, was a large but disused cocoa house. Beyond that structure, the road disappeared into the hinterlands where the cocoa estate lands were concentrated.

    Macaima's air spoke of nearby moving bodies of water. Although the river could not be seen, it could be heard behind the buildings on the western side of the road, tumbling down to the narrow strip of beach below. Franco didn't know the river's name, but said ole-time people called it *Wa-she*. He could say nothing of its meaning and didn't seem interested, other than to say that the river was the life blood of the estates around Macaima. The river emptied into Goodbye Bay. Los Valientes Bay was the official name but it had been dropped long ago by the villagers.

    After a fifteen-minute walk that seemed an eternity, we reached Beach Trace, which turned out to be Church Street, according to a worn sign obscured by a tangle of love vine. Most of the road's asphalt surface had disappeared, leaving a sloping track of compacted gravel. We passed the stone ruins of a church, partially hidden by overgrowth. Franco didn't give the structure so much as a glance, but its derelict condition explained the current church-school arrangement. He deposited my suitcases before the house that was to be my home for the year and beckoned me to follow him.

    He wanted me to see that the beach could be reached by the

footpath at the end of the trace. The plan had been to extend Macaima's main road to connect the south coast to the east coast, by way of Guaya, but that hadn't happened. Another river further along from Church Street cut across the road. A bridge was required and the foothills would have had to be cut through. As the district declined in importance, the plan was shelved.

Through the greenery that curtained the bay, I could see the ocean's silver eyes blinking as the breeze disturbed the leaves.

– How far is it?

– Maybe half-a-mile down that track. Since '33, when storm hit, we lose some coast.

– What storm?

– Hurricane. What age you have? You look like you born with Hitler war.

– Maybe I brought it on.

I thought the quip might help repair the tension between us. I had been unnecessarily defensive about my name. The idea engaged him more than I anticipated.

– Doh call bad on yuhself, Miss. Hitler war was pure wickedness. He is no company to keep! Anyhow '33 was a blight year. Sea come straight in like it take special aim for Beach Trace. Nature give account to nobody.

Apart from the remnants of the church, my rental was the only house on the road. Built to suggest rustic simplicity, the structure was elevated on pillars that were high enough to provide a clear view of the bay. It seemed to stand sentinel over the track that led down to the beach. Franco explained that the lumber used for the construction, mostly mora and teak, had been extracted from De Valremy's land. The lower floor was an open area, bordered by a low wall on the southern side – perhaps an incomplete project.

– Elton will check on you later; but before I head back, Miss Bridgemohan, take a little friendly advice.

– Sure.

– Ease yuhself. Doh look so frighten.

– Frightened – who me?

– Yeah. People go think yuh carrying guilt or yuh fraid to live.

I laughed, but without warning felt my stomach drop. Beach Trace vanished.

CHAPTER 3 – A SHADOW ON THE TRACE

Things are never quite what they seem. From my very first evening in Macaima, a meeting took place that to this day I cannot fully explain. After it, I had fallen into a heavy sleep. Time had slipped away. When I finally woke, the slow pulsing shadows of softening light, along with a cooling breeze perfumed with the tang of salt and musky earth, told me sunset was nearing. I lay riveted to a mattress, drifting in and out of sleep. I had never known such exhaustion, possibly the culmination of the last two months of decisions, ruptures, departures – loss. I had no recollection of how I had gotten onto the bed, or who had brought my suitcases into the house. I knew nothing past the fact that one minute I was standing on Beach Trace and the next moment I was no longer there.

Through the haze of a mosquito net, my eyes trailed the hypnotic to and fro of gauze curtains. Back and forth they sailed like delicate wings, or gently fanned mist. In the near distance, the broad swash of waves kept up a shuffling turnabout metre that held me on the threshold of consciousness. A voice intruded.

– Anybody home?

I strained after a note of recognition.

– You inside, Miss Bri?

A name finally emerged: Franco. I heard him moving about the yard, first along the side, then at the back of the house. Booted feet clobbered, disturbing what sounded like gravel strewn under the eaves. The property, I remembered, was not fenced. I held still. Wind rustled leaves. Water washed over the beach below. The silence told me that he, too, had paused, listening. There had been something unsettling about his manner, a confidence that verged on brashness, coupled with an appetite for provocation.

There was something more. Just under the surface, I had sensed an instinct for guardedness. Why the disregard he had shown for the derelict church, walking straight by the ruins as though the lot were empty? Surely the church was important to a place like Macaima? Was it just an innocent omission – a sign of familiarity? I sensed something more deliberate. He purposely did not take notice of the structure; he did not want to tell its story.

He was calling:

– Upstairs – anybody there? A body in yuh yard, Miss Bri.

Boots crunched as he moved to the front again. I managed to get myself into a seated position. The room tilted like sand in an hourglass. I stumbled barefooted towards the veranda, my limbs feeling bound by invisible cords.

– Ah-ha, I see you up-an-about, Miss Bri. I bet sea breeze make you sleep like baby. How yuh head?

A hand instinctively reached up to the sore spot at my right temple.

– Did I fall?

– You could say so. Coulda be worse.

– Must have been the heat.

– Could be. Big rain near, I sure.

The late afternoon sky was cloudless.

– Rain – really?

Franco ignored my question and went on to explain why he had returned to the house: to deliver a message on Mr Elton's behalf.

– Bossman say Monday morning he go check on you. Business keep him outside. De-*tained*.

He stretched out the last syllable until his mouth broadened to a grin. I tried to receive the news blankly, unwilling to show any sign of dashed expectations. But Franco clearly enjoyed having to relay his messages, and I sensed a dynamic that was interesting. Perhaps Mr Elton did have a legitimate emergency that needed his attention. I was certainly not a priority. Yet the main part of his promise had been honoured. The house was ideal. Even so, I was curious about the man that Franco seemed so eager to serve – and he felt obliged to say more about Mr Elton's absence.

– He tired-tuh-dead after d-service.

– Service – is he some kind of priest?

He paused, as if to savour my puzzlement, then moved on to other things. I guessed that this was his way of demonstrating that withholding information was a privilege he not only valued but enjoyed.

– As I say, Monday he going to catch up with you. I have something for you. D-lady send a parcel.

I was not sure whether he meant *his* lady or Mr Elton's, but assumed the former.

He handed over a canvas-handled bag and stepped back to observe my reaction. Carefully tucked under a warm kitchen towel was a flower-patterned enamel bowl. The aroma of cooked food greeted me. I was truly grateful. Some crackers and guava jam were all I had brought to tide me over until I got settled.

– Please be sure to relay my thanks.

– Look-an-see what inside.

In the enamel bowl was a neatly arranged meal of rice, a slice of macaroni pie, red beans, callaloo and stewed meats of some kind. The day's disappointments paled a little.

– That is curry-stew yard-fowl and gouti I hunt myself. Macaima is wilemeat country.

He beamed at his revelation and maybe saw my cringe.

– You have to have belly for hunting. Is not for everybody but when pot cook is another matter. Everybody eating.

He stared provocatively at the bowl.

– Maybe so. But is this hunting season? I read something a while ago about October to…

Franco had clearly anticipated a more enthusiastic response. A deep frown was etched on his brow as he jerked his head towards the lush mountains that climbed steadily from the coastal road.

– I know law pass, but plenty beast roam Macaima forest. Hunting season is any time in my book. I have my own law: I doh kill animal with young. Never once!

He spoke bluntly, but I felt compelled to hold my ground.

– Well, there must be a good reason for the law. The animals must suffer so much – being chased.

– Miss, animal hunt animal every day. Hunting is no different. Nothing rush my blood like when I track down dem beast.

– Being hunted by a human being is hardly the same as what animals do to survive in the wild, but I suppose, in one way or another, we each get a turn to know what it means to be both – hunter and hunted.

I wasn't sure exactly what I meant.

– You full with correction today, Miss Bridgemohan. If a time like you talk about ever reach, I going to have my gun ready. Survival, balance-a-nature, is bush law, and I doh see you objecting to eating what kill.

Maybe my question had come off as judgemental. I smiled and he saw my retreat and moved to claim the last word.

– Different strokes for different folks, right Miss Bridgemohan? So how yuh like d-place? I prepare it myself. Doh fraid to say your complaint. Me-an-Elton go back far. I could talk to him direct. His place fix with telephone.

I registered the prestige that went with the possession of a telephone here. I supposed only government offices and a few private residences enjoyed the privilege of having one. Franco was evidently nudging me to enquire further into his boss's whereabouts, but though my curiosity was stirred, I held back.

– Since you ask, the house is a little out of the way, don't you think? My only neighbour is that derelict church. What happened to it, anyway?

– Yuh find down here too lonely?

– I meant isolated, not lonely. They're not the same thing.

Something that bordered on a tease played in his smile. After all, I was a woman alone, a stranger taking up a job in a remote village. He must have thought me an oddity.

– Nobody will trouble you, Miss.

I tried another approach.

– So, does the Valremy family still own the house?

– Yes. Elton in direct contact with him. Thomas is boss now, but he doh come inside here too often. He in construction. Is new times. Cocoa days done.

So, Franco's real admiration was for this Thomas De Valremy. Mr Elton was only his surrogate. I wondered at his connection to the family. He needed no encouragement to continue.

– All these lands belong to De Valremy. Up Mountain Road and down to Salvador side is cocoa, coffee, plenty timber. My granpappy plant over fifty acres with crop; little good it did him.

– Why so?

– He make contract with De Valremy. Perez was his name – everybody know him.

– You mean your grandfather planted lands for a price?

He lifted his hat and scratched his head.

– That was how cocoa business went. He dead poor like church rat.

His voiced drifted away.

– Did De Valremy cheat him?

– I never claim so. All I say is he only had small change to show for all dem years he work. I build up my place on a little plot he leave when he pass. He was from Vene, and he meet up with De Valremy over by Cedros side. Was the time when Spanish start coming over to work cocoa lands.

– I suppose that was Thomas's grandfather.

– Yes, d-one-an-only Francisco.

He scoffed and spat.

– Was he also from Venezuela?

– Nah. He travel down from somewhere up-island and decide here is where to make his start. You could say that he catch scent of a future when he meet up with my granpappy. He teach De Valremy all he know about estate work.

Franco's eyes glazed over. He had made an unplanned detour and seemed to surrender to its current.

– From cane people out in Railway is where he find his lady.

– Your grandmother?

– Yes. Ten she make. My mother was lagniappe. Now she old, she make me see trouble. Sugar. Cataract. Blind like bat going on five years. She don't want to bathe or change clothes. She don't want priest or doctor, like she holding protest against this world.

– Blind – goodness! I hope she has someone to help her.

– Fourteen years she was when I born. I was first. She like to say I turn over a whole century. From day one, I was everybody salt-fish. People call me *Lil Cisco*.

A confusion of emotion swept over his face much too quickly for me to untangle its meaning. I caught, though, a shift from a proud facial uplift to the downturn of what seemed hurt. A story was in the transition and I instinctively reached for it.

– Why?

– Foolishness. Anyhow, change start when De Valremy get his marrid wife. He was smart and had brains to make money grow. French creole mostly own estate lands. He slip in with some Marseille people from over by Sando and reap big when Venes come to work; but all fall down when blight reach. Kill off everything.

– Maybe one day the crop will make a comeback?

His eyes brightened for a second before he spat hard and ground his spittle into the dust as one would a cigarette butt.

– So what happens on the estate now?

– Nothing much.

– Did the first De Valremy have only one son?

– Well, let me put it proper for you: he wasn't shy with skirt-tail.

He laughed heartily at what he considered his effort at tact but couldn't resist making himself plainer.

– Up to when he dead, he was troubling people girl-chirren.

If I recoiled, he didn't seem to notice.

– I meant did Francisco De Valremy have more children with the woman he married?

– Every one count.

– Of course. I was asking about the immediate family.

– He make Joseph with his church-wife, Marie. Joseph make Thomas. Second is Julien. He settle up in Canada. He doh set foot here again.

– How come?

– Life must be nice where he is. Like I say, Elton in control. Bossman say what he want done. Elton put everything in place.

– And you – what's your role?

His face hardened.

– I never work one day on Ave-near. Now Thomas say he done with estate. I glad too bad.

– Did Joseph have any siblings?

– Like I say, plenty could claim him as pappy, but I know for sure they never do right by all. Before he dead, first one he make inside here, he call a Judas.

– Why was that?

It was a puzzling back and forth between father and sons.

– I cut my own path. Estate wuk not for me.

– Really, why not?

– Scorpion. I get out from in there soon as I able.

He showed me his right shoulder. I saw nothing but understood that he meant it was the spot where he had been stung.

– Dry rafter is where they like to res. One night he drop down – and WHAM!

Like a ghost reaction his arm swung up and slapped his shoulder as though he had been freshly stung.

– Worse bite in this whole blasted world – excuse my French.

– Should I be worried – about scorpions?

– House-an-grounds clean out and spray good. I use diesel; but still watch out. I was sick fuh days from that one sting. Up to now I suffer from bad-bad headache. I stay far from forest. Everyday I tend my animals. Do my maintenance work. I have no complaint.

Franco took off and replaced his hat. I noticed the uneven line of perspiration that ringed the crown. The hat had evidently become part of his self-expression, like a language.

– No more bushlife for me.

– What about your hunting?

– That different.

He scratched his shoulder and looked away.

– Like I say, Miss Bridgemohan, any problem let me know. Elton will take care of everything. De Valremy trust him – hands down.

I asked nothing further, but saw that Franco was not ready to leave. He told me that my rental had once been used by the family as a holiday house, their getaway from L'Avenir. Now, only occasional friends from town and *foreign* made use of the place. The trace, he said, was once far busier than now.

– I suppose the church was in use back then too.

He eyed me uneasily, perhaps recognising I had picked up on his reticence about the building. Maybe not.

– Everybody come to hear Mass at *Our Lady of Victory*. From as far as Salvador. That was until storm mash it up.

We both looked towards the structure. Although blackened by sea blast, I could see the statue of the Virgin from where I stood. It remained surprisingly well preserved in what was left of the grotto.

– No joke, Miss Bri, nature is boss. Hurricane then witchbroom show De Valremy who stronger. Lands in here see plenty trouble. I live to see Ave-near come to nought. One time gov-ment send agriculture people to give cocoa estate injection, but it didn't take.

He laughed and swept off and replaced his hat, enjoying, I thought, his allusion to the calypso that Neville had left us with earlier that day. He went on side-glancing me; I pretended not to get the reference.

– So why wasn't the church repaired?

– Too much wrong in that foundation from day one.

– What do you mean?

– Older folks say a woman get rape over so.

He gestured to the church site.

– A setta-dem Carib-people from church-mission fight back, kill priest and then hightail. That happen long time back. Who didn't drown in Goodbye get send back to d-mission. Is better they dead.

– Why did they run this far east?

– Doh know. That is longtime history. Maybe soldier block off sea access over so.

He pointed southwest towards Cedros where the crossing was shorter.

– Some get trap inside Macaima. Nowhere to run. Anyway, big official decide to build church to mark the place. *Our Lady of Victory* is how they call it.

– It certainly wasn't a victory for those who ran.

A cough caught in his throat as though he realised, for the first time, the irony of the naming.

– Some see it different.

His tone was sharp. I didn't want to agitate him more by pushing the point further.

– Did anything happen, other than the storm?

He cast me a suspicious look.

– I mean to the church?

– Like I say, Elton will pass early Monday morning. A pleasant good night to you, Miss Bridgemohan. I have my animals to bring in.

★

Now that I have the time, I do a great deal of remembering of that first day.

The more I remember, the more light shines in, though memory is a tricky business. I can only tell it as I lived it on that first Sunday. I had watched Franco walk away up the darkening trace, and always wondered what *he* remembered of that evening. He had not gone far, for he must have seen me fall and returned to help me. True, it was almost dark. Beach Trace had no streetlights, but he must have seen the woman cross paths with him as he was leaving to pen his animals. I never put the question to him, but I often wondered whether he had seen the woman go right up to the grotto, put some flowers by the statue, then blow what looked like smoke into its face. Or had he passed her without noticing, in the way that happens when something becomes familiar or as indistinguishable as shadows?

The light wasn't good. Her head was covered with some sort of veil or mantilla so I couldn't see her face, but when she left the grotto – and this I will never forget – she paused on the far side of the road, turned towards me and said:

– Welcome, Miss Anna. Time finally reach to settle.

That was all. The voice was clear as day. My blood ran cold. I could offer no response. Who was she and what did she mean? More than that, she had used the name by which I was usually called – not Annabelle, but Anna. I didn't know the lady from Adam and I had never before set foot in Macaima. She moved away, lightly, like a shadow on the trace.

CHAPTER 4 – LOOKING AROUND

On Monday I rose early to watch the day begin from the veranda. At first, dawn eased awake, quietly shifting shades rising to soft yellow, until light speared out across the bay like the opening of shutters. The riptide became visible then. Waves, as if not satisfied with their arrival, reversed themselves to keep an appointment with an over there, before they returned to shore again. The waters of Goodbye Bay touched the South American mainland; towards their northeast was the Atlantic. You could say that Macaima had its eyes set on two bodies of water, two shores, at the same time. It neighboured a channel that funnelled an entire history into the island.

So many people cross your path, but few really stay with you, find a place in you. Thea was one. She was many things, including our in-house historian. Once she had joked that Columbus must have pissed himself when he saw land on the left and right of him, that day of his arrival. He was so desperate to prove himself right, he must have thought, *To hell with them! I find my China.* Discovery, she said, was always a misnomer. All anyone could hope for was to encounter what was already there. Otherwise, she said, we risk becoming trapped in misdirected narratives and the horrors suffered by the lost.

One day remains with me because we had been chatting during the lunch break, just days after the big Chaguaramas march when the chorus, *Uncle Sam, give we back we lan*, still echoed around the country. We had gone as a group to hear the speeches in the Square. The Premier was expected to speak. That was in '60 – April 22nd. Thea was from accounts. Yolanda and I worked the counter and Miles was in the sorting room. Miles called her a *highbrower*, but she wasn't like that at all. It was the first time we had met. That day she wore black, bell-bottom slacks and a loose, multicoloured kaftan-style blouse; her hair was like a full moon and two beautiful silver hoops hung from her ears – all against dress-code regulations. The Americans had to go home, the Premier had insisted, and the entire Square was one with that call. The war was long over and the military bases were no longer necessary. It was also about the inauguration of the West Indian Federation. Chaguaramas was to be its capital, so the march encompassed the future of the island and the region.

We had linked arms – Miles-Me-James-Yolanda-Hamid-Kimberly-Horace-Thea – marching in the rain, telling the Americans to take up their business and go home. We were telling England the same thing: *Give we back we lan'*. From Woodford Square to Chaguaramas, James-Yolanda-Horace-Me-Thea-Miles-Kimberly, all of us marching side by side. We were one body that day, connected to the ground beneath us. When the sun came out our bodies glistened like some marvellous wonder come up from the deep to breathe. After the march, splitting-up was a quiet sadness, the kind I had felt the previous year when, for the first time, I had played mas with George Bailey's *Relics of Egypt*. For two days I was Cleopatra, chipping royal behind *Invaders* steel band, with Miles, Horace and Yolanda. When the sun began to set in the Gulf and the band started to disperse, when every one was spent but happy, and carrying the conviction that *here was home in truth,* I had wanted to embrace the whole place, so instead I had hugged Miles, and he kissed me. After, we had danced in a circle, with Horace and Yolanda joining in, singing into the dusk: *Dis mas cyah done!* Now I know that sunsets can nest ironies.

At that April march in the rain, all of us were together again in the open street. That same year, we had played in *Ye Saga of Merrie England* just to so we could wine down on all that history. So when the march to Chag started to move through Port of Spain, we marched with what we had found together, thirsty for the transition that would confirm our right to determine our future, together.

In the weeks that followed, Thea spoke cautiously about where we were with what we sought, even as the raw promise of it had glowed as much in her as it did in the rest of us. She moved in political circles, we knew that much, and she would have been aware of the tensions that brewed beneath the surface of the day's protest. They would eventually destroy the dream, but in those post-march days, we rode a current of optimism. A lunchroom meetup began, almost spontaneously, to chat about politics, Federation, the Americans on the Base, independence, the unions. Sometimes tempers flared, but people listened to Thea, even if they disagreed with her. She had an unsettling way of stripping away the dross. Her resolve was that the Americans should go, but her argument, I thought at first, was ambivalent, until I grew to understand its core: *Yes, they must go, and yes this long England saga must end. For me a flag, when we get one, signals our presence and participation in this world of neighbours. This thing about you over there, I here; you this, I that, is secondary nonsense. Difference or nationality, call it what you want, is not a divider but a shape of the whole of who we must be, together.*

Maybe that was what she meant by home. The Americans had to leave to reset the terms of our relationships. Her hope was for the unification of the islands. No more small-island-big-island foolishness. The region would be one nation. It was a season of dreams and the woman could preach! The Chag march always returns to me. It had introduced me to who I was, and with so much else going on, I needed time to work it through. I owed that much to myself. Those early days in Macaima, I kept those thoughts at a distance, the way one returns to a treasure – captivated, allured even, but not at all sure about what should be done with it.

*

Having some time to spare that morning, I decided to explore the property before heading up to the post office. The De Valremies' vacation house was not large, but it had been carefully designed to make the best use of its space and surroundings. The interior was in perpetual shade because of the wooden finish, a tall gable with its rafters exposed and, of course, the deep veranda that bordered each side, except at the back of the house where the kitchen was located. A staircase allowed access to the backyard. There was only a latch to keep the door shut – clearly no fear of intruders. I asked Franco about putting in something more secure. After all I was alone on the trace. But Franco had insisted there was nothing to worry about.

I appreciated most that the space was uncluttered. Furnishings were bare essentials, which gave the rooms a pleasant airy, even austere feel. The house was not intended for long-term stay. Double doors and louvred windows opened onto the veranda. A framed picture of the Sacred Heart hung over the front entrance, the only decorative feature. That same sparsity marked the undercroft, though that space seemed unfinished. The floor was raw concrete; a crocus-bag hammock hung in the cooler northern section and there was a wooden table covered with a plastic tablecloth patterned with bunches of intensely purple grapes. Two benches stood on either side of the table. Brown stains on the untiled floor and wire hooks attached to the rafters suggested that produce had been stored there and left to ripen. All in all, the house had an air of intentional simplicity that counterpointed the fact that the De Valremy family was no doubt the wealthiest in the district.

I returned to the veranda to look at the surrounding area. There was nothing accidental about the house's construction. It was aligned so that it commanded a panoramic view of the bay and Beach Trace. Its structure, though, stood aslant in its plot, so I felt that in spite of the expansive view it offered of the bay, it mapped an incomplete story – the same way you can look at a photograph and find yourself straining to see what is off the edge of the picture. There was the story about what had happened on the trace and down at the bay that I wanted to ask more about. Perhaps Franco had told as much as he knew, but there were others and time enough to learn more.

I wished, though, that I had brought my camera with me instead of asking Yolanda to keep it safe until I returned to the city. The landscape was breathtaking and photographs have a way of revealing more about the truth of things. Maybe they press at the past more than we recognise. Not just the histories they conjure but what they hint at beyond their timeframes. They talk, Mr Cunningham had said. He was the instructor of the class Miles had encouraged me to join. I supposed Miles had noticed the interest I took in the stamp designs, especially those with local landscapes. We even collected stamps from earlier periods and had a good laugh at how representations called *First Boca* and *Queens Park Savannah* failed to capture the intensity of colour and the aliveness of the place. They were placid and pale landscapes that belonged to another climate.

Photography taught me about looking. So much was about light, perspective, angles – and that language seeped into our conversations. I practised with my Nikon SP, a neat rangefinder I had bought off the instructor. It had a versatile 50 mm lens and was a great camera for a beginner. Miles, though, wasn't convinced that he wanted to invest in a camera of his own. His father's Target Brownie, a box Kodak that used hard-to-find 620 black and white rolls, did the job and won him the nickname *Antique* from the group, a joke he liked. He never bothered to get an updated model.

On the journey back from shoots we talked about the attributes of different lenses, like the wide-angled and telescopic, which Mr Cunningham gave us opportunities to practice with. I enjoyed how they could be used to frame a shot, bring what is far near or pack more into a frame. In the end, though, I always preferred the 50 mm. It seemed closest to the normal eye, though I soon learned that what you saw and attempted to frame was never quite how the eventual picture turned out. My looking was one thing; the lens did its own revealing.

Miles had a deeper objection to using enhanced lenses. Both, he declared, facilitated the photographer's visual entitlement and represented a contrived vision of space. I had no problem with the optical illusion they afforded if it helped the viewer to see unconsidered relations among things. Miles wasn't sold for that very reason – too much information without well-defined boundaries. Such lenses were fine for aesthetic purposes, but the bottom line was that they toyed with the real. Maybe so, but I felt the camera wasn't simply a mirror. Even a 50 mm could be used to manipulate reality. I liked the idea that we could have another view of the world. He preferred things as he thought they should be.

Those months of learning photography had exposed our differences in a way neither of us had foreseen. Maybe we began to wonder what had drawn us together in the first place. Early on, he told me he had abandoned teacher training for a job in the mailroom as an affront to his parents' insistence that he find a "respectable" job. I had found his commitment to making his own way admirable, but what he thought was a capacity for rebellion was mostly grumbling directed at authority figures. I discovered they were not the same thing.

I had spent most of my life resisting my mother's vision of the world that circled her choice to stay appended to the Hendersons' household. When we moved into our own rented house after Mr Henderson, rather unexpectedly, resigned from his post to follow his wife back to England, my mother sulked for the old days, but we never spoke about the source of her grief. It never leaves me: that annex and the backyard of my childhood. I knew the number of footsteps between each fruit and flowering tree. I knew exactly where the sunspots were under the Julie mango and avocado trees. I knew how many of my giant steps it took to cross the yard to the landing that led to the kitchen of the big house. I could predict when the ants would begin their seasonal marches and where the yellow lilies would sprout after a heavy shower. I knew the times Mrs Henderson liked to come out to the gazebo to rock in her hammock.

I missed my mother, but needed to put space between us, though she held the answer to a question I had never put. In the mix of all that I had brought with me to Macaima, my mother and I were unfinished business. No light had been switched on to illuminate the shadow that hung between us. I hoped that Macaima would be the switch. I was setting out to make sense of the place. I did not know then that the place would make sense of me. The familiar wave of sadness I felt when my mother came to mind broke over me. I pushed it aside. There was work to be done.

I had no clear plan for my future but I knew I didn't want to settle for any life that boxed me in. I wanted to be far away from Miles, and in some impossible and impractical way, I also wanted to escape my mother. Thea, I had to reflect on. Maybe Goodbye Bay would be the portal.

★

De Valremy's house was a world on its own so it was almost

possible to forget about the junction, the village, and the estates in the interior. Though Beach Trace was always in view and, of course, the church, it was the bay that beckoned, its expanse and tireless churn. The house, I thought, gave the impression of having only a partial immersion in the place.

Not much thought had been given to the layout of the garden, with randomly placed hibiscus, oleander and croton shrubs. At the far boundary, but still in view of the house, a small concrete building sat beneath an unruly overhang of branches – perhaps it had been occupied by a caretaker. When I got closer, I saw that the padlock on the door hung like a gaping mouth. I released it from the clasp, pushed the door open and peered in. There was no electricity supply and with just one window on its northern side, the space did not receive much natural light. From the layer of dust that coated the bare floor, I could tell that the room had not been used for some time. Maybe it had left behind its original use and evolved into a storeroom for broken and discarded things. It had an aura of disregard, an untended sorrow. Cardboard boxes and pieces of furniture, including a pupil's desk, lay scattered about. When I ventured further in, I saw that a bunk bed was jammed against the wall so that when the door was open, it was screened from view. I caught sight of a massive spider's web suspended over the cot, its delicate curtain hanging suspended in space, threads glistening razor sharp when they caught the light. Its creator lurked at its centre, like the pupil of an eye. I decided to store my suitcase there, the one that had remained unopened since my arrival. It contained nothing that I immediately needed, only what I later realised I did not want to let go unremembered. I was certain that its contents would be undisturbed. I made a mental note to ask Franco about the key for the padlock.

When I set off for work and reached the main road, I took a moment to look out from the land's elevation. Except on the Beach Trace end where the sea had encroached, the village was considerably set back from the sea, tucked into the foothills of one of those three peaks that Columbus had supposedly sighted when his ship sailed into the channel between the island and the mainland. The three peaks were not visible unless you were out at sea, but they were there and Macaima was nestled in their shadow.

Everything comes to light in its own time, Thea would say. Her voice came to me in waves. Not by any rhythm that I could anticipate, it arrived unexpectedly, as if from nowhere, but making you think it has always been there, continuing a conversation that never feels intrusive for being so familiar.

When I reached Mountain Road, I ran into a Mrs Austin, who evidently already knew who I was.

– Lovely day for a fresh start, Miss Bridgemohan. I hope all's well with you.

She introduced herself as the wife of the school's principal and assistant to Mr Elton at the warden's office. I soon realised that along with Franco, she buffered the warden's unofficial absences. There couldn't be that much to do at the office, judging from the palpable sense of pause in a place that seemed a shell of its former self. Mrs Austin turned out to be a friend of a friend of Mrs Bailey's, the woman who had put me in touch with Mr Elton. A sharp inquisitiveness ignited her rather small eyes, which seemed to rarely blink, as if determined not to miss anything.

– I'm fine so far, thank you. Macaima is gorgeous.

– Glad to hear it. We have our advantages. I hope the house suits you.

– It's great. Feels like I'm on holiday. Thanks for asking.

– Maybe you need the break. Merrill told me the whole story.

She paused as if gauging my reaction. I said nothing, waiting for her to lead on.

– Anyway, she's on an extended stint in Tobago. A new grand arrived.

– I see. Well, I hope to meet Mr Elton soon – to say thanks for the arrangements.

– No luck in that department either. He's not in the village and may be away for some time.

– Oh?

– Yes, a troublesome situation turned up. He's a bit of a fixer, you know.

– I hope it's not too serious.

– Nothing to bother yourself with, Miss Bridgemohan. Macaima can be messy.

I took this as my cue to move on.

– Well, please extend my thanks to Mr Elton for the rental whenever he's back in the village.

– I'll be sure pass on your message. Elton is family, you know.

– Really?

– Everybody is family in Macaima.

The admission came a little stiffly.

– Anyhow, my dear, so glad you've settled in. You're in time for some major changes, according to the chatter. It scares me a little to think what may come with the development frenzy. We must be careful not to throw the baby out with the bathwater, if you know what I mean. Good day to you, Miss Bridgemohan.

She excused herself and headed towards Johnny's shop. With Merrill, Mrs Bailey's contact, away in Tobago, Mrs Austin was my sole connection with what I had left. Our exchange was pleasant enough but I couldn't help but feel that she wanted me to know she was well-informed and that I wasn't as much of an unknown stranger as I imagined myself to be. I told myself I had no interest in speculating about the story Mrs Bailey had passed on to this Merrill and then she to Mrs Austin. What Mrs Austin or Mrs Bailey thought about me mattered little. I cared more that Miles had spared me nothing in his reaction to my decision not to have our child. I had acted alone and acknowledged my responsibility in isolating him, but he wasn't satisfied. Blood, he said, was on my hands. Of one thing I was certain: although he was entitled to his anger, I wanted to be free of being constantly reminded of it and of the moral high ground on which he had perched himself. There was something more. I knew I had to figure out where Thea fitted into why I had chosen to end the relationship – if in fact she did.

★

Time didn't wait for me to ask Franco about the woman on Beach Trace. Macaima was an unfinished book and people brought me their chapters. Not all at once, but page by page, letter by letter, people gave whatever part they wanted to tell. You could say that a world came to meet me in that very first week. Spectral at the beginning, the way a place gradually takes form at dawn, showing in stages what is there to be seen and would have to be seen again and again. The post office provided a space for people to talk their stories. Or maybe I was the space, the outsider, and because I didn't know their backstories, people took the opportunity to tell their side, or create the self they felt they could live with – or wanted to find the courage to welcome. My own troubles were gladly pushed to the sidelines as new stories came my way. And they did, from the very first day.

It didn't surprise me when Franco arrived with news that Mr Elton would not be passing by that day. Mrs Austin had suggested as much, but I let Franco have his moment in the sun.

– Bossman send for him.

He spoke as though the identity of the person he called *bossman,* presumably Thomas De Valremy, was a shared familiarity.

– As light break, he head out. So it is sometimes; but he tell me make sure to give you his apology, personal.

I glimpsed a mischievous glint in his eyes that made me wonder whether the open admiration he had displayed for Mr Elton, the man that I had initially thought he served so selflessly, was more a cultivated performance and carried its own coded irony. I pressed to get his version of his boss's whereabouts.

– Gone? Where?

– Town to see after a case. Could be a day, or two. Depends.

Was he being deliberately vague or was he genuinely unable to be precise about Mr Elton's location or return? Certainly, he wanted me to recognise that he was withholding information. Our conversation of last evening had revealed that reticence was not his natural disposition, only a restraint that waited to be lifted with a little prodding.

– I hope it's not too serious.

He flicked off his hat.

– That story so long it can't done. Some people doh know how to bury what done pass and move they life on. Bowl another ball. Look at we now. England not in charge. And I glad when people decide to leave Macaima. Here is not all, but here is home for me. What happen, done-an-gone.

I had never even left the island, but I could not miss that Franco spoke at cross purposes, as though the currents of his thinking tugged in different directions all at once.

– Maybe the issue is whether you can make a home wherever you find yourself.

He eyed me closely, weighing what I had said.

– Sure-sure. People have to decide to move where they feel life could be better. If here troublesome, pick up an' go.

He indicated with his eyes an imaginary divide that I automatically followed, a nowhere spot that he quickly abandoned when he realised that I had tacked his glance. He replaced his hat and pulled himself upright.

– A body can't sit down nursing wrong or waiting on miracle to happen. Look at you – out here all by yuhself. No man. No chile to hold you back. You move as you want. Not so?

– Maybe. No one is ever totally unhindered.

Something was clearly eating at the man and I was sure it had little or nothing to do with my being in Macaima, but I wasn't inclined to be the subject of his speculations or a decoy for whatever was bothering him.

– Look, Miss Bri, take or leave my foolish advice. Happiness is what you make for your own self. To hell with who try to tief life from you. I doh mean to say changing a place is solution.

– Sometimes a change of place helps with some other deeper change.

– Yuh mean like how you run quite out here?

– Maybe. But tell me: who put you in this quarrelsome mood, Mr Franco?

My directness stumped him.

– Nobody is your boss, that is all I mean; but let me go my way. Time wait on no man. Pleasant day.

I watched him walk away, heading in the direction of the school. He stepped heavily in his tall tops, a swiping cutlass and a crook stick in his hands. He was a tall man, but carried his weight a little unevenly. I had missed that detail when I first followed behind him as he carried my bags to Beach Trace. Possibly an uncorrected curvature of the spine troubled him, compromised his gait, robbed him of his full height. For certain, he seemed in a provoking mood. Maybe he was more invested in Mr Elton's case than he had let on. He was not the same man I had met yesterday. Something or someone must have tipped whatever kept him in balance.

Franco was right about one thing: time waited on no one. I set my mind to do the work at hand, but it was not long before the swipe of a cutlass at the back of the building drew me to investigate. Franco stood in a tilted stance on the sloping land, swinging his arm in a wide circular motion. The action was effortless and precise. The blade glistened as it arched smoothly skywards and back to earth, creating an alluring, but dangerous symmetry. Perhaps he sensed that he was being watched. He paused to confirm and immediately caught sight of me at the window. He smiled broadly and touched his fingers to the rim of his hat before continuing his rhythmic motion. I left him to his task, thinking how much more at ease and at home in himself he seemed as he worked. When I returned to the front of the building, I saw that across the road, in the yard of the warden's office, a young man, who looked like a younger version of Franco, was doing the same thing – cutlassing. Small world.

CHAPTER 5 – A WHITE ENVELOPE

Mrs Gomez, I discovered, had been a meticulous worker. Everything was in perfect order. She had even tucked a handwritten list of the few outstanding tasks inside the accounts ledger for whoever would be her replacement, so getting a handle on how the office worked was not difficult, and in a post office like Macaima's, there wasn't much to manage. Mail moved in a triangle from Railway to Macaima and then Salvador. They were the catchment points for the smaller communities scattered across the district. Mrs Bailey had informed me that there were discussions about the possible closure of both the Macaima office and the Salvador outpost. The postal service was trimming away nonessential sites and upgrading key ones. The proposal was to consolidate everything at Railway, which made a kind of sense, but disadvantaged the Macaima community as everyone would have to travel for service. Change was indeed on the way.

Truth be told, the possibility of the new arrangement was why I'd got the post. Mrs Bailey had been clear on that score. The assignment was a temporary one that would give me valuable work experience with minimum risks, though nothing final was likely to happen before my stint was up. So, although I was committed to maintaining standards, I felt no pressure to overextend myself. I was the stopgap until a decision was made. I didn't mind. It gave me the space and time to figure out what my next move might be. I had already begun to weigh my options: possibly apply for a degree in something. I was yet to decide on exactly what. *The sky's the limit,* Thea often said. Her optimism about the future was daunting. I had not even begun to dream of what mine could be.

For all she found so much wrong with *the system*, as she called it, Thea believed in the future. *We're all flawed, Anna; so don't bank on us ever getting it right, but that's the fight – for a more just world. That's what I'm willing to invest in.* I had asked whether our idea of what we called justice was itself flawed. I think that was the only time I actually saw her pause to turn over what I had said, whether intrigued, challenged or just struck by my naivety I could not say, but she was the sternest I ever heard her when she replied: *What's flawed, Anna, is our tendency to clean house and leave spider behind. I can't live with that – sweeping out cobweb every time I turn around. I doh have time or breath to waste.* I understood then that she really believed in something – with time itself as a corrective. She believed in a future, even though her discomfort with the regime we had launched on the road to independence was clear. The rat, she said, had appeared in the deal brokered at the Tobago Convention over the USA's occupation of Chaguaramas. The extension of their lease was exchanged for green-backed development money, and in the midst of all that had come the ousting of her beloved Comrade Nello, the PM's one-time confidant, and the sudden death of the Federation. Most of the nuances passed me by. I wasn't that interested in politics, or perhaps Thea read me correctly when she said that my nonchalance was really my default for living on the defensive. She had an opinion about everything – irritating as hell sometimes, but maybe I had hoped something of her sense of purpose would rub off on me.

*

I settled into sorting letters, monotonous work, but a completable task that kept me focused. Not long afterwards a girl appeared as if from nowhere. Two plaits hung like hooks at the sides of her face and shorter strands curled into a disorderly muff above her forehead. She could not have been more than thirteen or so. A hand reached out, offering me a white envelope. She said nothing.

– Can I help?

She gave no answer.

– Do you want to post that letter?

Her head swivelled from side to side and pursed lips indicated that she did not. Her eyes remained fixed on me. I felt looked at deeply, seen through by brown wells, fathoms deep, yet, disturbingly flat, revealing nothing. They were the eyes of someone who had learnt to survive by holding the world contemptuously at arm's length. Something had toughened her into a shield; but so young! I tried to find an approach that would make her more communicative.

– Is this envelope for me?

– Yes, and you name Miss Anna.

The words rifled from her mouth. That was the name I had heard from the woman on Beach Trace, who had perhaps mistaken me for someone else. I could find no other explanation. Now this girl, a perfect stranger, had addressed me with the same familiarity. It was my turn to stand mutely before her, my inclination to upbraid her rudeness lost in astonishment. There was, too, something about her burnt-brown complexion and freckled cheeks that I recognised but could not immediately account for. Quite visibly, she carried some hurt.

– My name is Miss Bridgemohan. If you want to post that letter, I can help you with that.

Perhaps she had expected a reprimand for her abrasiveness, and because none came, her tone softened.

– I know. I bring it for you.

Before I could take hold of the envelope, she left it on the counter and sped through the door. I watched the faded colours of her cotton shift disappear down the Mountain Road. When I flipped the white envelope, I saw that it was indeed addressed to *Miss Anna*, the letters deliberately, carefully, formed. If the girl had written it herself, how did she know my name? The paper bore signs of smudged fingerprints, maybe from cooking or lamp oil. Inside was an even greater mystery. A single, lined copybook page with just four words. It read, *Dear Miss Anna*, and at the bottom of the page a scribbled signature that had me puzzling over whether the name was *Maria* or *Marie*, or possibly both. There was nothing more. The entire middle was blank. Was it a hoax – a Macaima-style welcome prank? Who was Maria/Marie and what was her relationship to the ill-mannered girl who had delivered the envelope?

Franco came in and saw me brooding over its contents.

– Ah Miss Bri, I glad to see mails reach for you to handle.

He released himself onto the bench and leaned back against the wall, his face sweaty and reddened from his cutlassing. I folded the page and slipped it into the ledger.

– Do you know anyone around here by the name Maria or Marie?

– Could be anybody.

– Really. How so?

– De Valremy wife name so and plenty people find they like it.

– Which one and which name: Maria or Marie?

– You full with question today, Miss Bri. Marie was De Valremy marrid wife. Pure angel and quiet-quiet. She sit down in church – always front pew – cover over with pretty mantilla. Same way she was on big-house veranda. Dress nice. No talker. A little sickly, but heart like gold. She like to help people: clothes, dry goods, money. Nearly every girl-chile born in Macaima christen Marie.

– That can't be true, Franco.

– Why you think I lie? Madam was from French creole stock. Not panyol.

I registered the prejudice as well as his admiration for her privileged role as matron of the village.

– Cisco fall in with Marseille who own estate lands over on Salvador side. So he come out good when he marrid. Biggest church wedding ever hold in Macaima.

– He certainly knew how to make his way.

Franco's demeanour tensed.

– Like I say before, he could do business and was well connect to who-is-who in Port of Spain.

– De Valremy is not a name I'm familiar with, and I get to know many in my job.

He appeared puzzled and a touch annoyed.

– Maybe it bogus. Plenty people craft dey own name or somebody make mistake when it write down. Once he tell me to my face his own mother cut cane. Nobody to say is true or false. Maybe De Valremy come from everybody. Maybe plenty people doh want nothing to do with who his people was. We doh have a choice when it come to what blood we end up with. However yuh look at it, now De Valremy dead, that history gone!

– The name is unique. That's all I meant.

I could not fathom Franco's moods. He seemed offended by what I thought was a harmless observation about the De Valremy name. Equally mystifying was his defensiveness about the class that his own family had laboured for and no doubt suffered under. Some attraction to or affinity for the man and his group that tugged against an unspoken resentment that breached his efforts to suppress it? I kept my thoughts to myself. I did not want to risk losing him as an informant on the inner workings of the village.

– Anyhow, name like Marie and Maria knocking dog in here. Why yuh ask?

– A note was brought to me signed by a Maria or Marie. I'm not sure which. A girl delivered it. Two plaits, a little mean.

– Damn foolishness!

– Do you know them?

– Yes. I know.

– Who – Marie and Maria? Or the girl that brought the letter?

He rose abruptly from his seat and replaced his hat. I half expected him to leave but he didn't.

– The girl is Pixie. Maria is Joseph own by Miss Ana. Son and father no different when it come to skirt-tail. Fruit doh fall far from d-tree.

A laugh that was a cocktail of approval and reproof filled the room.

– Maybe so, Franco, but I like to think people are free to choose different paths.

He cast me a sceptical glance.

– I doh disagree, but sometimes I have to pretend not to see. She like to play martyr, like she alone on this earth know what it is to suffer wrong.

– Who was wronged – Maria – Marie?

– What I know is that I claim my own self – but blood strong.

Was this an indirect invitation to connect the dots about how he and the women fitted into the De Valremy saga? Maybe I was wrong about his desire to maintain the illusion of disconnection. If, as I suspected, De Valremy blood ran in his veins, his situation was hardly unique. Or was there something else in his story that fed the need for distance, even as he sought to own it. My questions about Maria and Marie seemed to have provoked the beginnings of an unintended disclosure, that whatever he was withholding lay close to his skin.

– What's the story with those women and the De Valremies?

Brows knitted, he shook his head, slowly, as in an effort to shake off an unwanted memory.

– I not one to talk what I doh know. I wasn't on d-spot. I keep my distance when Maria have to take lessons. About Marie, you have to ask Roland. He put ring on Marie finger. Church-an-dance, but all fall down. I stay out of man-an-woman business. Same with Maria. I stay out.

This cross-stitch of stories had lost me. He flicked off his hat once again – a sort of personalised ellipsis for whatever he was reluctant to voice but wanted to suggest.

– If anybody is to tell you about Marie is Roland.

– Who's he?

– He around. Mostly down by Goodbye. He is the one to ask bout Marie.

Franco averted his face.

– Why not Marie herself?

– Dead doh talk.

– Dead! What happened?

– Drown. So police conclude. Two maybe three Aprils back. All we hear is Roland chase and she run straight inside Goodbye. She never come back out.

– You mean he forced her into the sea?

– Miss, I never say force! I have no warrant in blame. I doh judge. I not no slacker, Miss. I take my responsibility serious.

I wasn't sure what he meant.

– Danny is my son but big as he is, I would cut his tail if he do like foolishness. All I saying is that Roland run quick-quick to church. Now look at the result. Six children I have, but I never reach no altar. I proud to say I mine every last one.

I failed to follow the logic of the link he was attempting to make. I thought it best to shift the conversation to pick up again the Maria thread.

– Maybe Pixie knows whether that note she brought me was signed Maria or Marie.

– If she come in here again to bother you, let me know. She is Mason concern.

– Who is Mason?

– A brother. He settle in Railway. You should see him either tomorrow or next week. Mail van pass most fortnight on a Tuesday. Like I say, not to worry with what Pixie tell you. Elton should come back tomorrow. Pleasant day to you, Miss Bri.

The floorboards groaned as he left. It didn't occur to me then, but I later realised the source of Pixie's familiarity. Franco and his son looked very much like her.

CHAPTER 6 – A CASE OF FLEAS

My immediate concern as I walked to the post office that Tuesday morning was to figure out how I could learn more about the identity of the Maria or Marie of Pixie's letter. I wondered, too, about the lady on the road, the woman Franco had chosen to pass by unnoticed on Beach Trace, the day of my arrival. Was she Maria? Ever since that first day, my eyes were drawn to the spot where the Madonna stood amid the ruined church. The bouquet the woman had put in the grotto had remained fresh. The flowers were the hardy types that grow with little attention in people's yards: ginger lilies, ixoras, heliconias and crotons – all my mother's favourites, which she arranged throughout the Hendersons' yard. Mr Henderson was an Englishman who had come to the island with his wife and daughter to be a big somebody in the bank on Marine Square. I knew the bank. The sign on the red and clay-coloured building with its high Roman arches said *Barclays Bank.* My mother wanted me to know she had once worked there, cleaning the offices and then serving tea morning and evening to men who wore suits like Mr Henderson. It was her first job. She wanted me to know the work place of the man who had employed her when she most needed a job. *One door closed and another opened*, she had said – part of a prayer answered when she had gone back to her birth home in Siparia, to pray to La Divi for a way forward. I had long guessed that there was something she had chosen to keep to herself – the story that was ours.

I knew, though, that she loved flowers. A pretty yard was the closest picture she had of whatever heaven might be. Neither of the Hendersons paid any attention to the garden. My mother, though, freely took on the landscaping of the property, taking special pleasure every second week of the month in going about the yard, including the perimeter of the annex where we lived, and instructing Mr Lutchman which plants to prune and where to plant the cuttings she had acquired from neighbours, by what she called *Zara's ways and means.* In rusty pans of water to which she had added her secret ingredient, she miraculously coaxed almost any sprig to send out roots. Those plants were her pride and she was not shy to celebrate her way with growing things, as it was her habit to celebrate all her *talents*, as she called them, no matter how small, like the razor-sharp seams she pressed into trousers and sleeves, and her *sweethand* cooking that Mr Henderson never tired of praising, especially when they had company. She claimed these talents like a pact she had made with herself to value whatever mark she was able to leave in the world. As she said, it would never value you more than the value you put on your own self.

As a child, it bothered me that the Henderson household got the best of my mother and, as I got older, I wondered whether it was a compensatory generosity for more than just being employed and housed by them – her *good luck*. She had settled for an ancillary life and, as buffer for that choice, surrounded herself with growing things. It had long puzzled me why she never picked the blossoms she grew. I discovered why the day when Mr Henderson came home with a huge bouquet of red roses, wrapped in heart-patterned transparent film. It was an anniversary gift to his wife. I happened to climb the veranda steps in time to see my mother arrange the bouquet in the crystal vase on the centre table, taking each bloom from the wrapper and settling it in. She was alone and there were tears in her eyes as she worked. To surprise her, I had gone into the garden and collected blossoms from the yard and made a vase of an empty gin bottle Mrs Henderson had left in the gazebo. That day, I saw a shadow of disappointment descend as she stood by our kitchen table and fussed with the flowers until they were better settled in the bottle, her lips pursed, brow furrowed. My mother, I realised, wanted flowers that came from shops, like those that came to the big house, and that Mrs Henderson instructed her to place on the coffee or dining table. She never picked the flowers that Mr Lutchman planted about the yard under her direction. They blossomed and died on their stems. She wanted flowers that came bunched in plastic, held with ribbons, or arranged in green oases, complete with their little appreciation cards, tokens of love that never came.

★

When I got to the post office, I saw that someone had posted a sign, written in red, on the front door of the warden's office: *Closed Until Monday.* On closer examination, I saw that the initials F. D. or F.P. had been squeezed in at the bottom. The communication of essentials was clearly not enough as the script was notably different from the precision of the sign-maker's. Perhaps there was a need for the person who had included the initials to make known their identity as the authoriser. Perhaps a similar compulsion lay behind the altered sign I had seen in the schoolyard during my exploratory stroll up the hill the day before. The sign-maker had written in bold script: DO NOT PICK THE FLOWER. In the spirit of the garden theme, a scalloped border in emerald was added. No confidence was lacking in its creation. The word *flower* had apparently been thought sufficient as a plural marker or else the writer had miscalculated and run out of space. Some other hand, though, had deemed it necessary to squeeze in a tiny "s". I assumed the correction had been the principal's, but just then, when I encountered the parish priest, I discovered otherwise.

– I see you're getting your bearings, Miss Bridgemohan. As you can see, we're vigilant about standards in Macaima.

– So it seems.

He was perhaps in his early thirties but had an air of smug self-satisfaction that told me he was recently ordained. My less than enthusiastic response must have unsettled him as he diverted to introduce himself.

– But forgive me, we've not met. I am the unworthy leader of the flock in these parts. Father Xavier, at your service.

– Nice to meet you. I see you already know who I am.

– Villagers like to keep me updated on the goings on.

He was too pleased with himself and the authority that came with his presence in the district. Perhaps Macaima was his first assignment.

– I hope you are finding things to your liking. Macaima is a far cry from Port of Spain. It took me a while to adjust.

– So we are newcomers together, then?

– Diego born-an-grow. I went to school at Saints.

– Then we might have crossed paths. I was at the convent next door.

– Look at that! I should have recognised the…

He paused as if searching for the appropriate word.

– The what, Father?

– Never mind. We are glad to have you. Do you know that we've nurtured scholarship winners in our little school, including our very own Mr Elton – but as you can see errors are inevitable.

He gestured at the sign.

– Seems fine to me. Beautifully made actually.

I saw his disappointment at my response but he recovered quickly to lead the conversation into what I initially thought was an unrelated direction.

– Don't you think, Miss Bridgemohan, that following a religion is akin to learning a language?

– Never thought of it.

– Sure. A language respects rules and laws, doesn't it?

Did he think that I was in need of his instruction?

– Of course, and languages change and reinvent themselves, carry new awareness – don't they?

– I see what you mean, but that's not entirely the same thing. Faith has a text – a tradition. Case in point: this embarrassment of a sign, which *my* principal had no problem with. The man even defended the thing. His position is that people know what it means, so why *hurt the maker* by altering the wording. Imagine that! I think he's losing his grit. We must not fail to correct in love, Miss Bridgemohan.

– Maybe he has a point. People get the meaning. I did.

– Is it really that simple, Miss Bridgemohan? Think of what is sacrificed. It isn't correct.

– Maybe the problem is yours. From what I see the sign is doing its job.

– Maybe so, but that doesn't make it right. I assure you, Miss Bridgemohan, structure is essential; without it we are lawless. The said *person* is his wife's cousin. Lovely-lovely woman, but, as you see, language is not her gift. Anyway, she's over in Tobago doing grandmother duties so I took the opportunity to step in.

I immediately realised that this was the same Merrill that Mrs Austin had mentioned, the friend of Mrs Bailey. Father Xavier caressed his crucifix, observing me closely.

– I am guessing we are of the same cloth, Miss Bridgemohan? Though I see you are a bit of a renegade.

He settled his crucifix centre breast. I did not respond.

– Why not come up to Mass on Sunday? We should not neglect the faith – our beginnings.

– Sometimes, Father, it's a good thing to make a rule of forgetting – even the rules of a language.

Bars appeared between his eyebrows.

– My dear, one never really forgets a first language. So be careful how you travel. Forgetting is not forgiveness.

At this point he was done with his impromptu religion class. His *children*, he said, were waiting to hear about a reluctant prophet and a whale. He turned to enter the gate and his black cassock flapped like a sail, leaving a whiff of musky cloth and burnt incense. I watched him disappear into the belly of the schoolhouse. It was not long before I heard the chorus of children's voices sing, *Good afternoon, Father Xavier,* and I wished I had asked him if the whale, too, had a story.

★

The sign by the warden's office remained something of a mystery, though I was almost certain that the initials F.D., possibly P., were Franco's. He had never revealed his full name but he did say at our first meeting that his grandfather's surname was Perez. It signalled, though, that the elusive Mr Elton was unlikely to make an appearance any time soon. I was beginning to think that the man was merely a name that blew in the wind of people's conversations. The voice I had heard over the phone need not have been his. Macaima was becoming a place inhabited by shadows. Mason, the mail-van driver, had also not yet turned up.

Franco, though, stopped by a little before closing time. He was on his way up to the school. Like a metronome, his right hand tapped the swiper's blade against his boot. I supposed that his task, now that the sun had cooled, was to cutlass the grass in the schoolyard. I discovered later that he served as a general maintenance man for the post office, warden's office and school. I asked about the sign next door. He glanced at the shut-up building and then back at me.

– I hope nobody trouble you since we talk, Miss Bridgemohan.

I guessed at his reference but waited for him to clarify.

– Let me know if Pixie pass in here with any foolishness.

– Why would she? Shouldn't she be in school?

I could see his disdain.

– She stop learn. Best she stay home and help out she grannie.

It sounded like a punishment.

– Do you think it fair to keep her away from school? Maybe something is bothering her?

He kept up his rhythmic tap-tap.

– Mason stop in yet?

– No. Why?

– No reason. Mountain Road not easy. Accident could happen.

I wasn't about to let him get away with a diversion.

– Don't you think Pixie should be given the chance to learn?

– Miss, I never went to school and I turn out good. I not no fool. I listen. Doc say education is key. Sparrow sing, an-all sing so. Pixie get enough school. She could read and write. More than I could do. Now she only want to cause me embarrassment. She better off home.

– She's too young to be taken out of school, Franco. She has a whole life ahead of her. Maybe she wants to…

– Miss, you just reach inside here. What you know about what Pixie want?

I had crossed a line. It was best to ease off. Franco stormed out to the landing and spat into the yard. On his return, anger issued from him like a current.

– So what's up with the warden's office?

– Fleas. A bitch put down a litter. I already see bout them. River takeway every las one.

– You didn't!

He smirked, relishing my distress.

– Is only strays. Nobody to claim them. Look at trouble they cause me. I had to spray everything top to bottom. Fleabite is itch to drive you loco, Miss Bridgemohan. We can't have pest inside gov-ment building. A pleasant, good-day to you.

I watched him trudge up the hill with his slightly lopsided gait, his figure growing smaller as he drew closer to the school where Pixie would not be present, if he stuck to his decision to keep her away. What he had done was simply horrible. There was no excuse for it. All those pups drowned. The son, the one he had called Danny, emerged shortly after from somewhere at the back of the warden's office. The cylinder of a hand-pumped sprayer was strapped to his back like a piece of artillery. Maybe the school was also to be sprayed. He paused to heave his shoulders upwards to adjust its fit, then ran a few paces to fall into step behind his father. They cast one shadow as distance enveloped them both.

For the remainder of the afternoon, I heard only the wash of the river that flowed down from Mountain Road and passed through the estates to empty itself in the bay. Franco had said the river's name might be *Wa-She*. I heard only its ceaseless weeping.

CHAPTER 7 – LOOK TROUBLE

At first, I felt she was trouble. A succession of high-pitched *you-whos* that sounded like a day-owl looking for a perch preceded her. After a good minute or so, the owner of those shrill calls made her entrance. Maybe memory exaggerates the scene, but on that particular morning everything about her attracted attention. She floated into the post office, stepping not too lightly in block-heeled, bowtie pumps in tan leatherette. A collision of *Oil of Olay* and *Apple Blossom* battled it out, gobbling up every ounce of breathable air in the room. The woman was an image straight out of McCall's – which was in fact the subscription she had come to enquire after. Pressed-thin hair, generously greased to obediently lie flat, was pulled tightly into a single ballerina bun, so that her face was pulled backwards in a look caught between surprise and alarm. An oversized handbag hung on one arm. In the other was a book, cased in black leather, which she held cradled to her bosom. She announced herself, style-wise at any rate, as being irreconcilably caught between a 1960s carefree flair and a slightly prudish retro.

    I took in the presentation. She positioned herself as though in the spotlight of a stage, yet there seemed, in the ever so slight angle of her body, an instinct, perhaps unconscious, to shield herself from observation, despite the flourish. All this complicated what was perhaps a simple desire – to display a new dress profusely patterned with peach and yellow roses that sported a cuff-sleeved bodice with a little puff, accentuated by a V-neckline, not-too-low. The bodice fell to a loosely fitted, knee-length skirt; but what really caught my attention was the empire waistline fitted with elastic to accommodate an unusually high stomach. My initial inclination to want to laugh quickly dissipated. The woman was around my mother's age, who also wore those elastic-waisted skirts which I loathed but she said gave her room to breathe as she went about her house chores. Was this why I found myself feeling a degree of protectiveness towards her, as for something endangered or wounded? Before I could speak to offer her assistance, she piped:

– Oh my, oh my, *dat* is a heat!

In her elocution was a strained effort at informality. Through the fanfare of her arrival, I remained an ignored witness, though I could see her side-glancing me as she vigorously fanned her face, neck, then face again with the most delicate looking handkerchief, complete with a crocheted border. Her head swivelled from side to side, like a peacock showing itself, an antic that allowed her to surreptitiously assess my person and take stock of the room that must have been long familiar to her. Once she had decided that the bench was where she would perch, she made a point of thoroughly inspecting the surface. Satisfied that no harm would be done to her ensemble, she freed her hand of the book, made a dramatic sweep along the back of her dress before she sat, and readied herself to acknowledge my presence.

– Oh my, where have my manners gone!

Her voice hung on the brink of song in a pitch that seemed to express surprise at discovering me standing there behind the counter.

– I am Eunice-Marie Gomez. My mother was postmistress here before…

Her composure disturbed, the fanning resumed, but this time her eyes remained fixed on me, though from over the frame of her glasses. It was an odd way to be looked at, but I returned her gaze. After a deep intake of breath, she continued:

– My mother would have retired this very year. Life can certainly throw you a lemon.

A nervous laugh escaped her. She fanned some more. I waited.

– It's simply blistering out there.

I felt compelled to offer some relief.

– Can I get you anything – a drink of water, maybe?

– Oh, don't trouble yourself. I'll be fine. It's probably just me. Season of change.

She looked me over.

– But you, my dear, are ages and ages from that drama.

Another nervous laugh burst from her throat, followed by some fussing with her clothes and the positioning of her oversized handbag on the floor.

– Anyway, c'est la vie! Enough of me – and you are?

Her question caught me off guard and I found myself announcing my name like the answer to a quiz.

– Would that be Mrs – or Miss?

– I'm not married.

– Never married. I see.

– I said I'm not married.

– Well, never mind. That makes us both.

Her quip suggested that she had taken my response as a concession to a shared predicament.

– It's a modern world, Miss Bridgemohan. We women have to forge forward.

She fired a clumsy, unconvincing punch at the air. She seemed such a pleasant eccentric that one could not help but think her harmless – especially because she appeared so happily unaware of her strangeness.

– I'm sure you'll like Macaima, Miss Bridgemohan. By the way, I'm in charge of the choir at our little chapel. You should come to hear us. We practice on Fridays and, hint-hint, we need VOY-ces.

She sang the word.

– Thank you, but I'm not a singer.

– Oh, nonsense! Everyone can sing. It's a fact. You merely need to find your range. I'm sure you've met Mrs Austin across the way.

She indicated the warden's office.

– Well, she's with us. We've been friends for ages. Went to Holy Innocents Mission School in Railway. Macaima had no school back then. No small feat, let me tell you, travelling by mule cart back and forth. My father was an estate driver for L'Avenir so he organised the transport. We had a ball back then – our little band.

– Band?

– Mr Elton, Thomas and Julien De Valremy, included. So great expectations and all that sorta thing hung in the balance… Ha!

Her eyes drifted off to some personal destination before she made a flick of her head, as if to throw off an unpleasant thought.

– Joseph De Valremy was many things, some of them pretty awful. That's no secret. But he did fight for the building of the school in the village. Not his father.

– How do you mean, awful?

She returned to the composition of her choir.

– Did I mention Lucille? She has a useful mid-range voice, but we can't always count on h-*er*. She's what I call a hopper, but my policy is to let people do their searching until they settle. Eventually we all do.

She paused, allowing time for what seemed to me an insinuation to settle in.

– We're in need of an extra voice, Miss Bridgemohan. Macaima folk are not much into volunteering.

– Why's that?

I had my suspicions about the drought in membership, but felt that her explanation would at least be entertaining.

– I'm known to be a bit of a taskmaster. And if I may say so, I consider myself progressive.

– Interesting.

– I don't mind sharing with you that the parish council has at last agreed that the choir would benefit from the inclusion of a drum. All at my insistence! It took years of lobbying, and the council, let me tell you, amounts to one man, Mr Cabral. A fossil of a man! You won't run into him for a while. He's in Tobago with Merrill. They have a new grand. I suppose you already heard that from next door. You would think I was advocating for fêting in the aisles. Anyhow, we have our drum, at last. We have to become ourselves, Miss Bridgemohan.

She clasped her hands and seemed to momentarily drift away again before she surfaced with a whispered query.

– By the way, have you met Mr Elton? I was hoping to see him.
– I'm yet to meet the man.

She paused as though expecting me to speak, then ploughed on.

– I suppose you've met Pixie?

– Yes, she came by yesterday.

– She plays the drum now that we've lost Roland. It's not ideal, and not her real talent, but we have to do our best. The girl has the most BEA-u-ti-ful voice; but she's difficult.

– In what way?

– Let's just say she's special. Anyhow, out of the blue, she has refused to sing.

Miss Gomez retrieved her book and hugged it to her even more tightly. I couldn't help but think that, like Franco, she was a hive of paradoxes, but far more likeable for all her quirkiness.

– Be careful with that one, Miss Bridgemohan. She's a bit of a storyteller.

– Is she?

– Oh yes. I hope she hasn't already come to you with some nancy story about that mother of hers sending for her?

– No. We haven't spoken at length. She seems shy.

– Far from it! I suppose you've heard about the fight?

– No, I haven't.

She perked up, eager to share the details.

– Yes, guilty as charged for brawling with those boys up at the school. Maybe she's not to be blamed. Her grandmother is not well, and the mother cut ties and hightailed to New York. Then that Maria is another story.

The name jumped out at me.

– Maria – what's the relation?

– I'm not one for gossip, Miss Bridgemohan. All will unfold in time.

She flicked her head towards the warden's office.

– By the way, do you know why next door is closed?

– Something needs attending to, I think. Maybe Franco can fill you in.

– Franco, fill me in? Hardly!

Either the suggestion had caused offence or she felt I was being unnecessarily reticent. She dabbed her forehead delicately with her handkerchief.

– I suppose he's still in town. His prayers apparently didn't work. You know he has his own church, but I can't vouch for his prayers. I mean, I haven't had the benefit of them.

– Who is he praying for?

– Long story. Well, Miss Bridgemohan, happy to make your acquaintance. I hope you enjoy your stay with us. And my offer still stands…

– Offer?

– The choir – we need more VOY-ces, and I won't divulge who suggested that you would make a good recruit. Who knows, you may be an undiscovered rose. Think about it.

No doubt the nudge had come from Father Xavier.

– Anyway, I'm off. Bible class is in my unworthy hands.

The waistline of her dress rode up the unusually high mound of her stomach like a pregnancy that wasn't one. She righted it again.

– Good day to you, Miss Bridgemohan.

Miss Gomez exited, thankfully taking her perfumes with her. She seemed neither to belong to the place nor to herself. The blunt knock of her heels as she descended the steps paused, and the exclamation rose:

– Well, speak of trouble! Don't forget choir practice, Missy. And don't be late.

Pixie appeared holding a cardboard box. Her dress was soaked up to the waist.

– Miss, you read my letter?

– Hello, Pixie. How are you?

– I okay.

One bare foot moved to scratch the calf of the next. A puddle gathered at her feet.

– What do you have there?

I gestured at the box.

– Something I find. You read my letter, Miss Anna?

– Yes, I did. It didn't say much. Is there something you want to tell me? Who's Maria or Marie?

She glanced into the box and spoke as if to its contents.

– Maria is my cousin, Miss, and my friend is Miss Marie, but she dead now.

She concentrated on whatever was tumbling around inside the box.

– I'm sorry about your friend.
She shrugged off my condolences.
– I write it for you, Miss.
There was pride in the admission that I didn't let slip by.
– You have a beautiful handwriting.
– I write that one over there too.
She meant the one on the warden's office.
– I see. You are a good writer. Maybe you can tell me who is F. D.?
– Uncle Franco but he make mistake with D and P sometimes.
– Oh I see! Perez, right?
– Yes, Miss.
She gazed into the box, but a smile filled out her face. I felt I could push a bit further.
– Well, since you're the writer, you should have signed it.
– Not me, Miss. I only write what Uncle Franco say.
– Is there something more you wanted to say in your letter, Pixie?
– Pixie is not my name, Miss.
– Okay. I'm sorry. What is your name?
– Samantha-Marie Douglas is the whole thing, but you could call me Sam – though Uncle France doh like that name.
– Why?
– Because I born like devil.
– Why would you say such a thing? Who told you such rubbish?
She ignored my question and refocused on whatever was scratching about inside the box.
– Miss, I bring you something to keep safe.
I came around the counter and peered into the box she had placed on the bench. Two pups, their coats uneven patches of black, beige and white, shivered at the bottom. Oversized heads bobbed on thin necks. They were soaked through and could not have been more than four or five weeks old and badly undernourished.
– Oh, the poor little darlings!
– I know you would like them.
– Who wouldn't? Where did you find them?

– In the river, Miss. Keep them for me, please. I can't take them home.

I didn't need to know why. Not after this morning's encounter with Franco.

– My brother will pass tomorrow, Miss. He going to take good care of them. He going away from here.

– Do you mean Danny? Won't he kill…

– No, not he. My own brother.

She swept a quick hand over the wobbly heads, then fled before I could accept or protest. The pups whined and rolled about at the bottom of the box. They were so small and obviously in some discomfort, cold and hungry. I wrapped them in a towel, made a hurried trip to Johnny's for some powdered milk, thinking nothing about how I would feed them. On my return, I was lucky to find a dispenser in the medicine cabinet that would work fine as a temporary feeder. They took the milk slowly, a little reluctantly. I wondered if they would survive, and whether Sam's brother could really come for them in the morning.

CHAPTER 8 – BRENDA'S BATTLE

Next morning, a single, almost stern, *Mornin* was directed my way. The greeting came from a woman who stormed by. She wore a checkered cotton blouse and brown skirt that was bound at the waist by a broad belt. Her green head-tie reached up to the mountains that loomed above us. From the set of her face and the pace with which she mounted the hill to the school she seemed to be on a mission. Two children were in tow, and a third, perhaps in his early teens, trailed behind, his face downcast. So determined was her passage that I could not make a return greeting in time to catch her ear. I settled the pups in the back room and as I opened up the windows to let in the cool breeze that blew off the hills, I watched the woman marching her children up to the schoolyard and waiting with clear impatience for the last to pass through the gate before she followed. Something was clearly up.

The pups moved about in their box, nuzzling at the towel I put in for warmth. They had awakened me at the crack of dawn with agitated yelping, and I did my best to feed them with the dispenser. They were definitely underweight and much too young to have been separated from their mother but, as I discovered, they were tough little troupers determined to live. As I think about it now, those pups brought me an unexpected responsibility that, in those early days, became a source of grace. Having to care for them provided an anchor in the current of my own turmoil, which had also been caught up in Sam's mysterious crisis. She had done her part in fishing them from the river. Now, in addition to her strange letter, they linked us. I tickled their little pot bellies and watched them sleep. They seemed so uncomplicated. Eat. Tumble. Sleep. I felt a little regretful that they would soon be gone – if Sam's brother turned up to collect them.

At about an hour later, a second *Morn-in* greeted me. The woman, minus the children, released her weight onto the bench with a heavy sigh and introduced herself as Brenda Solomon. Her gruff veneer softened as she relaxed into her seat. I could then see that she was probably Miss Gomez's contemporary, maybe slightly younger, but her opposite in dress and manner. There was nothing diffident about Brenda, whose business was to enquire about a letter from *America*. She said the word a little dismissively.

– I call. Then I write. No reply.

She had been trying to track down a cousin.

– I don't know if Kizzy change address or phone number. Not a word come for months. I tired bother Mistress Gomez, rest her soul. I hear up there not easy. I ask that chile over and over: Kizzy where yuh going? She say more opportunity in America, but I know is run she run from the trouble she bring into this world.

– What trouble?

Her eyes became furtive. I tried to put her at ease.

– Maybe she's busy. Or, as you say, moved and can't find time to write. No promises, but if you have her address, I will see what I can find out. It's almost impossible to trace unregistered mail. Perhaps for some reason your letter never left the island.

She handed over a very worn slip of paper. I copied the name and address of Kizzy Douglas, more than sure that Yolanda, who was still at head office, would come up blank if she checked to see whether it had been cast aside as undeliverable. I decided to keep to myself the link Kizzy's surname confirmed rather than risk shutting down Brenda with another intrusive question.

– It will take some time, but yuh never know.

– I appreciate any help. She make a free choice to go with that man, and when the result come, she run. I say, *Kizzy, carry Pixie by Sando hospital*. She didn't want to hear, and Mama Gloria, who was midwife, didn't help. She say Pixie bless-an-special. Wonderment and what not. I have no objection to that, but I can't worry over Kizzy concerns again. I have enough on my plate.

I could see that Brenda was burdened and, as she intimated, by more than her cousin's silence. It was not hard to guess the source.

– Are those your children – the ones I saw you with earlier?

– Yes. All mine. Patrick, the oldest, is the one who have me in Mr Austin office, listening to speech on how to raise my own chirren. He and Miss Gomez out-a-order!

– Oh?

– She is one miserable woman! Making claim that my Patrick is ringleader in fight. How he interfere with Pixie in class and bacchanal start.

– Over what?

– Patrick say all he do was ask if God could make mistake, and Barry (he is Mr Austin son), push in and say like what happen to Pixie.

– What did he mean by that?

– He say she is a double-chenette.

– A what?

– Hai – imagine! I bet he didn't come up with that chupidness on his own steam. I myself had to correct Patrick on that nonsense. This same human race we like to claim as ours not cut-an-dry. And we know so, but pretend otherwise and swear God only make day and night full stop!

There was no doubting her sincerity. Something had hit close to home. Sam had been cruelly insulted and there was a fight for which Patrick was singled out as instigator. But I guessed much more had been going on.

– You have chirren, Miss Bri?

I indicated that I did not.

– I try my best with my own. I give them what I know. Miss Gomez carry wrong news on my boy. She run quick to block for she family.

– Who's that?

– Mrs Austin.

She gestured at the warden's office.

– Oh, I didn't know they were related. But why would Patrick want to fight with Sam – or anybody? Isn't that the name she prefers, by the way, and not Pixie?

Brenda ignored the question. Her focus was her son.

– Day-in, day-out, I drill in him to stay far from trouble. Study his lessons. I only want him to hold on until I find a trade for him to learn. He is not to end up on no estate. He is no saint, but I sure-

sure he not no ringleader. Pure wickedness make dat foolish woman frame my boy like some criminal!

She slapped her thighs, grabbing and releasing her skirt as she did. I could hardly untangle what had been revealed in the rush, but I couldn't quite accept that Miss Gomez would have implicated Patrick without cause. But nor did I doubt that Brenda was aggrieved, and probably for good reason.

– Perhaps there was a misunderstanding in how the news was relayed. It happens.

– So you say, but I see Eunice in here yesterday. I bet she come to give you *her* story, and to ask after Elton?

I noted the switch to Miss Gomez's first name and that she had added another matter to our conversation.

– As a matter of fact she did stop by.

– I know so. She feel Elton is some kinda magic man.

Maybe she had judged my silence as incredulity.

– I talk only facts. She run hidee-hidee to ask Elton for prayers. I know up there they have plenty problems with me.

She lifted her chin towards the school.

– Not my concern. I have no explanation of anybody. I cross over to a church that speak direct to me.

She pointed to her own person.

– Elton church lift me up. Eunice want his prayers, but she call what we do when Sunday mornin come simmy-dimmy. Well, if that is how she think, I for one thank God for my deliverance. Foolish woman!

Brenda was on a roll. I could offer nothing but a listening ear, and maybe that was all she needed.

– I don't know your politics, Miss Bridgemohan, but I glad too bad independence come. I was right there in Port of Spain for Liberation Day when we put fire to that kill-life constitution and everything else that sell we out to whoever. Deadly sins, Mr Premier say. One by one, he cast straight them to hell. So I glad he is PM now. He going to represent we affairs proper. I was there: me, my mother, my sister. We went right up in front that bandstand. I – we put down wreath to bury that history. Maybe now this place will be for everybody. Like how we march to Chaguaramas after – hand in hand.

– You were in the Square, Brenda? So was I.

Brenda looked at me as though I had uttered what she could not believe.

– You?

– Yes. So we marched to Chaguaramas together. Imagine that!

She seemed to be processing the veracity of my claim and I voiced what became the chorus that accompanied the burning of the documents.

– *To hell with it!* Remember?

– And *Uncle Sam give we back we lan* as we march down!

She searched my face for confirmation. I nodded.

– Nobody must forget how we march. Plenty people long before I born break back-an-soul-case over this place. I march for them and for the freedom everybody want. So, Miss Bri, it look like we meet up already.

We looked at each other with new wonder. A flood of memories came rushing in about that day. I had to push those thoughts aside as Brenda moved on with her telling.

– From that day, Elton was neck-an-neck with this party we vote into parliament. He want to bring change to Macaima. He get that gift. Anyhow, now Eunice meet with sickness, she want prayers, but won't stop talking rubbish about how we choose to pray. I try not to lack charity when it come to Eunice, and if you ask me, she like that same junction we pass on everyday – split two ways.

My head reeled with all that Brenda had disclosed, and with an energy that made the post office thunder. She was a mountain sitting on that bench, her fists pressed into her waist and her feet planted wide. I sensed, though, that whatever truth lay behind her grievance, the anger she displayed was fed by some hurt to her very person. I advanced as gently as I could to the source.

– What's wrong with Miss Gomez? Is she sick?

It was a bold question, but one I sensed that Brenda would welcome.

– Fibroids. Yuh see how she belly high-high. But that is only half. She pass it off as gas cause she shame to say.

– What's there to be ashamed about?

– I will say this much – what make Eunice sick is all the years she stay lockup inside a shell tight-tight from whatever she fraid more than fear self. She is a good-good woman, but she doh believe so. Home to church, home to church is how Eunice live. In-an-out confession box like crab from hole and swallowing Communion like tablet, like she commit some crime against the self that is her very own.

Brenda sighed and retreated to the privacy of her thoughts. I waited on her. She had made me witness of much more than her grouse with Miss Gomez over what she supposedly said was Patrick's role in the fight. She had offered a reading of a life: *her* sense that Miss Gomez had in some way sabotaged her own living. More than that, whatever her choice, it had for some reason deeply wounded Brenda. I let her talk on:

– Whatever part Patrick take in that fight, I will deal with him. I raise him to respect people. Those up so doh know (she cast a surreptitious glance at the school), but first chance I get, I moving out my chirren. Alisha is my last. She turn six this month. Obadiah is nine. I don't want no belief to take root that make them feel they less bless than anybody else because of the church they attend or how God choose to make them. I know no God like dat, Miss Bri!

She was speaking, I felt, about two issues at once. Maybe she saw them as one and the same thing. Maybe it was just her way of approaching the difference. I felt her burden. Outside, the sky was so clear, so very high and so-so blue without even the company of a cloud. Brenda grew quiet, as if emptied.

– Maybe you should have a word with Miss Gomez about the incident.

– I talk more than I come here to say. I have no argument with Miss Gomez, but it hurt me that only now, when water more than flour, she feel Mr Elton could cure that belly of hers.

How Brenda claimed to know so much about Miss Gomez and the supposed ailment she had not herself disclosed was unclear, but in a place like Macaima, where everyone was so interconnected, confidences would not be easy to maintain. If Patrick had in fact participated in the schoolyard incident, whatever version Miss Gomez had given, he was culpable,. That was the disturbing truth Brenda would have to face and hopefully help him to *deal* with.

Just then a Corporal Luke came in. His booted footfall was heavy on the board flooring. His purpose was to purchase stamps. I wasn't at all sorry that his presence put a stop to our conversation, which had unleashed a web of issues. I was a little relieved at Brenda's departure, taking with her the worry she carried over Kizzy's silence or disappearance, Sam's hurt, Patrick's bullying and, somewhere in the mix, Miss Gomez's search for relief from whatever was her ailment. I needed to breathe. Macaima was giving me no space to lay down my own burden, though, truth was, I welcomed the distractions.

Thankfully, the Corporal was not interested in socialising beyond the expected courtesies. He paid for his stamps with exact change and carefully arranged them in his black notebook, around which he slipped a thick rubber band – all with the show of the meticulous attention to detail of one trained to follow fixed procedures and to uncover deception. His hands moved smoothly, economically, like a magician's. I noticed how perfectly his nails were clipped. When he was done, he touched the visor of his cap and left with measured footsteps that gradually faded out of earshot as the pups began their hunger cries.

CHAPTER 9 – BONES

A panel van pulled up in front the post office at about 1pm. The driver who mounted the steps looked like an aged teenager. He introduced himself as Mason Alexander.

– Everybody call me Bones, but you, boss-lady, could call me what yuh want.

He was all teeth.

– I'll stick with Mason.

His alias was too cruel a truth. He sat like an apparition on the bench. Despite his smile, life, it seemed, had sucked him dry. Even so, he cultivated a youthful, jovial demeanour, which I thought was meant to dissuade anyone inclined to think that he had been beaten by whatever he was fighting, or that was fighting him. He tore off his aviator sunglasses to reveal hollowed, weary eyes. Nothing about his physique suggested any connection to Franco, who had identified him as *a brother*. My guess was that they shared the same mother and he carried his own father's name. An interesting detail. Franco bore his mother's surname, Perez. But what had befallen Mason? There was an air of illness about him that undermined his readiness to joke and propensity for what seemed meant to be self-irony.

It turned out that he wasn't working the Salvador route that day but was on an unspecified personal errand in the hinterland. I didn't ask further, although I noted that he had no qualms about using the postal van for his private business. Our conversation, though, opened up realities about the estate that Franco had been reluctant to divulge or was vague in his offerings. L'Avenir estate began, he said, about three miles up Mountain Road. Salvador, though, could only be reached via Macaima because the western entry had remained a bridle path accessible only on foot or by mule. Otherwise, to arrive at Salvador you were required to overpass the bridle road and use Mountain Road on the eastern end, then track back to it – a journey in reverse. I had obviously missed the sign, but he said that there was one about five miles before the junction. At the top of Mountain Road there was a Y-shaped junction similar to Macaima's, so you could either continue inland, from which point the road became Salvador Trace or else turn seawards, following the bridle road that rejoined the main road west of Macaima junction. There was more.

– La Divina in Siparia – I sure you hear bout her?

– Yes, I heard some stories from my mother. She was born in the village and she still goes to the devotions.

– Yuh, see! My kinda people.

The detail excited him, but that was about the extent of my knowledge. My mother had offered a vague story about having received a personal favour when she was a teenager. She never shared the whole of the miracle, only that my birth was in some way involved and her continued devotion was part of the deal. She had made a promise in return for the life we lived – which was to never want for anything.

Mason explained La Divi.

– She belong to people from Vene-side before Catholic take over.

– Oh, I didn't know.

I supposed he meant the Warao. I knew a little about these people through our few visits to my grandparents' home, the place my mother had left to find work in the capital and then made a life for herself working for the Hendersons. The connection had come from my grandfather's side. I remember little about him, but the only picture my mother kept of them in her Bible showed a slender, mixed-race man who, she said, loved singing bhajans and weddings songs more than the cane-cutting that fed and clothed them. My grandmother, I learnt, was Bajan with pure Igbo blood in her veins, and that supposedly accounted for her business sense and that other thing – her mistaken *redness* that had caught her husband's eye. She made cakes and sweet bread, sweets and jams that people came from miles around to purchase. My mother said that through them three continents ran in her blood, and I had brought a fourth. That was how she explained me. She never went further but I did the math to make up for the silence I could not get her to break.

Mason, meantime, was going on with his La Divi story.

– Plenty people from Macaima make pilgrimage to ask for favour. Old, young, doh matter. I go myself and ask for help. She working on me all now.

His voice dropped to intimate sincerity.

– Every year I present myself. Sun or rain.

– How is that working for you?

His brows knotted.

– She promise me a cure and I waiting. Faith take strength. Is not a now-fuh-now matter.

It was his way of letting me know that he didn't share my scepticism. I wasn't so much interested in his devotions as in what more he could tell me about the goings on in the village. I felt the opening had been made to ask about the couple, Marie and Roland, whom Franco had mentioned.

– So did Marie go to see La Divi?

– You mean Roland wife? I doh know. Maybe she shoulda go if she didn't. She woulda be alive today.

– What's the story behind her death?

– Like plenty story done pass by you already, boss-lady.

– Not really. Her name came up. What happened to her?

– Sad-sad business. She drown inside Goodbye.

He cleared his throat at the revelation.

– Yuh know Mitra? He work taxi between here and Railway.

The name didn't ring a bell.

– He is Marie brother.

I didn't see the relevance but let him continue.

– She was a nice-nice girl. Thomas doh talk to his own brother up to this day. And Mitra stop talk to me for whatever reason.

– What caused the rift – between the brothers, and you and Mitra?

He sighed and leaned forward, propped his elbows on his thighs and hung his head over clasped hands like a penitent.

– Best man to ask is Roland.

– Did he chase her into the sea?

– Maybe. Maybe not. Talk is he get fool at the altar.
– She was pregnant, then?
– So people say. Things turn out real bad for her.

His story about the drowning and pregnancy matched Franco's. Both cast doubt on the child's paternity, but Franco had stopped short of insinuating Roland's possible role in Marie's death. Mason had preserved that possibility. Compared to Franco, he seemed more personally impacted by what might have happened.

– Did you know Marie?
– Nobody is stranger in Macaima.

Something simmered beneath what he had said, some detail held back, perhaps something too self-exposing to be shared. I wanted to know more, but decided that a less direct approach might be the best route.

– Were the De Valremy brothers close?
– Those two grow up like Bim-an-Bam.
– What drove them apart?
– As far as I see, it centre on what happen three Aprils ago when Julien was last here.
– Thomas's brother?
– Yes. They send him England to study doctor but he never come back permanent. He settle for Canada; but if you ask me what happen with Marie finally kill Joseph. He didn't last a good year, and after that Thomas move from Macaima and say he in contractor business.
– Why do you think that?
– From all that bacchanal. Police start to investigate. Then case drop.
– What case?
– A girl get rape on De Valremy estate. Reporters board Macaima like corbeau-on-a-dead but that whole story disappear.
– Who was the girl?
– That same Marie. Maybe no rape ever happen. Yuh know how young girl stop. They get in business, then bawl rape.
– A woman gets raped and you're blaming the victim! Come on!
– I only mean we doh know what happen. I not God.
– And I'm saying all the more reason to drop that nonsense.

– Okay-okay. All I saying is that what happen went inside Goodbye with Marie.

Mason leaned back onto the wall, withdrew a washrag from his back pocket and vigorously wiped his face. The phone rang and I excused myself to take the call.

– You fix up. I in no rush.

He sounded strangely exhausted and relieved to be left alone. I returned to discover that he had retreated to the van where he sat in the driver's seat, not so much reclined as with his head thrown back, his throat exposed, He wore his sunglasses. From where I stood, he appeared to be asleep but responded to my first call. He settled back onto the bench. This time he did not remove his sunglasses. I figured it was best to lay off the Marie incident and Roland's possible role in it for now. I wanted, though, to tease out further the identities of the women who were behind the letter Sam had delivered.

– What about Maria? Who is she?

– What make you ask?

– No reason. Franco mentioned her the other day.

– Sound to me like you meet up with everybody already.

– Well, I didn't go looking.

He laughed.

– She is Joseph own with Miss Ana. She name after his marrid wife, Marianne.

– Strange he should do that.

– If you ask me, he wanted to make it plain that from where he stand, Maria was like inside family. She was his eyeball.

– I wonder what his wife felt about that?

He sidestepped the question.

– She like to walk the road like Mama Gloria.

– Mama Gloria?

– Roland grow with her. She is a healer like Papa Menz.

– This Mama Gloria's father?

– Yes. Everybody blood mix up now, but he was pure from across d-Main. Mama Gloria help birth plenty people inside here. De Valremy sow these mountains with more than cocoa, and was proud to say so. But mother and daughter stay here like ghost.

He looked at me blankly. It was not the first time that I felt like

I occupied two timeframes at once. Ana was a new addition to the growing but still blurred list of names and relations. I wanted to know more, but Mason continued along another line before I could ask.

– I didn't know ole man De Valremy so good, but everybody know he was watless and proud same way.

He laughed at some private joke. I figured he was talking about Joseph's father, Francisco, based on what Franco had said, but couldn't be sure.

– So Joseph's wife is still on the island.

– No. After Joseph pass, she went up to Canada by Julian and never set foot here again.

– I see. And where was Miss Ana from – the estate?

– She was from Salvador side, but crop time she use come over. De Valremy build house for that one, but every fortnight she run back home.

– Why is that?

A smile framed his otherwise inscrutable face.

– She couldn't tame. Near send Joseph mad. She had certain powers.

– I don't think a woman could have *too* much powers where the De Valremy men were concerned.

– Tru talk. She could turn into bird, tree – anything. That was how she use to hide from him. Warao blood could do that. Ana was a changer – like Mama Gloria. Maria maybe same way too, although people say she mad.

His tone dared me to question his conviction.

– You're full of stories, Mr Mason. Maybe all those women had good cause to change their skins to survive the place.

– No lie in it! Right this minute Miss Ana up in those hills.

He fell silent as though entranced by his own tale, then looped back to my original question.

– That business with Marie hurt me bad though – real bad. After that I move out from here. Too much bacchanal. She was a nice-nice girl.

He shook his head in disbelief, then sprang to his feet.

– I heading out now. You have to take yuh time on Mountain Road.

He folded the washrag, opposite sides to meet in the centre and then once over before tucking it into the back pocket of his trousers.

– So as you know what in the pipeline: I put in for a transfer. My case settle. I tell them I want to reach my retirement alive.

By my guess, he was possibly another ten years from retirement, but I understood the desire for a change.

– What prompted the request?

– Eye trouble.

He indicated his temples before removing the sunglasses to wipe away some accumulated moisture.

– Too much pressure behind here mash up my eyesight. Yuh know Corporal Luke from the station?

I recognised that he meant the officer who had bought the stamps, but I was more struck by his being so explicit about his health issues.

– Well, he sour like lime since I tell him I put in for my transfer. Years now we hunt together, but that done now. Once they find my replacement, I gone.

This seemed to contradict his claim of having had his application approved, but I let him go on with his story.

– Mountain Road could be like night in midday hot sun. Deer run wild. One time I hit one. BAM!

– Gosh! Did it die?

– By the time I mash brakes and look back… Nothing. No animal. Like it was wind I hit.

– Maybe you ran over a log.

– No. Deer. You won't believe me, but when I bounce the starter and glance in my rearview, guess what I see?

He paused, locked onto my eyes, as if he wanted to make sure I was in the story before he told it.

– A woman!

A sound erupted from me that I could not precisely name, an utterance of astonishment or doubt. Mason arrived at his own interpretation.

– Laugh all yuh want. As God is my witness, she hightail like devil-self was in chase. Head was cover-over so I didn't make out a face.

He sucked in a deep breath and drew his skeletal frame upright as though his own body were a burden too heavy to carry.

– Maybe it was only a shadow that appeared to move across the road.

He shook his head.

– I must take you to Salvador side one day – so you get to know the place.

He must have noticed my hesitation.

– My mother still live up there, but she blind now.

– Blind, your mother and Franco's – and Sam, yours?

– Mine? If you mean Pixie, she is Franco concern, but he quick to say different.

– Why would he do that?

– Long story. We doh go down good again. Pixie is his, but he never take full responsibility and the mother run to America.

Was this the cousin Brenda was trying to reconnect with? I kept that thought to myself.

– Up to now she can't send for Pixie. She better off up there, if you ask me. They have all kinda doctor.

– Better off – why?

He replaced his sunglasses. The pups began yelping just then and caught Mason's attention.

– You have company in there you never tell me about.

I brushed the comment aside, thinking it was best to leave Sam's rescues out of the conversation. Mason took the cue.

– Anyway, is time I push off. But tell me: yuh like pommerac? Season almost done but last crop red like blood and juicy too-bad.

He didn't wait for my answer.

– When I passing back, I will leave a few for you.

I nodded my gratitude and he made to leave.

– Welcome to Macaima and stay lovely, Miss Post.

He was almost out the door when he added:

– You know, you could pass easy-easy for one-a-we inside here. No joke.

– I guess I have a face like that.

– Maybe you have pumpkin vine family in here.

I laughed off the suggestion. The tight knit nature of the village had also been Mrs Austin's description of the place. For Mason, though, the possibility seemed to intrigue. I watched him walk to the van with a bobbing-bounce. He'd left me not so much with a promise, but with a long trail of incomplete stories. He left me, too, with the realisation that he had given me another name – Miss Post.

Franco stood on the opposite side of the road watching me watch Mason carrying away his bones.

CHAPTER 10 – A GOLDEN THREAD

Next morning, I could hear hammering all the way from Beach Trace. When I got to the junction, I saw the construction of what looked like a platform was in full swing in front of Johnny's. From beneath the cover of the shop's eave, Franco was boisterously directing two workmen.

– Come Cray, pull yuh hand. We doh have till next week.

– Then we shoulda start this work yesterday.

Franco made no response but continued to stretch and release a rubber band he had looped onto thumb and index finger like a slingshot. The man named Cray stopped his nailing to take a long drink of water at the standpipe beside the shop. Franco kept a stern gaze fixed on him, which only fuelled Cray's commitment to quenching his thirst. I was certain that Franco had seen me, but he was pretending to be too busy with his project to give me the time of day, no doubt still smarting over our conversation about Sam's non-attendance at school. I was determined not to let him off the hook on that score. His disregard suited me fine. I had the space I needed to keep my little charges safe. They were Sam's secret and I was determined to protect it.

Cray eventually resumed his hammering, at which point a woman I supposed to be Johnny's wife shouted something from a window about the *blasted noise*. Franco moved from under the eave to stand closer to his workers.

– Any disturbance my men cause, I responsible, Miss Claudette. Gov'ment business.

– You agree to start that commotion when shop close today. Not so?

– Time too short, Miss Johnny. Sorry to trouble your peace.

She sucked her teeth and slammed the window shut. Franco

retaliated by grunting a curt instruction, this time to Cray's companion, who complied with mocking obedience. To this man's delight, Cray broke into a calypso I immediately recognised as Spoiler's, "My Shadow". He sang: *Pardna, from de time ah small / Meh shadow wouldn't give me a break at all / (Oh meh darlin) Sometimes I will run / to see if I could get away: but he still stick on. / Oh Lord!...*

The song was a favourite of my mother's, mostly because she had picked up on its riff off a Stevenson poem she had memorised and often recited to me. It came from a book she had found in the main house. I learnt later that all the books I had read and thought mine, she had *borrowed* indefinitely from the Henderson's bookshelves. So my first library belonged to their daughter, Emily. She had long outgrown them by the time we arrived at the annex. My copies of *Jane Eyre, Treasure Island* and *Little Women* had come from the same source and were stored in a box under my bed, *for safekeeping*, my mother said. As Cray sang his calypso on the junction to taunt Franco, it brought me face-to-face again with the unfinished business I had with my mother and the half of my story she had chosen to withhold. It was a shadow neither of us could dispel. It circulated through our days like the learned distance I had navigated in the Hendersons' yard.

Staying out of the Hendersons' way was easy, living in a separate annex. Mr Henderson was mostly at work and his wife spent most of her time either in the gazebo with her gin and kola tonic and magazines, or out at the country club. My mother said the reason she drank too much was because she missed Emily; she had left, first for university and then to be with her American husband. I believed this to be true because Mrs Henderson sometimes joked that I was what Emily had left behind. Sometimes, she spoke to me in riddles when I was sent out with the refilled ice bucket with instructions to return right away.

The gazebo was built close to the seawall on the opposite side of our annex. I did not know what she meant when she said to me: *You're such an angel – our little golden thread*, or when she sang: *Golden thread, golden thread, our little golden thread* to the rhythm of the hammock's swing, back and forth, back... Her speech was slurred on those days. I never knew her meaning until I read Dickens's *A*

Tale of Two Cities. I had read it just before my sixteenth birthday and found in its pages the story of a golden-haired girl named Lucie, the golden thread who connects the main characters in the novel. She was the girl Mrs Henderson referred to when she drank too much gin and called me her little *golden thread*. There was never gratitude or admiration in her voice. Only something sour, like blame.

★

Cray had finished his calypso and work continued in earnest as I went on my way, but that scene remained with me, as did so many things that happened during my time in Macaima. I saw how the men were not at all intimidated by Franco's bossiness. It backfired because they knew how much value he placed in playing the role of boss – when they also saw how beholden he was to others. There seemed no real malice in their attitude towards him, perhaps even a degree of compassion, or maybe the hope he would abandon the phantom that rode him and hollowed him at the core. He was vulnerable, and whether or not he harboured some measure of contempt for me seemed more and more inconsequential. He was compensating for some deeper wound and Sam, I felt, was paying for it.

★

I settled the pups in their usual place, feeling increasingly doubtful that Sam's brother would come for them. They were not as yet weaned, so leaving them at home all day wasn't an option, at least not yet. They were, though, out of danger and I no longer worried about whether they would survive. I would have to think about finding them a home, though it would be sad to see them go. Sam's situation worried me. There was something at the root of it about which I had, as yet, no inkling. Something had been uncovered in the bullying incident at the school. Was that also behind Kizzy's abandonment of her daughter? For all his foibles, Franco had stepped in to care for her, which suggested a deeper personal involvement than what he had initialled claimed – that she was Mason's *concern*. Sam, though, must have been deeply hurt by the schoolyard assault and needed support. I wasn't willing to let the matter rest and I suspected Franco knew so.

★

The morning drifted on. There was no sign of either Sam or her brother. At about noon, someone called out to me from the road.

– Mornin-mornin. A minute for me please, Miss Post-lady.

I went to the gate to meet the woman I recognised as the dancer at the junction on the day of my arrival. An enormous bunch of plantains was balanced on her head and she carried a heavy crocus bag of produce in one hand and a cutlass in the other. Her name was Lucille Figueroa.

– I stop to offer my welcome and to leave a little gift from my garden.

Without disturbing her load, she reached into the bag and extracted an assortment of vegetables and provisions: okras, bodi, tomatoes, pimentos, a slice of orange pumpkin and sweet potatoes.

– Nothing much but I give with a good heart.
– Thanks, Lucille. This is wonderful!
– Harvest must share. I not stopping long. Market tomorrow morning and I have more goods to bring out. Maybe we meet again when bacchanal start.
– What bacchanal?
– Yuh didn't hear?
– Hear what?
– PM coming to talk. I want to be up front. I have a question or two for him. We have to make demands on who we put in parliament. I didn't give my vote for nobody to tell me how to live. So, I want to ask my question. If I not satisfy, my vote going elsewhere next time.

I was intrigued. Lucille, it appeared, had not signed up for an independence that amounted to what Thea called a creeping dictatorship spurred on by a heavy dose of nostalgia for the colonial state. Lucille, like Thea, evidently believed the government belonged to the people that elected it to serve them, not the other way around.

– Come tomorrow, I want to put my question plain. A pleasant day to you, Miss Post-lady. You will see we are a kind-an-lovin people in Macaima.

I watched her thump down the hill and wondered what were *her* concerns. When I got back to the office, the pups were making a racket that I recognised as their hunger yelps. They were livelier than yesterday so feeding sessions were becoming a rather tedious process of having to do frequent repeats with the dispenser. Should Sam's brother turn up, I would have to draw that to his attention. The pups needed a feeding bottle. If there was another no show, I would stop by Johnny's on my way home to purchase one.

Later that afternoon, I discovered more about the PM's visit from Mrs Austin. She had dropped in to check for mail.

– I can hardly believe it! Our own Prime Minister, here, in Macaima – in person – to meet his people.

She radiated genuine wonder at the prospect. The *Face the People* project was his post-election initiative, part of his mission to travel to every corner of the nation, no matter how remote. He wanted to educate, assess needs and at the same time spread his message that he was at the service of everyone – toute bagai. Equal place for everybody. That was his mandate. He had, after all, made political capital of his decision to put down his bucket on the island, refusing attractive opportunities elsewhere. These islands were sufficient. That decision had bolstered the nationalistic current that surged through the place when Federation suddenly expired. How his efforts to befriend the people would evolve was yet to be seen. Mrs. Austin withheld nothing of her admiration and optimism. She was not alone; even his strongest opponents could not dismiss his gifts.

– I expect you'll be there, Miss Bridgemohan?
– I haven't given it much thought, Mrs Austin. Maybe.
– Oh, but you must! I'll not miss it for the world.

At heart she seemed an amiable woman whose natural inclination was to bolster, but the notion that her son could be a bully made me wonder what lay behind her public face. Brenda had suggested that Barry's derogatory name-calling had its roots from right inside his own home.

– What time is the meeting, anyway?
– I'm not entirely sure, but it will be made clear soon. Franco will take care of that. Even Barry wants to attend – but he's confined to home until further notice. I suppose you heard of the schoolyard scuffle.

She searched my face for confirmation.

– Boys will be boys, Miss Bridgemohan.

– I hope not at any cost.

– Of course. Anyway, tomorrow we will make history in Macaima.

I couldn't help but feel that her disclosure of her son's punishment was the real reason for broaching the subject of the PM's visit. She was possibly aware that Brenda had stopped by and wanted to register her position on the incident. She wasn't, though, inviting conversation about what I thought was her rather glib assessment of Barry's behaviour. I could hear her in conversation with someone on the road. Her tone was buoyant. I didn't share her enthusiasm about the PM's visit. I had shared Thea's disillusionment when it became clear, for those who wanted to see, that the new PM had used the plight of ordinary workers as a tarmac. Thea had stood firm with the independence movement, but the witch hunt following independence that targeted the major unions was intolerable to her, as was the dash ahead to nationhood that left the death of the Federation unmourned.

We watched her drift away from us into a world of new, more radical political affiliations, but it was hard to ignore her energy or not be moved by her convictions. Her idealism could overwhelm in a single sentence: *Hummingbird doh build nest like semp but both must rest somewhere, some place, though they fly the same sky.* She had a way of weaving the collective with the personal that mesmerised me: *I don't want us to disappear, Anna. I want to be fully present and I also want to become whatever I can't even imagine I could be, because you and everyone else are here.*

Most people thought her too intense – too brainy to endure her company for more than a few minutes in the lunchroom. But friends and followers were not her focus. In fact, she was much too busy to bother with our after-work office limes and weekend outings. She always had business elsewhere, was always dashing out to some appointment or meeting that couldn't be missed. In a sense, she remained an enigma to me, even though the general feeling among the others was that we were friends. I don't think any of us really understood what she was after. Maybe she herself didn't know, not the full of it. In truth, I felt her post-election disappointment somewhat exaggerated, even premature. We were only just days old as a nation. She insisted that the writing was on the wall and that history would judge us harshly for not using all the gifts we had been given. I knew that she meant Comrade Nello. I could not agree or disagree. To her, I was a political infant. She was not wrong. Politics was not a matter for discussion in the Hendersons' yard. My mother showed little interest in anything other than caring for the needs of the occupants of the main house. That was her world, her politics.

In those early days in the village, I moved in a daze thinking about those different endings. What had first brought us all together, and seemed so tangible and unshakeable from that march in the rain, had not held. Maybe we did not believe enough in the possibility we dreamed. Miles felt her politics were too radical and I should not be so much in her company.

★

– Thea Dennis is an instigator, Anna. She looking for trouble and will find it with her union talk. Management going to make her pay.

– At least she is willing to risk herself for something, Miles. I think she's great. She makes me think I've been asleep all my life.

– Be careful. That's all I saying.

– Of what?

– For one, you're still on probation. You don't have the safety of a permanent job, so be smart.

– She is perfectly fine to me – in fact, she's more than just a little interesting.

– You don't want to be labelled. That is all I mean.

– Labelled what?

– A little too red for one.

– Well, that is not new.

– Come on, Anna, I'm being serious. Once you get pigeonholed it's near impossible to shake the label.

– What label is that, Miles?

He had hesitated.

– Forget it. I hear what I hear. Talk done.

I didn't take him on.

CHAPTER 11– EQUAL PLACE

By late afternoon that day, the platform was ready but for the final decorative touches. A larger crowd than usual was already congregating in the vicinity of the shop. Amid the general gaiety, the men drinking at the bar were noticeably more spirited than usual, but this was a Friday evening, with an event to anticipate. Like a mascot for a pending performance, Franco's voice had thundered through the village, announcing the time and place of the meeting. A mega speaker was mounted on the pick-up he had hired to spread the message. He sat strangely hunched over a microphone, which he held close to his mouth, repeating a memorised message that changed slightly with each round of the announcement: *Attention. Attention. Fellow villagers of Macaima-an-environs. Tomorrow – Saturday. Six o'clock sharp. I repeat: tomorrow, Saturday, your duly elected leader go be here. D-man have-a-plan. We own Prime Minister. Come out in your large numbers. D-man have a-vision. Attention. Attention. Feature address by we own leader who we elect to lead, who in parliament for we – all-a-we. Come out villagers. Turn down pot. Put down wuk. Come out. Meet D-man…*

His voice became an irritant I wished would stop, but it went on and on.

Sam appeared at around closing time, looking distraught. She wore the same faded shift, and her hair was a tangle of frayed plaits.

– What's the matter, Sam? Haven't you been home?

She shook her head and sat on the bench swinging her legs. I sat beside her, hoping she would say more about what troubled her.

– Where have you been?

Sam shook her head despondently.

– Your granny must be worried sick. Did you stay with Franco, then?

– No, Miss. He don't want me by him. I live by Granny. Me and Maria – but she gone days now. They take she far from here.

– Who took her where?

– Franco – and Mr Elton. She gone to get better is what Granny say.

– I see. She'll be back soon, Sam. I know you must miss her.

– I not going back home. Ever.

Tears rolled down her face. She sobbed uncontrollably.

– How can I help, Sam?

Her sorrow was so raw. I struggled to keep my suspicions at bay. The last thing I wanted to do was to jump to any conclusions that might only estrange her further. She had to tell her story.

– Where did you spend last night, then?

– Nowhere.

– Tell me how I can help, Sam.

She tracked back to my initial question.

– I stay by Roland, Miss. He let me stay sometimes.

– Did he – hurt you?

– Who? Roland? No, Miss. He let me stay sometimes. He never say bad things about me.

– Who would say bad things about you?

She sobbed some more.

– Pay no attention to what people say, Sam, especially the ugly things. That's mostly all about them.

– They say I shoulda dead in my mother belly.

– Who says such rubbish? Children at school?

She nodded.

– Well, they're wrong. And if they continue, they will have to deal with me!

– With you, Miss?

– Yes, me!

I could tell that she was doubtful.

– I going far-far away from here.

– Where will you go?

She hesitated.

– Is your brother going with you – and the pups? They miss you, you know.

She permitted herself a brief respite.

– They doh know me. How they could miss me?

– Oh they know you alright. You're their hero. You saved them from the river, remember.

She smiled, but kept her head bowed.

– Everybody laugh at me. I shoulda dead before I born.

– Say no such thing, Sam! You're a good and beautiful girl. Is your brother still in the village? Maybe we can tackle this together.

She locked eyes with me so fiercely I flinched.

– I my own brother, Miss.

Again, she dashed through the door and disappeared up the hill, leaving me more perplexed about what I could do, but beginning to wonder if what I had at first dismissed might be true.

The puppies began their hunger cries. I did the necessary, but my heart was heavy with what Sam had said. Could she mean literally what she said in metaphor? She spoke so negatively about herself but possessed such a strong, independent disposition that I hoped she could escape from being overshadowed by whatever troubled her. I looked at the pups; their eagerness to get on with the business of living was contagious. Sam deserved to thrive, and that meant solving her riddle. That, though, would obviously take time. For now, I had to see after the pups. They quickly devoured the milk in the dispenser. I had to get them a proper feeder. They needed names. I decided to call the female Day. She had more of a tan and white coat. The male was Night. So at day's end, I made the trip to Johnny's before heading home with my charges.

★

A heated discussion was in progress when I got to the shop. A man called Balkissoon was holding court.

– If you ask me, we put a bookman in parliament. I doh grudge him that, but he know nothing bout land and what it mean to have dirt under yuh fingernail. Plus, he fraid people.

– Sure he know book, Balkissoon. He not into bush politics and he could talk. Place pack with people so they could hear d-man talk.

– That doh change what I say. Maybe he prefer a stage.

– Everybody in here know your politics. So be careful not to make claim with no foundation.

The caution had come from Cray, the singer. Balkissoon paid him no mind. He was asking about why Macaima was given a last-minute pick for the PM's *Face the People* campaign.

– Doh fool yuhself, Macaima. Land is not a priority for this government. They have gas brains and we have no oil inside here. At least Railway stand firm and blank him outright and make case for what role agriculture should play in this nation. If we sideline food for oil that go be a big mistake.

I picked up from the crosstalk that Balkissoon had unspecified connections with the Labour party that enjoyed widespread support in Railway and the surrounding villages. Macaima remained somewhat of a marginal constituency – or that was the claim. Cray, though, was not finished with him.

– Balkie, Railway-an-associates turn dey back on who we elect to lead. What you and your party need is one or two lessons in respect, at least for how people choose to vote.

Supportive murmurs rose from the shop. Claudette, who was weighing out rice in five-pound brown paper bags, intervened. She had been listening in from behind the counter.

– Dis-party, dat party. Allyuh not tired fretting over who in charge. What we want to make this place? Ask that question for a change.

She went on with her work. Cray pressed on with his point.

– Not to worry with Railway, Balkie. Mr PM put one parry on dem. It was brutal.

The shop hung on, waiting for Cray's account.

– What he say, Cray?

He became circumspect. No doubt timing his punch line.

– His exact turn of phrase slip me, so doh say I say.

– What he say? Bring it nah man!

It didn't matter who had asked. The question was the entire shop's.

– I doh intend to misquote nobody, but it went something like this.

He cleared his throat and proceeded to do a bad imitation of the PM:

– *My brothers and sisters, I have no patience with the brown sugar mentality of certain detractors in this constituency.*

Laughter erupted. Balkissoon countered.

– Yes, laugh, but hear me good: if we tie the future of this place to oil, we better make sure it good to eat and it doh run out.

Cray strode out of the shop to join a group of men gathered around a game of draughts under the eaves. A woman, whose head was a balloon of pink rollers, added her two cents as he left.

– My PM is in charge, so who vex lorse! He ready night-an-day to put all-dem clown in dey place. Why yuh think light always on inside he car?

Balkissoon wasn't prepared to let things rest there.

– Light on so he could see what he reading behind dem dark glasses. Macaima blind like bat to think he really seeing we.

The woman wasn't convinced.

– Doh talk dotishness, Balkie. D-man have his reasons. Is he who see what we could be.

Balkissoon changed gear and was quick with a comic comeback, making a gesture to his ear as if turning up a hearing aid.

– Who jus talk? O-ho, is you Ora. I ent hear one damn thing yuh say.

– Watch how yuh disrespect people, Balkie. It go come back to bite you in d-arse.

At that same moment, amid the kiff-kiff, Franco and his driver came in for a break from their rounds with the loudspeaker. Mason was in trail, and he jumped right in to the banter, deliberately misreading and undermining Balkissoon's intent.

– Balkie, why yuh feel nobody see or hear *you*? Look, I see you.

His tease opened the way for Franco.

– Tell me what really sour you, Balks? Come, talk plain. I all ears.

– I have no gripe with nobody.

Balkissoon's tone was bitter. Franco seized the chance to provoke him further.

– Well, what vex you then?

– Okay Franco, answer me straight: how come Lennox get hire tuh drive? How come I didn't get pick?

Franco laughed and gave Lennox an approving slap on his shoulder.

– Be-cause Lennox is a well-certify dri-VA.

Lennox pulled out a washrag and made a show of wiping a grin from his face to the delight of the onlookers. Balkissoon took the bait.

– You make bad-bad accusation, Franco.

He proceeded to extract his license.

– Who is me to doubt your credentials, Balkie?

Franco was the picture of sincerity.

– I jus worried you might drive me off some cliff so people never hear my news. *Dat* is my concern!

All three men went over to the bar. Balkissoon continued his grumbling, but he had lost his audience to the general feeling that his complaints were merely sour grapes. I waited at the counter to be served as he launched into an angry tirade about the unfairness of the politics in the country. He railed and railed.

– Independence Day we sing *where every creed and race find equal place.* Equal place? We cyah be serious!

I had not seen when Lucille entered the shop, but she had obviously been present long enough to catch the exchange.

– Balkie, anybody could look at *your* own children and see race is not *your* problem, but that doh mean it not real. Equal place is what we have to work on. So doh knock we anthem. Is a future we have to make for everybody. We now start to finish make what we sing.

No one felt the need to add to what she had said and that was not because her point had no resonance. I knew as much. In the lull that followed, Johnny had made his way over to my side of the counter to launch his own indirect taunt at the disgruntled man who was close enough to catch the comment and, with it, Johnny's political leanings.

– Doh study Balkie. He always chookin fire. Motor car is motor car, not so?

Balkissoon shook his head a little wearily and moved away. My feeling was that the man deserved a hearing. He made a worthwhile observation about the political landscape, but the dynamics of Macaima were still a blur. I had already crossed a line with

Franco over Sam's education and I don't know what else. It was better to stay focused on my purpose for being in the shop than to speculate or engage.

I was out of luck with the feeder. Johnny said he was expecting a fresh supply on Saturday. One more night with the dispenser would make little difference. Johnny, though, had more to say about the demand for baby products in the village.

– Plenty young-girl belly big in here. Money-money... (he brushed his thumb against his fingers).

Claudette overheard the comment and didn't allow him to say more. She took him to task.

– O-ho Mr Johnny – is so? Man share no responsibility for when young-girl get pregnant. So is mystery then?

Johnny's face grew sheepish.

– You too foolish, man. At least action taking place somewhere, because it certainly not happening here.

Claudette went back to her stolid manner of serving, unconcerned that she had publicised some private disaffection between them. It troubled me, though, that Johnny had so easily painted the young mothers as mere hustlers.

Lucille, who was standing near enough to witness the exchange, joined in.

– What pass there is exactly why I have a question to put to Mr PM.

– What question is that?

– Miss Bri, I have two girls, eight and ten. No man leave shoes under my bed. My choice. But I want to ask Mr PM why he advise that if a man like to run after every skirt-tail he see, responsibility is for every such woman to get up from where she is and leave?

I didn't immediately get her meaning.

– But she should get out of such a relationship.

– Hear me. What I, Lucille Figueroa, want to know is *why* Mr PM doh address his own kind direc when it come to that subject. Why woman should take either blame or responsibility for however a man choose to behave. Woman cyah tote load for man and deyself too. I for one not no pushover Eve. I want to know if *he*, Mr PM, ever sit down to study what history and economics behind *dat* foolishness!

CHAPTER 12 – SAME RIDER

Dusk was just settling in when I made my way back to the post office to collect the pups. Night came early to Macaima because the mountains backed the village on the northwestern side. It took some getting used to – their closeness and the early disappearance of light. I made my way towards Beach Trace mulling over the day's events. There were so many unexpected convergences, beginning with Cray's calypso rendition that morning. Pasts hung close. We were a new nation with a great deal to face about what it meant to occupy this space as equals. Thea always said independence was like a marriage that had to be worked at and continuously refreshed. Johnny's chauvinistic assessment of the young women in the village revealed so much about how we saw each other. He painted the young women crudely as hagglers, trading their bodies and babies to survive. What were their dreams and disappointments? He sought to dismiss their story by reducing them to a type.

Anger burned in me. This was the logic behind Thea's sudden transfer to the San Fernando office. It had followed the lunchroom conversations about why we should join the union. James, the resident news carrier, was of course present. Her comments that the PM's attack on the unions was dictatorial had no doubt reached management's ears. The materialisation of that "special" project was the beginning of the end for her.

As I headed towards Beach Trace, I saw Mason propped up against a lamppost on the junction.
– What load you carrying, Miss Post?
He stepped forward to glance into the box.
– Dogs to guard yuh place. Nice move. So yuh putting down roots in Macaima. Come, let me give you a help.

I declined, but he didn't seem to mind and went on explain his purpose.

– I waiting here to tell you we have a little change to the Salvador run next week. I passing Monday, not Tuesday.

Some obscure explanation was offered about one of the postal vehicles being out of service so an adjustment to the schedule was needed. I wondered why he had waited until this late to relay the change, but wasn't in the mood to think about work. But since he seemed in the mood to talk, as we turned onto Beach Trace, I pressed him with a question I had been carrying.

– What was Thomas's brother like?

– Who? Julien? I can't say I knew him.

I walked on, sensing that it might be more comfortable for him to talk on the move. I was right.

– He was more with Roland and Marie. They around same age. Well, he a little older. Sometimes Marie use to stop by my mother to ask if Pixie could go to Mermaid Pool with them. She treat Pixie like a little sister.

– Mermaid?

– Nice bathing spot inside Ave-near. Deep though. They say mermaid drown a man inside there. That is why we call it so. He was from foreign. Mermaid wanted him for keeps.

– That can't be true. Maybe he couldn't swim and got into trouble.

– This world is more than you think, Miss Post. Anyhow, I use to think back then that Julien would be the one to step outside his crease when he marrid.

– What makes you say that?

We paused at the site of the derelict church. Mason tapped a cigarette from its packet. A struck match sizzled to life. I switched my position to up wind. He noticed and tucked the lighted end towards his palm. When he spoke again, it was to begin at another branch of the plot.

– How he like to hang around Marie. They three roam all over Macaima, but it always look to me like Roland was the tag along.

– Really? So Julien was interested in Marie?

Mason chuckled. Just at that moment we passed the church and he switched tack.

– You know you was asking me about De Valremy and what happened to the church? Well, De Valremy was always a church-going man. His own money went into building that church.

– Which De Valremy – Joseph?

– No, his ole man – Francisco. He finance everything, and after hurricane mash it up in '33, he pay for repairs when war end.

– Franco mentioned the storm damage but didn't say the church was repaired.

– I bet he didn't tell you that same church kill Francisco.

– No. What happened?

– That story follow Franco up to this day like a ghost he can't shake. I wasn't on spot, but when peace declare, De Valremy had fête. Everybody get invite. He put up tent. Rum, gouti, lappe, deer. Parang. That same day he announce he was going to fix the church back to when it was in its prime. Since '33 it had no roof. Priest had to say Mass under carat shed. De Valremy fix over everything bran-new, down to pews. They plan dedication ceremony with bishop and officials to come. It was his gift to Macaima – what he wanted people to remember him by.

– Hmmm. Sounds like he was cleaning up his legacy.

– That was how he was – splash and show. When building finish, men start to take down scaffolding. Franco help. De Valremy was there giving instruction. That was how he was – always dishing out orders. Yuh know he never plant a single tree on his own estate. Franco could tell you. People say Franco was De Valremy personal jackass. If you ask me, it no different today – only d-rider change.

Mason's story snaked its way out, gliding this way and that. I tried to follow his twists and turns.

– Yes, that story haunt him. Watch this: from twenty feet high, a 2 by 4 fall from Franco hand like a hammer straight from heaven. Men say it was like when scorpion tail strike.

– Did it slip?

He ignored my question and went on with his tale.

– It happen like in slow motion. Nobody could move a muscle, like every man sign contract to stand witness to that blow. De Valremy see it coming, but he had appointment with that lash. He couldn't move. It take aim, drop down and res flush on his chest. BAM!

My body involuntarily tensed. Mason was pleased with the effect of his dramatics.

– Franco bawl louder than red howler. Tru-talk. Three days later, De Valremy was dead.

– Gosh! What happened to the church after that?

– Fire. Nobody could say how it start. Plenty bacchanal happen in Macaima; but I talk too much.

The red rag I had seen before appeared. He seemed easily exhausted. Perspiration glistened on his face. Without another word about the matter, he said goodnight and began the trek back to the junction.

I stayed put a moment to absorb the new information. The Madonna, with that familiar veneer of serenity looked out at me. Life was hardly that unruffled, but the image conjured a peace no doubt suffered for. The pups began yelping. They had lost their mother but were rallying on. Loss itself was perhaps seldom the real issue – not in the long run. We all lose. No exceptions. Maybe loss makes it clear that life must always be remade, and that is the larger part of what's involved in mourning: having to find the way forward. I sucked in a lungful of the cool evening air. For much of the first half of my life, I never felt I had lost anything. The Hendersons were our good luck, my mother always said. Maybe so. She spoke very little about her life before coming to work for them. It seemed she didn't want anything to be known about the part of her life inbetween leaving Siparia and coming to Port of Spain. I didn't probe. It seemed easier that way – for both of us.

There was a saying my mother liked to repeat: *I here when I gone: I coming home when I leave.* It was what she said her father often said when he left for work on mornings to do his cane cutting. I like to think it was his way of daily renewing his commitment to his family – and he had made good. By the time I came along, he had already *gone to be always here* and my mother had set off for the capital. Banks, insurance companies and the like were hiring cleaners, tea ladies. She often said she had no regrets but one – not going back to Siparia enough. The Hendersons had most of her attention and, I suppose, mine by proxy. Thea, of course, had found my distance from my family odd. To me, it never really figured much. She, though, felt family was super important. She called it *rooting* and said I should try to connect the dots before it was too late to know and not be defined by that missing piece. That conversation stayed with me:

– *What was your mother so afraid of? I know both my parents but pieces get lost before them. A missing grandfather on my mother's side, for instance.*

– *I don't think they matter – the missing links. I make my own decisions.*

– *Of course they matter. Listen, history dealt us a raw deal from the start. It can't be our path forward to accept as lost, connections that can be recovered.*

– *It's impossible to find all the pieces, Thea. You know that. In my case, I don't see the value in knowing for certain what I suspect.*

– *And what is that – about your father?*

– *It doesn't matter.*

– *That's precisely why you need to verify your suspicions, Anna, because it does matter, so you can know what to do with the information. If you can bridge the gap, do it while you can. Until you do, life will be too much drift – amorphous.*

★

We had never finished that conversation but I realised that my mother had settled for fixing our life as taking place in the Hendersons' yard and blocking off everything else. I barely knew my relations. For whatever reason, she had robbed me of those connections. Maybe Thea was right, I needed to fill in the blanks before it was too late, for better or worse.

CHAPTER 13 – FACE THE PEOPLE

The whole of Macaima converged at Johnny's shop that Saturday evening. The shop's eaves were draped with crepe-paper garlands in the national colours. Erected at the back of the stage was a huge banner with the PM's signature statement: *Massa Day Done*. A microphone and two speakers had been set up. Fiery floral tails hung from the perimeter of the stage and on every lamppost in the vicinity. I supposed this had been Franco's work behind the scenes.

It was very much a display of political allegiances touted as a national event. No one cared to consider the blurring of the two. The *Face the People* forum was not supposed to be a campaign meeting – but that didn't matter. The party was the nation. In truth, Macaima had outdone itself. Spirits were high. Entertainers arrived early and took their stations close to the three steps that led up to the stage in readiness for the cultural segment that would precede the PM's talk or speech. Nobody could say which. They comprised the usual reduction of the nation's ethnic diversity to a drummer and two dancers, one dressed in leopard skin and a black leotard, the other in sari, veil and ghungroo bells. Amidst a crush of bodies anxious to claim one of the token party T-shirts, Franco took stern charge of their distribution, commanding the crowd to *behave*. A tense calm followed, only to be shattered when the first T-shirt appeared. To Franco's exaggerated chagrin, the store of shirts quickly disappeared as hands stretched towards him and bodies pressed in, hoping to collect the freeness.

I saw Brenda. Two of her children darted through a crowd that included people from neighbouring districts. There was no sign of her oldest, Patrick. A couple I had seen and spoken to outside the closed Warden's office was also there. An older woman stood with them, expertly cradling their baby with one arm and shifting her weight from one foot to the other to make a rocking motion. At intervals, the mother wiped the infant's face with a sky-blue washrag. The husband positioned himself slightly apart, scoping out the scene. His wife whispered something to the woman who held the baby. They both smiled in my direction and made me feel less of a stranger as I navigated the tight cluster of people under the shop's eaves and inched my way towards the counter. Many more than Johnny's usual quota of customers vied for his attention. As well as locals, those who had come over from Salvador and other communities all wanted to complete their Saturday shopping before the start of the meeting. Johnny was manning the bar where he conducted a swift trade in rum and beer. Claudette covered the shop.

A woman whose name I did not know, but recognised as the lady with the pink rollers, began swaying her body from side to side. With arms outstretched, she was crying:

– Oh God, Johnny, save me from this perilous sea. This ship not steady!

Her tactic amused the other shoppers and served to get her closer to the counter. In the general congeniality of the mêlée, I saw Miss Gomez in all her flowers and bangles, standing on the edge of the crowd, her handbag held before her like a shield. She saw me and waved vigorously. I acknowledged her, but quickly weaved my way to the opposite end of the counter. The school principal and his wife joined her soon after and I felt relieved to have escaped her fanfare.

After a long wait, Claudette turned her attention to me. She fetched my purchases, moving with deliberate pace from one end of the shop to the other. As I waited on her returns, I could not help but hear the boisterous talk that spilled over from the bar. Only a partition, which was really just a reconditioned blackboard plastered with advertisements, divided the space. The banter was all politics: the good that the party would bring to the country, the exceptional man that the PM was, his degrees and travels to America and England, so nobody could tie him up like market crab. He was going to educate and prepare the nation for the future. His trademark slogan raised toasts: *Massa day done, done, done* – followed by triumphant laughter.

The atmosphere was charged with hope that I wanted to share; but I agreed too much with Thea's view about how pride in nation was being hijacked for narrower racial and political ends. I tried to shift all my attention back to the buzz in the shop, to be in the present of Macaima's anticipation. Through the gap in the partition, I saw Franco in the midst of a group of drinkers seated at one of the square-metal tables on which empty bottles were displayed like trophies. With him were Mason, Danny, Cray and Lucille, who sat next to the man who had worked on the stage with Cray. Mason had the floor. He did most of the talking and joking, even performing a fairly creditable impersonation of the PM's raspy microphone voice: *My friends, slavery was first and foremost about economics. Capital. Educate people. Put money in poor-people pockets. Change is going to happen... If Barbados is Little England, then Trinidad is destined to be the New York of all these islands.* Whether or not this was an accurate account of the PM's thinking didn't matter. The bar applauded. No one was interested in debating limitations. For Macaima, on that evening, there was a future to anticipate and gains to celebrate. A toast was raised to more money in poor-people pockets. A man addressed as "Spanish", because he was from the Main, and possibly emboldened by the jubilation, exclaimed:

– Sí, dame mas mo-nee!

There were more cheers. Spanish felt encouraged to say more.

– Vene gi Trini CRIX. Entonces, pásame mucho dinero!

The man sitting next to Lucille intervened.

– Spanish, I grateful for yuh CRIX, but I hear biscuit is not what *you* come over here to sell.

Spanish laughed nervously and pretended not to catch on.

Lucille took him to task.

– Doh play chupidy, Spanish. You well know what Razor mean.

She threw a hand across her companion's shoulders. Spanish smiled from a flushed face and swallowed his drink.

In the midst of the merrymaking, Danny sat self-consciously stroking an emerging beard, the contents of his glass untouched. I guessed that he must have been about seventeen, and was, I thought, apprenticed to his father in more ways than one. Our eyes made four and he reached for his glass, nudging his father as it contacted his lips. Before I could turn away, Franco pushed his chair back and crossed over to the shop.

– A-A, is you, Miss Post? Beg pardon. I mean, Miss Bridgemohan. I forget you prefer your proper name.

All eyes converged on me. Franco had taken up Mason's naming – wanting me to know that they had shared a conversation about me. I knew he wanted to provoke a response, but I held my tongue, certain that any show of resistance, with so big an audience, would only fuel his desire to attract attention. The best part of me wanted to believe that what Franco enjoyed was the banter – more than an intent to diminish me for intervening in Sam's affairs. For a moment, with nothing to spur him on, he seemed to relent. It was, I soon discovered, a temporary retreat.

– See how we get bright in Macaima, Miss Bridgemohan? Like you bring a light with you in dem two suitcase?

I felt a lurching in my stomach and bile in my mouth. It took me back to the parting words Miles had spat at me. *Murderer.* No matter how much I saw he was trying to bully me back into the relationship, and express an offended sense of male rights, I couldn't free myself from feeling guilt.

Meantime, Danny, Mason and Spanish joined him from the bar. Razor stayed where he was. Lucille had slipped out into the night. Mason held himself aloof, as though we had never met. He looked on in anticipation of the entertainment that the scene promised. Franco beamed. He had the audience he desired.

– I doh want to take in front, but is development PM coming here to talk. Plenty more than cocoa inside Macaima. Who want to stay sweet on brown sugar, let them stay. We moving on.

Laughter burst from those who recognised the much-repeated reference to the villages in the sugarcane district. The entire shop hung on Franco's words. This was his moment to shine, to flaunt his insider's knowledge, the source of which I could only suppose was the still invisible Mr Elton. Whatever Franco was allowed to know was sure to be much less than what he brandished. A ravenous hunger to be seen and acknowledged possessed the man. Someone took the bait.

– What coming, Franco? Tell we.

– Change coming. And faster than yuh could blink.

The gathering buzzed.

– What kinda change?

– Allyuh going to get details tonight from Mister PM-self. I only his humble foot soldier.

He would say no more on the matter. I saw he wanted to intimate some pledge of confidentiality to which he was unshakeably loyal. It was then, with the shop's thirst for further details unquenched, that he redirected his attention to me. In between dealing with other customers, Claudette had been slowly creating a small stack of my purchases on the counter. His eyes made a quick scan of the items and then of my person.

– I see you stocking up, Miss Bri, but like you forget to bring bag to hold yuh message.

Claudette had heard and made a loud steupes. She disappeared through the door that led to the unseen section of the building where the family lived, calling out irritably to someone about a burning pot and instructing Johnny to see about my purchases. Franco called Johnny over from the bar.

– What wrong with you, Chinee? You can't see this lady need a bag?

Johnny carried on serving at the other end of the counter, ignoring the scene that Franco was attempting to create.

– Come Johnny, d-lady want service!

When he was finished with his customer, Johnny took his time to make his way over to me and my purchases. No longer a young man, he moved with an arthritic shuffle. Both he and Claudette operated as though they had agreed upon a certain mode of service to maintain proprietorial distance. When someone expressed dissatisfaction with an item or its price, Johnny waited patiently for the complainant to decide on the purchase. He was never rude nor disrespectful. The supply of the villagers' needs was in his hands, and they knew it. When he finally reached my end, he looked blankly at Franco.

– What happen, Franco – PM raise your blood?

– No, but like you get plenty mouth tonight.

Franco was ready for a war of words, but Johnny was done with him. I called out what more I wanted. He wiped his damp face with the towel that was slung over his shoulder before reaching into the glass case that ran the entire length of the counter. He extracted a baby's feeder in plastic wrapping, with a yellow-haired, smiling infant on the label, and placed it beside my other purchases. The item caught Franco's eye.

– What! Miss Bri, you move like sprat in water. Baby reach already.

A loud guffaw came from Danny, who stood in the gap between the shop and bar. Johnny gestured to a boy who sat on top of a pile of rice bags behind him. He had Claudette's complexion and his father's eyes. He disappeared behind the curtained doorway and returned in no time with a cardboard box. Franco gestured to Danny. He moved forward hesitantly.

– Come, son, help out d-lady.

I had no intention of allowing Franco any liberty with my affairs.

– No need, I'm fine.

Amusement played on Franco's face as he watched me pay for my purchases.

– Danny young-an-strong. He could help you out, Miss Post.
– I'm fine, thanks.

By then Lucille had returned and moved right into the centre of the scene.

– I leave to take a pee and these fellas causing you trouble, Miss Post-lady?

– It's okay. I can manage.

– It doh look so to me. Put this man in his place one time. Franco, haul yuh arse somewhere else and leave this woman alone. She say she doh need *your* help. Dat is plain English.

– Okay-okay. She is independent woman. My mistake.

He made a show of scanning my body again, peeling away layers. Lucille nudged me towards the door and accompanied me outside.

– You have to shut Franco down one time. Forget polite. Doh fraid to hear yuh own voice. Is so to handle people like he. See how quick he boil down like bhaji.

– I hear you, Lucille, but he's so – awful.

– D-man plain rude-an-outta place. Listen, take my advice:

Forget nice. Stand yuh ground or he eat you raw. Anyhow, I have to go. I want to be in front row when meeting start.

I was glad to melt into the crowd that had packed into the junction, sore that I had not stood up to Franco. He seemed to enjoy being obnoxious. Lucille was right. I would not be his target ever again. I found a place next to Brenda, who stood with her sister. We chatted easily about expectations for the country: a new school for the village and a better water supply. Like Lucille, Brenda's sister planted short crops and she hoped the farmers in the district could get help with learning how to better fight off pests like bollworms, slugs and mealy bugs. Brenda, though, was sceptical. She thought it was best to stick to natural methods because the government people would only get farmers dependent on chemicals. It was all foreign to me. These women ate what they grew and sold what they could to keep their families alive.

Not long after, the news came: the PM wasn't coming. Johnny had taken the call. The crowd grumbled and fussed. People wanted to know why. After an eternity of waiting, punctuated by Franco's two or three ascents and descents from the stage, consultations with Johnny over the call, and with the drummer and dancers who were still waiting in the wings, Franco mounted the podium again and tested for sound. Waited. Tested for sound again and announced in a stammering style that urgent business had made it impossible for the PM to appear. He would come another day.

Murmurs, cuss words, suck-teeth circulated – but there was a concession. Franco from some place of found or feigned confidence made the announcement:

– Villagers, we suffer a setback, but we already get compensate. Tomorrow, Sunday, the Women's Coalition going to come here and talk. Four p.m. sharp. PM promise to…

The microphone screeched so loudly that his parting words were inaudible. Much of the crowd started to depart, enfolded in thick night. Others lingered by the stage, and the bar gained a few more customers before closing time. I saw Lucille moving off with a small group of women that included Brenda. She had lost the chance to ask her question. Maybe she would have a new one if another opportunity came. Music blasted through the speakers.

I was happy to head home. The scene with Franco was

troubling to say the least. He'd displayed an unusual degree of antagonism towards me. Maybe he also felt blindsided by whatever he supposed Mason might have said to me about Sam, so I was now included in the network of ambiguity surrounding her paternity. It was true that what Mason said had painted Franco in a different light, made him appear like a man floundering with unreconciled responsibilities for his daughter. Perhaps his attitude towards me was a displacement of his anxiety over Sam's situation – whatever it was. There was, though, no excuse for his obnoxious behaviour. Not knowing how to help her weighed on me. I had to find a way.

★

Cool air embraced me on the way to Beach Trace. I looked up at the stars. They appeared tranquil and untroubled from this distance, their music or rumblings lost to the ear. They were so much more than the shining we enjoyed. It felt good, in that moment, to be one with the night – to be just an anonymous body beneath the sky. But Lucille was right in so many ways. You can't fear your own voice – no matter what. Thea might have said the same thing. She said what she believed, and I suppose had paid the price. I had not attempted to get in contact with her after her departure and wondered if she would come back after she finished her studies, though she had said it was her intention to return, but things change. With Thea I had begun to feel myself to be a different person – more aware, less believing that there was nothing I needed to fight for. Why would I think that anyway – that the world was simply what it was?

I had lived in the Hendersons' yard surrounded by silences, including my own, and had mistaken my love of solitude for what was really the neutrality of distance between the annex and the main house. This protected me from knowing what was really happening. It blinded me from understanding why my mother would want to conceal Emily's books under her bed in the first place and why there were those strange days when Mrs Henderson would make impromptu, unannounced visits to our annex, especially when my mother had gone out to do the shopping for the main house. She would drift through the two rooms, her fingers trailing over the kitchen table, counter, backs of chairs, and saying nothing to me, as though I were invisible. Maybe she wanted me to disappear, but could not say so.

I thought of Sam. Her fascinating beauty was also her pain. Was she just tomboyish or was there more? I had not heard the phrase "double chenette" before, but was beginning to guess what it pointed to. I walked on, enfolded by the night. I could sense that the village, or maybe more so Franco, was trying to place me, pushing me to give an account of myself. Maybe there was gossip from Mrs Bailey circulating of which I was unaware. In truth, I both cared and didn't care. Whatever they thought they knew about me or what measure they had already taken of me was their concern, not mine. I wanted only to do my job until it was time to leave – do what I had come for, and find a way forward. For now, it was enough to be a body alive in the world – nothing more, nothing less. Wasn't that enough? I thought about Mason's story of Ana's *gift* of being able to change her form. But what had fuelled the story that had grown around her – and her daughter? So much about Macaima was withheld. So much came as second-hand knowledge, twice, or more, removed from the source. I would have given anything to hear more of the women tell their own stories.

★

Danny, unexpectedly, fell into step with me. He must have followed me from the shop.

– Miss, let me help carry yuh message.

I could hear the plea and apology in his voice.

– Doh take on Franco. He get carried away sometimes.

– Carried away is putting it lightly. He was plain rude.

– Sorry, Miss. So he is – but only sometimes.

I saw his effort to defend his father. He knew him more than I ever would – or feel inclined to. My mother always said every man jack has a store of good, no matter what. There was little benefit in dismissing Franco entirely. For all his faults he did care for Sam, Maria and his mother. Danny was perhaps hoping I could see that side of his father. I did not immediately respond, wondering whether the intention behind his offer was genuine. He was so much under Franco's wing. But when I eventually consented, I saw his shoulders relax as we set out together, carrying my purchases as though they were weightless. He had perhaps taken my consent as a token of a forgiveness I had not spoken, but he clearly wanted to hear. I wasn't ready to go further. Franco had been grossly out of line. If he had any decency, he would have been here instead of his son.

We walked in silence. I wanted to be alone with my thoughts and Danny, I could tell, was cautious, maybe a little uncertain as to whether his offer of help was a sufficient apology. He managed a question at the bottom of the steps.

– Miss, I see you buy bottle for yuh dogs.

– Yes. How did you know about them? They're not exactly mine.

I had not anticipated his reply.

– I fish them from the river.

– You did?

– I know Pixie woulda find them. She always down there hunting crayfish and she woulda never let them drown.

– You were right. She did save them.

– A pleasant goodnight to you, Miss.

I watched him jog up the trace, glad to discover that he was much more of his own man than I had initially thought.

CHAPTER 14 – WRITING ON THE ROAD

On Sunday morning, before daylight stitched through the trees that screened the sea at Goodbye, I could hear the pups beating around in their box. It was the sound of play. They were coming into their own. Day was the more active of the two. She rushed to feed first, was more adventurous and ready to stir up a fight. My purchase of the feeder was possibly unnecessary. I was learning as I went along, learning, too, how easy it was to love them. A louder than usual thud told me that the romping had overturned their temporary house. I found both comically draped in the towel I had used to create a warm bed for them. The house captured an almost steady stream of breeze off the mountains, so nights could be chilly. I sat on the floor and watched them enjoying each other as they romped about, trying out their legs, jaws, yelps, and even their little growls. It was Sunday morning indeed.

I spent much of that morning in the yard, weeding a patch of ground that had once served as a kitchen garden. Hardy clusters of turmeric, Spanish thyme, a few exhausted pimento and hot pepper shrubs were all that remained. I found a rusty cutlass and rake tucked away in the rafters beneath the house. There was also a pair of tall tops, but I abandoned the idea of wearing them. Franco's scorpion story was still fresh in my mind. With Night and Day nearby doing their nosey wobble-about in the grass, I managed to clear enough ground for about five beds. The land, being elevated from the beach and with enough distance from the sea, looked rich enough to grow almost anything. Macaima was interesting that way, being coastal but with an inland feel at the same time. I figured if I could get good seeds I could try with corn, okra, tomatoes, and pigeon peas. Johnny seemed to stock a bit of everything, so I supposed he carried some agricultural products as well. If not, asking Lucille or making a trip to Railway were my other options.

By late morning, the puppies started their feed-time noises and I was about to do the needful when I saw him – a young man standing just on the boundary of the yard where the concrete path led up to the house.

– Mornin-mornin. You Miss Anna?

– Yes, I am. Who's asking?

I protectively moved closer to the pups.

– Roland – Roland Mendoza.

Of course, I knew the name, but he was younger than I had imagined, pencil slim in his well-worn khaki trousers and a visibly stained, mint-coloured, long-sleeved shirt. He wore it unbuttoned at the front and cuffs. A cigarette was tucked behind each ear and his hair was cropped close to the skull.

– How can I help, Roland?

He eyed the pups with an approving smile.

– I see they doing good. Sam ask me to check on them.

– Have you seen her?

– Not since two days now. I hear she home by her granny.

– How is she? Do you know?

He looked towards the derelict church. I thought it an odd place to cast his gaze just at that moment. The pups began protesting, being robbed of their feed time.

– Not so good. She talking about running away from here.

– Did something happen at her house?

– No – down by the river.

– What do you mean – what happened?

– Some young fellas – they rough-handle her and…

He could not complete the sentence. He tried another approach.

– They say she is not no girl. So she tell me.

– Who said that and why?

– Barry, fuh sure.

I noticed his response was only to the first half of my question. I let it go.

– Shouldn't the police know about this?

– Police will say is only horseplay.

110

– This is the second time, for Christ's sake! Has anyone even bothered to lodge a proper complaint on her behalf?

It could have been perspiration that he wiped from his face just then. I regretted my distance – and my suspicion of him.

– You know how people stop… They quick to beat down what different from them.

– This is awful. What can we do, Roland?

– Better she go away from here.

– Is that an answer?

He dug his hands deep into his pockets, looking perplexed. I didn't feel I should press him further. It struck me that I had asked a question that was really my own, about my escape. When he spoke next it was to shift his attention to the ground I was working on.

– I see yuh making garden, Miss Anna.

– Yes, I thought I would get it going again.

– I could get some seedlings for you – okra, tomato, pepper, and some corn grain, too, if yuh want.

– That's perfect. Thank you.

He reached down to retrieve a crocus bag I had not seen.

– I heading out now.

I watched him move off, carrying himself quietly, lightly, with a gait that was much older than his age, as if giving himself to the road he travelled. He walked, I thought, mindfully, like someone who had come to learn that neither haste nor resolve was any guarantee against disappointment and, yes, pain. Whether that stride was defeat or acceptance, I did not know.

My thoughts turned to the arrival of the Women's Coalition that afternoon. I planned to be there. I gathered the pups up and went in.

★

Big confusion was in session when I got to the junction. Franco was at the centre of it all. There were no witnesses – or at least no one was willing to say they had seen the culprit. During the post-lunch lull, some phantom hand had painted an aspersion on the road, exactly at the foot of the stage on which the PM had been expected to speak. Johnny made the discovery and Franco was roused from his siesta to deal with the situation. From all reports, he had acted quickly by painting over the offending word, using the only paint he could put his hands on. White oil. Unfortunately, the effort had failed. Somehow, in the rush, he managed to leave two letters, N and G slightly visible. The vandal had used red. People put two and two together. Franco, after all, was not a reader and so could not be blamed for the unintended exposure of the slur. The remnant caused a storm. Speculation about the likely offender circulated. Accusations flew right and left, the target being Balkissoon, who was not present to defend himself.

Fortunately, the coming visit by the Women's Coalition helped to cool tempers. There was a meeting to prepare for. Another effort was made to conceal the crime, this time in black oil. Razor mused philosophically as the final concealing coat was applied.

– Yuh think paint is cure for a history? It right below this same road we travel on. Scratch the surface and it jump out.

Lucille, though, saw the whole matter from a different lens.

– To me, it look like we well-an-proper blend.

No one responded to either claim.

Franco was, understandably, not in the best of moods. Cray and Razor were directed to barricade the steps to the stage. It was designated off limits to everyone, including the Women's Coalition. Given what had transpired on the road, vigilance was the best course. In any case, the structure had been set up for another purpose – the PM's speech or talk. An alternative space for the meeting had to be found and Franco wanted the propriety of his rationale for devising a different arrangement for the Coalition to be well publicised.

– How it go look to put D-Man to talk from a stage people already prance-up on? Look at the commesse some fool put on gov'ment property. Certain people have no blasted respect for nobody.

No one voiced an opinion, choosing silence or just grumbling among themselves. Perhaps they were in shock that the underbelly of an unhealed wound had been so crudely exposed and they needed time to process the reality. I felt that Franco was probably not acting on his own in making the stage a restricted area, though his ill temper at having to reorganise the meeting's venue at short notice lay behind the point he wanted to make. I remained on the fringes, observing developments, along with the ten or so women who had already arrived for the meeting. Eventually, after some discussion that required seeking permission from Mr Austin, the schoolyard was decided upon as the venue.

We watched Cray and Razor transfer a few chairs from the warden's office to the school. What would serve as a head table? Johnny was not disposed to lending any furniture from his bar. He had already given up space for a stage that was not going to be used and probably not going to be dismantled in the timeframe agreed upon. The idea emerged that two desks from the infant's classroom, one placed on top the other, would suffice. Those seated at the head table would simply have to be careful not to topple them. The Mrs Somebody carded to be the main speaker – Franco had neglected to ask her name – would also have to make do without the help of a podium or microphone. Those sourced for the PM were also deemed off limits, indeed unnecessary, given the scaled-down nature of the event.

A few more women arrived as four o'clock neared. Mitra dropped off his wife, Sandra, parked his taxi on the opposite side of the road and settled down to wait out the meeting. Miss Gomez breezed in, looking as though she had not changed from her church clothes. She took a seat in the front row of the modest four rows of chairs, three abreast. Brenda had again chosen to stand at the back. Alisha and Obadiah chased each other, dodging in and out of the arranged seating. I wanted to talk to Brenda about Patrick and what Roland had revealed about the river incident. The principal's son had again been implicated. That, though, would have to wait. This wasn't the place to broach such a conversation. Brenda was with three women I had met at last night's cancelled *Face the People* meeting – her sister, Deborah, and Marissa and Baby. Both lived deep inside L'Avenir, the place Brenda had one day simply packed up and left. She had talked about this decision on one of her stop-ins to ask if I was working on Kizzy's address. I listened. It was all I could offer her.

– I can't explain how it happen. Maybe independence take me when our anthem sing. Maybe it was when Elton first read out Doctor King speech, I have a dream. I look at my chirren and I tell Paul, I leaving inside here. Estate life done for me. I want them to be part of this nation we start to make.

So I take up myself and walk out. We temporary by my sister until I could see a way. On a Saturday, we sell souse, sweetbread, pone in Railway. Better so. First, I try to do my own hustle in Sando but police say I breaking the law. I say, Mr Officer, I here trying to make a living so my chirren could eat. Law is law he tell me. So I in Railway now – me and Debbie. So far we good. I taking a chance on Independence, Miss Bri. If Paul want to stay sleeping, that is his choice. I moving on to better – for me and my concern.

I thought Brenda's courage was amazing, but nothing could have prepared me for what transpired at the Coalition meeting. I don't think anyone gathered that afternoon saw it coming.

★

Minutes before four o'clock, the Coalition rolled in, a modest motorcade of two or three cars and a minivan. The women, serious-faced and purposeful, made their way to the school yard. Franco left, with his workmen in trail, after a brief exchange with one of the leaders. Three women took their positions at the head table, exuding confidence as they exchanged whispered comments and cast inscrutable glances at the gathering they were to address. Miss Gomez was in her element. She perked up, sitting with ankles crossed, clearly admiring the women's ensembles that suggested a get-it-done work ethic balanced with an unmistakably feminine accent: tailored skirts and sleeveless bodices in checkered and floral prints, matching accessories, lightly styled hair, bright lipsticks and stylish stilettos and pumps. The Coalition's supporters, in maidenly skirts and blouses (they seemed to favour white), filed into the seats behind Miss Gomez.

A little after ten past four, we were encouraged to come closer. Miss Gomez frisked from her seat as though she had been paid a personal compliment. Baby and Deborah exchanged comments behind curtained mouths, mischief playing on their faces. Miss Gomez fussed some more. A few of the accompanying members tried to draw the rest of us in. Nobody moved. The Macaimans remained on the outskirts looking on, stubbornly noncompliant even as urgent deliberations ensued among the lead members. They wanted to begin. The main speaker, a Mrs Somebody, adjusted her posture in her seat, dusted away something from the surface of the large notepad on her lap. Her companion blotted perspiration from her brow. Another invitation was issued for us to draw nearer. I decided it was time to yield but wondered at the reluctance of the other women. It wasn't exactly shyness or timidity. Brenda remained where she was. After more consultations, the member elected to do the introductions, a Mrs Ottley, called the meeting to order, trumpeting the party's well-known platform boast, touting its greatness that would prevail and so on. She ended with an exuberant: *Welcome, sisters of Macaima!*

A round of applause followed, the cadence unsteady. We waited. Introductions were made. We learned that the main speaker was a Mrs Alphonso. Mrs Ottley directed an appreciative round of applause her way. The supporters joined in and their effort caught on in pockets among the Macaima women. Mrs Ottley spent considerable time outlining the important role the Coalition had played in winning votes for the election that had freed the country from England. Its members were the invisible backbone of that victory, and so on. The party had them in its debt. The members clapped and nodded their agreement. Mrs Alphonso rose and directed her applause to the members in white before she indicated to Mrs Ottley that she wanted to say something to the gathering. Mrs Ottley gave way, returning to her seat in the stooped gait of someone trying unsuccessfully to be inconspicuous.

– Sisters, ladies, women of Macaima, I want you to feel comfortable and at home. I want you to know that the Women's Coalition of the People's Independence Party is fundamentally interested in *human* rights and we are dedicated to improving the condition of women throughout this blessed nation. Be assured, our meetings are meant to foster unity and to support those in cabinet whose appointed task is to lead. Do not be afraid. We are not, as some might have you think, unbridled feminists. So, ladies, let us get to work. Unity is strength. Welcome.

Her comments were intended to put the gathering at ease, but they served more to unsettle. Amid the general shifting around were whispered queries about the word *feminist*. What did it mean – and should we care? Mrs Ottley was instructed to carry on as planned. All were invited to stand for the Coalition's prayer.

Members passed around printed copies. The head table rose in unison. Deepening her voice to a pitch that she felt would not just be heard, but command authority, Mrs Ottley began:

– *O Almighty and all wise God / We dedicate this meeting to thy care and guidance, / Unite our hearts in the oneness of purpose…*

… and so on and so on. Each word was precisely enunciated in a way that distracted more than invited real listening for being so forced, but the moment was Mrs Ottley's. She prayed on:

– *Keep us, O Lord, from pettiness / Let us be large in thought, word and deed / Let us be done with fault-finding and leave off self-seeking…*

And so on…

Things, though, started to collapse with the reading of each verse of the prayer. Some of the interjections I heard, but could not immediately identify the source. At first, not a sound had come from the gathering in response to the prayer. Not until the first, *Oh no!* – almost inaudible – intruded at the end of the "*leave off self-seeking*" supplication. Mrs Ottley scanned the small gathering, as if to reassure herself that she had been mistaken, that no-one was attempting to interrupt her praying. She continued.

– *May we put all pretence aside and meet each other face to face…*

… and so on and so on.

It was, in truth, a very long prayer and maybe too ambitious in the work it had set out to do. With every verse, every petition, the voice from the back of the meeting grew more insistent with its *Oh-No!* So, by the time the goodly prayer reached an entreaty to the Almighty to: *Make us grow calm, serene and gentle*, a very audible, unmistakable objection exploded:

– No! I say, No-No!

Some paused from their conscientious following of the words on the slip of paper in their hands. Others opened eyes that were squeezed shut in a show of concentrated sincerity. They raised bowed heads and looked about them. Mrs Ottley would not be fazed. She persisted with what she had been elected to do, pushed through to the very end with what I later discovered was an adaptation of the Mary Stewart collect prayer. The Coalition's version was dotted with petitions for the protection of the political leader and his party from the *snares and fiery darts of the enemy, for Jesus sake.*

We saw Mrs Ottley's eyes change from a disbelieving squint to oversized buttons of alarm trained on the woman at the back. She had suddenly become front and centre stage of the meeting's gaze. Pushing against the surging current of dissent, Mrs Ottley read on and on in denial of the brewing protest. She lifted her voice to a shouting pitch in an effort to drown out the disturbance, but to no avail. A hurricane was on its way.

– I say, NO! What on earth you telling me here today? Not me. I, Brenda Solomon, who jus walk outta estate life and into this thing we call Independence. You cannot expect me to be handmaid for no damn party. Not when we live for years-plus-years saying Y*es-Suh-no-Mam*. You asking me not to find fault, not to have grievance or opinion – and to seek nothing for myself! I-me, all-ah-we here, who know what it is to satisfy with seconds, to work for pittance so *Mr-Dis-&-Mrs-Dat* could live big. Oh-No! Not today! Not I-ME-WE, who had to make a study of *pretence*, playing *quiet, calm and gentle* in the face a plain selfishness and boldface injustice. I who had to take backseat in school, in church, you not asking me to pray to God to save me from whatever *you* call *petty*. No-No, Miss-Lady, Not so! Is not Brenda Solomon, you asking to not *forget to be kind,* like I know nothing about my own human heart! And to make matters worse, you sound like woman alone equip for bad-mind, small-mind and mauvais langue. Miss-Lady, I say, No! Not today. You cannot come here in my place to welcome me – WE. You cannot say *your* prayer like Sandra and Devi not present. Look, Yasmin right here, and Baba Cortney wife. Look Mama Gloria here too. What about their heart – and their God? I have to wonder where, in all that betterment that you say you want, all-ah-we fit in? And I mean everybody here, and those who on dey way, or elsewhere. So I say, NO. Not today, Miss Coalition! *You* not ready for *WE*.

Brenda untied the wrap that bound her hair to signal she was done, grabbed Alisha and Obadiah by their arms and stormed away. Mitra blew his horn. Sandra knew that it was time to go. Lucille, who had been silent throughout the whole turmoil, looked directly at Mrs Alphonso, her eyes ablaze:

– Brenda is right! Massa day far from done. Not yet. Not until *your* politics change.

She too walked away. We all looked on, stunned. The members at the head table froze. Speechless. That was the end of the meeting, or you might say the start of something else.

CHAPTER 15 – A RETURN

The lower reaches of the hills were already in shadow when I left the junction. Evening rays caught the leaves of towering immortelles in the hills of L'Avenir, so although it was not their season for flowering, they appeared to glow like brief flames before nightfall. I walked home canopied by that beauty and rage. Brenda's emphatic *No* had upstaged the meeting. The sheer energy of her refusal was infectious. We were all, I imagined, a little out of our depth and unready for her objection, which had certainly run ahead of the Coalition's mandate and vision. Even so, I felt the reverberation of her voice awaken every cell of my being. Her objection had surfaced, it seemed, from every age and circumstance to touch the unvoiced protest that we each carried concerning the prayer's unconsidered or deliberate omissions. It ignored the collective history of the very suppressed voices and lives the Coalition ostensibly sought to liberate and recruit in the work of the nation's development.

I walked home, upheld by the possibilities she had opened in us. Maybe some would feel she had overstepped. I had overheard Yasmin's hushed complaint to Sandra, whose wide-eyed confusion remained intact, when she asked, *Who Brenda feel she is to talk for we?* That Yasmin had found it necessary to insist that *she* was not voiceless was itself a gain. None of us were. That was the evening's greatest gift – the recognition that to speak is both risk and responsibility. Were we ready? Brenda had introduced us to that question. Was I ready?

I released my body to her word's defiant current, as if to test my own limits. The toasty sweetness of the cooling earth, mingled with fresh mountain breeze, pushed at me past the remains of *Our Lady of Victory*, past the De Valremy holiday house, right down to

Goodbye Bay. I could not think of the bay without remembering those drowned runaways or the violation of a woman at the site of the church. Possibly there were more than one. They were my grandfather's people, and also mine. Somehow that story of the unnamed had endured. Whether truth or fiction, it wanted completion. Who was she – and what does she, and so many others, yet demand for her life? I had turned to catch a glimpse of Mama Gloria when Brenda called her name at the meeting, but saw no one that could match the face I imagined. Maybe I had long failed to see her.

And what of the promise my grandfather had supposedly left with his family: *When I leave I will return.* It depended on a shared recognition – that someone would know the one who returned. My mother had refused me part of my history that was not so much lost as concealed. I had never challenged her silence enough. Perhaps, I, too, wanted to keep the balance she saw as *our luck*. And what of the woman on Beach Trace? The recognition she extended to me, mistaken or not, I could not return. Who was she and from what past or present did she belong? Some part of her history wanted to be known, or to make itself known to me. Maybe Macaima wanted me to share its own complicated story or to recognise that I already did. Thea had once said what I thought the oddest thing when the rift between Comrade Nello and the PM became public: *It was the first major failure of our democracy.* When I asked why, she sighed. I must have disappointed her tremendously because her only reply was that *Half of a heart can't beat properly.* In that moment, I realised for the first time that what I have most keenly felt for most of my life was grief. I still had to discover that true loss – as opposed to concealment – can heal, because its substance is real and, though changed, persists into our present.

With the few buildings clustered at the junction at my back, with all they echoed of the estate Brenda had left behind, and all that the meeting had thrown to the surface of my consciousness, it was a relief to allow the fast-arriving presence of night to take over: the singing bush, the river's insistent wash down to the waiting bay and the push and pull of the waves against the shore. I felt I had slipped backwards in time to the very beginnings of the place, the island, the land, before its naming and making into a human habitation. My thoughts drifted further out, to the moving channel between the island and the Main, and into the open ocean, and above to the endless sky. That expanded space held me, became a breathing lung, a rhythm to which the life of the place seemed to answer.

Into that chamber of nature's sounds, Brenda's protest travelled like a beginning, a word searching for a response, a *yes* to a future. It followed the road all the way out to Railway and the acres and acres of canefields, the sweat-soaked land of cocoa and citrus, fragranced by fresh and rotting green, running rivers and salted coasts. Her words spanned the entire breadth of the island from St Madeleine to Caroni. They touched the valleys and mountains to the north of the island, in Diego Martin and Petit Valley, Paramin and up to Maracas, Blanchisseuse, and across to Matelot, Grande Riviere and San Souci. They found every shore no matter how inaccessible, every village and town, suburb and yard, before swinging by Galera to pay homage to those who flew from its height or swam back home. They travelled down the east coast to Matura and cut a path through Sangre Grande and Valencia, reached Cumuto and Brazil, then travelled the length of the east-west corridor all through Arima and Curepe, St Joseph, Mount Hope to San Juan Junction, Barataria and Laventille to Port of Spain, and finally to the Gulf before whipping across Chaguaramas and Carenage. They flew towards Mucurapo, St James and Woodbrook to end up in the People's Parliament at Woodford Square, where they hovered over the Red House and stirred the bones of every violation and injustice buried in its foundations. Had they been there all along, present at my first political meeting as it spilled out into the streets and took the road to Chaguaramas?

★

…I could not forget… We were all there that day, in the Square, pressed tight in the crowd that hung on the Premier's words. Miles and Yolanda had insisted that I go with them to hear his speech. Miles had said it would be my first education. So that Friday, I found myself there. April 22nd, 1960. That was the day we stood together in the belly of the *People's University* and felt in ourselves the opening of a future. We stood drinking in his words, watching his every move as he burnt those *seven deadly sins*. With him, we chorused as the flames rose: *To Hell with it!* We were all there, part of the ritual at which he was high priest, exorcising the burden of history, or at least wanting to believe that it would be possible to begin afresh. Each document was part of a chain we had to break: from the colonial constitution to that thorn-in-the-side, the Chaguaramas Base agreement with the Americans, and every other shackle, from the ownership of newspapers to the telephone ordinance that represented Union Jack control. Everything went up in flames. Smoke spiralled up from the bandstand in Port of Spain. Then the wreath was laid and, like an affirmation from heaven, the rains came and the march started. Singing: *To hell with it!* Together, we were making a world, a new day from those flames: *To Hell with it...* That was the promise...

And there was Thea and her tease that I had not yet found my fight, but that I would. I hear her words now: *Oh but you will, Miss Bridgemohan – once you have really loved somebody and something deeply enough...*

★

... And what of Brenda's *No*? What did it have to say to me? I listened to it travel along the western coast, keeping company with the Gulf and all it contained. It went past Caroni, Claxton Bay until it reached San Fernando, La Brea, Point Fortin to Cedros, Icacos, Erin and Moruga before it boomeranged back to Harris Promenade and the Naparima Hills, Siparia, Penal. It swung back across to Fyzabad, Rio Claro, Princes Town to Mayaro. It hit Guayaguayare and Galeota and finally landed in Macaima, where that stalled Women's Coalition meeting had trickled to an end, and we had each, in some way, confronted what united and divided us. Were we really all that different? We wanted more or less that same things.

The shuttle of the tide at Goodbye grew stronger as I neared the house. The bits of story I had heard about the runaways returned. Those Warao, if that was in fact the tribe, had found it necessary for their living to reject the mission's enclosure, its order, language, faith. They had travelled east until they ended up at the foot of the hills Columbus had named and, no longer wanting to live exiled from themselves, had opted for a return to the Main when they entered the sea at Goodbye. Perhaps the piecemeal stories of that fatal day the villagers passed on was the endless *return* their farewell had anticipated. Maybe those runaways were trying to say that they had made a choice to save themselves, and those who would remain, so no one should ever again have to make the choice they had to make.

★

Before I came abreast to the house I could see that someone was sitting on the front steps. It was Franco, but he must have been preoccupied with his thoughts because he did not see or hear my approach. He jumped to his feet at my greeting.

– Oh is you, Miss Bri? Your footfall soft like ghost.

– Ghost? I'm very much in the world, Mr Franco.

Now that I understood him a little more, it was easier to shut him down before he could strike and I got sucked in.

– I know you here, Miss Bri. Maybe I doze-off. After all d-prepare-I-prepare, look at what transpire. I hear Coalition meeting buss.

He was genuinely disappointed.

– I wouldn't exactly say so. It didn't go as planned, that's for sure. Brenda had the floor. She was brilliant! You should've been there.

– I glad you profit from it.

– Yes, it was very instructive.

– Yuh going to hear real intelligent talk when d-Doc reach. Coalition get credit for rallying all-dem woman to vote but they too hurry to take charge.

– I didn't get the impression that taking charge is the Coalition's aim at all. Quite the opposite, which is perhaps part of the problem. Maybe as the group evolves, its agenda will change from being merely mouthpieces for the party. Who knows? In any case, I am very certain that *intelligent* talk is not the exclusive facility of the PM, Mr Franco.

– I not clear on yuh big-time words, but I hear you, Miss Bri. I didn't come down here to pick no fight.

– Who's fighting? We're talking.

Whichever, I wasn't disposed to an uphill battle with him over his views. Better to change the subject.

– So how's Sam doing?

– If you mean Pixie, she right where she should be – with her grannie.

– She doesn't like the name by the way. Do you know she's still being bullied by those boys?

– What happen now? I don't have it easy. I have plenty on my plate. That nex one up-an-down to all kinda doctor-an-priest. Money spend but no cure.

– Do you mean Maria?

He hesitated but chose to ignore my question.

– She stop talk years now. De Valremy raise that girl like she born to his own marrid-wife. She spend holiday in this same house and learn book right in that room over there.

He pointed to the structure I had called the storeroom.

– Not a man could go back there when lesson giving. He was strict too bad.

Though Sam's situation had been sidestepped, I let him go on with his Maria story. I noted that he slipped seamlessly from father to son. Whether he referenced Francisco or Joseph no longer mattered. They had been fused into a single identity, a paternity that I thought he both wanted to claim and reject, and that this very ambivalence was the chasm into which he had fallen and had become a perpetual place of torment. Perhaps that blurring was his way of shielding himself from confronting some truth about his relationship with the man I suspected to be his father.

– What did Joseph think about the attention his father paid to Maria?

– Nothing. Estate work never done. Joseph was busy night and day. When work done, he make Maria recite for everybody whatever she learn on that same veranda up there. I doh read or sign my name proper but now Maria doh even want to read book. She get too much. That is how I see it.

– Too much of *what* may be the appropriate question, Mr Franco.

He grunted, removed his hat and glanced uneasily over at the church. His hand moved to rub his shoulder at the spot where he had supposedly been stung by a scorpion. I thought of the room where my suitcase was lodged. It had been Maria's classroom. Franco said that she was the source of her own tragedy. I began to suspect otherwise. My heart sank.

– Like I say, I not here to quarrel. I come to say Elton reach back from town.

He spoke a little tight-jawed.

– Oh he's in the village?

– Yes. He bring back Maria.

– I hope she's better.

– She could never better, but that talk done. Elton passing by here tomorrow. Something to do with yuh place.

– Is there a problem?

– Tomorrow he go explain everything. I gone.

Fatigue took the edge from his tone, but it was clear how much Sam and Maria were the cause and target of Franco's frustration and anger. Maybe they reminded him of some other source of helplessness or shame that he resented having to carry, but was unable to confront or name. I could not let him go.

– We need to help your daughter, Franco.

– My daughter? What you know bout my business, Miss Bridgemohan?

– My only concern is for Sam's wellbeing. And that should be yours, even more than mine. Please, think about her and what she needs.

My plea had somehow reached him. He slumped to the steps like all the breath had been taken from him.

– I never ask for the trouble she bring. All I could say is that I do my best.

– What is the matter with her? Whatever it is, there must be a solution.

– She better off up on Ave-near.

– Is that fair to her, Franco? Why are you trying to hide her away.

– Life never fair, Miss Bridgemohan. I learn so from small.

– You're right about that, but we can try to make it more just, at least.

– Pixie is what she is.
– What on earth do you mean?
His sigh was more a groan that filled the silence of Beach Road.
– All I could tell you is that she…
He fell silent and looked about the yard.
– She like that hibiscus flower. That is what dem boys expose.
– She's what?
– She born as two.

The revelation opened like an infinite horizon before us. A pair of emerald parrots screeched overhead. Franco followed the frantic pumping of their wings and unconsciously flipped off his hat.

– Look like we getting some rain.
– She prefers to be called Sam by the way. Why does that upset you so much?
– I not responsible for how she turn out, Miss Bri. Not me, but I still here, not Kizzy. I stay even though she and Bones leave me in doubt. I choose to deal with her best I can. I know life one way, Miss Bri – simple. I make six children. Pix… Sam… she bring me only upset. But she is my own.

It was the first time that I had heard him claim her.

– Maybe, Franco, a body is more than we make it out to be, like a place…

He paused as if to absorb the largeness of his claim – to settle into it.

– I born on this island, right here in Macaima, but I would be a liar if I tell you I know it through and through. Every day, I see different with the same. Every day, I see this place born and die and come back new again. Maybe I am the one doing the changing. Maybe we happening together, the way Sam come into this world and change everything I think I know…

Words escaped him. He rose, replaced his hat and made his way back to the junction.

I went to the hibiscus bush Franco had recruited to explain his daughter. This was Sam. Now understanding dawned. I too had been thinking of her as though she was defined by an error. She is who she is. Franco was right about that. I cupped a flower with both hands. The family had chosen to conceal her secret. Things, though, had fallen into place after the incident at the school and

Franco's decision to keep her at home. It was difficult to tolerate his insensitivities and prejudices, but I was beginning to understand more about what lay behind his behaviour towards Sam. He could not manage the complication that she represented and he suspected that she had taken me into her confidence much more than she actually had. No doubt he felt exposed. I could not know the all of it, but I knew that Sam needed support and help. That was the bottom line. The girlhood she had worn externally was over. Or was it? Her fascinating beauty was also her pain. I wished there could be some other way. Dark had fallen when I entered the house.

CHAPTER 16 – MONDAY'S CHILD

On the Monday that came to be known as Storm Day, I walked up Beach Trace as usual, only this time there was a great deal more to mull over. It was my third week in Macaima and I had begun my experiment with leaving the pups alone in the house. It no longer made sense to lug them to and fro, especially since Sam's riddle had been, in a sense, revealed. The kitchen was now their domain. I knew there would be a mess to be cleaned up when I returned to check on them at lunchtime, but that was okay. I hoped, though, that Roland had passed on to Sam my message about their wellbeing. That would make her happy. I had never imagined that she was also the *brother* I had been waiting on. That was something in itself. The world is full of wonder.

My walk to the junction took around fifteen to twenty minutes, depending on my pace. Its distance from the junction and the absence of a telephone had at first made me feel cut off from the village, but as time went on my discomfort dissipated. The sheer serenity of Beach Trace took hold. It was a joy simply to stroll along the deserted road with the rustle of leaves and the wash of water for companions before entering the junction. This was never bustling, but was, nevertheless, a reconnection with life and its demands. Each day brought to my attention something I had failed to notice before. Franco was right about that – about being renewed by our seeing.

I paused at the shallow pool by the beam bridge. From my very first day, it had become one of my favourite spots on the trace. The water collected there before exiting to join the main tributary that tumbled down behind the church-school and warden's office. The flow at the bridge was much gentler and provided a resting place to which I easily surrendered. On sunny days, the water was so clear that nothing on the bed was hidden. A variegated combination of jade and emerald moss grew on the rocks that bordered the banks. Delicate fanlike filaments rippled and trailed in the current, their graceful dances leisurely scribbles in the water's flow. It was like seeing through the surface of a mirror, right into its submerged underworld where that alluring script drew me in only to obscure its meaning. It made me think of those occasional notes my mother passed to Mr Henderson as the *Ford* backed out of the yard. Some request or reminder, maybe, that she wanted to go unnoticed. Their secret bond grew into a void that I felt would consume me unless I could give it a shape and a name, but her silence refused to let me in.

The pool held me captive until a cloud sailed overhead, shielding the sun for no longer than a second. In the fleeting gap, when the cloud's shadow was cast upon the river's surface, my own reflection met me, surfacing as from a deep place, and with it the rhyme my mother sang to keep me out of her way when she worked at her washing or ironing for the main house. She sang it, too, so I could do what she most wanted me to do: learn. Education, more than the little that she had got, was what she wanted for me. The rhyme began: *Monday's child...* I was born on a Monday. When I asked her what it meant to be *fair of face*, she cupped mine between her hands and said, *You, Anna – you, inside-out. Monday's child is Annabelle*, she sang. *See. I make it mean who you are. Doh end up like me.* Another time, when I had complained that *Annabelle* didn't rhyme with the line about Tuesday's child being *full of grace*, she stopped her work of hanging out Mr Henderson's white shirts on a line to consider the puzzle. The front of her dress clung to her like a second skin. After a moment's thought she said, *Well, Missy, if is so, we rhyme however we please. That rhyme talk foolishness anyhow.* From that day on, every day ended with *Annabelle* until, in quick time, there was no more need for singing the rhyme.

In her own way, my mother sought to make me see myself as sufficient. Perhaps what she meant to say, from some need of her own, was that I had my place, even as she hid a major piece of my puzzle to safeguard the life she believed had saved us both. The Hendersons' house offered her survival, and she had settled for her portion. I could not know for sure. We never spoke of such things. *Bloom where yuh plant* was her motto. She was alone with a daughter to raise and going back to Siparia was impossible: *Go home for what? Nothing there for me.* Over the years, though, I had collected her maxims that sought to affirm the life she had made for us. *You can't leave good to end up in worse…*

But I knew the weight of the silence she maintained to keep what she had found – a life not quite full, though no life, she said, ever was. Maybe Mrs Henderson felt the same as she sat installed on the front veranda or under the gazebo. Even when she smiled, she had the saddest eyes. They had a look of incompleteness, unattended dissatisfaction, like her constant asking for more ice or whether the *Ford* had swung into the yard. Time revolved around her husband's leavings and arrivals. His homecomings, I remember, were like a brief but anticipated breeze that brought life back to the house – the *hello* that followed a playful sip of whatever sparkled in his wife's glass, then the drop of his feet, sure and confident, on the polished floors, the clatter of dishes and cutlery as he ate what my mother had cooked, served before his disappearance into his room of newspapers, books and LPs.

To me, he was my endless store of peppermints and quarters that he put into the palm of my hand, winking as though we shared a secret. In the midst of his comings and goings was my mother's patient dusting, sweeping, polishing, her washing in the big sink behind the annex and her Sunday afternoons sermonising on her gratitude for having what she most wanted in life – me – to fill in what was missing. I could not blame my mother for her choice; I could not say that Mr Henderson or his wife had been unkind to us, only that the unspoken had its immeasurable, indescribable cost.

The shrill cry of some bird I couldn't name startled me. When I looked again all I could see was the riverbed at bottom of the pool. *Monday's child is Annabelle* – those rhymes that meant nothing and like my own birth remained unexplained. It was time to move on.

★

Entering the junction was always an immediate reminder of the importance places like Macaima enjoyed when cocoa pods lit the hills. Everything was at hand – a whole city in the bush. Now it was a forgotten backwater, waiting for its chance to cash in on the promises of independence – education, modernisation, technology, sustainable development – that kind of talk. Hemmed in as it was by mountains of stalled and rotting estates, you could say that Macaima carried its history on its back and, at the same time, looked out towards a future that was yet to unfold, but which was already harnessed to the growing importance of oil and gas. Balkissoon's was a lone voice warning about the danger of neglecting the land, but no one was prepared to take him seriously, even when he made a worthwhile point. He was with the Labour Party and that mired him in the suspicions of a political culture that, from its infancy, had been snagged in a stubborn divide, summed up so crudely by words like the one the unknown vandal had written on the main road. Balkissoon was singled out as the prime suspect, a charge that he vehemently denied but could not disprove.

Mitra and Johnny were locked in an intense discussion outside the shop. From their glances and gestures, I could tell that their conversation was focused on the unused stage. No news had arrived about the PM's rescheduled visit, if indeed there was going to be one. The structure was now an obstruction, a reminder that the priorities of the PM had shifted elsewhere. I stopped to take in the scene. Someone, maybe Franco, had already removed the pennants and banner which, in the light of the events of the last few days, seemed a premature victory cry. The garlands were also gone, but the party's symbol, a hardy species of flower, remained pinned to the stage, beginning to show signs of wilt. Franco was nowhere to be seen. I was happy to pass by unnoticed.

The warden's office had for some days been open for business. The alleged flea infestation had no doubt been successfully eradicated. Mrs Austin, I supposed, had arrived early and was somewhere within, readying herself to carry out the business of the day. Whether Mr Elton would turn up was another matter. Brenda called out to me on her way up the hill to drop off her children at the school. I returned her greeting. Patrick was not with them. I had not seen him since the day his mother had stopped by after her visit to the principal's office, and I guessed that he would have usually accompanied his siblings to school. Based on Roland's story, I knew that his alleged accomplice, Barry, was still at large. The bullying of Sam had to stop. It was a good reason to catch Brenda on her way down.

After the Coalition's meeting, I felt that I owed her a word of gratitude for what she had done on behalf of us all. The criticism she had levied was brutal – but necessary. Whether or not the group was conscious of it, the prayer announced the group's politics. Not everyone had approved of Brenda's interruption. I saw Devi shield her face with her veil and Mrs Austin averted her eyes. Maybe they were embarrassed and thought her behaviour discourteous or unwarranted. I was among those who had stayed on to witness Mrs Alphonso's labour to regain control of what was left of the meeting. She had struggled to deliver the speech she was scheduled to give and to salvage what little there was left of the event after Brenda's departure.

I had made my own exit with most of the other remaining women when the registration exercise began. The anticipated avalanche of support from the villagers was not forthcoming, but even so, my decision to stay to hear Mrs Alphonso say her piece seemed almost a betrayal of Brenda's critique of the group's purpose. The sight of her resolutely climbing the hill to the school made it clear that hers was the gift of fight that perhaps not everyone had in the same measure, or possibly needed: a body, a voice ready to call up the fight from deep inside, and to give themselves permission to stop holding the strain of whatever life they had been expected to accept as their lot – that *bloom-where-yuh-plant* philosophy that was my mother's. I had never wanted it to be mine if that meant settling for life in someone else's prayer. Brenda had risked herself to oppose what she could not abide.

★

Mason appeared when I was in the middle of my letter-sorting. I had forgotten about the adjustment to the Salvador schedule he had mentioned a week or so back. We exchanged packages and paperwork without much talk. I sensed a strain that I suspected had to do with the scene Franco had created in the shop and he had stood by and watched. I didn't feel I needed his intervention, but he had hung back like a stranger while Franco needled and bullied me. Perhaps he habitually deferred to his brother, or preferred to give that impression. Was there, too, some unease about the apparent link he had with the man called Spanish? People and goods were trafficked regularly across the channel from the Main. Spanish was known to the villagers as a trader of some kind. He had what appeared to be a more than a casual acquaintance with Mason, who struck me as being more at ease on the fringes of relationships, despite his projection of a jovial disposition. Then there was Corporal Luke. I knew little of him. Only that he and Mason hunted together. That required trust and more than a small measure of familiarity – to be in deep forest together all night and armed. If not trust, then something else bound them – but what?

When it was time to leave for Salvador, Mason attempted to break the ice.

– I didn't forget you and those pommerac I promise.

– You know where to find me, Mr Mason.

– I hear you, Miss Post. I hear you.

The last thing I wanted to communicate was that I harboured any ill-will about his behaviour in the shop. I seemed to have him on the back foot, so I chanced to test my suspicion about his connection to Brenda's cousin, Kizzy. I was more than certain that she was Sam's mother.

– Do you happen to know if Sam's mother changed her address?

The question surprised him. He hesitated. I was on target. I pushed further.

– Brenda's been trying to make contact. They've apparently fallen out of communication. I've been helping to find out if her Brooklyn address is still the same, but there's no evidence of returned mail on our end.

I didn't need to say more. He wrote the details down with a sprawling script and made as if to go, then stopped in his tracks.

– I don't mind telling you, Miss Post. You look confidential.

He paused for some sign of confirmation, but already had his answer. What did it matter what I knew? I would be gone in a few months.

– I help Kizzy leave Macaima. She choose Franco over me, but I never hold that against her. Franco put blame on her for how Sam turn out. I hope Kizzy not in trouble over there.

– I'm sure it's nothing to worry about.

– Let me know what you hear.

He made another attempt to leave, then paused.

– By the way, I run into Mama Gloria in Railway yesterday. First thing she say is how much you look like Maria.

– I didn't realise she knew me?

– I suppose not. She say you was in the Coalition meeting and you could pass for Maria.

– Oh, I see. What drew the comparison?

– Maybe how you mix, like Maria and Miss Ana.

– Did Mama Gloria know Miss Ana?

– Fuh sure. She use to stay by her place off and on – when she run from Joseph.

– Run, why?

– Man-woman troubles. He was quick to lash sometimes – but a little licks does sweeten love.

He smiled mischievously.

– Nonsense! I seriously doubt Miss Ana saw it that way.

He shrugged off the comment.

– Anyway, Miss Ana pass away young.

– How come?

– Cocoa branch swing back. WHAP! Straight here.

He pointed to his chest.

– Talk say it rotten out.

– My God! What do you mean?

I watched him wipe his face with that familiar red rag. I wanted him gone. I didn't think I could bear to hear another word, but he continued.

– I only say what I hear. She see plenty trouble, then Maria come-an-shame everybody. Mad like hell. Night-an-day she roam Mountain Road telling people she making baby. Sad-sad business.

My head spun. I was bone tired of hearing these women's stories secondhand, and from the mouths of men like Franco and Mason who cheapened their pain and made jaded heroes of those

I was sure were their abusers. Even my new naming was theirs. It was like being trapped on a carousel. Brenda's hurricane swirled, but Mason kept talking, oblivious to the rush of rage he had stirred in me.

– Anyway, Maria reach back from Port of Spain. She going to be quiet for a while. You know is Thomas who pay for her treatment.

Mason stuffed his rag into his pocket.

– Time to go. Later, Miss Post. Stay lovely.

I couldn't fully grasp all that he had revealed. Who was responsible for what has so traumatised Maria that she seemed mentally stuck in the shock and shame of what she had suffered? Had she been pregnant? Whatever, it must have happened when she was quite young. On the surface, Joseph's son, Thomas, appeared to have taken on the role of a caretaker of sorts. But why? Something wasn't adding up. There were a million more questions I wanted to ask.

The start of an engine drew my attention. The mail van pulled off. I was in time to see Corporal Luke in the passenger seat, dressed in civilian clothes, his eyes concealed behind inscrutable sunglasses like Mason's, though his sported bluish mirror lenses. Mason said something and the corporal laughed. Without the policeman's cap and with his elbow resting on the window, he looked more relaxed than when he had first come in to buy stamps. I remembered that his hands were noticeably well cared for.

CHAPTER 17 – STORM WARNING

After the mail van sped off up Mountain Road, leaving me with what felt like the broken strands of the betrayals suffered by Maria and her mother, and a question about Mason's real purpose that day, tidying up the office once again presented itself as a good way to make sense of what I could. Already September was at its end, and I had attended to most of the minor administrative tasks. Indeed, I could see the good sense of combining postal services with the running a country parlour. I had time. Franco and his son were contracted to maintain the exterior of the building, so I assumed the interior was my responsibility.

When I returned, armed with broom and dust cloth, a vehicle braked loudly at the gate. Doors slammed shut and hurried feet ascended the stairs. Standing in the doorway, accompanied by a young corporal, was a man of average height and impeccably dressed in charcoal slacks and a white, short-sleeved shirt. A row of black, blue and red pens lined to his breast pocket. He introduced himself as Joshua Elton.

– At last we meet, Miss Bridgemohan, but circumstances could have been better. I have urgent news to share.

He wasted no time getting to the purpose of this visit.

– Tobago is about to take a direct hit from hurricane Flora. The advisory came much too late to orchestrate a proper response. The government is at this very moment doing its best to issue warnings to Trinidad in case the system should do the unexpected and swing south. A state of emergency has been declared. The police, army and coastguard are on high alert. Disaster preparedness personnel on the island are doing all they can to reach people. I have been charged with the responsibility to help with that process. The government has taken the initiative of distributing free candles to all citizens. The best approach, given the grave and present danger of the storm, is to exercise extreme vigilance. Readiness better than regret. It would be remiss of me not to say how grateful we must be to the US Navy reconnaissance aircraft that confirmed the existence of the system. We must be grateful for our neighbours to the north. (His hand smoothed over recently barbered hair that had been generously greased, parted at the side and brushed to a shine.) Please stay tuned to your radio, Miss Bridgemohan. Updates will be communicated on all available channels. We must prepare for the worse.

I watched him closely. His demeanour was not unpleasant, though more than little puffed up. He spoke as to an imagined audience, not really making eye contact. Something about his style struck me that I could not name until he was ready to leave. He was the bossman in absentia and had chosen the PM's voice to convey his message. When his speech was done, so was the officialdom in which it had been cast.

– Forgive my bad manners, Miss Bridgemohan, but I busy like a bee – and now storm turn up from nowhere. I know Franco has been seeing to your needs. Are you settled?

– Yes, the rental is perfect. Thank you.

– Happy to hear, but that makes what I have to tell you even more difficult. That, though, must wait for another time, but allow me to formally welcome you to Macaima.

He took his leave, followed by the young police officer. Joshua Elton was not the man I had imagined him to be, though this was clearly a persona he'd adopted to execute his task. I was sure there was more to the man, more than the mask he had chosen for the role.

I was dusting the pigeonholes that were mostly empty of letters and thinking of Mr Elton when someone disturbed the wooden bench. Sam was sitting there and looking straight at me like the eye of a storm. She wore a pair of blue jeans and an oversized T-shirt. Her hair was a fabulous tangle, which told me that she had not been to her grandmother's house, and when she pulled back the strands that obstructed her vision, I saw the unattended wound over her right eyebrow.

– What on earth happened, Sam? Did those boys hurt you…
She protectively shielded the cut but didn't let me finish.
– I not going back home, Miss Anna. I going away and never coming back.
Her face remained remarkably expressionless in spite of the turmoil that racked her voice.
– Were you in another fight, Sam?
Tears welled up. She seemed poised to make another dash for the door.
– Where will you go, Sam? Let me help you.
– Help me?
The words torpedoed from her mouth, charged with so much disdain I felt unfairly blamed for whatever grievance she carried.
–Everybody, even Granny, say I cause too much trouble. Everybody fed-up with me. So, what make you different?
– Did Barry or Patrick interfere with you?
– They lock up Maria again. Somebody must pay for that!
– Who did – Franco? Where is she?
– In that nasty shed. She only get worse when she inside there.
– Why would he do that?
– He shame she like to walk. That is why. But I let her out and she run away faster than deer. Somebody going to pay, Miss Anna. They feel we ent know what they do. I see. Me and Maria – we see everything.
– Who did what?
– Uncle but he and that other one going to pay.
– Uncle?
– Bones.

I had never anticipated Mason's involvement, and who was the other one? What did they do? I wanted, though, to get Sam talking about her own circumstances, although Maria's situation seemed just as pressing and disturbing to her.
– Calm down, Sam. We will figure things out. Have you seen Roland?
– He say how my puppies get big. What name you give them?
– Day and Night. Do you like those names?
Her eyes softened for a second, but then were steel again.
– Everything will be fine, Sam. Let's deal with things one at a

time. First, tell me how you got that gash? It needs attention.

I motioned to take a closer look, but she drew back.

– Were you in a fight?

– He say he like me.

– Who said that, Barry?

– Yes. So I ask him who he like. He say Sam. I say she doh like not one bone in he body. He shove me down for that.

– Was Patrick with him?

– No.

– We will have to deal with Barry, then – once and for all.

– I done deal with him, Miss.

– You did?

– One hard cuff.

She gestured at the spot and I watched her re-enact the scene of her retaliation, which involved doubling over in fake pain when the imaginary blow landed. We both laughed.

– Good for you, Sam!

I let her enjoy her triumph, happy to see her spirits lifted a little and her face come alive.

– We will have to tell Barry's parents, but no more fighting. Okay?

– Nobody to fight for me but me, Miss.

– I understand how you feel, Sam, and it was great that you stood up for yourself. Now we must look for another way to deal with those bullies. Mr Austin must be told…

That was her cue. She pelted through the door, leaving me to wonder what it would take to get her to sit through an entire conversation. I needed to figure who could help with her needs, as well as to find out more about Maria's situation. Franco was clearly out of his depth on both scores. He would prefer that Sam disappear into the recesses of the dying estate. Her grandmother was herself no doubt tired and burnt out. Something had to be done for Sam, and Maria, but what?

CHAPTER 18 – UNDER GOD ARMPIT

With the storm fast approaching, the village converged once again on Johnny's shop. People were frantically stocking up on dried goods: rice, flour, sugar, Crix, and anything in a tin: sardines, corned beef, beans, condensed milk. I paid for my purchases and made for the exit. Franco was in conversation with Cray and Razor outside the shop. He saw me before I could escape.

– Miss Bri, nothing to worry about. Hurricane doh hit Trinidad. When last storm pass by here?

Razor answered.

– '33. Wind take way roof De Valremy pay for. Payback, people say.

He spoke with mischief in his voice. I knew the roof story from Mason. Franco folded his arms across his chest. He evidently didn't appreciate the connection.

– Payback for what? You wasn't even born. All I say is storm doh pass by this side. I repeat it for Miss Bri benefit. She mus be frighten-an-concern.

Cray looked on, seemingly amused that Franco had assumed the prerogative to speak for me. Razor, though, was too eager to press his point to allow room for an intervention.

– De Valremy shoulda leave church construction alone. Twice he try, all fall down. I hear he get spite first time. Fire was next. Eh, Franco?

– Razor, why anybody would sabotage what they build? That is pure dotishness. Storm mash it up. All I saying is Trinidad is God country. Storm doh pass by here.

– You too foolish, Franco. If what you say is true, where that leave all my family in Tobago and everywhere else – in hell? You not talking sense.

– I never say dat! No storm passing here. Period! We safe beneath God armpit.

Razor saw his opening.

– Then we better hope God doh sweat like you, Franco.

It was a brutal hit. Razor abandoned the circle and Franco sought to recover by directing attention onto me. Thankfully, customers were too taken with their panic-buying to care about his banter.

– Miss Bri, you sure you didn't walk with a storm in dem suitcase? Wind doh have to blow too hard for current to go in Macaima. I hope yuh buy candle.

– PM promise everybody free candle, not so Franco? You should know that.

The comment was Cray's.

– Correct is right. His word is gold.

– You sure bout that? It look to me like storm going to come-an-go before we get to light one.

– Cray, d-PM is no magician! Dat is what people fail to realise. If he say we getting candle, we getting candle. Yuh should thank God we in Macaima have light switch to turn on.

– I doh have to be grateful. Light, water, road, hospital – all that is why we put this party in power. We doh have to be grateful. Responsible yes, but we owe him nothing but the respect we give to anybody.

Cray moved towards the shop and Franco continued.

– Yuh see how ignorance prosper, Miss Bri. Some people feel gov'ment is God. I put my head on a block. No storm passing here. We safe under God armpit. Even so, yuh better doh stay on Beach Trace tonight. Stay by me. D-madam doh mine. If storm really come, you going tuh see trouble.

Maybe Cray's victory had tempered him. It hadn't occurred to me that my location would be dangerous, but I had no desire to be in close quarters with Franco.

– Thanks, but I'm sure I'll be fine. As you say, everybody safe under God's armpit in Macaima. And *God has no favourites.* I'll be fine.

He smirked but I could see that he was caught off-guard by my ready rebuttal.

– Suit yuhself. I say my piece.

Beneath the declaration was more than a hint of rejection, and what followed uncovered it.

– Somehow I feel... now how to put this?

He scratched the stubble on his chin and grinned sheepishly.

– You doh favour the likes of me for protection.

I hadn't seen it coming and I could not help but wonder whether Mrs Bailey had been up to speed on office gossip and had said something to her friend Merrill. James must have been busy running his mouth about what he had seen in the lunchroom. Everyone had returned to their posts and Thea had asked me to stay back. She wanted to leave me a book.

★

– To remember me by.

– Oh, it's by your favourite person.

It was a historical work about the Haitian revolution by Comrade Nello – I had not read any of his books. Thea insisted it was a necessary education.

– And signed too, so keep it safe. Give it a read. Write me and let me know what you think.

– Thanks, but I'm sure you will have more to say to me about it.

– Why do you discredit your thoughts?

– What I think is that you should get out of here as quickly as you can and don't look back.

– That's precisely why you should read it. Okay, I'm leaving, but I'm coming back, Anna. That much I know.

– I'm just sorry you have to go.

– Management will be happy I'm gone. It's all politics. But seriously, I think this building spot makes people antsy.

– I'm trying to say we'll miss you.

– And you? – I bet you didn't know that the Emancipation Act was announced from this very site.

– The Treasury? No, I didn't know.

– This used to be the Governor's address and now we humble postal workers get to share it with the Treasury folks. But with the same breath that the Governor announced emancipation, he drop a six-year apprenticeship bomb on people who wanted freedom. People get blue-vex. Rebellion buss out one time. Martial law had to be declared. Here's another titbit. They're

moving the post office to a new location by next year. That's the word at any rate. This building is going to be all about the money.

– I had no idea.

– Managerial gossip seems to find its way to me. The upside of being what they call around here, too political. So on another matter of politics, are you and Miles still an item?

– Why are you asking?

Her curiosity was understandable. The transfer had kept her out of the loop.

– Yes, we are.

– What's the attraction?

– What do you mean?

– Just curious. Maybe what I really want to say is that I'm leaving at the end of the month.

– This July? So soon?

– Yep. I want to roam a little before I get tied to a classroom and library.

– You seem to have a thing with disappearing.

She had laughed.

– You seem to notice when I do.

It was my turn to laugh.

– Do you remember the Square, and that march in the rain, way back when?

– Who could ever forget?

– I always felt we missed an opportunity that day.

– What opportunity is that?

– Well, we didn't burn all the deadly sins in that fire…

– Oh, what did we omit?

– I suspect that you already know.

– Do I?

– To hell with it… Remember…

Her voice dropped to a whisper.

– Yes, I do…

Her breath on my face… The ground shifted. We were left with ourselves. Then James was in the doorway.

– I hope I'm not interrupting anything, ladies…

CHAPTER 19 – REVELATIONS

Thunder boomed, though far off to the north of the island, as I entered Beach Trace. The sky had grown more clouded. By the time I got to the bridge, it was well past one o'clock, and with the coming storm I was sure the puppies would be both hungry and frightened. I allowed myself only a brief pause at the bridge and saw my face silhouetted on the water's surface. I thought of the postcard I had included in the mail bag for Mason to collect on his return trip from Salvador. I hadn't been in touch since my arrival. I had written two words to my mother: *All's good*. She would recognise them. They were her rote answer to anyone, including Mrs Henderson, when she asked how things were going with us. Her way of politely keeping people out of our business. *Keep your own counsel*. Another of her maxims. I wondered what she spoke of in her *meetings* in the annex with Mr Henderson when his wife had gone to the Country Club and it was my duty to wash the Sunday dishes, dry and replace them without breaking anything unless I wanted to lose the payment of a silver coin.

I saw again the neat hedge of crotons that, inch by inch, extended to the border of the annex *to brighten up our place*. As the plants flourished, the fence they formed became our boundary inside the Hendersons' world. The backyard opened to the Gulf, which was quiet when the tide was high, and always looked so vast. My eyes hungered for that far horizon in those days.

Now Franco was trying to hedge me in with his taunts and insinuations. *You decide*. Those were Thea's last words to me. After the farewell we had organised for her, I had returned to my post at the counter and the letter was there: a single L: red on a white page. I had gazed at it until my eyes burned with tears and

I was probably shaking. I did not notice when Thea entered the room.

⋆

– *Jesus, Anna! What are you doing to yourself?*

– *What do you mean? Can't you see what they did?*

– *That's exactly my point. You're giving them permission to fence you in. Just throw this shit where it belongs – in the bin.*

She tore the page to pieces.

– *I'm sure it was James. Do you think he saw?*

– *What he saw or didn't see is his affair. Whoever did that crap is not worth the time of day. What happened, happened. I regret nothing. But that's me.*

I could not respond.

– *Be careful not to build your own fences, Anna. Don't do that to yourself.*

– *It's not that simple, and you know it.*

– *Listen, I made a pact with myself. I decided that this world is where I belong. Every corner of it. I am here. I didn't choose to be born, but what I choose is to accept that it is my responsibility to live. To live. Nobody is going to take that right from me. In fact, to hell with them who try! Moreover, no one letter is going to reduce me to a small plot of ground. So decide, Anna. You decide.*

⋆

A light drizzle began; perhaps we were on the storm's outer band. Tobago was no doubt in its grip. I hurried on, hoping that Sam had found Maria and they were both safely indoors. An unexpected visitor was awaiting my return to the house. Startled by the voice, I slipped on the wet step and lost hold of my storm supplies.

– Doh frighten. Is only me, Roland.

– What on earth are you doing here?

He emerged from the undercroft, his head inclined to avoid the beam and immediately began to collect the items that had fallen through the gap between the stair treads. I watched him scrambling around. The shoulders of his shirt were damp. He must have only just arrived. There was no saving the eggs. Half a dozen yellow yolks and their plasma lay splattered on the ground. I could see from his knitted brow that their loss troubled him.

– Sorry about yuh eggs.

He handed over the items he had gathered up.

– Never mind. What brings you down here? Don't you know about the storm?

– I worried bout Sam. She pass by me today in a state. All she talk was how she going away. I not sure what she plan.

He waited, holding himself upright, his face tilted upward, open, not pleading, but strangely expectant as though I could provide a solution. I glanced at my watch and saw that it was just approaching two o'clock. Things could get worse, weather-wise. There was no way to be certain that the system would not reach landfall. Tobago, given what Elton had said, could already be in its grip. I didn't think Sam would do anything to harm herself or anybody else. At least, I hoped not, but if Roland had anything to share about her situation, I wanted to know. I told him to wait for me in the undercroft. He allowed himself a smile and I heard a match strike as I entered the house.

The pups trotted towards me in their awkward fashion. I gave them each a firm hug. They had managed to get through the day on their own and were bundles of joyous, curious energy, simply happy that they would be fed. The kitchen floor was a total wreck but a clean-up would have to wait. I had given them the full run of the space. I put the kettle on, filled their bowls and I watched them devour their meal, then prepared some coffee, with them tripping up my steps as I moved from stove to cupboards to sink.

By the time I descended the stairs, I found Roland sitting on the low wall. We were alone on Beach Trace when everyone in Macaima was taken up with their own worries over what was happening in Tobago, and whether Trinidad would be next to take a beating. Apart from what Franco and Mason had said, I knew so little about him, though he seemed genuine in his concern for Sam and I was curious about the bond between them. Seeing me approach with the steaming cups, he quickly extinguished his cigarette and accepted the mug with a warm smile. I was sure he could see my discomfort. I guessed that he was somewhere in his early twenties, though it was hard to tell, and I knew he had been through a great deal.

I sat side-angled on the wall so that I could better face him.

He spoke first.

– Sam not doing good, Miss Anna. Not since what happen in school.

– I would be even more worried if she did appear to be doing well. What happened to her is nothing less than criminal. Has there been another incident?

He took a noisy sip from his mug.

– I doh think so, but she change. She was always a fighter, but now a sadness take over, even though I could see that she pushing it back, swallowing everything.

– She's been carrying a great deal. Where is she now?

– If I know Sam, she heading up Mountain Road.

– To her grannie's place?

Roland took another drink, then placed his cup on the wall between us.

– No higher up.

– Why would she – and in this weather?

– If I right, Maria could be there.

He drained his cup and set it down.

– Sam only take up staying by me after Marie pass. Nobody pay her much attention. Marie was like a sister.

Both Franco and Mason had made Roland sole keeper of Marie's story, as though he alone bore responsibility for whatever had happened to her. If I wanted to know more, it would have to come directly from him.

– How did you come to know Marie?

– We grow up together. I work with her father, Mr Samuel, sometimes – when he wasn't working for De Valremy. He tend a five-acre on Salvador side; but since Marie pass, we doh talk.

He evidently assumed that I knew who else was involved in the story. I let him talk on.

– Julien, he in Canada now, but we all use to go traipsing around estate land. We do all kinda thing: river-an-sea bath, we pick mango, hunt parrot, catch crayfish. You name it. He was okay. He was like one-a-we, never mind he was a De Valremy. Sometime, though, he like to show off.

– Who for? Marie?

He nodded.

– One time, he stand up on a fowl neck. I watch it beat up till it nearly dead.

Roland shook his head. The incident obviously still disturbed him.

– Why would he do that?

– He like to play wild, when he was younger. I wanted to cuff him down for doing that, but instead I keep quiet. When push come to shove, he is De Valremy son. He could do what he want.

Roland seemed to be fishing for understanding.

– Is that all that happened?

He shrugged his shoulders.

– That is what I see. Then Marie meet her trouble.

– What was that?

– First she say that she and Julien hike up Mountain Road to collect jumbie bead. She like to make bracelet, chain. She even make nice earring from cedar seed, polish smooth-smooth like glass.

His voice trailed off. We listened to the silence together.

– What did Julien have to say?

– Story change when questions start to ask. Marie say she went alone and two fellas come from nowhere. She never see who. Next she say the whole thing was a lie. Nothing happen. When police question Julien, he say he was in town. Mr Joseph vouch for him. Next thing we hear case drop. Julien jump on plane quick-quick and gone.

Roland's eyes welled up.

– You must have loved her very much.

He passed his forearm roughly across his face.

– In my heart, I never believe it was Julien. I tell Marie we okay even when she start to show baby was coming; but she wasn't able. She run straight into Goodbye same day she was ready to birth. No matter how I try, I couldn't reach them. Current was too strong. We never find a body. Macaima never see Julien again.

– What about the other men who were supposedly involved? Was there any evidence?

– Case drop. Marie say nothing happen. She fall down in some ditch up there. That is how she get bruise up. That was it. Nobody to charge with nothing.

– Roland, I'm so sorry. There must be some way to reopen the case.

– Nothing to do now. Nothing could bring back Marie, though that pain stay with me. Is Sam I worried about, Miss Anna.

We sat with his pain. Had Thomas lied to protect his brother, and the family whisked Julien away to avoid involvement in any possible litigation, and maybe responsibility for the pregnancy? Why, though, would Marie lie? To protect Julien? It didn't make sense. But Marie was gone, and Sam could be helped. I reached for my mug, which I had set down next to Roland's.

– Watch it!

I froze at his shout. He flicked a spiky caterpillar from the handle.

– Be careful. You don't want to get a sting from shinney – they poisonous like hell. They all over these days.

– Gosh, thanks.

– No problem.

– So what can we do to help Sam?

– I know she was mad-vex how Franco lock up Maria. Sometimes Maria hike to High Point. That is before Mountain Road start to dip down over by Salvador. Sometimes Sam go with her up there.

– Is that good for Sam – her spending so much time with Maria?

– Maria stay like she is twelve years old. Sam go to keep her safe. She like to dash across just before vehicle reach High Point.

– That's dangerous – that spot must be blind!

– Yes, I know. Up there is where I would search. Better I head out now before night fall.

He reached behind the wall to retrieve his bag. The same crocus bag I had seen him carrying before.

– What's in the bag?

He slung it over his shoulder.

– Jus some things I have to put to rest.

The drizzle intensified as Roland walked up the trace in his cloud of worry. Night would surely meet him before he reached his destination and make the effort futile. Roland had told a confusing story. Something had happened on the estate and the truth had died with Marie. He, though, was definitely aware of the connection between Julien and Marie. I suspected she had chosen Julien over him. I felt I was in a giant labyrinth pursuing a many-headed beast.

Shadows from a heavy sky blanketed the trace when I climbed the stairs, and as I entered the living room, the strangest thing greeted me: singing. It came from the kitchen. No one should have been in the house. The voice, soft yet crystal clear and beautifully plaintive, drew me forward. I knew immediately whose it was: Sam's. She sat on the floor, cuddling the pups. They were absolutely at ease, their heads flattened to an almost supplicant bow as she stroked them, eyes drowsy and restfully turned down. Questions about how she might have gotten in unnoticed, or whether she had been there throughout my conversation with Roland, would have to wait. She sang a soulful "Amazing Grace", and though she must have known I was standing in the doorway, chose to remain taken up by the song she both offered and was enwrapped by... *O how sweet the sound... that saved...*

Somewhere during the singing, her voice took flight to demand an even deeper attention. Then, as though releasing herself from that pitch which was just below a bird's cry, she stitched in a story about a garden and a tree: *Our tree, she had eyes – four. We see everything. Two deer play and fight – kiss and play a fight until they do together what was and wasn't fighting at all. Then hunter-beast storm-in with nasty talk and gun cock. No face on them but tree see all. Boy deer take-off like wind. Beast laugh bellyful. They snatch lady-deer. She toss one from the other like stick in rough water. Big beast take he ride. Bony one watch like he want to run-an-stay same time. Then he too ride. Tree close eyes. Cry. We run far from that garden as from a snake. We never tell a single soul what we know.*

Then Sam fell silent. I sank to the floor as realisation dawned. A rendezvous had turned out to be a tragic crime instead of a coming-of-age story. Julien may have been an irresponsible scamp, or coaxed to lie to avoid scandal, but he was no rapist. Too paralysed to say or do anything, I watched her leave as she had entered the house – through the kitchen door.

CHAPTER 20 – A WOMAN IN THE ROOM

I must have fallen asleep because when the pups began their whining, it was already pitch black. With no hum from the refrigerator, I guessed there was no electricity. After some stumbling around, I found and lit a candle. My wristwatch said six-thirty. An early night had fallen. Roland should have been way up Mountain Road by now. And what of Sam? Had she been in the house all along and how had she got in without my knowing? And where was she now? I hoped that she and Maria weren't out in the storm and that Roland had found them.

The pups reminded me that they needed feeding, so I chunked up some bread in their dish and added milk. I watched them fall on their meal. After some romping, they soon settled down to sleep. Eat, play, sleep. Repeat. It was comforting to just look at them napping, snuggled together, their full stomachs gently rising and falling. The trauma of their near drowning appeared to be behind them. They mirrored perfect contentment. My thoughts drifted to Tobago. It was hard to imagine what the island must be suffering. Merrill, whom I had not met, but from my interaction with Mrs Austin, was a link to my past, was on that island. We were sure to receive word about how she and her family had fared.

There was so much to figure out, so many loose strands to gather, although I could see that some histories were beginning to disentangle themselves. I had no doubt that the second pair of eyes in Sam's sung parable was Maria's. She still existed only as a name to which I had attached a few inconclusive scraps of stories I had heard. Yet she seemed to be at the heart of so much, and now, with the detail Sam had allowed me to see, I was sure I had been let into the awful secret that Marie had taken with her into the sea. Who those masked hunters were seemed all too clear, and if I was right, they were still at large. I felt that a responsibility had been laid on me. Marie was gone but could there be justice for her – and Maria? Their story needed to be heard, but could the case be reopened on the basis of Sam's story? That I doubted. Would anyone would take seriously a tale told by a disturbed young woman and a girl like Sam?

Then there was Marie and Julien. They had been lovers, I was sure, and maybe that was her reason for dropping the case. He would have had to give evidence. Perhaps she didn't want to implicate him or felt it would be futile to do so. The unborn child that the sea also took could have been his – or Mason's, even Corporal Luke's. Roland had done the brave thing in choosing to marry Marie. He must have been deeply in love, but that was not enough. Maybe Marie could not carry the pain of the rape and Julien's betrayal. Whatever the case, the crime she suffered refused to buried. These histories flowed in the very veins of the place – and in the foundation of the church I passed every day.

Before I knew it, an hour had passed. Sleep wasn't an option. I wanted to be awake if Roland returned with any news. From the kitchen window, I saw that a slight drizzle persisted, and the moon was almost completely blanketed. My view of the backyard was of an eerie canvas of silhouetted leaves quivering above the sheen of wet grass. Interrupting the chorus of the usual night sounds was an occasional creak and bang that came from the direction of the caretaker's hut. I had not snapped the padlock shut and had forgotten to ask Franco about the key, if one existed. The door must have been blown open by strong gusts.

Another bout of banging came as the wind picked up. I strained to see more. It was dark, but not so dark that I failed to see a figure dash from under the house, heading in the direction of the hut. I could not tell what or who it was. I had only a glimpse of a form, not much bigger than a child's, scurrying through the night. Could it be Sam? Maybe she had chosen not to risk the hike up Mountain Road in search of Maria. But why was she out in this weather in the dead of night? Then it struck me that the suitcase I had stored there was unsecured. A lock hadn't seemed necessary. I was alone in the house and the hut was clearly no longer in use. So much had happened since my arrival that I had delayed dealing with its contents. Now there was chance of it being uncovered should the intruder decide to rummage about. I needed to retrieve what was mine. I quickly put the packet of candles, along with some matches, into a plastic bag, made sure that the pups were okay, noticed that the backdoor had been unbolted, then dashed out into the night.

As I suspected, the door was swinging on its hinges. The room stood before me a mute and formless void. Someone or something was in there, but I dared not venture further. I called out:

– Anybody there?

At first, only the night noises chorused on. I listened more closely. The door creaked on its rusty hinges whenever the landbreeze pushed seaward. Nothing more.

– Anybody there?

Leaves fussed. Bamboo groaned. The scurrying form that had entered the hut was real. I was sure of it. I inched closer to the threshold, listening for any indication of a presence. There was nothing to see. The door kept up a distracting creak. I grabbed hold to steady it. The most excruciating pain riddled my right palm and maybe from the shock of the sting, I tripped and found myself propelled forward into the cavity until I connected with what must have been the opposite wall. I do not know which was more painful, the spears of fire darting through my palm or my shoulder, which had taken the brunt of the blow.

The room, a boundless, withholding dark, roiled like a churning wave when next I opened my eyes. Almost instantly, I became aware of a putrid smell. My stomach convulsed but nothing came, only a sensation of being hurtled back and forth, my ears singing. A lit candle stood in the middle of the dusty floor; it became an anchor that told me that I was not alone. Shadows leapt about as the solitary flame pulsed and flickered. A draught came from somewhere, maybe from beneath the door and the window behind me. I felt strangely exposed, visible to who or whatever had found cover in the shadows. With all the strength I could muster, I eased myself into a seated position, conscious of the awful, numbing pain that travelled up my arm and lodged in my armpit as the poison from whatever had stung or bitten me took effect. I must have also severely bruised or dislocated my shoulder as I could not raise my arm. No matter how I positioned my body, I could find no relief from the pain, so I slid again to the floor and lay on my left side, the candle's flame my only anchor. Expanding and contracting shadows danced about the ghostly space.

From the blur of my fever, I saw that my suitcase stood exactly where I had placed it at the foot of the empty cot. The sound of urgent knocking intruded. Again, the nausea swept over me, and this time the initial shock was as of cold steel on warm flesh.

Someone was banging on the door – from inside or outside, I could not be sure.

– He go kill we. Open this door nah. He go kill me…
– Who's there?

My voice returned like an amplified gargle, the sound of talking underwater. No one answered. I dragged myself closer to the door, not trusting my legs, feeling exposed. Naked. Cold. I forced myself to a seated position, and with my back pressed against the door, pushed all my weight against it. No use. Something must have fallen across the doorway. I tried again. It would not budge. Too exhausted and too dizzy to move, I sat where I was and surveyed the pulsing room. It was not long before movement, like feet shuffling around, caught my attention.

– Is that you, Sam? Open this door at once!

Laughter erupted, its pitch deafening in the small room.

– Open the door – please!

Silence.

Leaves rustled in branches that overhung the hut. Something fell on the zinc roof. I heard the clash of an instrument in a stainless steel tray. Determined to give the door one more try, I used the handle as leverage to get to my feet and pushed until a new sound interrupted my effort. A dull thud like the palm of a hand against a glass pane. But where did it come from? The window was behind me. I spun around much too quickly. The room flipped over and I again found myself clinging to the floor, desperately trying to hold on, as though at any moment I would be dislodged and fall into an unfathomable abyss.

The call for help became more urgent. The room tilted up. Fear such as I had never before experienced gripped me. My bladder released itself. Warmth. I strained to see through amniotic space to the other side of the pane. At first, I looked into a frame that had dissected the world into neat 8x8 BRC wire squares. Diced blocks of myself looked back at me. An image gradually presented itself, a face regathered, distorted by the rain-washed pane.

– Miss – Ma-dam, he promise to kill we dead.

A woman, draped in a blanket or robe of some sort, looks directly at me.

– Miss, you know me – and see my condition. I have nothing to hide. Is them so want to hide me.

She gestures to the house. My lips move to form another question, but before I can speak, a deep-voiced command blasts through the room:

– *Say your letters for me, Missy. Come on: A is for what? Come, child speak!*

My ground gives way. Catapulted against the door, realisation registers. The voice is a man's. The woman beckons me, head bowed, eyes focused on her belly as if she is pregnant. Cramps grip me. I was told they were to be expected. The body grieves. The blood will stop. I think maybe her waters broke. Maybe it is just the rain. I am crying and shivering now. The clamps were so cold. When she lifts her face to the pane again, the answer returns in a childlike murmur to the question:

– *Apple Pappy De-v.*

– *What's next? B is for what?*

The voice coaxes but is coiled to strike. The woman adjusts the blanket as though it is an uncomfortable veil. When she speaks again, a woman's voice, but a borrowed one, commands attention:

– *Children, my dear little ones, A as in A-dam… Who is he?*

She answers herself:

– *The first man. Make an A word. Follow me: A as in A-ngel. Gabriel is the Strength of God. Raphael is the Healing of God, Michael is…*

A girl's voice answers, with confidence:

– *Like God.*

– *Good. So B is for? B-aby and B is for B-oy. Who is the baby boy?*

The girl says:

– *Je-sus!*

– Excellent. Don't forget B is for this big word too: B-lasphemy – means something that is unforgivable... So be careful. Learn to be good boys and good girls. And what do you say now?
– Yes, Miss.
– Class address me correctly, please.
– Yes, Sister Michael-Mary.

The man suddenly intrudes:

– Look at the chart, Missy. A for Apple and B for Bat. C for...

The woman's giggle is a girl's. She spins around and around with her arms extended, and when she comes to a stop, she is not herself. The deep, rough voice booms.

– Everything begins with A. Remember that. A as in A-pple. Come, I know you bright. Sit here and say it for me.

The woman pats her lap agitatedly.

– Sit here and we will read the chart together – top to bottom. No De Valremy is a dunce.

Again, she gestures impatiently for me to sit.

I remain where I am. She slaps her thighs in annoyance and gets to her feet, drawing herself up to her full height so that her head almost touches the low ceiling, or so it seems. When the lesson begins, a woman speaks:

– C is for Christmas when the Baby lies in the manger. Back now to A as in Angelus... the angel of the Lord said unto...?

She waits, swinging her torso from side to side and holding herself as if she was an expectant mother.

– Class, this is why I have to go down on my knees for every one of you... The Angelus is all about whom?

She no longer has any lips. With her head uncovered, she spins around. From a face that glistens like wet glass, wild eyes stare. Lips pursed. She is not the same. Another appears. She sings mockingly, as if in response:

– A as in St Ann. ... St Ann, St Ann, Ah want ah man...

She doubles over in a bout of raucous laughter, then abruptly claps a warning at the darkness, becomes still and with eyes closed and head bowed, prays like a supplicant child.

– The angel of the Lord said unto... who is M-A-R-Y. And she is without... spell it: S-I-N. So we girls must strive to be full of grace. Not dis-grace! Remember that!

I listen from the cloud of my own delirium. The poison throbbing. Numbing. The woman's eyes hold me transfixed as she continues her instruction:

– *So who did the A-ngel appear to with the news about the baby? Come now, class, this is revision.*

The woman waits for her answer. She begins to speak. A girl cries out.

– *Me, Miss. Is me.*

– *Child are you crazy?*

She falls silent, sobbing. Muffled sounds of scrambled reprimands and curses that could only be self-directed fill the room.

– Please help me, Miss Anna. Please. I so tired.

I hear the plea, but I cannot respond. My body is riveted to the ground. The woman expels a long steupes, and whips off the blanket. I follow its flare and curve through space like the arc of a scythe or falling star. My eyes hold to the wide swing of its circumference that expands to enfold the entire room. Wider and wider it swirls to embrace the unseen regions that spread across the mountains of Macaima and beyond until there is only space. No time. I hear a voice speak into the void – maybe hers. Maybe us, both:

– *Who is she – and who is you? Woman, what you gone and do?*

A powerful wind, furnace-hot, sweeps in, whipping up the dust and sending me into a fit of coughing. Crouched over, I bury my face in my hands. The voice thunders:

– *Doh play with fate, Miss Lady. Doh play with God-people.*

Air is sucked from the room. The woman shrinks as the flame of the candle burns lower. When she speak again it is in a whisper:

– You know that one ent, Missy? Our Lady conceive without sin, pray for us… You know – who is you?

Maybe I had lost consciousness because when next I scan the room, the woman is huddled in the far corner in the narrow space between the cot and the wall. I could hear her suppressed sobs.

– Lady, are you alright?

My question or the sound of my voice – maybe both – is enough to make her retreat even further, like a frightened animal.

– What is your name?

Despite my fear, I recognise, with slight wonder, the endearing strain in my tone. She offers no answer. The odour that issues from her body is stifling, almost miasmatic, like the sea when it is washing itself, or a swamp – the rot and renewal of a world all at once. I try again.

– My name is Anna. Annabelle Bridgemohan. What is yours?

This time, with her face still buried in the wall, she blurts out:

– I tell you already. Maria, Maria, Maria – every kinda Maria.

An almost airless silence presses down upon us in the aftermath – the eye of her storm. She must have sensed my puzzlement as an incomprehensible mumbling begins to issue from her corner, like the tumble of clouds, God moving furniture around, rearranging space, a wave bashing itself into a trillion pieces against a rocky shore. She launches into a vehement, many-voiced medley of voices:

– *I Maria / hail Mary, Madame Marie&Marianne of big house, Maria of mountains and snakes, Soparee Mai, Marianne, too, sifting sand down by Goodbye, Mary of Little Lamb, Aye-aye Maria, Mary-Mary quite contrary, Mary who Lord Blakie sing* (her voice altered to a baritone): *Ma-ria, gyal I love yuh so bad / Ma-ria if you leave me now will be hard… Oh jeez zan! Music too sweet. What yuh go do when we Sparrow sing – not dance? Hear he nah: to see Miss Mary, she big and hairy. One Pound. Yuh see she mudda, yuh see she daughter… And he: Oh-oh-oh-O Maria, Darlin I must go. Unfortunately, we must part… What I tell yuh is plenty bloody Mary! Is music-music that doh mean nothing. What wrong with you? Like you 'fraid to dance? One Pound! Who – who is you? Hai-ya-yai – tell me! Who de hell is you. For Carnival dis year I have Miss Mary here…*

I press my back against the wall to keep the room steady and ask what to her must have been the most foolish question she had ever heard, judging from her reaction.

– But which Maria are *you* – Ana's daughter?

She roared with laughter.

– How much time I have to say it over-an-over… I-all-a-dem. I play saint and jammet – whatever yuh want. But I doh want he to ever touch me!

– Nobody is here to hurt you. We're safe, Maria. I promise.

– Safe! Promise! Say A for A-sssss! Ha! Here is where? I tell you where here is.

Her voice alters and she begins to sing:
– *Maria… girl I tell you flat / if yuh leave me, you sure to come back…*

I did not know what to make of her vexed and sardonic self-narrative, only that there was a violation, a pain lodged in her very sinews and cells, a memory trapped, undigested, unhealed.

– He go kill we, dead – dead, if I tell. I Maria. And you is who? Answer me that?

Whipped of fight, she turns and almost wriggles back into the corner, making herself into a tight ball. A fresh bout of crying begins, low sobs that cause her shadow to mount and descend the wall. I wonder what the time is, but my watch is broken, perhaps when I collided with the wall. There is no way of knowing how long we have been in the room together. Outside is still dark, but I guess it must be way past midnight. Soon her sobbing begins to subside. She must have been exhausted. I, too, am so very tired, my body a numb weight. I find a spot that allows me a clear view of Maria's corner. Morning could not be far off. I feel we had been in the room for decades.

The woman's question swirls in my feverish brain: *Who-you?* I try to listen to the tide shuttling over the gritty sand down at Goodbye. I try to anticipate the waves breaking back before the surf rolls up the shore. It is the rhythm I'd met when I first arrived. Now, a net of stories, though tangled and incomplete, moves with the beat of the sea. Mine, too, is there.

I drift into a fitful sleep.

A second, a minute, an hour passes. I cannot tell, only that the sound of a world crashing around me wakes me. Books lie tumbled over like demolished cities. There is no sign of the woman. The stacked boxes must have collapsed during all the commotion. A red-covered *Nelson's Reader* is among the books. The series was a childhood favourite. The book lies open at the sixth lesson. I read aloud: *Here is a clock. Can you tell the time by it? If you cannot tell the time, you should now learn to do so.* I read those opening sentences several times. *If you cannot… you should learn.* The words on the page burn.

The woman returns. I did not see her approach. She grabs the book and begins frantically flipping through the pages, back and forth, as she moves in hyper-concentration towards the candle's flame. I slip into the shadows, terrified, but she does not seem to notice. The room somersaults and falls as the pages turn. I want to lie flat on my back in the hope that the turmoil will stop, but am afraid to make myself so vulnerable. The woman is much too agitated. Back and forth, the pages go, fanning the flame into a consuming fire that encircles us before she settles on the one she wants. A girl's voice reads in a singsong fashion: *When I was sick and lay in bed / I had two pillows at my head...* Something about the lines strike her as extremely humorous. She slaps the book against her thighs, clasps it between her legs and doubles over laughing.

– Oh Gawwd, Miss Anna, lesson not done. You know what I learn? A word is a met-cin put in yuh mouth and you have to swallow, but be sure to say me-di-cine! Pronunciation make a person rise up. Here is what I think – you have to spit out plenty word and do like this!

She flicks a hand under her chin, but then drops like an emptied bag onto her haunches.

– A criminal offence when they force you to swallow a word whole til it take you over. It get inside yuh blood. That is met-cin to make you sick. Sick like dawg. Word could make you dumb – dummy – dunce – duncey. Dead like this damn baby!

She slaps her belly. Freezes. Her head is tilted, eyes wide open, like a doll's. Then with the utmost sincerity she says:

– Yuh know, Miss Anna, if ever you want me to read for you, let me know. I am a reader. Th-at big veranda over th-ere is my special stage. I-Maria, am going read – for you.

She springs to standing, does a quick curtsy and inhales deeply.

– *Hear th-is one.*

The voice is girl's.

– *I lived first in a little house / I lived th-ere very well...*

She stops abruptly. Dissatisfaction imprints her face as she flips quickly through the pages.

– No-no, not that one. Listen to thi-s one. It's the best. In fact, better than best. Perfect!

She inhales, regains her composure and begins again.

– *I once had a sweet little doll, dears, / the prettiest doll in the world / But I lost my poor little doll, dears, / As I played in the heath one day...*

Without warning another voice thunders. I'd heard it before. The room cracks.

– No. Damnit! The w-o-r-d is hea-th not heat.

She dashes the book to the ground, stamps on it and kicks it into a corner.

– How many times must I say it. / Put your tongue behind your tee-th. / Blow a little. / Come on, say it for me: hea-th – hea-th. / Come-come, feel my breath. / Use your tongue. / Push a little. / Not heat – th-at is another word with an entirely different meaning. / Now say it like I taught you, Maria… Hea-th!

– What is a blasted heaTH!

At that word, her face is crestfallen.

– Let's do B, okay.

She has a word for me.

– B is for Betrayal.

– What do you mean?

– What yuh mean – what I mean? You spend a whole life making question for what yuh done know already. Try this on.

She takes the blanket that she has been using as a veil and flings it towards me. I react in time to avoid the dank fabric that is so close now I could scarcely breathe.

– Answer yuhself! C is for?… D is for? Th-at my girl is how the world turns. Oppose a man and the first word he throws in your face is c-u-n-t!

The reprimand is a blow, blunt in its effort to be clear.

– Listen to me. Doh bother to read this foolish book, Miss Anna. Watch. I serious.

She shows some pictures.

– All I get to do in this book is pick-an-break cocoa in hot-sun / break cocoa / break co-co… I so tired, Miss Ana. I so-so tired…

The room shrinks to a dark cavity. I watch the defeated figure, a formless shadow, crawl to the corner, pausing only to glance at my suitcase as though seeing it for the first time. In spite of all that Franco, Mason and Miss Gomez had shared, I remain puzzled over the different personalities that evidently inhabit the woman who calls herself Maria. Maybe it did not matter. I, too, am in the dust. I cannot feel the ground. All around is darkness, a void. I have fallen out of time itself…

★

... A voice thunders. Splits space. Jolts me awake.
 – *Yuh see this breast?*
At first I am not sure who has spoken. The voice is not familiar. I listen for more. What returns is a cry so unable to be heard, it draws every last breath from my lungs. I clasp my ears, gasp for air, tear at my own throat. How to survive this – this body in pain? The mind is what hurts – is wounded first. You learn its agony. I cannot look at the afflicted part. I cannot know.
When she faces me again, she is clutching a bared breast.
Look at what happen to me! Oh God chile – Oh God!
I see only a breast.
The woman laughs almost fiendishly and moves towards the window. Her shadow grows tall as she approaches the wall. I remember her story.
– Are you Ana?
– Funny how you and she have the same name, eh? Well almost. Here watch it.
 She turns. Shows me the breast, again.
– *Cocoa branch beat me. Not my Tom-Tom. Swing back. WHAP!*
She cowers, protecting herself with her hands.
– *Now look at my good-good tot-tot. And let me tell you, I wasn't fraid to hit back. Licks doh go one way. A little pleasure: plenty pain. Ha!*
Somewhere in the room metal falls onto a tray. I remember thinking how such bright lights were shining up what's most private.
You never feel comfortable that way.
– What you mean... to never birth... Who you carry? That dearie is apple, pommerac and story. Doh interfere!
– Did you say something?
– Who, not me!
The woman laughs.
Count backwards from ten and begin again.
But where – to begin a beginning?
– Foolishness! Is H-ow-ow! See how I walk this road? I put my body on it. Lordie-Lord! Keep a little oil in my lamp...
She wasn't done.
– *Hai, Maria, I shoulda see what dat ole lagahoo was aiming to do –*

162

say he teaching you to read… Want you to dance for he… brown girl in the ring tra-la-la-la-la… Sugar plum – plum – plum. Nice-nicey. Ole goat!

She whips her hips.

– I shoulda see what that lagahoo was up to. Bad go fall on he! Mark my word! Hush chile. In God-own time. No more crying… Yuh hear.

I could not figure who the speaker might be. Maybe another woman close to Maria. Franco's mother maybe. I watch her return once more to her corner. Bits and pieces of pasts, maybe spoken to her and overheard, had somehow stitched themselves into her person – into a single body. One burden. One circuitous story. I suddenly realise that tightly held bits of my own burden had entered the space. Had she heard? A laugh cracks the darkness.

– You too foolish, Miss Anna.

I surrender my body to the dusty floor. Think my last thought. She is several.

CHAPTER 21 – INSIDE

– Miss Bri! You inside there?

The voice was Franco's. Light streamed through the half-opened door. Dust frolicked in the rays. I did not answer but remained fixated on the swirling dance of countless particles, tumbling, orbiting each other in the light. He called again. I was not immediately visible to him because the cot near which I lay was jammed against the wall. I remained still. Wood grated against bare concrete as the door was pushed back until it connected with the wall. More light flooded the room. Franco was all silhouette, but the burst of light illuminated the spider's web that hovered directly above me. I leapt up from the floor as from an unwanted touch.

– Is you in here, Miss Bri? Yuh didn't hear me call?

Franco moved further into the room, but held back as though reluctant to advance too far beyond the threshold.

– Yes, it's me.

– I look all over for you.

I turned to assess the corner behind the cot. The space was empty. The room was in far greater disarray than I had first met it. Broken furniture and storage boxes – some capsized with books strewn about. My suitcase lay on its side, the clasps undone. I moved quickly to check its contents. Everything was intact. I scanned the room again. No one. Just an unused space starved of light and air. Was it all real – last night? Franco stayed where he was, following my every move. I imagined him to be a little amused, but he had news.

– We find Maria.

The revelation puzzled me.

– But Maria was here all night – with me. I...

Franco interrupted.

– She here in true, Miss Bri, but sleeping and smelling strong on your kitchen floor. She and your two dogs. I never know yuh had dogs, Miss Bri.

– Maria, in my house – how?

– My guess is that she pass in through the kitchen. Door wasn't bolt. But what bring you out here?

– She was in here. That is what I said!

– Okay, Miss Bri. I ent here to fight what you claim. I hustle down here to Beach to tell you Sam in hospital.

– Hospital? How?

– Long story. Later, for all that. I see you sweating a fever.

– I saw something last night. Somebody ran right inside here, then I couldn't get the door to open. I was locked in.

– Locked – how? That door was swinging like a loose mouth when I reach. Maybe a branch jam it. Or maybe it swell. When weather damp that could happen.

– I was locked in – from the outside!

– Ok. Like I say, I not here to fight you. What happen to you?

– I was bitten or stung. I don't know by what.

– Where? Show me.

I showed him my hand. The pain had lessened considerably, but the swollen lymph nodes under my arm brought back the ordeal. Franco's proclamation in the bar about God and armpits returned like an ironic joke that was certainly on me. He turned my arm this way and that. Felt the nodules in my armpit.

– Oh-ho! I see. You grab onto shinney. Doh worry, yuh go live.

He chuckled at his diagnosis.

– And Sam – what happened …

– Never mine all that. Fever still have you in grips. Better I get you home.

– Home?

★

Someone lays my body down on sheets cool and soft as cloud. Rain falling on the galvanize of the roof electrifies the room, draws the rafters and the walls closer, like being hugged. I know that I am not alone. On the night table there is an earthen mug, its contents steaming an aroma of herbs and spices I cannot quite distinguish. I smell orange peel, ginger – but there is more. Some hand brings the warm mug to my lips. I sip. There is no hesitation in me. No question. I drink again and lie back. Now the room is raining. The room smells of sun-dried cloth, rain forest, tobacco. Streams flow from the corners of my eyes. I surrender to being held – rocked as in a vessel on the bay when the sea is calm. A white net descends like an elaborate veil. A shadow standing behind the mesh is tall above me or that is how it seems. Chanting enters my cells. I open. A vast landscape and sky welcomes me. *So this how it is – peace?*

The voice, like a bird's sings:
– *Sleep now, Anna.*
– I will. Thank you.
And I did. I slept, weightless, released of myself…

★

…When I open my eyes, I am curled on the bed like a question mark. I roll over and look up. Brilliant light bursts through an open doorway. The light hurts my eyes, so I blink, shield them until they have grown accustomed to its intensity. A silhouetted form holds up the sun, turns it this way and that, beholding its entire circumference, as though wanting to see everything.

– What you have here, daughter?

It is a woman who speaks from the shadows. She gestures to me with her eyes to see along with her. I sit up and begin to look at the small sun that she holds up before the window. What is it – a star? Light bounces off glass. A glass jar – that is what she holds in her hands, turning it this way and that to catch the light. I can see now what has her attention.

– How could you? Who gave you the right to…
– I see you bring all your worries with you, sister. Who is this you have lock up inside here?

Her tone is curious and not the condemnation that I had feared.

– What are you doing? Who gave you the right…

I reach out as if to take myself back into my self, but I cannot carry my own weight. I am pinned to the ground.

– Peace, sister. I only looking at the burden you bring all the way here to Macaima. Strange that you still have her with you.

Why you keep her, dou-dou? Look how she sleeping inside that water, like fish.

– I said, you had no right to…

My voice booms into the void then dissipates. The woman examines the jar again as though seeing its contents for the first time.

– Peace, child. You can't see that all this time she want somebody to find her? Maybe that is why you keep her. Maybe is she you looking for all this time. Give the girl a good word, nuh.

I babble through sobs. She allows me to empty myself to a nakedness that hurts. I want to cover myself but my hands feel like weights at my side. The woman appears not to notice my struggle to move. My body will not obey what I require it to do and this confuses me, at first. The experience is both familiar and strange. Whose body is this then, if not my own, and why will it not obey a simple request to lift my hand, or turn my head? For a moment, I think I am misplaced. I must be in someone else's body. There could be no other reason for this disconnect between what I tell my arm to do and its refusal to move. The bed waves beneath me. My eyes scan the portion of the room that I can see. The foot of the bed, left and right side where there is the wardrobe, the woman, the side table with the mug. Small details that tell me I am still in the world. I cannot see directly behind me. I know a window is there with the sheer curtains. I can see part of them. There is a wall I cannot see. A blind spot, though I know it is there but cannot turn to see its colour or feel the texture of the laths. I think it is cedar. Or is it mahogany? I cannot resolve the question. I cannot move. My bladder releases itself and I am in its sea. I look down at my feet and feel betrayed. Why have I left myself?

– So why you keep this girl lock up in that grip so long, Miss Anna?

– Please, help me.

– I go tell you something, sister-daughter; this is the only help I can give you. Is something I learn. When a woman decide on anything she should never feel she have to convince herself, plus this whole world, that she right to have a mind of her own, and to choose how she choose. Answer youself why you want to give somebody else that job an I promise you, you will take your body up from that bed and go where yuh tell it to go. So if you feel you have to bawl, then that is what you should do – bawl. Open a space for yuhself… That is the only way I know healing come.

– And about **B** is for…

– Let me stop you right there, daughter! I never learn that alphabet and I don't plan to start now. You ask for my help, so I tell you what I learn. Every choice have a cost and make you responsible to join in the life that flowing on. This place is where your body bring you, so make room for yourself where you feel none remain. Make door and window for you to pass through – fly through to whatever sky calling to you. Make life with your salt and sound. This world, those stars – they already know and want you. Then I tell you a story…

After my storm she is quiet, so quiet I wonder if she had heard a note of my wailing. She is focused on the glass jar. Her wonder is without force and I begin to look for what she sees.

– You know she look to me like she make for the ocean. Why you have the girl lock up in that grip?

I cannot answer.

She gazes with wonder at the jar.

– But look at this one, nuh. See how easy she resting. So peace. Not all so, yuh know – not all. Some we have to avenge. Come tend to your girl now. Look with me. She want you to see who she be.

I move in closer – towards the light.

– That is it. Doh fraid. No shame. Tell her why you choose and let her go. Forgive yuhself, if forgiveness what you need. She going and say what she want from you, if anything at all. This is between she and you. Nobody else.

I look into the flame that was the backdrop of the jar. They are the same – she the curled wick that makes the light that is also her.

– BRITE.

– That is it. See who she is. She not holding no knife to your throat. She not talking no hell to you. Is a serious thing to send back a life even when sometimes life come with no love, no agreement in the making; but any which way, it is a precious thing. It demand respect. I not asking you to beat up yuhself with wrong or right. I asking you to grant your own self permission to get back in flow. River don't stop unless it dry. Brite settle her case with you, but you in this world. Now sleep… I going to talk you a story my own mother give me to carry. I going to talk it til you dream your own dream.

She begins:

– Look a bowl, a calabash, a gourd – if you look only with the dark side of any word, like that word whatever it is that stole you, broke into you, condemned, buried you – any such word – you will see only bones. So break it – hear it. Crick. Now listen good:

…There was a gourd but it was full only with dry bone – all kind we say dead. Here – now hold this gourd, hold it firm in your two hands, like a full belly. Look first at the outside story. Look, see with me this round belly – suns, moons, stars. Look. Turn. Now see with me: fish, bird, flower, scorpion, dog, hunter, deer… Look – a fruit-bearing tree. O Go-ur-d – so-so pretty, beautiful pretty, on the outside. How come when you look inside you see only bones? Look. Spell what bones you see. Start with whatever you know. How they teach you: A – that is apple that grow heavy in you. All them words that beat you to naught. They make you sick. Look. See how they make spider-web inside you. Now hold that bowl. Shake. Shake. Listen to the sound. Shake. Be that breaking sound. Shake. Turn over everything until it break up and come back alive. Start with that first sound: A-ahh! Break it. Break it! Break it! Crack! Here, daughter, spit it out like a poison. Spit. Now breathe. Breathe. Look now. What do you see – inside the bowl.

– Fish.

I see or dream them moving, spiralling through dark water.

– Fish not bones. Good. Now eat. Here: hold on to this feather. My people say we come from sky. Put that inside your heart. Here hold this machete, too. Keep it sharp. Oil it with your tongue. We have to live in this world where wolf must live too.

CHAPTER 22 – A CERTAIN KINDA MIRACLE

... I woke to the hypnotic shuttle of sheer curtains. The world outside was a distant place from which I had been released. I was happy to lie weightless on a cloud of sheets, drifting in and out of a drowsy calm. Bird-songs entered the room unbarred, filling the space with their choruses, sounds piped and rustled with the churning sea at Goodbye. Along the length of louvred windows, luminous lines were drawn, empty of anything but their radiant script that danced and softened as evening came to rest upon Beach Trace. If I wanted, I could ascribe meanings the birds did not intend. I could create histories, make them texts, but I wanted nothing – only to be cradled in an alphabet of pure sense, if that were possible, with no desire to understand or plan, like a world in its infancy.

A wave crashed heavily on the shore and surf swashed up the beach. The tide had begun its change and I, too, needed to do something: offer a farewell to what I had been holding onto like a ball and chain blues. Laughter burst from me at the image. Of one thing I was certain: it was time to move on.

★

A series of pitched *you-whos* told me that Miss Gomez was in my yard. I went out to find her perched on the veranda.

– Oh my, Miss Bridgemohan, I hope I didn't disturb your rest. I heard from Franco that you had quite a night locked in that room back there. How are you?

She looked at me over her glasses, her eyes lit with curiosity.
– What day is it?
– Wednesday, my dear! You missed everything. I suppose you heard about Sam and that awful affair on Mountain Road?
– Not really. Please, tell me.

– You won't believe it! Sam and Roland had gone up there with an intention.

– Roland too?

– Yes. Apparently, over some time they had figured out a pattern with guess who? Bones and Corporal Luke, my dear.

– Pattern?

– Yes, a contraband ring and more.

– But why would they get involved? What about the police?

– Cop and crook are sometimes the same fish.

– Do you mean…

– Uh-huh. An awful trade has been going on right under our noses. Maria and Sam accidentally uncovered the scheme. But goodness, those two were reckless!

– What scheme? And reckless – how?

– You're really out of circulation down here, Miss Anna. Where to start?

She sighed and fanned, her body tense with excitement.

– Here's what I know: every other month or so, the mail van comes from Salvador with cargo in the back. One time when Sam and Maria were up there, doing God-knows-what, Maria ran straight across the road. According to Sam, the van near plummeted down the mountainside. Bones must have been scared stiff. He left the vehicle unattended to go in search of whatever had startled him. That was when Sam heard a commotion inside the van and had a look. You wouldn't believe what she found!

Miss Gomez drew in her breath and sat back in the chair, eyes wide open, apparently too overwhelmed to go on. I waited, allowing her theatrics to play themselves out.

– A young woman – in the flesh! Can you believe it? Oh, the devil is a busy-busy man!

– You mean Bones is trafficking women?

– Yes, girls have been on occasion among the booty. Imagine, right here in Macaima. And Bones is deep in it! All this time Salvador has been a holding bay. The smugglers come in somewhere along the coast and take their contraband and what-not up the old bridle path.

– But that doesn't make sense. Wouldn't they have to pass the station on the way out? Why not just head straight to Railway?

– I asked myself the same thing! But you see, that way they avoid the police station and should there be a roadblock further out, a mail van would not draw suspicion. In any event, Corporal Luke would be sure to be there to keep things moving. It was the perfect decoy. Anyhow, when the time is right, Bones turns up to collect the merchandise under the cover of his mail run to Salvador.

I wasn't clear where she was heading, but I let her talk on.

– Now we know that the one they call Spanish is involved in more than contraband whiskey and meat – and why the Corporal and Bones are thick as thieves. Spanish has since disappeared. No surprise there; but both Bones and Luke are in hospital under police watch. The past few days have been just awful! But thankfully the whole scheme is now all in the open.

She slumped back again, vigorously fanning herself, but also assessing my reaction.

– It's almost unbelievable, Miss Gomez. So carefully orchestrated with connections across the channel and all.

– My grandfather was from the Main, you know. He slaved on that cocoa estate to send all his children to school. Oh, I can't bear to think what would have been the fate of that poor girl. But, oh my, miracles happen. They do happen!

She searched my face, I thought, for any sign of scepticism. I gave away nothing.

– Sam, I hope, was not badly hurt. Franco mentioned she's in hospital. What happened?

– Oh, she twisted her ankle in the scramble, trying to avoid the van.

– What was she doing in the road?

– They planned a ambush. Can you believe! Thank goodness Sam can move like the wind. It seems that she stood in the road with Roland beside her.

– They did what? They could have been killed!

– My thoughts exactly. I'm not entirely clear about all the details.

Miss Gomez went on to tell with unbridled enthusiasm a fantastic story about Roland and Sam waiting in hiding for the van to cross the ridge at Hight Point. When it arrived, as expected, the first thing that Bones encountered was them standing in the middle of the road. Sam was decked out in Marie's wedding dress with Roland at her side. His worse nightmare! And this part she confessed was close to impossible to believe: a deer dashed across the road, forcing Bones to swerve and collide with a tree. He went straight through the windscreen and *kissed wood* – Franco's words. The deer vanished into thin air.

She released herself once again onto the backrest of her chair and sighed, exhausted with her telling. I let it all sink in, suspended between belief and disbelief until Miss Gomez provided a plausible resolution to the events she had shared.

– All ludicrous, if you ask me, but I suppose the whole truth's somewhere in there.

I had already concluded who the woman in the room had been, but I asked, for the sake of certainty.

– Where was Maria all this time?

– Roland made sure that Maria was safely locked away at your place, so they could carry out the scheme.

– You mean in the storeroom?

My question caused her pause. I could see her turning over the information.

– I suppose so; she was definitely tucked away somewhere. They didn't want her mixed up in their plan. Once Franco had realised Maria and Sam were missing, he would figure out they had gone to High Point and go after them. That was their thinking. Franco's not the endearing type, but he checks on his mother every day, especially since she lost her sight. They banked on that and they were right. I know it's hard to believe, but there's a caring side to him.

It was almost too much to process. I had been cleverly played. When Sam was telling me her garden story, Roland must have doubled back to stash Maria. He evidently knew Sam's story and about Marie's rape. Maybe he hadn't known of the affair with Julien when he offered to marry her; maybe it didn't matter. Now the jammed door made sense. I was no doubt baited to go out to the storeroom. Maria and I were both safely out of the way. And God, those shinneys! Had he…?

Miss Gomez, though, was going on with her story.

– Bones and Luke are pretty battered. I can't give the details; but it serves them right! Luke especially should be so ashamed – an officer of the law. The LAW, Miss Bridgemohan! What has it become? I shudder to think that justice has no true guardian in this place. He should be lost in jail. The girl was barely fifteen years old. At least she was saved and maybe their arrest will be the end of that ring.

I was sceptical about that, but my thoughts had already shifted elsewhere.

– What are we going to do about Sam, Miss Gomez?

– You know, I came here precisely to talk about just that and got sidetracked. Something came up that may be the light in all this terrible business. I had a chat with some friends. They know of a congregation in the States that runs a hospital that can get Sam the help she needs. Of course, we can't do anything without Franco's permission, as the mother has been out of touch. Even Brenda can't make contact. I think it's a great chance for Sam – if we can get Franco on board.

It was the first time that I realised that Brenda and Miss Gomez were working together to find Sam's mother, and that there was a friendship there in spite of Brenda's anger over her alleged role in implicating Patrick as the instigator of the schoolyard fight. I let my role in the search slide.

– It sounds like a chance, Miss Gomez. But what does Sam want?

– That's just the thing – I don't think anyone who really matters to her has asked. She needs to be involved in the decision-making. We can't decide for her.

– Yes, I agree. She must have her say.

– Leave everything to me, Miss Bridgemohan.

As she said this, it struck me that Miss Gomez had matters of her own that needed attention but had been so generous in pursuing Sam's needs that she'd ignored them.

I had to find a way to broach my concern.

– Forgive my intrusion on your affairs, Miss Gomez, but are you alright? I ask only from concern.

I allowed my gaze to linger on her stomach. She self-consciously adjusted the waistband of her shirt and crossed her ankles.

– Oh, I see, you've been listening to gossip. Well, let me put your concerns to rest, Miss Bridgemohan. I'm fine. Just a simple case of *fibroids*.

She whispered the word.

– They're not uncommon, you know.

– Isn't it better to act quickly?

– It is, but in my case…

She looked around as though wanting to ensure that we were alone.

– Well, we're not exactly strangers, so I suppose I can be plain. It's been a difficult decision.

– How so?

– It would mean not having a chance at being a mother.

She fussed some more with her clothes. A tear spilled from an eye. She delicately whipped it away with her pinky as she rose to leave.

– But, my dear, that's behind me, now. I've decided on the procedure. Dreams will be dreams. I have my choir and my flowers. Have you seen my orchids and anthuriums, Miss Bridgemohan? You must see them. They are gorgeous! Do come to see them one day soon.

She floated up Beach Trace, like a butterfly flitting through the garden of her own blossoms and perfumes. I would never claim to be an expert on understanding people, but as Miss Gomez breezed away, I saw how much I had misread her, made fun of her eccentricities and judged harshly her biases. Beneath it all – the fussy aloofness, uncharitable dismissals and criticisms that were possibly habitual deflections – she had a real concern for Sam that went beyond empty sentiment. Moreover, she had dreamed a life for herself. I watched her go. My eyes welled up.

CHAPTER 23 – RITUAL

After Miss Gomez left that morning, I was ready to take care of what I had brought with me in my luggage to Macaima. A revisiting of the storeroom where so much had unravelled was necessary, perhaps to confirm whether all that I had experienced in there was in fact true. Maria had been in there. That was certain. Brite had been there with me, too.

From the threshold of the room, I saw the wreckage that had been left behind. A scrambled map of footprints tracked the dusty floor and in places large patches were wiped clean, but the miry smell that had enveloped the space was no longer there. The window in which a dizzying pageant of phantom faces and pasts had appeared was shut, the pane broken. The books that had tumbled from stacked boxes still lay scattered on the floor. My eyes settled on the *Nelson's Reader*, the one that Marie had read from. It was open at Lesson Six. I read aloud again the opening sentences: *Here is a clock.* I repeated the words slowly, listening to their sounds. I read the question put to the reader about the skills needed to make sense of its operations: *Can you tell the time by it?* The lesson appeared so singular in its purpose. With each repeat, the lines reverberated with what hung in their shadows. A clock was necessary to order the passage of a day, for shaping a life. What would life be without this power to navigate the world?

The lesson, though, was structured as an obligation: *You ought to learn...* how the world turns. Time, too, had a language. So much must be unlearned. All those years of living behind the line that divided the Hendersons' house and our annex. All those years of looking at my world from distant and oblique perspectives: my mother's silences, her unwillingness to share with me our story. All those years of keeping time with what ought to be, in a yard that was not her own, and where she planted, as in a fever, anything that flowered but left the blossoms to wither on their stems, looked at, but never brought into the house that was not ours, not even the books that I first read.

For me, the bottom had fallen out of that world long before Mr Henderson had ended his tenure on the island and gone back to his home, his wife – his life. Maybe that is what I had come to resent without fully understanding – the statement his leaving had made. I was sixteen and he had given my mother money for the cake: fruits in yellow batter. Pink rosettes on white icing. He had found his way to have his cake and eat it, and my mother had agreed that was enough for her – for us. Thea had accused me of the same thing, after that day in the lunchroom when she told the history of the Treasury and we had made it our own. It was hilarious really. Maybe I had loved Thea in those days and Miles was a detour from myself. I still wasn't certain of any future, only that I was here. What I did not want was a world of secrets like my mother had lived. I didn't anymore want to live the life others thought I should.

The ground beneath my feet was solid. I stomped on it with both feet. Tomorrow was more than possible; it was necessary. What about Maria – was tomorrow possible for her? She deserved another story, another beginning. I saw that the cot with its wafer-thin mattress was in the same corner. Maria's childhood violation was not mine. Or was it, now that I shared in her story? She had made me a witness. So, too, had Sam when she sang of Marie's rape on the estate. We had all learned how time *could t*urn. Maria must have read that lesson for her grandfather again and again – to perfection. Now I wanted to be time's story's maker, not its casualty or its keeper. What would be the story I tell of time? Not my mother's. Not the Red Reader's. No more *Monday's child*. I would have no more of that haunted rhyme, caught in its rhythm even when the words changed. Who was Annabelle? I flung the book at the bed, capsized the frame, kicked at the mattress, lifted and smashed the vile thing to the floor, wanting to burn it to ashes. With the bed behind me, I saw through teary eyes, a bundle tucked into the corner, in the same spot where Maria had huddled and wept. I moved closer to investigate.

– I was just coming to collect that.

The voice boomed in the small space. My sudden turn caused a collision with a pile of broken furniture.

– Careful, Miss Anna. Doh frighten. Is only me – Roland.

I righted myself, conscious that our last encounter had produced a similar request – that I should not be frightened.

– What are you doing here, Roland?

His shadow loomed, tall and slim like a vertical line drawn down the middle of the doorway that was otherwise framed by blinding light.

– I come to collect my belongings. I hope you doh mind. I wanted somewhere safe to put them.

– What's wrong with your place; isn't it safe?

I moved as far as I could to the opposite side of the room, arcing so that I drew closer to the open door. He noticed my manoeuvre but said nothing as he reached into the corner to retrieve the bag he had tucked out of view.

– What's in there anyway – gold?

He lifted the sack as though gauging its weight, giving more consideration to my question than I had intended.

– You could say that, depending on what you put your value in. I keep a few things in there that belong to Marie and the baby. No shame in that.

I sensed a challenge.

– I suppose not.

– Anyhow, is time to let them go. Everything finish now. But maybe you understand that?

He glanced at the wrapped package I had placed on the floor and left the room, leaving me with the suggestion that he knew about Brite. I could be wrong. Everything about that night was a muddle. I picked up my own belongings and followed him.

It was refreshing to return to the open air where I found Roland squatting easily on his haunches in a sunlit spot. Smoke jetted from his nostrils and curled up, filtering through the cover of leaves that the garden offered. His eyes rested in soft concentration on the sack that lay on the grass before him. It couldn't have contained much, but whatever was hidden inside absorbed his attention. I could have been invisible. He possessed a capacity to keep the world at bay, a concentration that could appear to be indulgent self-absorption had it not also been evidence of a kind of determination to do right. That ambivalence irritated me. I snapped.

– You could have asked.

He looked at me dreamily, not comprehending.

– You could have asked me about using the room to store your belongings.

His thumb flicked. Ash fell.

– Yes. I should have. Sorry fuh that.

He drew again on the cigarette, sucking air into his lungs and hissing on the exhale. He got up, using his knees for leverage, his arms extended downwards so that they looked like the frontal limbs of a quadruped. He appeared to be under no pressure to speak. We had not spoken of the Mountain Road events that now seemed so much in the past, but there was more to hear about that, and he alone carried the truth about Marie's last moments. That remained the missing piece. What I did know was that he had some accounting to do. I had been used in the scheme he had concocted with Sam to trap Bones and his accomplice.

– I think you have some explaining to do. I was locked in that room with Marie and you know it – you and Sam.

He didn't appear surprised by the accusation.

– Well, did you?

– We put her in there, Miss Anna – before Sam sing for you. She meet up with me on the junction after; but that thing about locking you in, we never do that part. We only wanted to keep Marie out the way. Sam stay with her 'til she doze off. Once she fall sound asleep, she doh usually wake til morning. We know Franco woulda come up Mountain Road to look for Maria.

– What made you so sure, he would?

He seemed surprised by the question.

– Franco is a hard man to understand. He rough and plain foolish in how he reason sometimes. He doh know how to manage with Maria or Sam for that matter, but he would never let them stay out in no storm.

– I saw someone or something out there that night. It drew me out here.

– Maybe it was deer. Nighttime, they roam all over.

– What about the shut door?
– Nothing to do with me or Sam.
– And those awful shinneys?
– Shinney in season, Miss Anna. That wasn't me.

I didn't know what to think. He could be telling the truth. Nothing, though, could excuse the deception, and to think that he got Sam to go along. She liked and trusted him, but the whole masquerade was too much. What else could he be capable of pulling off?

– I real sorry for all the trouble we put you in, Miss Anna. That part wasn't what we plan. Anyway, I glad to see you alright and I hope what I bring back for you would make up the difference.

He spoke quietly, flicking away the cigarette butt like a timed full stop. In one fluid motion he swept the bag up, rose to his full height and strode off. I followed, hanging back a little to gauge his intent. Excited yelps greeted us as we drew near the house. I immediately knew. Night and Day were waiting for us. I ran to greet them. They were either happy to see me or just happy to play. Roland remained in the yard observing the scene.

– They remember you good, Miss Anna.
– Yes they do, and I didn't forget you beauties for a second.

I nuzzled their faces. They had grown chubby and their thickened coats shone.

– What have you been feeding them?
– That is Mama Gloria doing.

I was so absorbed in the play that didn't notice Roland had slipped away. I was just in time to see the pale blue of his shirt disappear down the track that led to the beach. I felt our conversation was not finished. There were still questions to be answered about what he and Sam had revealed. I fell in behind him but kept my distance. If he were unaware of my presence, I would have been surprised. He possessed the stealth and alertness of an animal. I watched him as he gathered a few dried coconuts, which he placed in his bag. Stripped of his shirt, he ventured to the water's edge at the place where the riptide surged, then waded waist-deep into the sea, his body struggling against the current.

I realised then that we had both made a similar appointment with Goodbye Bay that morning – to release the past. That was encouragement enough to close the distance between us, certain that he had registered my presence. The excited yelping of the pups would certainly have caught his attention. They overtook me and ran back and forth with the retreat and advance of the tide as he surrendered the bundle to its pull. He waited until it was no longer visible before vigorously splashing water onto his chest and face before he dunked under, returning to the surface with a burst of exhaled breath, water cascading from his head and shoulders. His body was polished in light as he waded to the shore, pushing against the outgoing current. There he lunged onto the beach, spent. He lay flat on the sand, face upturned, eyes closed. The pups gathered close, sniffing at his drenched body.

– Your turn now, Miss Anna. She waiting on your offering, too.

There was no need to answer. I walked into the water as far as I could manage, steadied myself as the current churned around me, tore away the wrapping that concealed Brite, took one more look at the sleeping form and let her go. I waited until I could no longer see anything but the glistening waves.

I returned to find Roland propped on his elbows, watching me intently in that detached way he had, which made you feel simultaneously seen and free. I sat beside him and listened to the world that teemed around us – the surging surf and whisking breeze, cloudy with sea spray. I felt immensely small beneath a sky that was endlessly blue and feathered.

He spoke first.

– You know, Miss Anna, Warao is water people. I have that nation in my blood.

– I didn't know.

– Yes, from my father. Mama Gloria is a great aunt, but she is Natu to me. When Franco bring you out from that room, she is the one who stay to care for you.

– I guessed that, but she left before I could thank her.

– She is a healer. Since small I live by her. I tell people I luckier than most to have two mothers; but is Mama Gloria that teach me how to live in this world.

I could hear pride in his declaration, though I remained a little sceptical. I still felt uneasy about him – the self he presented and the stories that he gave – but I had no concrete case. There were only coincidences and gaps that I supposed would remain a mystery.

– Everybody know that Natu was the only person Miss Ana trust to raise Maria. That was her choice, but De Valremy say no.

– Why?

– I figure he didn't like that his woman could find comfort by Mama – when she run to Mama from the beast he could turn sometimes. Nobody could get between them when Miss Ana was there. Mama treat her like her own.

– She was lucky to have her.

He nodded in agreement. His story changed direction.

– I believe Marie went back home when she walk into this sea – she and the baby. I couldn't reach them. Current was strong that day, but Natu see it different. She say they turn fish and swim away. She make story for everything. See that out there?

I followed to where he pointed.

– She would say that is caiman crossing from the Main to bring blessing.

We both focused on the object bobbing in the water, slowly inching to the shore. We soon saw it was only a log. I wondered, though, at the journey it had made, and all the crossings that for centuries had joined the shores between us. If I looked east there was another landmass across the Atlantic, and another further north. Always an *over there* from wherever we call *here*. I was never interested in travel. Not like Thea, who spoke with enthusiasm of getting to know *her* world. Travel, she said, would introduce her to it, not as a tourist. The world was home. I could not share that feeling – the sense of being at home not just on the island but on the planet. I had not as yet allowed myself that expansion. Thea fought for the place she wanted the world to become because she believed she had a place – a role in it. She always said I was too much a spectator. Maybe she was right.

I watched Roland as he began to slowly, meditatively, to gather up sand, which he rubbed over his damp body, limb by limb, becoming the beach, the place where the sea arrived and departed. Once he was completely covered in sand, he sprinted into the sea and returned again, washed.

– I can't remember much about my father, Miss Anna, but this song I learn from him. He sing it to put me to sleep: *U-na-na-ka ta-me / o-ba-e-ta-no re / ma-na-to-ro sa-nu-ka re / hi-da-ne du-wa-re / hi-da-ne du-wa re / hi-da-ne du-wa-re…*

– That's beautiful. What does it mean?

– Not sure. A lullaby. Natu would know. I like how the words sound. They touch somewhere in me that I don't always know is there.

– What happened to your father?

– Long story. But the short is 'mortelle tree fall on him.

– Goodness! Sorry to hear.

– But song make him feel close. I feel like I more than know him, and that feeling put a light inside me. I can't explain.

– I guess we all carry plenty history – all kinds that make us innocent and guilty same time.

Roland looked at me puzzled, then found resonance.

– Natu always say, once we breathing this air we likely to be crocodile that foolish enough to steal from God. I have plenty deciding to do, Miss Anna, but I know my part with Marie finish now. Time for me to see what is my next step. Maybe I should see what life outside could bring. All I know is Macaima, and maybe is time for me to know more about this world I living in. You take care, Miss Anna.

He began the trudge back to the track that led up to Beach Trace. The pups raced behind him with joyful yelps. I sat a while longer, wondering at all these leave-takings, including my own, whether they were temporary necessities for different kinds of returns. For a little while longer I wanted to be there on that beach, unsheltered from the wind and the churning tides, savouring the quiet and release granted by my own farewell. Grateful, too, for the mercy of the sea that had wrapped Brite in the surge of its immaculate folds.

CHAPTER 24 – THE STAGE COMES DOWN

On my first day back to work after Monday's *storm day,* another commotion was in train in front of Johnny's shop. All the village's conflicts seemed to converge there. People stopped to watch. The stage was at last being dismantled. Stationed on the opposite side of the road was the man who had introduced himself to me as Mr Elton. He oversaw the men who were extracting nails and knocking apart boards. Noticeable, too, was that Mr Elton was not dressed in the clerkish slacks and shirt sleeves in which I had first met him. The oyster dashiki and matching trousers offered a different face of the man. I did not know what to make of either version.

Franco was nowhere in sight, which I found odd. He had given the impression, in Mr Elton's absence, that he was his right-hand man, and Mr Elton, as far as I had gathered, was himself a proxy for the still unknown Thomas De Valremy. I supposed that Franco was about his own business, possibly making travel arrangements for Sam. My one-dimensional view of him had been complicated. I was under no illusion about his capacity to be a bully and downright insensitive, but I had come to recognise that he was much more – a man shaken to his core by the reality of his daughter.

A dispirited silence prevailed in the small group with whom I stood watching the gradual disappearance of the platform. Even Johnny made a rare appearance from behind his counter to stand witness with the rest of Macaima. Mr Elton crossed the road to join the gathering. I could tell that his presence was important to the villagers. More than the dismantling of the stage was in play. The men worked with a quiet and efficient fervour. Gone was the playfulness I witnessed when Franco had supervised the construction. Maybe they sensed some sort of era had come to an end, and Mr Elton was signalling a distance between himself and the party he was once dedicated to representing, and that *he* himself, not Franco, was responsible for engineering the removal of the most recent public sign of that affiliation – the stage on which the PM did not appear to speak.

The junction pulsed and echoed with hammering and the blunt thud of discarded lumber as each lath was painfully pried loose and thrown aside like a broken promise. Mr Elton called some instructions to the workmen. Cray stopped what he was doing to listen above the noise of the demolition. No good. He shouted to Mr Elton to repeat what he had said. He nodded and began piling the unbroken laths neatly at the side of the shop. Whispered conversations filtered through the gathering about the suspension of the *Face the People* campaign, *until further notice*. The PM had gone on a personal retreat. He was at his residence, thinking – and writing. Rumours circulated that some minister or the other had vexed him. Then new information surfaced about the real issue behind his chosen stint of solitude. Somebody from up the islands, a fellow leader of a government whose country had escaped Flora's path, had made a bad joke about the hurricane that flattened Tobago. The comment leaked out: it was God's belated correction for the PM's *one from ten leaves nought* arithmetic. Blame requires a target, so the claim was that the math drove the last nail into the Federation's coffin and that history would one day prove the PM wrong on that score. He had a chance to really lead and he chose to go home with his marbles instead. The PM was infuriated. He was adamant that he would not surrender the nation for the rest of the region to freeload off. Any other talk was pure badmind. The *Face the People* meetings were put on the back burner. He would run the nation remotely from his home office and concentrate on writing more books – to give them *economics in dey backside*. He was done talking.

The whole business sounded like pure foolishness to me, but people liked to find reasons for things. That was my thought when Lucille whispered to me that Thomas De Valremy and Mr Elton were no longer on speaking terms.

– Yuh see how Elton dress like is Sunday church? He decide he done with politics and De Valremy.

– What's the grouse?

– Anybody who put that question to him, Elton say *When yuh find snake inside yuh house, it make no sense to ask how long it is. All talk done. Kill it!* De Valremy thought he could blow smoke in he eye forever.

– What on earth do you mean?

– De Valremy sell Ave-near. He sell we out, and everybody know he give big money to the party.

– That was sudden. What's behind the decision?

– We waiting to discover. But Elton take it hard. He well educate and coulda go far, but he choose Macaima. I never trust Thomas – always playing nicey-nicey. Elton take a chance on him but he is flesh and could make mistake like everybody else. So I standing with him through his trouble. We have to learn together – and if nothing doing, well, then I have to make a different choice.

– Maybe Thomas initially meant well and got sidetracked along the way.

– I can't argue with what you say. But, Miss Anna, for all that, he sell we out and not one word to a soul inside here. And as for Elton, he was like blindman in the middle. I better play a whe-whe mark on he.

Her reading of the end of the Elton-Thomas alliance was persuasive, but I suspected all had not been told. As Thea would have said, the government was showing its hand on development policies that were more about wooing foreign investors to stake their claims to oil production than working with the rank and file who were eager to be a part of all the talk about nation building and development. That was clear to anyone willing to look the beast in the eye. The PM had opted to play the game of big capital with the sharks. Only time would tell where it would all lead. Unless she had changed her tune, there was one thing that could be said of Thea: she wanted a future that put people front and centre. We were all too caught up in the theatrics of nationalism to think clearly about what nationhood could mean for ourselves and the region. Education certainly, but what exactly were we building and what kind of people were we shaping to take hold of tomorrow?

If Mr Elton was sending a very public message to the village that he was no longer De Valremy's lackey and no longer convinced by the direction the government was going, what was his plan? While I knew nothing directly about Thomas De Valremy, it seemed probable that he had felt it beneficial to court the loyalty of Mr Elton, who was certainly respected by the villagers. Now something had changed. In his Afro-styled outfit, after Lucille's revelation, I saw a man who had been blindsided and was anxious to recover his wounded pride. Whatever had transpired between himself and Thomas over the sale of the estate, he had been rudely awakened. Mr Elton was presenting himself as a reformed man of the people. Beyond the visible change of clothes, the truth of that would have to unfold.

I walked on to the post office with the noise of the demolition trailing behind me. The place felt strangely in hiatus. I opened all the windows to let the breeze blow through and instinctively knew that my time in Macaima was coming to a premature end. I was going to have to inform Mrs Bailey that I did not think I could continue on at Macaima – not after all that had happened. That would not go over well, and my resignation might be required. The thought was daunting. Begin again. I, too, was unfinished. In that space of recognition, and perhaps decision, which brought with it an extreme sense of aloneness, Mr Elton came in.

– Happy to see that you are back with the living, Miss Bridgemohan.

– Yes, Mr Elton, I am.

It wasn't the entire truth. My own storm was far from over, but it was what I could offer him. We were barely acquainted, but even the bonds I had formed with some of the villagers were uncertain. I supposed that they felt the same about me. Macaima, I had come to learn, was not the quiet, uneventful place I had imagined it would be. I had been draw into a giddying drama of convergences. Now all was laid bare, I felt bruised, more than somewhat tender, and a little healed but far from resolved. Where was I to go from here and what was I to do? Maybe Macaima pondered similar questions. Nothing was the same. Not for me, Brenda, Sam, or even Mr Elton, no matter how composed he managed to make himself sound.

– I owe you an apology, Miss Bridgemohan. I have not had the time to welcome you properly. It has been an unusual few weeks.

– I would agree with you on that score, Mr Elton. As for apologies, you owe me nothing.

He appeared a little put off. Although a late arrival to events, and in the background, he had been involved throughout. In that brief encounter on *storm day,* he was a reporter's voice, a mimicked monotone he thought necessary for the role he had assumed. Now the man in the dashiki was a different person altogether. Still very much composed but less formal. I felt that I was seeing him for the first time.

– It look like Franco manage to hold his tongue on this news.

It was my turn to look puzzled.

– An unforeseen problem with the lease.

– What do you mean?

– Well, I hope it's not a problem. Mr De Valremy decide to terminate. Sorry to bring you this news – and it is my last work for him. We're no longer associates.

– Can he do that? I signed for a year, Mr Elton.

– Yes, he can. The mutual termination clause – one month's notice from either side. It's in black and white.

– I see.

– But if it's any consolation, you have three months to vacate.

– I suppose I should be grateful for the grace; but why the termination?

– Nothing to do with you, Miss Bridgemohan. He give notice to all his tenants. All the lands sell.

– Yes, but I didn't realise I would be affected.

– He sell everything – every tree and stone. Not even my church get exempt, so we all in the same barrel.

His voice choked with a renewed hurt.

– What's behind it, Mr Elton? The Beach Trace property isn't exactly part of the estate.

For the first time, he appeared shaken, barely present, just a shell of the self-assured news-bringer of *storm day*. Perhaps he was more self-possessed than I was able to see at the time, but I saw a man caught in the shadowland of the new self he had to become, having suddenly found himself face to face with betrayal and the collapse of the leverage he once enjoyed as De Valremy's right-hand man.

– That is how money people operate, Miss Bridgemohan. When greener pastures elsewhere, they move on. It will all come to light; but perhaps you should find a new place sooner rather than later. I already put your case to Johnny. I hope you don't mind me taking that liberty.

– Why Johnny?

– Sometimes he offer the room above his shop for rent.

– Thank you, Mr Elton, but no thanks. That won't do at all.

– I thought as much, but to find anything better going to be hard. I could have a word with Mrs Austin. She might have a room to spare.

That alternative was equally unappealing, not with the family's connection to all that Sam had suffered.

– In that case, Johnny's might have to do. As you say I have a few months grace before I decide.

– I understand. Three months – that will take us into Christmas.

He shook his head disbelievingly.

– No room at the inn, Miss Bridgemohan. Even my church must start over from scratch. Imagine that. You know, something hit me today as I was watching that stage come down. It hit me how easy you could bury a history – wipe it out clean like it was never there.

– Somebody always remembers, Mr Elton.

– Maybe so, but I was a damn fool to believe that when Thomas De Valremy saw his own father burn down that same church his grandfather put his money to build, he would grow to be a different man.

– The church on Beach Trace – Joseph De Valremy did that?

He didn't confirm, but went on like the lid of a boiling pot had blow off.

– I thought Joseph learn a lesson for life that day. The grandfather was a twisted man. Everybody know that. We use to make joke and say his blood run too close to his skin. That was to compensate for what we didn't know how to confront. Not even I could challenge him on what he was doing, although I had to comfort plenty for his wicked ways. No excuse for that. We never act, Miss Bridgemohan. We turn a blind eye. But Thomas – I thought that what happened to Maria, who is his blood, would change him. Well, now I know that whatever guilt he inherit is not the same thing as responsibility. Responsibility is something you have to take up without force. You have to take it up free. Guilt is not atonement. Nothing comes of spending a life trying to appease a wrong, like sorry is the only word they could speak.

– What are you saying, Mr Elton? Did Thomas know of Maria's abuse? He must have been a teenager himself when that happened?

– I not here to lay blame for what I have no proof for. All I saying is that guilt could cause a person to play Samaritan and saint. That is not love. That is not responsibility. Not only that – guilt sit down inside you like Dry-bone on lookout for some fool to take away the burden. All these years I was that fool. I was nothing but jackass carrying load that all them De Valremy wanted to pass on.

CHAPTER 25 – A DEPARTURE

Life went on. I read reports in the newspapers of the *freak accident* up Mountain Road that had uncovered a criminal ring. Pictures of Corporal Luke and Mason were posted as key operators in the network. A passing mention was made of possible high-level associates. No names. An investigation was purportedly in train. Franklyn Perez was mentioned as having made the discovery of the van and praised for his single-handed apprehension of the fleeing corporal, who remained hospitalised under police guard with a concussion and broken ribs. Mason had been discharged from hospital and was held on remand pending a trial on smuggling charges. No mention was made of Sam and Roland. Franco had obviously kept their involvement safe from official scrutiny.

Little was said about the young Venezuelan woman found in the van. She was apparently an illegal seeking work on the island, and had been duly deported. The possibility of a regular traffic in girls was downplayed. The authorities were adamant that such a find was rare and that mostly they came of their own free will, or were foolish enough to be seduced by false promises. Much later, after I had left the village, an article appeared that caught my interest about the island being well-positioned to become a major transhipment hub for a growing Latin American weapons and narcotics trade with markets in the US and Europe. Then the story evaporated.

Franco and Sam were scarce after the Mountain Road incident. I heard from Miss Gomez that they were both staying with family somewhere closer to the city. It was a more convenient location for making all the arrangements required for the US trip. Franco had apparently opted out of accompanying her. A relative would go in his stead. His objection was that he wasn't leaving his soil and he wasn't no bird, but there was more to it. The main reason, according to Miss Gomez, was his discovery, in preparation to apply for a passport, that he actually carried his father's name. The story was sketchy but it turned out De Valremy had made sure that his first child on the island carried his name. The change to Perez was made later by his mother when she took up with Mason's father. Franco was too young to know this, and she had kept her silence. Did names matter? I carried my mother's, though I was more than sure who Mr Henderson was in relation to me. It mattered little; what I really wanted was for her to share our story. More than a name, I hungered for intimacy and openness, longing to end the loneliness I felt because, for as long as I could remember, we were like two people looking at each other from the opposite ends of a bridge.

I was more than thankful that Sam was on her way to getting the help that she needed. That was Miss Gomez's conviction when she had relayed the news of the US trip.

– Franco's in deep waters, Miss Bridgemohan. I don't think he can manage the situation; but not to worry. Cheryl will take charge. Her hurried explanation of the family ties that made Cheryl a half cousin she shared with Franco lost me in its complications, but I did grasp that Miss Gomez was godmother to one of Cheryl's children. Miss Gomez, though, was preoccupied with her own concerns over her decision to finally have surgery. She, too, had temporally left the village.

As the weeks passed, the village eased once again into the flow of life. The news that the estate lands were to be sold took centre stage. I remained on the periphery of developments. I didn't mind. I was quietly planning my exit, making inquiries about a place to return to in the city and writing to universities for a range of undergraduate brochures. Not that I was clear on any career path, but I needed to have something lined up. I wrote to my mother – another one-pager with a yes or no question about Mr Henderson. She had not yet answered my pre-storm card, but in all fairness, I had given her no opportunity to respond. *All was good*. There was nothing more to say. Maybe the second attempt was a little blunt, and while I was doubtful she would reply, I had lost the taste for sidling. I wanted to get to the core.

I thought sometimes of Thea, about her last days on the island and wondered whether she was enjoying her programme at the university in the USA. In our last meeting in the lunchroom, she had said that her choice of study was history and economics because the region needed to explore new developmental models as the islands gained their independence. She wanted to be a part of that conversation and making of the future. What she said remained with me:

★

– Connecting culturally will be like breathing, Anna. What we need is to cohere as a region. The possibilities will be endless. So far we're still hung up on singularities. We aborted the vision. Too many big egos.
– I suppose we feared we would lose ourselves.
– You're right about that. Power-mongering and money-wrangling aside, we're unpractised in radical collaboration. We're still hiding our copybooks and trying to outdo each other.

As was usual when Thea got into that intellectual fast lane, I was left walking. I was mostly a sounding board for the refinement of ideas that had caught her imagination, no doubt sparked in the circles she was involved in, beyond the office lime. It was no secret that she had grown close to the oilfield workers' union, connections she cemented during her stint in the south. She refused to be bullied into silence. The Commission of Inquiry to investigate subversives in the trade union movement had soured alliances and the lines were drawn. We were at war with ourselves.

Maybe there was a touch of the extremist in her, but her energy was infectious, and she invited me to think.

– So you haven't given up on Federation then?
– Never! How we manage ourselves in this shared geography – and I don't mean mere window-dressing – will be the real test of our civilisation.
– Maybe it was all just a dream.
– Oh, it was much more, Anna. We got scared of our own potential. Comrade Nello was our main visionary at the time, and look what happened to him.
– I suppose people were uncomfortable and the PM definitely thought he was too far left.

– The PM was too focused on not wanting to be found on the wrong side of how our big neighbours define democracy. That's the real betrayal if you ask me.

– Yes, the nation idea got snagged in the American and British set up.

– You could be on mark there. The single nation formula is a difficult ole mas to abandon. The region had a jump on remodelling that, but we messed up big time.

– Where do you get all this from, Thea? I feel I'm still on the shore and you're somewhere out there on the horizon.

– You just afraid to move out of your comfort zones, Anna – and I mean mentally move out. There're no dragons on the edge.

– So you say.

– Well, none that can't be slain.

★

One Friday, after work, when I stopped for some supplies at Johnny's, I happened to get a glimpse of Roland on the bar side of the shop, but by the time I was finished with my purchases, he had left. We had not spoken since our time on the beach, and I wanted to inquire after Sam. I could understand his avoidance. He knew I still suspected I had been used as a ploy and that I doubted whether all had been revealed. I, too, had surrendered to my own brand of avoidance. The isolation I felt, and somewhat relished in the aftermath of the storm, confirmed how much of a newcomer I was to the place. For a few weeks before the storm, time had been concentrated and I had been at the centre of a series of interconnected lives and stories. With the commotion of all that had happened behind them, people were now focused on what lay ahead. Time stretched out and the villagers no longer saw me as a novelty – or needed me as a confidant. Then there was the concern over Tobago and its recovery from Flora. Mrs Austin stopped by with news about Mrs Cabral – Merrill – and her Tobago trip.

– You may want to know, Miss Bridgemohan, that news came about Merrill. She and the family survived the storm. The house is gone, but, as she says, life and limb were spared; so they're thankful. They all squeezed in with the mother-in-law; the baby is their constant joy for being so completely oblivious to the loss.

– Happy to hear that, Mrs Austin. I suppose some were even less fortunate.

She nodded regretfully.

– You're quite right. Father Xavier is rallying the parish to collect clothes, linen, dry goods, tinned items and so on to send across. You can leave items at the warden's or there's a donation box at the school, if you're interested.

– Of course, I'll definitely give what I can.

– Good. I'm helping with the sorting and dragged Barry into helping with the boxing-up.

– Oh, how's Barry? I haven't been seeing him around.

– He's been spending some time with my sister and her family in Railway. All the donations are being sent to the main parish there; so it's a good way to keep him busy.

– I see. He caused Sam a great deal of pain.

Her eyes narrowed.

– As far as I understand, he was not alone and while I agree they may have been a little rough, it was just play.

She eyed me for a response.

– I don't think that what happened to her can in any way be called *play*.

– We're entitled to our opinions, Miss Bridgemohan. In any case, he'll be starting school there in Railway. Mr Austin and I agreed he would benefit from the change. He's likely to get a scholarship and Father Xavier is keen to ensure he keeps focused. Anyway, my dear, I'll be getting back to the job. Mr Elton is not in today. He's busy with the preparations for his a new church; but I suppose you already heard.

I hadn't, but did not invite her to provide details, making an excuse about pending phone calls.

Soon enough, I discovered that Mr Elton was at work on the structure. Before and after reporting to work at the warden's office, and on weekends, he gave his time to the project. The site was a small plot not too far east of Beach Trace. Word was that the land had been a parting gift from De Valremy as compensation for the loss of the old building due to the sale of estate lands. Mr Elton had obviously put aside his sense of betrayal to accept. I supposed it would have been foolish to refuse. He didn't strike me as a zealot, but a man who sought the possibilities of a middle way, which meant he was open to compromise and so capable of dealing with disappointment, even betrayal. His church needed a new site. He was offered a way. Though he talked of killing the snake, he was invested in keeping the house. I wondered what the village felt about his acceptance of the plot and whether they saw it as a damaging compromise or an opportunity to rebuild on their own terms.

On mornings, as I walked up to the post office, I watched Mr Elton first cutlassing the mountainous razor grass on the site, then nailing together the narrow laths that would profile the foundations. He worked alone. Soon, all that was visible of him, from the distance I kept, was the round of his bare back glistening like a wet shell as, inch by inch, he dug the trenches. He worked rhythmically, following his line, solitary, harnessed to his labour. Danny was there, too, every morning and evening, observing his progress. He stood riveted to his spot, chastened, his eyes fixed on the site and the man who seemed to be deliberately ignoring him and everyone else as he worked. That Thomas De Valremy, from somewhere in Port of Spain, had orchestrated the sale of L'Avenir right under Mr Elton's nose must have been a cruel wake-up call that forced him to stand back to consider the role he had been recruited to play. Maybe Thomas had intended a different evolution for the relationship. Who knows?

Sometimes, either in the morning or in the afternoon, Mr Elton's wife, Deborah, and their daughter, Nneka, joined him at the plot. We exchanged waves and nods of greeting. They usually sat under the shade of a tree, bonded in their vigil of support, a bottle of water, thermos and wicker basket between them. Once, I had seen Deborah take a steaming cup of something to Mr Elton. He accepted. They did not speak but there was a gentleness between them as he accepted the drink. I watched their interactions closely, saw the exchanges between them, the propped chins of mother and daughter and, on occasion, the wearied glances in his direction, witness to the path he had chosen.

Then, one afternoon, as I strolled home from work, I witnessed a heated exchange between the couple. Whatever its cause, the row ended with the two women storming off. From that day on, neither Nneka or her mother came to deliver the thermos and basket. I guessed that what they were offering was an acceptance of the task Mr Elton had imposed on himself as a penance, but not a commitment to his path. They had simply agreed to let him play the martyr he needed to be in those days of contrition. The muted standoff came to an end when Deborah arrived one morning and, ignoring her husband's objections, hitched up her skirt and began purposefully shovelling cement into two buckets that Mr Elton carried and emptied into the trenches. Danny, still hanging around, saw her initiative as an opening for him to step in, and soon he was taking instruction from Mr Elton on how to mix the mortar. The trio worked together, perspiration dripping into the earth that would be the ground for the church.

★

I crossed paths with Brenda on one of those mornings. She and her children were on their way to the bus stop. She lugged two suitcases and the boys each carried stuffed bags that they could barely manage. She looked a little caught out.

– Well, Miss Bri, it look like we had to meet up this morning.

The little ones, still sleep-dazed, held on to their mother's skirt. Patrick's eyes were glued to his feet. Brenda saw his discomfort.

– Patrick, take your brother and sister and wait by Johnny for me.

Patrick moved off a little reluctantly. When they were out of earshot, Brenda put down her luggage and inhaled deeply, grateful for the reprieve. She daubed her face with the washcloth that was draped over her shoulder.

– I heading out, Miss Bri, and I taking my concern.

Perhaps she felt it necessary to say the obvious, seal her conviction in the telling.

– Is time to make a move. Too much commesse in Macaima. Not even Elton know what was going on, and he suppose to know.

She looked towards the plot where Mr Elton and Danny were at work, mixing a mountain of cement.

– You see what De Valremy come and do to everybody, and the church we build up? I say I done with Macaima and I going to take my chances outside.

– Maybe the changes to the village will bring some good.

– For some, maybe. Time for me to move on and give my

chirren more to choose from. That is why I put that estate behind me in the first place. I harbour no regrets. So, I leaving to finish what I start.

It was a resolution that was still young, driven by disappointment and so still in need of testing. I heard in her voice the pain of her commitment, and the anger that sealed it.

– Where are you headed?

– Morvant. I have family out there. Patrick could learn whatever trade he choose, and I going to put the little ones in one ah-them new school that going to build. Education is key. You have to plan, Miss Bri – and I will tell you something else. I take Patrick quite Sando hospital to see Pixie when she was there.

– You did!

I was genuinely surprised, and ashamed that I had not taken it upon myself to make the trip to see how she was doing.

– Yes, and I make him speak his apology for what he do. He can't go on in this world passing on anger and pain to other people. I tell him: This world full with trouble. Whatever fight yuh want to fight, make sure purpose behind it. Be sure it make this place better for you and everybody else. I can't make his mind, Miss Bri, but I could show him my own.

There was no way that I could express the extent of my admiration.

– I wish you the very best, Brenda. Macaima will miss you. I will miss you.

She steupsed, but it was only a way to deflect her tears.

– You have to know when to move on, Miss Bri. Paul sitting down up on that estate like he waiting on his god that have no time with him. Yuh have to play your part. I tell him I not sitting down with my hands fold on my lap.

I had heard that story before. Maybe she, too, remembered and hurried on to another matter.

– So yuh hear how De Valremy offer Elton land as compensation. I say compensation for what? I put my own mind to study those two, Miss Bri, and I say Elton now realise that Thomas see his way out. Not just from Macaima – outta a whole history. He find a way to cut ties with this village for good.

I looked at her quizzically.

– Think about it. Now, he don't have to bother with Maria. He could move on from here and forget this estate. Wash his hands clean. And yuh see Elton over there?

We both turned to the plot.

– He walking to his Calvary, one he feel he deserve. Miss Bri, I have no time with that. Elton say we have to carry on. Shake off yesterday and look forward. I say he right, but I don't want to remember De Valremy every Sunday morning I stand up in my church to pray. I don't want to look no more day at Elton and see the loss in his face.

– What do you mean?

– Time can't wash out memory. Not in full. Something always remain. Marie come-an-dead and Elton play godfather running up and down with Maria, when he well know what part a De Valremy play in both.

– Do you mean…

– Is tru-talk. Elton help to ease they guilt. He well know what transpire. People carry their burdens to him. He get catch in overseer ole mas when he thought he was mending bridges.

– How could he be so blind?

– I stand up here and telling you that is how it play out.

I looked over to where Elton worked. It made no sense – his loyalty to Thomas – unless he really thought Thomas had become a new man.

– Watch him good. He now trying to claim back the self he give away. This place is for everybody, he preach. I say, yes, but that doh mean you bring snake inside your house, no matter the skin that show outside. So I gone. I want a fresh start, on my own terms.

She appeared to be fully convinced of her decision to leave, but thinking of my own coming to Macaima, I wondered what a fresh start really meant. The sound of Mr Elton's digging played between us. Was there ever such a thing – a complete break? The hope Brenda had for herself and her children hung full and delicate like ripe fruit on the tree of her dreams. I watched her take a firm grip of her suitcases, both tied securely with broad belts, knowing that I would probably never see her again. I stepped in and hugged her. She stood stiffly, at first, resolute in her decision to press on, then rocked her body from side to side like a ship in the ocean of her journey to new shores.

– You take care, Miss Bri. We have to keep marching on to glory.

We both held silent, then as if the sentiment that stirred us both was too great, a distraction to her purpose, she added:

– By the way, yuh hear how Eunice lie down sick in Railway?

It was the second time I had heard Brenda call Miss Gomez by her first name.

– Sick? I knew she had a medical matter to attend to. Did something go wrong?

Tears welled up but she fought them back.

– We use to be good friends from small. She wasn't so tie-up as she is now. We get into all kinda mischief together. I grow and choose my way. Who she now is, wasn't who she was.

She appeared to want to say more.

– What do you mean?

– Jus what I say. Life could kill your joy if you can't find how to answer back. But I talk too much already this morning.

The bus rattled to its stop opposite Johnny's. Brenda hurried to meet it. I waited until she and the children had piled in. Just then I thought of her cousin, Sam's mother, Kizzy. I had heard nothing. Maybe Franco knew more about Sam's progress. I did not know if she had already left the island. Miss Gomez would have surely brought me up to speed had she been here. As I resumed my walk to the post office, I felt my aloneness in the place and Franco's remark returned: *You just reach here.* He was right. Brenda waved from the window seat she had chosen. I saw, too, Patrick's face framed by the rear windshield as the brakes hissed their noisy release. He raised his hand to wave, tentatively at first. I returned the gesture. He smiled and waved back more firmly. I thought he looked relieved.

CHAPTER 26 – ...FOR THE SAKE OF LOVE

Some things remain locked in not knowing rather than mystery. That was what defined the news that Corporal Luke had been attacked while he slept in his hospital bed, sometime in the early hours of the morning. *Assailant unknown*, the reports said. Assassin would have been the better word. He had died of his injuries, and the authorities claimed an earnest search was being mounted. Speculation circulated that the homicide was an inside job to thwart the impending investigation of the corporal's alleged connections to a South American contraband and gun-supply ring that would implicate well-connected local associates. It sounded like a fantasy, unlikely that such an alliance existed. Alcohol, meat, birds and wild animals were the usual trades from the Main. Mason was apparently in the dark about the kingpins involved. He just did the driving. The corporal turned out to be the main middleman. Talk-talk-talk. The days passed and we looked on as the case was quickly swept under the carpet. The corporal's murderer remained at large. A *mystery*, people said. It all eventually disappeared like mist.

I went about my business, keeping my thoughts to myself as developments unfolded, but *the murder* took my thoughts directly to Roland. A motive he certainly had, and perhaps a case could be constructed if the right questions were asked of the right people: including me. I could not deny that I thought he had acted suspiciously during his unexpected appearance at the house to recover his belongings. There had been something about his demeanour, a preoccupied aloofness that bothered me. Maybe that was just his way, like his habit of suddenly appearing and disappearing. Yet the attentiveness and sensitivity that he displayed towards Sam was undeniably genuine. So was his long pain over Marie's passing. He did not seem capable of the horrid, calculated act that had taken the corporal's life. Even so I remained mired in uncertainty, though I most wanted to preserve my memory of him that morning when we had both made a ritual of letting go of our dead. Maybe we had more in common than I was willing to consider.

★

Not long after *the murder*, a telephone call came to the post office from a Mrs Campbell. She identified herself as a cousin of Miss Gomez, who was convalescing at her home in Railway. With a formality of register that reminded me of her cousin, but with a great deal more reserve, she revealed that Eunice had requested that she call me on her behalf. She would say no more than what she had been instructed to convey: a visit from me would be greatly appreciated. Before she hung up, she made a brief amplification.

– Might I suggest that you visit at your earliest convenience, Miss Bridgemohan.

I took down the address and promised I would be there on Saturday. The addition to her script suggested some urgency. All was not well with Miss Gomez. Brenda had already hinted as much on the day of her departure.

That Saturday, it took all the discipline I could muster to stay my mind from making assumptions as I journeyed to Railway in the front seat of Mitra's taxi. The talk in the car was of the PM's fight to root out the *commies* from the trade unions. The exchanges were energetically cavalier and although I wasn't in the mood for politics, I could not help but listen. Mitra was right in the middle of the talk, swivelling his head dangerously to make his points to the men in the backseat.

– I telling you flat. He sell we out long time since that Tobago meeting with dem American over that Chaguaramas lease. A little money blind d-man. War finish so long. Dem-Yankee is not homing pigeon. Is time they say bye-bye. Give we back what is we-own.

Arthur weighed in.

– Oh gosh, that done gone so long, Mitra.

– You see what I mean? We like to forget too quick. That was a sign. He favour big business and forget to put he foot down.

– Americans bring money. We shouldn't be so quick to push them out. My own brother build house and buy motor car with what he make on that same Base. War done yes, but I for one glad we getting help-out with security from that US satellite.

– Not to mention killing we with radiation. Them fruits down Chag going to kill we. Not me. Mitra Samuel not touching no grapefruit mark *Tucker Valley*.

– You too paranoid. American bring prosperity, jus like how Vene sneaking over here to help we wine-an-dine.

Razor jumped in.

– Kill dat talk. Lennox happy too bad with his Rosa. I see them come here and work more than I ever see *you* do in your whole life.

– Okay, I done talk. I done.

– Is you raise jep nest and now yuh running from sting. Cray, I not hearing you. How I talk?

Mitra glanced back at Cray, smiling broadly at his picong.

– My only business to is collect my van from d-mechanic this morning. I need to work.

– Doh try that. You always have opinion.

– Alright, if is opinion you want, all I have to say is all that was so in sixty. Now, we in sixty-three and free. Chag lease go be up in a few years, then is adios America.

Cray seemed to want to lighten the mood in the car, but Mitra persisted.

– Story never done jus so. Something show up in that deal and it going to come back one day to bite this country in d-arse.

– Mit, you sound like you vex we get money for betterment. Cray right, that done gone!

– See what I say? Nothing wrong with US money.

– Art, like I have to start calling you dollar sign?

Cray sighed loudly and, as if to release what he could no longer keep to himself, spoke up.

– Okay, serious talk now. Chag wasn't about one thing. You have to read the play. Federation needed a capital, so Americans had to go, but it was also about holding Independence in reserve in case all fall down. D-Doc had Independence as his trump card.

Arthur came back.

– Lawwd, I never see dat play, Cray. So is not Jamaica who start to mash up things with referendum? It was both-a-dem. Sparrow sing it right: *dog eat dog and survival of the fittest.*

– I agree with you on that, Arts, but more in d-mortar. I say Mr PM didn't want America-an-England to think he was a next Castro or Jagan, so he ease up on his politics when lease negotiations start in Tobago. He is no fool. He was singing for US development money on first base, and play for election support from workers on second, and then, like whiplash, he crack down on unions on third, an call that democracy.

– Oh Lawwd, Cray, that is why I like to hear your side. I never see that play. How you like that for opinion, Mits?

Razor slapped Mitra's shoulder from the back seat.

– Bulls-eye is all I have to say.

– Is anybody's guess what really went down, but now that I thinking about it, development money from America must be play big in why he blank OPEC when he get invitation to join.

– O-who?

The question was Arthur's. He was genuinely puzzled, but Cray had moved on.

– Think who start up OPEC – Venezuela and Arab countries. And look at who running oil in this country: Texaco, Shell, Apex. Saying no to OPEC to look good for d-west, as if we doh need nobody else. That was a big mistake he make. He going to regret it.

The idea intrigued me and I looked around in time to see Arthur lift his cap and scratch his head, genuinely flabbergasted.

– Cray, like you turn politician on we.

Mitra pushed in.

– We doh need no OPEC. Oil go to sell itself.

– Mitra, like you didn't hear one word I say?

Cray fell silent, maybe in a show of frustration.

Arthur chose that gap to sing a Sparrow rendition acapella in what I thought was a clumsy attempt to taunt Mitra on his Yankee-go-home mantra.

– *We reach the glamour boys again, / We are going to rule Port of Spain / No more Yankees to spoil the fete / Dorothy have to take what she get…*

The song, though, helped to take the edge off Cray.

– Fadda! Blind-an-blinder. Man, done with that chupidness!

Mitra laughed heartily and looked in my direction to see whether I was in on the conversation.

– What you say, Miss Bri. Yuh think we shoulda send dem Yankee home?

Turning so that I had them all in full view, I said,

– My concern, as I listened to your choice of song, is more a question.

I turned to look directly at Arthur:

– Why must a woman's body feature in every issue?

Mitra bellowed:

– O Gawd, Art, *dat* is a hit! O God, woman! Ouch-ouch-ouch!

Arthur feigned innocence.

– What I do? That is what Sparrow sing. Miss, what sour you so this early morning? Is only joke I joking.

I held his gaze.

– Well, maybe all joke is no joke at all.

Cray pulled down the visor of his cap so that it shielded his eyes and cupped his mouth with his hand. As if reliving the blow, Mitra howled again, shattering the silence. He turned to look at Arthur, almost pitifully, before he adjusted his attention to negotiating the twisting road with comfortable familiarity.

It was my first trip out of the village since my arrival. I remembered little of the terrain. The sea disappeared as we wound our way inland towards Railway. After a while, once we left the foothills of Macaima behind and approached the outskirts of Railway, it was like travelling in reverse to the beginnings of the country, to plantation, the sugar belt. The faint smell of burnt cane thrash breezed through the windows and the languid roll of green cane fields took over the landscape, walling us in on both sides with towering stalks, crowned, at that time of year, with cane arrows – resplendent flowers to which I wanted to attach no history, wanted them to just be. In vain.

Railway bustled with Saturday morning commerce. The mêleé of activities was invigorating compared to the lull of Macaima, but it was difficult not to see that a battle was in process. On both sides of the road, emergent businesses jostled for space with private dwellings, or were themselves extensions of family houses. Some proprietors had created store fronts by constructing galvanized sheds off the fence walls, which they enclosed with bricks and BRC wire. Customers were enticed into stores with bhajans and Bombay cinema hits that blared through speakers. The remnant of house owners showed their discomfort by the adjustments they made to their predicament. Like an army in retreat, they put up shields – kept their front doors closed, galleries vacant and windows heavily curtained.

Mitra let me off at a narrow street bounded on one side by a furniture store and a general retail enterprise on the other. Miss Gomez's relations lived three houses down in a cottage-styled dwelling. The concrete walls were painted in pastel shades of mint and pearl. Clusters of poinsettia, hibiscus and Christmas bush spilled over the front wall. It exuded a tranquil aura after the buzz of the main street. Mrs Campbell was sitting on the veranda in anticipation of my arrival and hurried to the gate to welcome me.

– Miss Bridgemohan, mornin-mornin. So glad to see you.

She was a bustle of nervous energy as she ushered me in, walking purposefully in her pink-puff slippers on highly polished floors. After knocking lightly on a door that was left ajar, I was directed to enter the bedroom where Miss Gomez lay with her eyes closed.

– Go right in. She's expecting you.

Mrs Campbell's whispered instruction lingered as she briskly retreated to another part of the house. I stood on the threshold but didn't focus immediately on Miss Gomez. Perhaps it was easier to first take in the space that she occupied – its economy as though built for a child – the walls freshly painted in antique white; the white lace curtains with embroidered rosettes at the window tied back to let in light and breeze; the single bed, the mahogany side table where a glass of water and an open Bible rested. The plainness of the space suggested a utilitarian, transitory quality. I entered and sat on the chair that had been placed so Miss Gomez would have no trouble seeing whoever might come to visit. The freshly laundered smell of sheets filled the room. Their crisp, unwrinkled neatness suggested that they had been recently changed and that Miss Gomez, by necessity or choice, had not adjusted her current position. I saw that the mound of her stomach had almost doubled in size, but my gaze did not linger.

On the otherwise bare wall that faced her hung a simple wooden crucifix with a silver corpus. Its design was similar to the one that hung over the door of the Hendersons' annex. I did not see when Mrs Gomez opened her eyes.

– Miss Bridgemohan, you are here.

Her voice was considerably weakened, but still upbeat.

– As you can see, I am not quite myself these days.

She chuckled in recognition of her understatement. I had come to see that her register, a brand of ironic humour that played off an effacing congeniality, was her strategy for negotiating the world. It suggested someone who had made a habit of, if not averting pain, living in anticipation of it.

I must have frowned and she noticed.

– Isn't life full of surprises, Miss Bridgemohan? But defeat is not an option.

She patted her distended stomach. I saw how perfectly her nails were manicured, rounded precisely at the fingertips. Hers were a musician's hands.

– As you see, after all these years, I am with child but, regretfully, immaculately so.

An attempt to laugh at her joke was interrupted by a coughing fit. I reached for the glass and steadied the straw at her lips as she strained forward to meet it.

She released her head to the pillow with a mimed, *Thank you-thank you*.

I saw that her eyes were fixed on the crucifix. They rested there so lovingly that I felt an interloper in a moment of the utmost intimacy, so private that the only expression of respect was to wait for her to speak, and as I waited, what came to mind was the time I had accompanied my mother to the parish priest to have her crucifix blessed, and on our return to the annex, she had asked Mr Lutchman to hang it over the front door. For some reason, the priest had felt it necessary to explain to me, as my mother looked on, the difference between a cross and a crucifix. *The crucifix*, he said, *is all about the suffering body. The cross just happens to be the instrument and so means little without the Lord's corpus.* He had emphasised at the end. *Do you see?*

The difference meant little to me then, and I had never thought about it since, but sitting in Miss Gomez's room that morning and watching her engage in some private communication with the object, the words returned and I wondered what cross she carried and whether she found solace in the object on the wall, which must also have been blessed. Brenda had suggested that she harboured some misplaced shame about the cancer that had so obviously ravaged her body, kept it secret and unattended for far too long, and even sought Mr Elton's spiritual intervention for a cure. Could there be more? I was preoccupied with that possibility when Miss Gomez spoke again.

– I want to leave you something. It's a little thank-you and I hope you'll accept.

– Thanks for what, Miss Gomez?

More than the surprise of her intent, it was her sheer, unforced graciousness that was almost too much to bear from a woman I felt had lived a defeated life.

– I know we've not been acquainted long, but somehow you were central to my having the opportunity to assist Sam, for which I am deeply grateful. I have not always spoken to you about her in the kindest of terms, and for that I am sorry.

Even at her most needy, she was the model of decency and that, I had to concede, generated its own measure of admiration. I could see that she was trying to find a path to what she would say next.

– You see, in a way, Sam's truth was my lie.

It was an unexpected disclosure and, at the time, a vulnerability I did not think she should allow herself.

– Miss Gomez, you shouldn't trouble yourself with such things. Rest. In no time you will be back in Macaima with your choir and flowers. Then we will talk more about Sam.

– If only that were true – my returning home. I have run short of the folly it takes to entertain dissembling. What I am offering is a small gift from my garden. Please accept it before the vultures descend. You will find it at my little grotto. This note goes with it. Please open it and read it when you get there. I hope it brings you much joy, and perhaps more so, purpose. I have found that purpose is much more dependable than happiness, though sometimes happiness is its reward.

I could not meet her eyes as I accepted the note. Already I knew she was saying her goodbyes – this woman whom I could not really say was a friend, though we had crossed paths in that season of over-turnings.

– Good. That's that! Now, on to Sam. I suppose you've heard of her decision.

I hadn't. I had not seen or heard from either Sam or Franco for weeks. Some time ago Danny had mentioned that she had arrived safely at the hospital in the US. Nothing had come my way since.

– Is there news? Was the procedure a success?

I was immediately sorry for my question. I did not miss the unintended discomfort it caused as Miss Gomez adjusted her head on the pillow and soldiered on good-naturedly.

– My dear, you're behind the times! Sam, though, should be the one to explain details as she chooses. I'll say this much – she has her own mind. She and Cheryl will be back on the island in a few of days. We've already connected by phone and I've asked her to do me a special kindness. Things have a way of working themselves out, Miss Bridgemohan – and in the least expected ways.

A knock at the bedroom door cut her off. Mrs Campbell peeped in to say that Sister Agnes Mary was outside.

– Please ask her to wait a minute, Maggie.

Miss Gomez unnecessarily smoothed over her sheets, her hands lingered at the high mound of her stomach and her brow furrowed. Another knock announced Sister Agnes Mary. Miss Gomez sang *en-TER* and I saw her countenance relax. Sister Agnes was not alone. Two women accompanied her. The room was suddenly crowded. We exchanged greetings. Sister took the seat I had vacated. The others gathered close and extracted rosaries that they shook free of tangles. Beads jingled. My cue to leave.

As I was about to exit, Miss Gomez piped, perhaps with all the energy she could muster:

– Miss Bridgemohan, what's a little suffering – for the sake of love?

– What indeed?

In the corridor outside the room, I heard voices unite in an intimate and sonorous prayer that trailed behind me. I wove my way through a forest of lace curtains and emerged again in the sparsely arranged living room where I found Mrs Campbell engrossed in a newspaper and surrendered to the gentle rhythm of a rocker. She immediately abandoned her reading and rose to see me to the door.

– It won't be long now, Miss Bridgemohan. We will be in touch.

We exchanged a brief consolatory hug before I walked quickly to the gate.

Once I had joined the bustle of Saturday morning Railway, I followed the flow of the street westward, ignoring the lure of shops, the merchandise on sale advertised as *100% pure or authentic this or that, superior quality this or that, reliable this or that*. The offerings of discounts and money-back guarantees stirred no interest. I milled about with the shoppers but without any desire to purchase or be laden down with anything. I did not feel I could find value in anything but my unfound answer to Miss Gomez's parting question.

CHAPTER 27 – NO QUIET REVOLUTION

Rain fell steadily for days after the Railway visit. There was still no sign of Franco or Roland, so I heard nothing more about Sam's return. There was also no chance of taking the walk up to Sunrise Trace where Miss Gomez lived. I didn't mind because I was uncertain whether I wanted to accept any *gift* she might have left. I was much too puzzled and not a little disturbed by her parting words, which, from the limits of my own understanding, seemed a motto for the life she had settled for. But I was in no place to judge. In that lull, to my great surprise, a postcard came from Thea. She must have gotten an address from someone from the old lunchroom lime – possibly Kimberly or Yolanda. I doubt she would have approached Miles, and certainly not James. Apart from the standard *hello* and *how are you*, there was nothing but a postal address. She wanted to be in touch. Our parting had been awkward, to say the least. What James actually saw, I would never know or care to know. So, Thea's question after my wellbeing, I knew, was loaded. Not ready to answer, I tucked the card away.

Rain poured on. Then, no more than two weeks after my visit to Railway, on an overcast morning in late November, when the world still reeled from the assassination of President Kennedy, and Tobago was struggling to recover from Flora, I answered the phone to hear Mrs Campbell on the other end. Miss Gomez had passed away peacefully in her sleep. I offered my condolences and listened to her relay the funeral arrangements. She had wanted to be interred quickly – no unnecessary delays. The service would be held in Railway. I learned, too, that Sam had returned from the States.

– We expect a packed church. Eunice was well known. That woman gave and gave. She will be greatly missed.

I listened to a litany of charities and groups with which Miss Gomez had collaborated: the Horticultural Society, the At-Risk Mothers and Needy Children Charity, the Helpers of the Homeless, Friends of the Environment, the Intercessors for World Peace, the Small Business Women's Support Group, the Music for Worship Society, the Teachers of Faith Corpus, and, of course, the Women's Coalition of the National Party... I was numbed. Mrs Campbell concluded her musings with what came across as a constrained compliment.

– She had her special struggles, as we all do, but she was a good-good woman.

I held onto the receiver, listening to the murmur of the dead line, suspended between Mrs Campbell's carefully constructed proviso and my effort to decipher more about the woman I had judged to be so outside herself on that first day, when she had sat in the post office in all her flourished uneasiness. I really did not know what had discomforted her. There were too many gaps in my knowledge, and now she was gone, with no capacity to ever speak for herself, I had an intense desire to know more. In the finality of that void, I saw again how uncharitable I had been in finding an excuse not to retrieve the gift she had offered me.

★

The funeral service took place on an overcast Thursday morning. The church, as Mrs Campbell had anticipated, was packed. Mrs Campbell approached the lectern to read the passage that her cousin had chosen from St Paul: *But by the grace of God I am what I am, and His grace toward me has not been void. Rather, I toiled more abundantly than all of them, yet not I, but the grace of God that was with me.* Her voice was clear and steady, a controlled solemnity that kept our grief in check, and held us attentive to the text until she was done. After a deep bow before the altar, she paused to tenderly touch the coffin that was positioned like a flower-laden bed in the crossing between the front of the nave and the altar, then returned to her seat next to her black-suited husband, whom I had not met on the day of my visit, but had glimpsed as a younger version in a wedding picture on the living-room wall. As then, both husband and wife were a picture of perfect composure as they sat in the front row reserved for family.

I focused on the flowers on the coffin, wondering if anyone in the congregation had recognised that the reading Miss Gomez had chosen was the very text the PM had included in his first Independence Day speech, an expression of suffering triumph with which she resonated. Thinking of this I saw afresh the journey I had made to her house. In a light but persistent rain, I had set out to retrieve the gift she had offered me as soon as I had put down the phone after Mrs Campbell's call.

Sunrise Trace opened on the mountain side of Macaima's main road. It was not a major thoroughfare and no more than a meandering footpath cut through the mountain and was passable only by jeep in the dry season. The initial climb was gradual, then the gradient steepened briefly before it plateaued, offering a respite before the ascent into the hills on the northern border of the property, a modest cottage-style dwelling. I puzzled over why the building was constructed so close to the front boundary of the lot, which resulted in the veranda being only a short distance from the gate and the trace. My question was answered when I advanced to the back of the property.

The house stood on a strip of level ground on the narrow ridge. What first met the eye was but a façade, as what initially appeared to be a rather choked plot of no more than thirty feet gave way to an expansive slope at the back of the house which dipped towards a veil of trees that obscured the property's eastern boundary. These must have been part of the original forest that had been cleared to accommodate the house. A solid retaining wall of stone, interrupted midway by three steps, divided the flat from the sloping land, which was landscaped as an orchard and flower garden. From a tiled patio that ran the entire width of the house, this was the view that could be seen beneath the partial shelter of a wooden trellis on which bougainvillea plants climbed to shield the viewer from direct sunlight. But this was not the distinctive feature of the space.

An extraordinary array of orchids roofed the patio. Given the age of the house, I could tell that the arbour was a much later addition – probably Miss Gomez's creation. The northern end was framed on two sides by huge baskets of breadfruit ferns that shaded a cozy sitting area from where you could enjoy the magnificent display. Suspended from the rafters were lines of spaced clay pots, baskets lined with halved coconut shells and bark-covered wedges of timber from which burst sprays of purple, pink, mint, yellow, ochre, orange, rust, red, white – every tint and shade imaginable. Exposed ivory roots trailed down, breathing the cool air. There were varieties too numerous and unknown for me to name, although I recognised flamboyant vandas, delicate cattleyas, and the more common dendrobiums. Lying under this broad spectrum of colour, a bare floor of natural blue stone provided a quietening counterpoint. But this too was subtly enlivened by exquisite nuances of light and shade, depending on the intensity and angle of light: darker or lighter tones of slate grey with hints of brown, plum and green. In that profusion of hues, linked spirals and the delicacy of petals, I felt upheld in a marvellous cosmic dance.

Then, like a release from an intoxicating swirl, a path that followed the contours of the land meandered through Miss Gomez's remarkable garden to the forest's entrance. The ground was slippery and waterlogged from the long period of heavy rain, so I took my time negotiating the slope. On either side, nested in moist coconut husks, were glossy clusters of flamingo-red, pearl-white, and oyster-pink anthuriums. Natural shade was created by what at first appeared to be haphazardly placed colonies of greenery: fan palms, elephant ears, ferns, red bananas, pendulous heliconia, the torches of ginger lilies. With fruit trees already in blossom for late-year bearing, and the rich humus that darkened the soil, the air was a jolting ferment. At the mouth of the forest path, I paused and turned to look up at the now elevated patio where the kaleidoscope of orchids married the expanse of sky. It was then that I saw something of Miss Gomez's intent. The journey down to the border of the land, where a track opened into the forest, was meant to conjure an approach to the source of life itself – womb, cave, grotto... The entire design was orchestrated to mean one thing: life. She had wanted to claim it with all her being, and that had been her labour.

★

Miss Gomez was gone. The church remained stilled by the reading that sought to lay laid claim to a life that had not been *void* or in vain. I glanced over at the rows of nuns who occupied the two benches at the front. They sat serene, upright. Black veils fanned out across their shoulders, each exactly spaced. Sister Agnes Mary sat with them, her head slightly bowed. Then I saw Sam making her way to the front of the church. I had not seen her since the *storm day*. We shifted in our seats, drew ourselves back from wherever we had travelled in the current of the reading as she walked up the aisle and climbed the steps to the lectern. She wore for the occasion what looked like an acolyte's white robe – perhaps at Miss Gomez's request. Sam, the anomaly who fitted no sanctioned category but her own, was the one Miss Gomez had appointed to offer her goodbye song to the world.

The congregation listened, suspended, I supposed, in some place of wonder and gratitude, as I was, by this new Sam, in possession of the calm and solidity of one who had fought and won, not a final battle, but the one that would teach her what she most needed to learn – that her dignity could not be destroyed unless she allowed it to be. This Sam, who stood before an assembly of persons who could say, *I know that girl from small*, was indeed *that girl* and beyond what we could ever know. She stood on the outside of every containable space or word, a question to every neatly packaged and sanctioned notion of humanity itself. Her very breath confronted any denial of her right to be. Then she opened her mouth and released the sound of that same *Amazing Grace* I had first heard on Beach Road.

The church, as one body gathered to say farewell to one of their own, was witness to those words… *O how sweet the sound…* like no other I had ever heard; so large and deep-bellied that it rose as from a maturity that was so much more than her years… Yes, *that saved* (she sang) *someone like me…* Her voice, attentive to every nuance of word and note, was a wave that filled the length and breadth of the church; it touched, traversed and embraced us all, affirming the whole mysterious and uncommon beauty, the pressed-down generosity and longing that was Miss Gomez's. In the plaintive stretch and expanse of each pitched word, in that making of unworded sounds, fresh words, Sam opened whatever doors people needed to enter to approach and make of their lives a touchable beauty and tender peace – a welcome: *I once was lost but now I'm found, was blind but now I'm free* – she sang. They were words Miss Gomez had requested, but they were now Sam's – entirely hers, and the gift she offered back to us, in that moment when we all ascended to reach the unreachable, the unapproachable, in our very selves…

★

…I had made my way slowly down the forested trail, the air fragrant with the birthing, growing and dying of things. Ferns dusted my ankles and sharp birdcalls quickened my awareness in that space of shifting shades where rays of light intersected and separated, like worlds folding and awakening to other beginnings, worlds alive in themselves. The sound of running water in the valley below intensified and through the leaves, I could see its glistening flow. The very base of the property was bordered by a brisk flowing stream, and on a mound close to the bank stood the grotto that Miss Gomez had made.

In the hollow was the figure of a cerulean blue Madonna, not at all the popular pencil-slim version, but a mature, full-bodied woman, pregnant with the world, and vested in a flowing gown of sunburst gold and ochre with streaks and swirls of indigo, red and silver. The gown fanned out from a pod or boat of some sort in which she stood, and draped down all the way to the base of the grotto. A single bench faced the image. Watermarks on the base of the structure told me that when the stream was at its fullest and overflowed its banks, water came up to the base of the grotto and the trailing skirt was submerged. Here before me was the woman who, in the words she had commissioned Sam to sing, was *free*, but my heart sank at what must have been her troubled effort to express the other side of her public self that was perhaps the unexplored undertow of her life. Had I not been directed there, I would never have encountered the sheer wonder of her creation.

I saw a tension there – the depths of the artist who pushed at the boundaries of her faith, interplayed with the woman who gazed so lovingly at the crucifix – but they were one and the same. I was so caught in the vexing paradox that I did not immediately see what she had left me as her parting gift: an orchid in bloom. I moved closer. Emerald leaves and a thicket of bulbs all but concealed the tiny blossoms, two or three on each spike. Rustspeckled cream petals unfurled like sails or wings. One formed a bucket-shaped container from which a ribbed neck in burnished gold and red extended. I gazed baffled at the design that was so alluringly strange in its clay pot. It was then that I remembered the note I had not opened and forgotten to bring with me.

★

Now Sam was bringing her hymn to a close. I reached into my handbag for the still sealed envelope. In it was a folded page. On the front fold was written in clear script the name *Coryanthes macrantha: Monkey Throat or Bucket Orchid*.

I saw again the hanging lip, neck and open throat, until the shape became its name. On the inside fold of the page she wrote: *I have not been entirely generous with myself…*

Unexpected rage ran through me. Why speak now? Why share that regret literally from the grave, like a cowardly reach for understanding? I could barely nod an acknowledgement to Sam when she waved to me as she returned to her seat, exuding confidence and composure. When I finally caught my breath, I turned and saw Sam seated next to Franco, who beamed with pride. I saw, too, Roland, Brenda and her children, including Patrick. They had all returned for her final send off. Brenda, with all her grievances, sobbed into a washrag and Roland, who had abandoned Miss Gomez's choir, sat with his eyes laden with unshed tears. Their grief told a different story, that perhaps the life she felt had not been entirely generous had been enough.

After the service, I wanted to speak with Sam, to hear more of her trip and the surprising twist Miss Gomez had mentioned, but she had gone ahead with the others to the cemetery by the time I had composed myself enough to leave the church. Sister Agnes had remained seated with her community as the congregation went out. She met me at the door, the last in line and greeted me warmly.

– Good to see you again, Miss Bridgemohan. Well, Eunice has left us and is at rest.

Her quick eyes caught my discomfort.

– She was a remarkable woman. We do best by living our best. And in that she was exceptional.

– Was she?

– Choice is never without cost.
– You're right about that. She must have paid dearly.

Her shoulders sank a little wearily, but she quickly righted herself.

– We all do, Miss Bridgemohan. Eunice, I assure you, was well loved. I believe she came to know that she was a friend of God.

– I would much prefer the assurance that she loved herself, Sister.

She folded her arms under her scapula and regarded me with an uninflected stare.

– We're in agreement over that, my dear, and now I must excuse myself.

She moved quietly away to rejoin her community.

I travelled back to Macaima with Lennox, Rosa and Lucille, who elected to ride in the tray with Juan, a cousin of Rosa's. He had recently made the crossing from the Main to give them a hand with building their house. It was a melancholy return trip under overcast skies. Rosa laid her head on Lennox's shoulder, and he stretched his arm along the backrest to accommodate her. I thought about my decision to leave Miss Gomez's goodbye token at the grotto. Perhaps I had been the coward for having delayed so long to retrieve her gift. Maybe she had been waiting, in those final days, for an opportunity to speak further. I could not know, but it must have taken tremendous courage for her to organise her funeral and to invest in Sam's uncontainable voice to deliver her final word to the world, as if, perhaps, she felt, to save herself from death itself. To have left the orchid for me at her grotto was an attempt to say something else. I thought immediately of the postcard from Thea I had not as yet answered. Seated in that cabin with Lennox and Rosa, and with Lucille playfully practising random Spanish words under Juan's guidance in the tray, I could only see the stream that flowed beside that remarkable work of art Miss Gomez had made and the bucket orchid, with its open throat, she had left for me to make my own.

CHAPTER 28 – WARNINGS

December rolled in. The rains persisted, though more intermittently. I heard from Lucille that Sam and Franco were once again in the village. Her grandmother was seriously ill. Early in the month, the season stirred in me no real sense of expectancy, nor did the spirited talk of bright futures that no one was actually clear about. Miss Gomez's passing had left a lingering sense of loss, though no one spoke about her, as if wanting to respect an absence that was slowly growing into acceptance. In the midst of that lull, Thea sent another postcard. This time she placed a single question mark under her greeting. She must have been uncertain about the accuracy of the address or whether there was a deliberate standoff on my part. I stored it along with the first and plodded on with my days to a less assured rhythm than the brisk, hopeful music that charged the nights as Christmas approached.

But a change of mood came over me. In those evenings, I found myself making a habit of sitting out on the veranda where I could better hear the music from Johnny's shop serenading the night. For hours, the racy expectancy of the Advent narratives, punctuated by high-pitched *Marias* and *Glorias*, tussled with the heated strum of cuatros and electrifying chac-chacs. Half-garbled verses in Spanish heralded annunciations that needed no conviction of faith. The music was its own sermon. On some evenings, I went to along with Lucille and her bunch to take in the merriment, and even danced a few sets with Lennox and Razor to stave off their good-natured picong about my primness and whatever. That was when Lucille would quickly intervene with that capacity she had to neutralise foolishness and make the world large. Before I could protest she would grab me by the hand and spin us around the floor, weaving expertly through the dancers to the delight and shock of everyone.

★

Life was going on. Maybe I was part of that flow of change but didn't quite know it. Most folks engaged in talk anticipating the promised development. Phase One would involve the upgrade of the road to Salvador by making the old bridle path accessible from both ends and by resurfacing Mountain Road. That way, the land in the middle of the crescent would be used to develop a nature reserve with spots set up for food and craft stalls and camping sites. Phase Two would be even grander: a deep-water harbour along the shore between Macaima and the Salvador Road entrance. Goodbye Bay, though, would be spared because of the barrier reefs that caused the rip tide. The future seemed bright. Business would come to the area. Ships would dock to offload goods, and so on. Salvador and Macaima could become tourist centres. There was a history to package and sell that would showcase the indigenous presence, the flora and fauna, local food, craft and what not. The district would be the envy of the entire region. Detractors were accused of political mischief with their claims that the project was voter-romancing or pandering to the interests of private business and foreign money. Who could know the truth? A future was in the pipeline. The villagers focused on that.

Things, though, were not adding up. De Valremy's sudden sellout remained a puzzle. Why expansion into the interior? The villages were small and the estates virtually dead. The new owners of the lands had not yet been revealed, although speculation circulated that quarrying was the hidden agenda behind the sale. Some said the construction of state-owned mega farms for the production of an undisclosed crop was behind the development. Millions would come to the nation's coffers. No need to worry about running out of oil when that time arrived. Every corner was a hive of talk. By and large, villagers chose to concentrate their hopes on the port and the tourist centre, as though blind investment in that promise was an antidote to doubt about the project's feasibility and their anticipated encounter with disappointment. In the middle of all the talk, an anonymous group, suspected to be party supporters, took it upon themselves to hang bold banners at strategic locations along the main road. These read: *We Want We Port!* People counselled each other to wait-and-see. What else to do?

The days turned over. We waited, regurgitating the scraps of information and assurances that we were fed by far-off officials and experts on this-and-that. Notices to vacate L'Avenir were quietly delivered to its tenants. I was roped in to read out notices to a few folk from inside the estate lands. They absorbed the news and went away numbed. Folk began to trickle away. Some found room with family in the district or risked squatting on a piece of crown land. Others moved out entirely, heading for Railway and elsewhere. A few stayed put on the estate in homes they had occupied for generations, choosing to ignore the letter in the hope that the demand to move would disappear – or until they were forced out.

★

One day, out of the blue, Balkissoon resurfaced in Johnny's. He said openly that what the government was planning was a road to nowhere. Arthur was furious.

– What horse shit yuh talking, man? Since when Macaima and Salvador qualify as no place?

– What I mean is the whole damn thing is a hoax to secure votes. Inside here is borderline seat, so the party laying foundation for '66.

Razor took him up.

– Doh try that, Balkie. Is only one person borderline inside here – you!

Nobody really took him on, despite their fears, dismissing what he had to say as self-interested canvassing for *his side.* The writing on the road incident had never been solved and they reminded him as such, but he persisted and I felt that there was some merit in the opposition Balkissoon offered, regardless of his suspected motives. Any voice asking challenging questions was worth attention. Balkissoon pushed on.

– When flour more than water, then is too late. The government going bout dey business and people suffering. Look at what happening with workers and trade unions in this place. Everyman-jack that dare to talk about justice and equality under suspicion. Poor people taking rain and boiling stone to eat, and nobody care.

Lucille saw an opportunity to tease:

– Doo-doo, if is shelter yuh looking for, then come inside, nah boi!

She opened her arms provocatively in a mock welcome, to the delight of the shop. It disappointed me that she would join in the banter. She was no blind follower of any party and was willing to ask difficult questions. I did not forget the question she had hoped to ask the PM or her public support for Brenda's interruption at the Coalition meeting. But here she was poking fun at Balkissoon, who made, I thought, too serious a charge to be diminished by picong. But it was up to the village to fight its own fights. I was becoming more and more a spectator. My time to leave was fast approaching and it didn't make sense to get further involved their affairs.

Things came to a head when Balkissoon brought in a firebrand from Railway to talk to the villagers about the government's development plans. That evening, I happened to be making my usual weekend purchases when he parked his pickup van strategically outside Johnny's and an impromptu meeting began. From the tray of Balkissoon's van, the man barked out his message.

– First and foremost, brothers and sisters, we sing how this country is for everybody. Equal place for every creed and race. Everybody must get a chance and the private sector must get on board with that. I have a question for Macaima. Anybody ask what really going to take place in the time between the road and that port d-government promise?

A few persons raised their hands.

– Good. We have something to discuss. People of Macaima, these leaders we put in power have a grouse with crop-land. Hear me out: look at how they treat farmers. Only when crisis hit, we go start to talk that we have to plant. People have to eat. Everything is oil-gas-gas-oil. Farmers suffering. This government have no heart for people who labour to bring a crop. Look at sugar. Same with estates inside here and that is reason to mash them up. Make them disappear.

Lennox shouted his objection from the crowd.

– Estate work dead long time, Mr Gentleman. Government promise road, a port and new business to follow.

The firebrand adjusted his stance. A fight was on.

– Yes, brother, I agree that we need road to drive motor car on. Nothing wrong with development. But while we sit down waiting, nothing happening. No crop planting.

– Is new business coming. Crop have no money in it.

– Maybe so. Cocoa price reach in dog house, but that is not reason to give up the land. What they hiding is that they building road for truck to cart away that whole mountain – one load at a time. Dat, brothers and sisters, is what this nimakharam government we put in power planning.

Arthur interjected.

– Sand and stone is what you come here to gripe about? That is no fish to fry, even if it true.

– All I saying is that Macaima should be wondering who going to benefit from all the quarrying that going to take place. I could bet De Valremy sell his estate to he-own-damn-self or whatever group he hug-up tight with. He need capital. Doh forget, he in construction. He well know what under these lands. Sand-an-gravel. Plenty money in that – tax free!

Loud suck-teeth and dismissive grumbles rose from the crowd. Arthur landed his ace.

– If what you say is his plan, then it have work for people inside here. What tax free is that US money you getting to cause doubt-an-division in Macaima and to destabilise this government we elect.

It was Cray's turn. His tone was dead serious when he took the talk in another direction.

– If we going to talk about division, let we talk. Why this Prime Minister start Commission of Inquiry to harass union members? Ask that! Ask, too, why anybody representing oil and sugar get burn from day one, if I remember right, *hostile* and *recalcitrant,* or encouraging *political subversion* were the words. Why we not listening to each other?

– Cray, dat is only platform talk, man. African and Indian unity is what this party is about. Look my good-good pardner Mitra right here. We nice. Scales balance plumb.

This was Arthur, whom Mitra now held in a fake neck hold to shut him up. A man in the crowd saw the opportunity to make the now familiar snipe at the firebrand.

– Mr Labour, what you have is a *mentality* problem that sweeten with too much sugar!

The comment was by then an overused anthem, but still it carried enough sting to stir the Labour representative to retaliate.

– Doh say I didn't try to warn Macaima. Go on swallowing whatever politician want to feed you. I go be the one to say *what sweet in goat mouth…*

He wasn't allowed to finish. Some fellas started rocking the vehicle, threatening to tip it over. Balkissoon was forced to start the engine and drive out so suddenly that the representative fell backwards. We watched his two legs, a splayed V, wave an odd farewell as he disappeared into a night that roared with laughter. I felt we had missed an opportunity to listen to another side of the debate, had given in too easily to the language of snide innuendo and brutal invective. Neither side could meet the other's challenge to find new ground. The gathering at Johnny's, though, had scored itself a victory. The parang side that was scheduled to play that night struck up and merriment took over.

CHAPTER 29 – DOG STAR

My mother had at last written. Her letter arrived just before the Christmas holidays. I was only half prepared for what I discovered. So much so that I rushed out of the house and stumbled down to Goodbye, tripping over the sand, letter in hand, my body propelled by a surge of blinding rage. I plunged ahead, wanting to be released from the very earth and air through which I tore until I threw myself down at the water's edge, lying flat on my back so that the expansive sky was above me as the surf washed over me. Only then did I realise that the puppies had followed me and were chasing around me, no doubt puzzled.

Her letter was brutally clear, and though I should have been, I was not at all ready for what I learned about my mother – about how she saw the world. What I read burned my mind:

Dear Anna,
I take this long to write because you ask me what I hope you never ask. I didn't want to have to explain what I know you already know. It shame me too much. I didn't want to cause disruption so I leave you to see what is what. But I will take my time to tell you.
Henderson treat us good, Anna. I was young. I know my place. Sometime he use to stay back late to finish work. We strike up conversation while I empty bin and clean. I never know to this day how it reach from one minute we talking and laughing to next –. I just freeze. Country-bookie in Port of Spain and he is big pappy. People run up and down that bank doing what he say. What I could do?
I not making excuse, and like he say, I never object. My own mother tell me look for my trouble and to make him responsible. So I let him know what is what. Is he who offer me a work and a place to stay and the Mrs in the beginning see me as a charity when he explain my

condition. Maybe he was sorry, as he say, for what happen. We never want for nothing, Anna, and all those years I tell myself, you and me, we have each other. I don't expect you to understand, but I find peace with what I come to learn. I grow a love for him and that make me stay in that yard longer than I should. If that make me a fool then so it is. I know we make the Mrs suffer. I sorry for that. She didn't deserve that hurt. I don't expect you to understand how my heart choose, but as your mother who love you even before I see you, I ask you to forgive me for whatever I rob you.

One more thing. Maybe two. Mr H always know you was a bright girl so he put aside a little something for you. 2,000 in England money Anna! That is plenty. Nobody perfect. And now the Mrs send to say he in a bad way and she need a little help. Emily in America with her own family to see about. So she want me to come up, Anna. He ask for me. She not able and it look like he not going to see the new year. Everything forgive she say. I tell her I will do it for all the trouble I cause. Everything fix. I going England for maybe three months. Nobody perfect, Anna. I always feel you hold up a standard that nobody could reach. Look what happened with you and that nice boy, Miles. How you take up and run so far in that bush. Doh feel I born yesterday. I put two and two together. I keep my peace and say truth will come to light. Take my advice and come down off your high horse before you end up with nobody.

Your loving mother,
Zara
Mr H is your father, Anna. Now you know so from me.

Her words soured in my mouth. How could I find understanding or the forgiveness she requested? She had chosen him over me, for whatever love she had developed for the man who was my father. Everything, our entire presence in that annex, was about her being able to stay within the radius of whatever care he had offered that she felt incapable of living without. Did she really discover that she loved him or was it the shelter he was able to provide that became the dependency? Whichever, she had sought to make me content to abide. I thought of those Sunday afternoons when I washed dishes for shiny quarters while Mrs Henderson went alone to the Country Club. In the end, it was still all about him, and her wanting to be close to the man with whom she longed to share an impossible union that would take her into his house. He had chosen to follow his wife back to England and, now that he was ill, asked for her care – pain care. I retched into the bay and watched the white froth sail away.

When I was able to sit up, the pups ran around me. Their warmth and excited licks were reassuring. They were here with me, and they were real. Not wanting to return to the house, to any enclosed space, I remained on the beach, emptied, watching the tide go through its tumbling change, as the sea gradually retreated and exposed more of the land. I dug my heels into the cool sand against the drag of the ebbing surf.

The weather was superb and the pups were happy to be out and about after so many the days of rain. Evenings in Macaima were especially magical. The land toned down to a hush, like an anticipation of the coming night when the demands of the day could be put down. The to-and-fro of the waves became a rhythm that unburdened me enough to see beyond myself and all that was still unfinished. I would come down to the beach and walk as far as I wanted along the shoreline, following its shifting arcs, listening to the waves keep their ferried time. Every now and then, I would pause to look at the gulls bobbing far out in the bay, permitting the embrace of the surf around my ankles and calves as the water rushed up the beach. The gulls sat on the water, content with whatever they had caught before the sun closed its eye behind the horizon.

It was possibly a good thing that my mother's letter had come when it did. News, too, arrived that week that the Macaima post office was to be closed earlier than anticipated. Head Office said something about budget cuts and reallocated funds to the new structure of its service to the district. Everything would be handled from Railway, and the transition was to happen as soon as possible, hopefully by the month's end, before the Carnival celebrations in February. I didn't see what the rush was about until it came to light that the spot where the post office stood had been earmarked for another project, at least according to the snippet that came from Mrs Austin. She couldn't or wouldn't elaborate, insisting that it was not her place to say, and I didn't give her the satisfaction of appearing too eager to know more. I would focus on the pending closure.

I had to let Mrs Bailey know, at my earliest convenience, whether or not I wished to return to my old position. I needed to be ready to vacate as soon as possible rather than drag things too far into the Carnival season. Given all that had happened, the news was not a disappointment. Thoughts of moving on had become more real, so I saw this development as an unexpected but not unhelpful exit route. What was next remained uncertain, although the idea of pursuing an undergraduate degree was surfacing more convincingly as a viable option. I had managed to accumulate a little savings and the government was offering scholarships in a drive to better prepare the nation for the future. I could apply. Going back to where I had started was not an option. Using my father's guilt money was also out of the question. I would make my own way.

As the sun began to set, I shifted to my usual spot near the rip tide and sat there trying to become its rhythm, not wanting to think of anything, wanting only to be a looker at the scene before me, in flow with the tireless current. *Things will work themselves out. Things will work themselves out* – my mother's anchor in tough times, but maybe in memory of Miss Gomez and the journey I had been both angered and touched by, I added, *in ways we least expect*, the line she had used in reference to Sam's American story of which I knew little. Those words became my mantra until I heard the dogs barking excitedly, then saw them racing to meet our unexpected guests – Sam and Roland.

They had called at the house, then figured I would be on the beach. Sam wanted to say her goodbyes. She was travelling back to the States in a few days. I had expected her to stay at least until after Easter. Roland, who appeared more relaxed than for some time, announced in an uncharacteristically jovial tone what was perhaps his own hope.

– Sam going, Miss Anna, but she coming back!

– And what do you say to that, Sam?

– Maybe I like it over there. Maybe I come back home. I doh know.

I was about to express my hope of seeing her again when

Roland put his fingers to his lips, as though to restrain me from giving away a shared secret. I was puzzled but let it slide. Seeing Sam again and having the opportunity to hear of her plans was enough. Roland took the dogs away for a walk to give us a few minutes alone. She had changed. I had glimpsed a difference in her bearing during her performance at the funeral, but seeing her close up was a confirmation. She was dressed smartly in a button-up blouse of multicoloured polka dots on a red background and a pair of black capris. Her hair was closely braided in a cute bob.

– It's so good to see you, Sam. You're – well, all grown up! Who combed your hair. It's beautiful.

She cast her eyes down, then, as if overriding an old habit, quickly adjusted.

– Thanks, Miss Anna. Granny. She could comb it with her eyes close.

She giggled at her unintended irony.

We sat in silence looking at the sunset unleash its colours.

– How is she doing?

– Not so good.

She dug her feet into the sand and bent to scoop up a handful.

– I'm sorry, but she's so lucky to have you here. How are you?

She turned to me and smiled.

– I going, but I real sad about plenty things.

– Like what?

– How Miss Gomez pass.

– We must think she's in a better place. She did a lot of good.

– I wanted to say a proper thanks before…

She gathered some sand and made a smooth ball of it.

– I tell them in the hospital over there that I don't want no operation. Franco vex, but he always vex.

– Sam, you know yourself best. Take your time.

This was territory I had to let her lead me through. She threw her sand-ball at the water's edge. I watched it splatter and rejoin the beach.

– How do you feel about the decision to wait?

– I good with it. I think I have to find out who is Samantha-Marie. I talk and talk to people over there and I come to know one thing: I have to decide how to be all who I am. I not doing no surgery. The counsellor-lady say that part could wait. The other part more important.

– What is that?

– She call it acceptance. I am who I am. No changing that story.

Sam spoke with easy conviction. I could tell that behind the jargon, which must have come from her counsellor, there was a genuine struggle to find a language for herself with which to discover her own answers.

– I still so mad-vex, Miss Anna: with Franco, Granny – everybody.

She kicked at the sand.

– That's a good place to start, Sam. You are the one to say who you are. Always remember that.

– I can't say I understand everything, only that I want good for myself. I know people born how they call perfect and right, but they act more devil than devil self. I don't understand all, but I know that is not me. That is not Sam.

– I am so happy to hear you say so, Sam. You bring me hope.

– For what?

The directness of her question was like light shone directly into my very heart. There was a new kind of strength and dignity in her language and bearing. Not the anger and aggression I had first encountered. She was discovering her right to simply be.

– This world needs you, Sam. It needs us all. We have to decide what gift we want to give to it, I suppose.

There were decisions that I, too, had to make. I saw her brows knit. Maybe I had lost her.

– What I mean is we can help to make each other better human beings. That's why we're here.

I had skipped ahead of her, but thankfully she had arrived at her own place of grounding and was in no need of my affirmation or preaching.

– The best part of over there, Miss Anna, is that some people want to sponsor me to go to a school where I could learn music and train my voice. They ask me and I sing for them. That is how it happen.

– That's wonderful news, Sam!

– My heart leap when they tell me about that school. I say, yes.

They going let me stay with them.

– Who are they – your sponsors?

– Prescott is their name. They had a daughter like me, about my age, but...

– But what – what happened?

– She died.

– Accidentally?

She shook her head.

– So they want to help me. The man, he from over there. He work in the hospital, and Karen, she from here but went from a baby. She teach music – like Miss Gomez. We talk plenty.

– They seem good for you, Sam. It sounds like a great chance.

– I think so, Miss Anna, but I will miss Granny – and Maria.

– You'll get to visit, I'm sure.

With her elbows on her knees and cupped chin in her hands, her eyes held to the horizon.

– You are the bravest person I know, Sam. So-so wonderfully brave and perfect.

She looked straight back at me with those piercing eyes.

– You too, Miss Anna.

It was my turn to look away.

Roland was on his way back with the pups skipping wildly about his legs. We sat together before the riptide that was busy moving away from Macaima, like it was hustling to carry a message to the other side, and rush back again with an answer. The last light of dusk was rapidly fading when Roland, in his quiet way, put his question to us.

– Who could tell me why that star over there so bright?

We followed his hand to where he pointed, low on the horizon. In truth the star was brighter than all the rest. I left the answering to Sam. It was her evening, and I had had my fill of answers.

– Because it nearer to us than all the rest.

He paused to give her answer its space.

– Yes, that correct-an-right.

He gave her a shoulder nudge of congratulations, then fixed his gaze on that one spot in the sky.

– I have another belief. I say that star so bright because it not alone up there. I have no proof, but I say company close by. So she happy too bad. You can't see with the naked eye, but she not alone. I say that is why they name her Dog Star. Company is what she love more than anything. Not so Day – not so, girl?

Day yelped with joy as Roland scratched and tickled behind her ears and underbelly, and Night, realising that plenty love was sharing, jumped right into the mix. There was no need to agree or disagree. In that moment, we were simply happy to be there, together.

CHAPTER 30 – TO PLAY-A-MAS

I spent a quiet Christmas Day on Beach Trace. Lucille had invited me to drop by her place, but I didn't feel like company. For most of the morning, I worked in the garden and later in the day, when the sun had cooled, headed out with the pups for a stroll on the beach. The pups were about four months old. Still babies, but more able to seek and enjoy their interests and pleasures, unafraid to venture out on their own, confident that they could reconnect with me whenever they chose. I left them to their frolicking in the sand and racing after the retreating surf. When they were ready, they made wild sprints to catch up with me, only to break away again, absorbed in their play. I let them have their freedom.

The bay was more or less deserted, except at the far end where a pirogue painted in white, blue and red stripes was anchored. The water was calmest there because of the shelter from the headland and distance from the riptide, which was closer to the Beach Trace end. It occurred to me that I did not know who owned the boat or took it out to sea when it wasn't in the bay. Maybe I had crossed paths with the owner on the junction or at Johnny's but had no clue. I watched the vessel bobbing in the waves, tugging at the anchor rope. Part of its story was missing. Did that matter? Parts of stories were always missing or lost – like the story of the Warao tribe that walked into the sea. Even Marie's story was incomplete. Such absences provoked their own questions – mine and Macaima's. The boat rocked and dipped. Waves slapped its sides. I decided that I would ask about the owner and retraced my steps, thinking that it was the boat that had done the asking – had by its very presence required that I fill my absences: the riddle of the riptide that took away the tribe and Marie; the puzzle of Miss Gomez's life; my mother's confirmation about Mr

Henderson; Thea's postcards. They were all asking questions, and while I tried not to think too much about them, they converged to form the void that tugged at me: *What next?*

When I returned to the house, Danny and Nneka were sitting on the front steps, locked in an embrace. They missed my approach and, at my greeting, they drew away a little embarrassed. Nneka had come to leave a gift of punch-a-creme and black cake from her parents and to invite me to hers and Danny's engagement ceremony on January 6th. Her hands caressed a small baby bump as she spoke. It was Danny's turn to look caught out. She reached instinctively for his hand when she emphasised that Mr Elton would be happy to see me. The intimated pregnancy explained Danny's eagerness to support Mr Elton with his building and to claim his place as family. Maybe Mr Elton had also yielded to the realisation that help was needed and he didn't have to walk, what Brenda had called *his* Calvary, all alone. He had trusted Thomas and had gotten burned. Bargained and lost. Danny put his arm around Nneka's waist as they walked away, no longer quite the shy youth who had followed me from Johnny's to apologise for his father's behaviour in the shop. Time was moving on.

My first Christmas in Macaima was probably going to be Sam's last with her grandmother, Maria and Franco. She was crossing a bridge into a larger version of herself. I was undecided about crossing or burning one. Thea's most recent card had said too much. It was something her father had said. I knew the story already. He had lost his teaching job for refusing to stand during the singing of *God Save the King* at an Empire Day celebration. He felt he couldn't do it anymore she had said. When she asked him what "it" was, his answer was the single line she had written on her Christmas card: *Suffering must not be confused with the fear of suffering.* Thea had been ten years old at the time, but her interpretation of that one line, she said, had made her an activist. What she had added further nagged at my thoughts: *We must heal ourselves from the fear of ourselves, Anna. Everyday. That alone will make clear our responsibility for this world.* I put the card, along with Miss Gomez's note, and my mother's letter, at the base of the Bucket orchid. Its fallen blossoms lay strewn on the coffee table.

On Boxing Day, I travelled to Railway with Mitra to Mrs

Campbell's house. She had called earlier that week to express her hope of seeing me before the season ended and I didn't want to disappoint her. She was alone that afternoon; her husband had gone out on some unspecified errand. It was a pleasant enough visit but with Miss Gomez gone, we discovered that whatever connection we had made prior to her death had exhausted itself. I did not miss, though, some discontent that lurked behind her well-mannered pleasantries and light-hearted chatter about the Yuletide decorations and the choir that had outdone itself at the midnight service.

Before I departed, something of the reason for her disheartened mood surfaced. Miss Gomez had left the house on Sunrise Trace to *the church*. The word had been emphasised and the collective anonymity that circled the word appeared the source of her annoyance.

– Imagine!

No more was said but perhaps enough had been said. True, Miss Gomez had no immediate kin, but the decision was evidently a disappointment to Mrs Campbell. She had stayed at her cousin's side to the very end. I thought again of Miss Gomez's extraordinary expression of imagination and spirit in her grotto and in organising her own funeral – her effort to push back on containment and exclusion. But what had she really achieved? The church to which she was apparently so committed wanted for nothing, at least materially, yet she wanted to give it her last worldly possession. What did she want to say – to her cousin or to this world that she struggled so hard to find her place in? Mrs Campbell dropped a hint of an answer as we said our goodbyes.

– Eunice had plenty taken from her, even as she gave so much, Miss Bridgemohan. I didn't expect her last wish would be to also give up the house. Maybe in the end she wanted to say more.

– What do you think that was, Mrs Campbell?

– I believe that she was more than what she agreed to lose, because, in the end, it is she who had agreed on the life she chose.

– Was she – really?

We stood together watching the flaming poinsettias mixed in with the milky Christmas bush, before we hugged again at the end of the narrow walkway before the gate closed behind me for the last time.

★

When January came, work began on the Mountain Road project. Progress was slow and messy as the rains resumed and lingered into the new year. Surveyors arrived in their pick-ups. Once weather permitted, they worked steadfastly beneath broad hats and umbrellas, looking intently into their instruments, jotting notes and motioning to assistants to move their ranging rods to the left or right, forward or backward. Others planted and painted pickets. It was quiet work until the bulldozers rumbled in, monstrous tanks that pushed down trees and raked, gobbled, straightened and flattened the ground.

Danny brought me a piece of his engagement cake and accepted mutely my excuse for not showing up because of a migraine. It wasn't exactly a lie. I was in no mood to witness any promises of *until death do us part* unions. So much was in flux.

I watched the mountain gradually ripped open. Day by day, it became a lengthening tunnel of unsheltered light, and the sky screamed with unhoused birds. Having lost their homes in the blink of an eye, monkeys, squirrels, even iguanas started making their way into people's yards in search of food and shelter. Villagers stumbled along, still banking on promises to materialise and taking what opportunities the construction work provided: shovelling, off-loading, digging, cutting bush and trees. A few women sold bake and fried fish, pelau and hot soup to the ever hungry workers.

On Friday and Saturday evenings especially, groups of workmen flocked to Johnny's bar. The shop, too, was busy. Johnny and Claudette moved energetically behind the counter with a new surge of energy. Rosa started serving more regularly on the bar side – wiping tables, collecting empty bottles and used glasses, glad for the wages to send back to her family across the channel. Lucille concluded that Johnny was smart too bad. Rosa was an additional attraction on the premises to draw customers, and she played the part well.

– Oh yes, mih dear, Johnny put Rosa to wipe table. Dem fellas glad too bad. Spanish fuh so: *Mas hielo senorita / me gusta chica / tengo mucho dinero*. She is no fool. She play dey game: dress nice, and smile and wiggle to get pay.

Lucille imitated what was supposedly Rosa's performance with a saucy sway of her body as she pretended to navigate tables and smile at customers. It was hilarious but I wasn't amused.

– So tiresome.

– Girl, sometimes you have to know when to play-a-mas and when to walk away. Money nice for Rosa since road start. As for me, the only mas I playing is *Lucille*.

We both laughed and took in Rosa's show, which was not at all as exaggerated as Lucille's version, but I saw her point. I wondered, too, about the self-knowledge that Lucille boasted and whether there was ever a completion – an end to the discovery of who we are. I ventured to draw her out further.

– So, who *is* Lucille?

From the wonderment that lit her face, I could see she welcomed my question.

– Miss Anna, she is somebody I like to be, and every day I learn more about that woman. Some good. Some troublesome. I not easy, but I love her same way and let her grow. Lucille is Lucille. She is me.

She smacked loud kisses on both palms and planted them on her cheeks. I was unprepared by what followed.

– I only wish Eunice coulda grant love to her own self.

– What makes you say that? She certainly gave a lot and the funeral was packed.

– People loving you and you loving the self you get to grow with in this world is two different thing, Miss Anna; but I not no preacher.

– I didn't think you were preaching.

She wasn't convinced.

– No sista, pulpit is not where I talk my sense. Anyway, I wanted to say that I see Sister-General catch you in talk after the service.

– Sister-General?

– Sister Agnes – she in charge. She use to come in here to teach Bible after Sunday church. Eunice was star pupil and she get to assist. But jokes aside, she was good to Eunice. Help her mend.

– Oh? Was she ill… I mean before her last trouble.
– Yes, but that was long time now. She suffer a set back.
– What do you mean?
– We grow together, Miss Bri. Friend was friend, no matter who was who. We went to school together, play and get in confusion together. How I see it, what transpire between she and Brenda is where it start.
– What happened?

Lucille showed reluctance to continue, but by bringing up Miss Gomez's past, it was clear she wanted me to know more.

– How I take it, dem-two had a little thing.
– What do you mean – romantic?
– I see what I see, and I ask Brenda direct.
– Saw what?
– Doh matter. It happen long time now. Brenda say it was young people foolishness… Eunice not here to speak her part, but I see the situation. They never know I was there.
– Where?
– Same place Eunice make her shrine. But like I say, Brenda swear it was nothing. Then she take up with Paul soon after and Patrick born. They together since. Maybe for Eunice it wasn't foolishness. Since that day was like when mirror fall from wall.
– Was she ill?
– You mean after? You could say that. Exam time come and she didn't win no big scholarship to go away. Everybody surprise. Nuns disappoint. Mr Gomez vex to kill. Eunice turn in and disappear for a year. When she come back, she wasn't the same. Church to home – like she fraid she own shadow. Sister Agnes was there to help and little by little she catch up.

Lucille's revelation was not what I had anticipated.

– Anyway that pass, and she gone now, rest her soul. But she leave a sadness in me. Belonging to a place is no passport anybody born with. You have to make a claim to it. Macaima no different from anywhere, and I not saying that Eunice didn't do nothing with what life she had. That would be a lie; but we bury a woman nobody ever really get to know. She give plenty, but whatever self was under all that she give, she chain down like a devil from hell. That is my sadness.

– Maybe we all contributed to that prison.

– I not saying I disagree, Miss Bri. I know what this place could give, but even if people choose to turn up at yuh funeral, nobody going to respect you for being too frighten to live. That kinda life is no legacy to leave.

– Miss Gomez was so much more than what you call her fear, Lucille. Look at what she did for Sam, and so many others. Maybe that was enough.

– I never say different, and she deserve her peace; but she play martyr, and it cost her plenty. People is people. Human being – that is one boat we all in. If yuh ask me, she get trap is a mas somebody else decide on. Nobody should walk that road.

Story is a two-way street. Lucille's disclosure stayed with me. She was a lovely woman but keeping confidences was evidently not her strong point and Miss Gomez and Brenda were not present to offer their sides of the story. They had a right to their truths, but the tale had shed light on the depth of Brenda's anger that day in the post office and maybe a little more about the *cure* Miss Gomez might have hoped to get from Mr Elton's prayers. I wondered, too, whether her concern for Patrick was connected to that period in time which she had relegated, according to Lucille, to youthful folly.

I, though, had begun to think I had been too easily absorbed by Macaima's stories. I had given little of myself to the place, but maybe the villagers had seen me more clearly than I imagined. Since then, I've come to learn that the untold is also its own story. That is the one people really want to read.

I thought of Mr Elton half buried in the trenches of his church. Who was he really? The public face had cracked. I could ask the same of Sam, myself, any one for that matter. Maybe the better question was: *who were we becoming*? To anybody who asked, I would say, in unoriginal jest, *What yuh see is what yuh get*. If I said I didn't want to be known, that might be the same as saying I didn't want to be hurt. Maybe those who are quick to lay out for the world what they claim to be are more self-deceiving than they realise. Maybe the deeper self is a much more private creature.

These thoughts preoccupied me. They were close to home.

CHAPTER 31 – A REQUEST

I regretted what I saw as the refusal of the villagers to interrogate the future they had been promised, their unwillingness to ask questions and demand answers about the party's promises. But I was no exception. My concentration was on the task at hand: the closure of the office. I was at the end of a chapter and with that knowledge came a detachment and calm that I mistook for resolution, even decision. I was moving on. My approaching departure was an option for limbo and without clear purpose. Not like Brenda. She had made a decision to leave Macaima. She had her children to think about and the road to a future she hoped to help set them on. Sam, too, was preparing for a new adventure and Roland had also hinted about relocating.

Out of the blue, during my final days in the village, I received a call from Miles. We had not been in contact since my arrival.

– You sound good, Anna.

– I'm doing okay.

– Country life suits you.

– Not too sure about that, but I suppose you've heard about the coming closure. I'm heading back to the city in a few days.

He had heard and wanted to be in touch before I disappeared. The word was out that I would probably not be returning to head office. It still bothered him that we had not parted on good terms. I had no reason to doubt what he said.

– I didn't quite get what went wrong with us, and… well, you just left. I don't think I will ever get over that.

I said nothing. Rehashing the hurt that had played a big part in my wanting to escape made no sense, but it all seemed so far away now. Miles was no longer on my horizon and I had no regrets about the end of the relationship. Macaima had given me that one clarity.

He spoke first.

– Maybe we work better as friends, Anna. How about a meet up when you get back to town?

The request came as a surprise.

– Let me think about it.

– No pressure. We could do something closer to Carnival. That was our season. Remember?

– Yes, it was.

Silence created its own distance. Maybe there was less enthusiasm in my voice than he had anticipated. Maybe not. I tried to fill the gap.

– What do you think of the calypsos this year? The papers say the tents are on fire.

That was enough get the conversation moving again.

– Bomber is tops. He could win king. "Joan and James" is my pick. Yuh hear it?

– No, I haven't but I picked up something in the newspapers.

He offered a few lines of the song.

– *Darlin, Darlin let we play little mammy, you is de mammy, I is de daddy...* People love it! Maybe we could hit a tent together. I'll bring Kimberly. You remember Kim, right?

– Of course. Didn't she get Thea's position in accounts?

– Yeah. By the way, how's Thea?

– Possibly in her element. Books and more books.

– Where did she land up, States?

– As far as I know.

– She been in touch? Not that I want to mine yuh business.

Another card had in fact arrived that week, which Thea announced as her *last-last-last*. Its message was an altered quotation credited to James Baldwin: *We can make [the world] what [the world] must become*. She had loaned me one of his novels. His first. Thea had said that is what happens when you succeed in making a fiction of your deepest hurt: art happens. She said she was no writer so she was living her story. I had no doubt that she would be at the centre of the civil rights unrest. But I knew nothing, and wasn't prepared to give Miles any information in that regard. He took the hint.

– I hope you could make that tent lime. Kim would be happy

to see you. I went and tie up myself. We getting married Easter coming.

– Oh! That's fast.

He laughed a little nervously.

– Not really. Anyhow, I have to take responsibility. You should know I doh run from that.

– Of course.

I held on to the receiver, though that familiar feel of wanting distance returned. This was the real reason for the call – to let me know he had moved on. His reference to the Bomber song made sense and took me right back to why I needed to put a wall between us and what he still wanted to punish me for. Guilt had not been sufficient for him – and I did feel guilt, although it took some self-searching to realise that had less to do with my decision and more with his expectations. He had taken the loss as a deprivation of his right to fatherhood and never tried to hear my part. I was the vessel. There was no going back, for either of us.

– You okay, Anna?

– Sure. That's great news. Congrats.

– Thanks, but I've really missed you, Anna. I wanted you to know that. Let's keep in touch.

– For what? You're such a prick, Miles!

I hung up before he could finish whatever he had started to say.

★

It was in that space between my leave-taking and my actual departure, with more time on my hands than I needed, just like that, my writing began: at first a note to my mother saying we should talk. I didn't understand her choice – the forgiveness she was able to offer that became love. I was clear about one thing. I didn't want the money. In the silence that followed, I began writing notes to myself, then mostly impressions, starting with my arrival in Macaima. I had brought my untold story to the place, so maybe it was my way of beginning the side of a conversation I had withheld. Although I was about to leave, the truth was I had never fully arrived.

That incompleteness, I realised, had begun in Mr Henderson's yard. Now that my mother had spoken, a certain kind of closure settled in me. Not that I felt a need to reach out to him;

he had all but abandoned me and attempted to buy a clean conscience. Maybe in some way he loved my mother, but she had settled for what he was able to give. That was her choice. Mine was I did not want to be bought. She could send back the money. When she eventually responded, it was to say that Henderson was dead. He had passed over the Christmas holidays and had been ailing for some time. She sounded broken, but I had no words of comfort for her although I was sorry for her pain. The numbness was its own agony. What could I say that would not be empty platitudes when she wanted understanding. She took my silence as grief and repeated that the money was there to make something of my life. He wanted me to have it. I left her with her story.

I did not, at first, write whole sentences, only sporadic words and phrases that I hoped to elaborate. My preparations for the closure of the office had unearthed piles of discarded envelopes. They became my pages. I did not see the irony of this until Lucille dropped by to share some of her produce.

– What is this, Miss Bri, you busy writing letter to yuhself?
Her voice was full of tease.

– That might just be the case, Miss Lucille.

– Nah, yuh too quick to agree with me. Maybe what you busy writing is a history that will connect up everybody.

– Not so ambitious. They're only notes.

– Well, connect them up. Story, history – once it tell. Past is what come to meet all-a-we and put we where we have to make a future happen. So write it for you, for Macaima, for this nation we in – and for everybody.

She saw I was doubtful but drawn to what she had said.

– I know one remedy for lonely, Miss Bri. You want to know it?

The assessment was a familiar one – Franco's when I had first arrived. I would humour her.

– Tell me, Miss Lucille.

– Let somebody, something, some place, love you, Miss Anna. So write what you have to say – if that is what you here to do. Maybe that is your love to give them back.

Then as though she had no more to say on the subject or felt the next move was my own, she took the conversation in another direction, telling me what was behind the hint that Mrs Austin had dropped about plans for the property on which the post office was located.

– So yuh hear we getting gas station in Macaima?

It was news to me.

– Yuh falling back sista. Harry-dem get elevate to gas.

Apparently, the owners of *H&W Hardware* had been awarded the dealer's licence from *Nation Gas* to manage it. The *H*, I learnt, was for Harry, which was the deceased corporal's surname: Luke Harry. The hardware was a longstanding family business that the corporal's eldest brother had inherited from their father. The *W* in the signage was less clearly explained but seemed to have a link to the mother. I had never met Corporal Luke's brother or wife in the months I had been in the village. On a couple of occasions, I had seen a car enter and exit the side gate that led to the large dwelling behind the store. Their names never came up and I had never asked.

– It look like Luke-brother was the real brains behind whatever business arrangement they make with Spanish, who, as you know, disappear like smoke. Luke and Bones only deliver.

I couldn't help thinking that, like a hydra, corruption continually grew new heads. News of the gas station was toasted at Johnny's bar as another plus on the road to the transformation of the district.

– Anyway, my dear, rope must run out. Harry-dem gone for higher. Now I have to mine where I heading.

She went on her way, walking with the purposefulness that I had come to know was only one side of the woman who was not shy to cross lines and dance in the road.

★

With more and more villagers choosing to do their business at the Railway post office, I had even more time to myself. I supposed that they were getting themselves accustomed to the new arrangement. And with Carnival in the air, I was left to my own devices. So much was happening. On one of those slow days, during my last week in the village, Roland dropped by, the usual cigarette tucked behind an ear. I had not seen him since the time on the beach with Sam when he had made that odd gesture of secrecy. Franco, too, had been scarce, but I knew he had to spend more time with his own affairs. His mother and Maria had to be moved from the estate house he had occupied since a child. Sam, too, must have already departed for the States. I had hoped to say a last goodbye. Now Roland stood in the doorway. There was the same quiet watchfulness about him, but his appearance was different. His hair was no longer closely cropped and a patchy beard covered his face. He had a message to deliver.

– I come to tell you I going away, Miss Anna.

I wasn't surprised, given all that had transpired, especially Sam's departure.

– Where're you headed?

– Town-side. Plenty building happening. I could get work in construction, if I want. So Brenda say.

– Oh, you've heard from her.

– Yeah, the sister she staying by married to a cousin on my mother side. My father was from inside here.

– Where's your mother now? You tell me that your father pass.

– Yes, when I small. But no scene. I doh really remember him much.

The beautiful lullaby he had shared on the beach told me otherwise, that he felt a deeper sense of loss. I had no such feeling about my father's death. My question had been answered and with it my obsession with knowing. He simply faded to the margins of my thoughts. We had shared no real relationship. From what I remembered, he related with no one beyond the usual pleasantries, though there were those Sunday afternoons and those shiny coins.

– And your mother, where is she?

– She cross to Vene-side not long after he bury and settle there. At first I went, but I give so much trouble she send me back. I go over every Easter. Maybe one time we could go together, Miss Anna. I bet you never cross over.

The invitation seemed odd but I figured he was making small talk.

– No, I haven't been over there, but maybe one day.

– Just tell me when. I go organise.

– Thanks. By the way, what was the secret you wanted me to keep from Sam that day on the beach?

– Secret?
– Yes, you signalled to me that there was something you didn't want me to disclose.

A light went on.

– Oh that! I didn't want you to tell Sam about the little thanksgiving we planning.

– Thanksgiving? I had no idea.

– Elton didn't tell you? Franco want Sam to get baptise before she go back.

– Oh she's still here.

– Yes, but going jus now. She woulda come to tell you so.

– Oh, I hadn't realised.

– She always ask after you, Miss Anna. Anyhow, service get postpone.

– How come?

– Sam granny really low.

– Sorry to hear.

– She is a heart case on top everything else. But this Sunday is for Sam. Elton plan to make it a thanksgiving for everything that happen. That is why he put up tent.

I had noticed a yellow tarpaulin mounted over the foundations of the new church but figured it was to stave off the bad weather.

– Franco want the whole village to be there. I guess he proud she going away from here.

He shrugged his shoulders a little dismissively.

I found the church baptism a curious decision on Franco's part. He had never struck me as the religious type, but this apparent show of admiration for Elton seemed more explicable. I was sure his conflicted loyalty to the De Valremies would have suffered a final blow with the betrayal of Thomas's land sale, and since Mr Elton had also made a public show of his decision to break ties with the family, there was a new motive to connect with him. Sam would be the first member in this new dispensation. I reflected how Brenda had expressed her distrust in this new arrangement. For my part, I wondered whether the church fully understood what its welcome of Sam might require. Time would tell.

– Is Sam okay with the baptism? It sounds like Franco's idea.

– I suppose she okay with it. I know she would rather be with the church that make here. She was never comfortable in Miss Gomez own.

– I'm happy she's getting a chance to go to school.

– Me too. She bless with plenty and it wasn't easy for her in Macaima.

– It won't be easy for her anywhere, Roland, but she's a fighter.

– Fuh sure. She doh play dead.

He tugged at the strands of his newly forming beard.

– I hope you come to the service, Miss Anna. We plan a little fete after.

– I don't think I've been invited.

– No invitation. Show up.

– I'll see. Sunday happens to be my moving day.

– I hear so, but Sam would want you there. Anyway, talk run far from the reason I here.

He moved in and sat on the bench.

– I bring a message for you from Mama Gloria.

– A message?

– Yes, she want to meet you by Miss Gomez grotto tomorrow morning. She have a word for you. Sun-up tomorrow. She going to be waiting. You will get to really meet her, and Maria too.

– Sounds like a showdown.

– Nah. Natu choose what fights is hers and you not no enemy.

The invitation was a strange one, but I was curious about the woman who had raised Roland and, of course, there was the chance to really meet Maria. They were both central to all that had unravelled in the last few months. Maria had been in the storeroom that horrid *storm day* and Mama Gloria had watched over me in its aftermath. She was the one who had introduced Brite to me – helped me to see another side, though I had not known that she was there at the time. I was between worlds that day. It would probably be my last chance to meet with them.

– And if yuh want, you could take Day and Night with you. I figure you would need somewhere to leave them.

– Thanks for that. I'd been wondering what was possible.

– No problem. I have a cousin staying by Natu that like to hunt. Night and Day is good hunting dogs.

– I didn't realise. How do you know?

– How the ears grow. I heading out now, Miss Anna. Take care.

– You too, Roland. Maybe we will meet up again.

– Mama always say that Warao goodbye is never forever. I doh know how true, but I like the idea. So dihana.

– Goodbye, Roland. Take care of yourself.

I sensed a hesitation to leave – that he had another reason for stopping by. He reached for the cigarette and placed it between his lips.

– I hope I doh cause offence, Miss Anna, but I have something I want to give you – to keep for me.

I only then saw that he carried a small knapsack from which he extracted an object carefully wrapped in what looked like tanned chamois. A knife lay there, its glistening blade about six inches long.

The request stirred again the suspicion I thought our conversations had dispelled. He saw my reaction.

– It belong to my father. He leave a flute too, but it gone missing. Jus so knife and flute disappear from my place. Then, the other day, I see the knife alone turn back up. Keep it for me – as a remembrance. Maybe one day, when I settle, I going to ask you for it back.

This did little to calm my uneasiness.

– The handle carve from deer antler. The flute that missing is from the shin. I never take much to Franco, but he teach me how to play it. He could make that flute talk. Natu play too. I bet you didn't know that Marie was a kinda niece to her.

– No I didn't. Doesn't that make your related – to Marie.

– In a pumpkin-vine way, maybe – not so direct.

– Complicated.

– You could say so; but if I had my flute, I woulda play a tune for you. I make it up myself.

– Maybe it will turn up, one day – like the knife did.

I could see him processing the thought.

– Maybe, but I want you to keep it safe for me, Miss Anna, until we meet again. I know we will meet up again.

What was Roland really asking of me? A match struck as he turned to leave, not waiting for my response. I looked more closely at his treasure: the knife's handle, smoothed and polished by use, his father's possession. Had it become something more? The missing flute – where was it? He was about to make me the keeper of what was his. Maybe he felt I would welcome the alliance – whatever it was. Or that I would not betray him. Maybe there was nothing to betray. Miss Gomez's note, the one I had read at her farewell to the world, flashed before me with its perhaps unintended complication of subjects. *You are the gift: I have not been entirely generous.* The entire address was to herself, as much as it was to me. So what more could she have given to the world – or was it to herself? In the event of her death, the question made no sense, but with Roland asking this curious favour of me the question revived. Why? Why, too, did my father leave me money? What was I to him or what was he to me – the fruit of a moment's indiscretion? He was the man my mother loved and chose to stay in his yard. The answer I needed for Roland suddenly surfaced. The knife was his. I would not accept responsibility for its safekeeping – and whatever history it carried. I caught up with him at the junction and handed it over. He made no protest. Smoke trailed in his wake. I saw in its ghostly lines the border that separated the annex from the Hendersons' house gradually disappear.

I was sure that Franco, who had been under the eave of Johnny's shop, saw the exchange.

CHAPTER 32– MARIA'S PARANG

I set out for Miss Gomez's house just after dawn. The pups followed. It was Saturday so the Main Road was already alive with folks looking for transport to Railway. Lennox pulled up beside me. I could tell from his *We done late* complaint that Lucille had insisted on him stopping. Her produce was loaded in the tray.

– I heading to market, Miss Bri, and this man have me late.

Almost her entire torso leaned over the window. Her face beamed health and mischief.

– Lennox, I not going to tell what keep you back this morning. That is between you, me – and Rosa.

Her voice played on the brink of laughter.

– Battery dead. I done tell you. No other truth in it. Say what you want.

He only feigned protest.

– Yes, Mr Lennox, only one truth in that story. Right, Miss Bri?

She winked at me. I declined to get involved in their banter. Lennox revved the engine.

– Girl, we go catch up in Sunday fete.

Lucille waved cheerfully as they drove off with a round of beeps. I supposed she meant Sam's thanksgiving. I had no details about the event and had neglected to ask Roland about the time. My best guess was that it would be in the morning. My arrangement with Neville was that he would meet me at the house at ten o'clock. That was the best he could do since he had a job that afternoon and couldn't risk running late. With any luck, I would be able to stop by the church at least to say my goodbyes and share with Sam an address where I could be reached, if she wanted.

Soft light showered through the mesh of greenery that lined Sunrise Trace. Not at all like the wet gloom of the day I had first visited Miss Gomez's house. The early morning air was an intoxicating blend of thriving vegetation and whistled choruses. I walked slowly, enveloped by a serenity that was its own welcome. The dogs raced ahead. They quickly disappeared down a sidetrack, emerging higher up the path, noses to the ground, tails whipping excitedly. Macaima would be a great home for them. I was grateful Roland had suggested that I could leave them with Mama Gloria. They would be well cared for and happy.

Before long I was at the ridge where the house stood. Already the place had the look of abandonment. I hesitated at the gate, which swung open. The lawn was overgrown and the porch was empty of furniture. I supposed the premises had been cleared by its new owners. Hesitant to venture further, I took in the vista beyond the property where the land dipped before making a steady climb to the beginnings of the estate lands. The empty space between that point and the Gomez's house was a long stretch of tall razor grass. The entry to Sunrise Trace, at least for about a mile in, was still in natural shade, which made the gap between the Gomez's house and the L'Avenir estate more noticeable, even odd, and I wondered why it had been cleared and then left uncultivated. Perhaps the trees had been felled for timber, or maybe there had been an abandoned plan to plant more cocoa trees in the valley. Miss Gomez's property was not on De Valremy land, so it had been spared what was happening to Mountain Road and beyond – the permanent loss of trees, of wildlife habitats, plantable soil and damaged water tables. I wondered, though, what plans the church had for the land.

There was no sign of Day and Night, but I could hear them yelping excitedly at the back of the house. They had discovered something. Before long, they both came pelting to the front. Day was shielding from Night something she held between her teeth. She approached me, tail wagging excitedly, and promptly laid her catch at my feet. It was a fledgling brown dove.

– Oh no Day – Night! How could you?

Puzzled and chastened by my displeasure, she retreated. Night followed. They lay some distance away, their chins pinned to the ground. The bird lay rigid, its toes curled, its tiny breast quivering. As I picked up the broken creature in my hands, I could feel its body warm, the flesh tremble on my palm, the tiny heart racing in its breast. The dogs looked on mutely as I stroked the flattened feathers, coaxing it to stir. No use. The body fell limp.

– What have you done?"

The question finally arrived – an address to the violence that was also mine. Who was I? I too had taken a life, told the universe I was not ready for it. Mother Gloria had said that Brite would tell me more – teach me more. She was right. The dove lay lifeless in my palm. I sat on the track dispirited, my face buried in my knees. The pups eased up and lay close, doleful, waiting for my flood to subside. Day whined her discomfort, no doubt confused by my mood. Night, too, came forward and leant his weight against me. They were merely living their nature – being hunters. I reached out to offer them both my apology with firm hugs, but it was not enough. They wanted to see my face as reassurance. I complied. Happy again, they sped off behind the house. I drew a deep breath, laid the dove's lifeless body in the nearby bushes and followed. Not with guilt or regret, only the dread awareness that I too possessed the power to kill, and a responsibility. My mother's words returned: *There was no going back, Anna.* We both chose – and maybe every choice leaves something behind that needs forgiving.

When I got to the back of the house, I was unprepared for what I saw: a denuded arbour. The trellis, stripped of all its orchids, framed the naked sky. Raw light streamed through, more hurtful to the eyes because I knew what was lost – Miss Gomez's prized orchids. The few potted plants that remained along the rim of the porch were starved of care. The violation filled me with sadness as I began my descent to the grotto. Day and Night raced through the space, chasing after scuttling leaves.

Laughter and clapping rose from the valley. The dogs scampered eagerly ahead. I followed, increasing my pace along the footpath. In no time, I was in view of the stream and, from where I stood, I could see that the clapping came from a squatting figure in a long-sleeved, oversized shirt, and wearing a wide-brimmed hat. I could not tell whether the clapper was a man or a woman, an adult or a child. Smoke intermittently streamed up above the person. The dogs paused briefly before they sped past the clapper to plunge into the stream, where they lapped thirstily. When I cleared the cluster of trees that shielded the deeper section of the grove, I saw that the clapping was accompaniment for a dancer who wore a tiered, two-tone skirt in brilliant red and sun-ripened gold. The tails of a cotton blouse were tied in a knot at her waist. Her loosened hair formed a wild puff of curls with a red hibiscus tucked in at one side. The dancer fanned her skirt vigorously as she moved amid the wreckage that was once Miss Gomez's grotto.

– What on earth happened here?

The young woman stopped her dancing and viewed me with the utmost defiance, as if I had intruded on something private. The clapper I could now see was an older woman, who must be Mama Gloria, heard but never really seen. She remained where she was, her skirt drawn tightly between her thighs, her feet bare. Her heavily bangled arms were the source of the music she made as she resumed her clapping, steadily, intently. I could have been invisible.

The dancer, whom I knew must be Maria, giggled and took her cue to resume the dance. She picked up her skirt and began her singing, moving now at a breathless pace in the clearing, circling the rim of the rubble:

– ...gría, alegría... nacio el Señor la-la el hombre ta-de-da-de-da-da... la Virgin María... es el niño... del Rey.

The missing words were inconsequential to the performance she gave. She allowed herself a brief interruption to retrieve a discarded bunch of flowers, then began again, making forward and backward steps, lifting the bouquet skywards as she did. I watched as she changed into a spinning motion, arms extended, flowers surrendered again to the floor. Streams of light broke through the tree cover and set her hair ablaze. The hollow was full of the sound of Maria's carefree parang and Mama Gloria's encouraging percussion, until a piercing *Ayeeeeeee!* brought all to a standstill and the dancer collapsed flat on her back, arms and legs spread like a star.

– I finish, Natu. I done-done!

She sighed loudly. My shock at the demolished grotto returned.

– What in heaven's name happened to the grotto?

– Mornin to you, Miss Anna.

The woman puffed contentedly at a pipe, but her eyes were sharp with disapproval.

– I'm sorry. Good morning. You must be Mama Gloria?

The woman nodded, as if in appreciation of my new approach.

– And our dancer is Maria.

An acknowledging *Ayeeeee* came from amidst the rubble.

– We glad you come.

– Happy to meet you both. I owe you a thank you.

Mama Gloria eyed me closely.

– No thanks needed. You had a bad-bad fever. I tend to you as I would anybody.

She focused her gaze on the rubble.

– Owners must be displease with Miss Gomez art. Make me remember how Joseph cut down all-dem trees up there.

I guessed she meant the empty stretch of land I had noticed on my way in.

– But why?

– When all that nastiness come to light about his own father, he lose he head for a time. Every day he come and cut down one-two trees until all gone.

– What on earth for?

– Vexation and grief – shame too – take him so he mash up what do him no harm at all.

She knocked ash from her pipe.

– You have to learn to walk light in this life, Miss Anna. Make friends with yuhself, with this earth, that river.

She puffed smoke into the air.

– One flow. Remember that.

I looked regretfully at the litter of rubble. She noticed.

– Who would have thought it necessary to destroy the grotto?

– Church-people. They making retreat house is what they say. Look like Miss Gomez vision didn't suit them. My story was in that work too.

She pointed to the remains of the pillars which had supported the grotto.

– Still, nothing too late in this life, Miss Anna. Look at Maria, how she blossoming like flower. She wanted to show off her talent – a little present for you to go back home with.

– Ayeeee!

Maria released her confirmation to the trees. The dogs took it as a signal to return to us. They sat close by, alert, taking in the scene.

– I see you bring my friends with you. We taking care of each other now. Life is a circle. We going round and climbing up same time. That is what Miss Ana always wanted – for me to care for Maria. Well, look how it come to pass. Nothing in this world can't heal – if we let it.

– Maybe you're right.

She sensed my scepticism.

– Yes, I right. Joseph De Valremy had his own foolish jealousy that keep him from doing right by Maria. We together now. So I glad you here with us, Miss Anna. You make a completion.

– What do you mean?

– Just what I say. You come to Macaima and help it heal lil' bit. You help Sam. I see with my own eyes she was born a miracle for this world. Maybe we in Macaima do something for you.

She exhaled a long trail of smoke.

– So walk good, Miss Anna. I have my pot to turn and Maria here promise to help me. She learning to care for herself. I not in this world forever.

Maria concurred.

– Yes, Mama!

I wasn't ready to say goodbye. There was so much more I wanted to say, to ask – about what I did not exactly know, only that my life gathered like a dam in my throat. Perhaps she saw exactly that.

– You know who was here just before you reach – Roland. He take the river trail back out.

– Roland was here?

– That is what I say. He had a message to leave for me. Come, give me your hand.

I obeyed as though in a trance.

– Sometimes knowing a wound is the beginning of a cure.

In a split second, steel sliced my palm. I had no chance to react. Blood filled the hairline wound.

– What the hell!

Fierce eyes mirrored mine. I recognised the knife. It had found its keeper.

– Remember that pain, Miss Anna. Feel it good. Know it. We have to forgive each other plenty in this world, but we have to demand more.

She walked into the rubble, looked at it with regret.

– This flesh we live in foolish, like caiman who mistake who he really is, when to satisfy hunger he try to steal from God. Wisdom is to know the difference.

– What difference?

– Knowing whether that god you steal from is really yours or belong to somebody else. Yours will remind you where you come from and who you are. That might feel like tough love, but it will feed you, bless you, allow you your power.

– And what if you prefer another story?

– Since you ask, you figure that one out, Miss Anna. But I tell you this much. You could make it light.

Maybe I had lost myself following the slow trail of blood that I let drip into Macaima's earth. Next thing I knew, Mama Gloria and Maria had left, taking Day and Night with them. I did not get a chance to say goodbye. *Dihana,* Roland had said, is never forever. *When I leave, I return* – my grandfather's version. I listened to the forest and heard the faint trail of the chorus Maria sang as the leaves stirred … *Alegría, alegría…* like the sweet singing of a flute…

CHAPTER 33 – THANKSGIVING

I didn't stay for Sam's baptism. At ten clock, I stood with my two bags on Beach Trace waiting for Neville and listening to the sea's fitful cadences. Someone had said goodbye: either the one who had chosen to stay behind on the shore or the one who had travelled across the sea. Did it matter? Macaima's lesson was that there are no real farewells.

In so many ways Macaima had come to be the light in my shadows. My mother had kept an important part of my life to herself. Maybe she did what she could, gave me what she could. She'd loved as she chose and I had lived clouded by her secret, though I had glimpsed something of what lay behind our lives on the day Mrs Henderson stormed out of the house and left the island. So much then was out of my reach and understanding; but I am here, and all of it will remain part of my story. That was acceptance enough, for now. Maybe one day I would need more. Maybe not. Then there was Thea. I had not responded to her efforts to reconnect. I was more my mother's daughter than I realised. I, too, did not want to risk a disruption. My thoughts churned on. I did not notice the car's approach.

– Look how we meet up again, Miss!

Neville beamed with the same good-natured disposition I encountered on our first meeting. He energetically piled my luggage into the trunk and hopped into the driver's seat. I settled into the backseat with Miss Gomez's gift at my side. The orchid's time for blossoming had passed, but there would be a new season.

– So how yuh enjoy country life? Nice ent?

– Interesting is the best word for it, Neville.

– What kinda word is that!

He grinned and bounced the starter, manoeuvring the car

slowly up the uneven terrain of Beach Trace. I glanced back at the trace, the house and the derelict church. Fresh flowers had been placed by the statue of the Madonna. I wondered whether Maria or Mama Gloria – or both – had paid her a visit. A heavy sigh escaped me that caught Neville's attention. He viewed me with open curiosity through the rearview mirror.

– Miss, like Macaima give you more than yuh bring to carry home.

I had no answer for him. I thought of Maria's elated parang, her joyful dance amid the rubble of the grotto Miss Gomez had created. That structure had been *her* response to whatever pain she had honed into a faith she felt could contain who she was and how she saw her place in the world. She had run her own race. Moreover, she had made a way for Sam. The children I had seen practising for their relay race in the school yard came back to me. Each ran a leg, passing on the baton to the waiting runner. Maybe that was the real measure of fullness, the collective running to the finish. What had I done?

When the car reached the intersection to the main road, I saw that a few people were already milling around the site of the church. Under the tarpaulin tent, chairs were arranged on the newly-cast foundations. I retrieved the slip of paper with my contact information from my bag and I asked Neville to stop the car.

– Give me a minute.

– No problem, but I have to make tracks – wedding this evening.

Lucille saw my approach and came over to hug me.

– So yuh leaving we already, Miss Bri.

She rocked me in a firm embrace.

– Yes, time to go, Lucille.

– Well, walk good but doh forget us inside here. Come any time. You have place to stay. I not going nowhere!

– Thank you. I will.

Lennox was standing nearby, an arm wrapped about Rosa's shoulders. She released herself to offer her farewell.

– Ayi chica, bye-bye. Cuídate, caio!

She pressed a cheek against each of mine and was about to retreat to Lennox's side when Lucille intercepted her.

– What happen, girl, how you lean-up on this man so? We have sweetbread and cake to slice. Juice to pour and a little spirits to sample on d-side.

She winked at me and blew a parting kiss as she hustled Rosa off in the direction of the group of women who were busy organising the eats for sharing after the service. Lucille's theatrics caught Sam's attention. She was dressed in white, her head tied with a scarf and seated almost in the centre of the space. She waved and was about to leave her seat to meet me half way when Franco gestured that she should stay where she was. He moved over to join her. Perhaps it was required that she be apart before the initiation service began. I did not know the protocol. Even from where I stood at the entrance of the tent, I could see that the table at the front was richly decorated with flowers, fruits, food of all kinds: brightly iced cakes and coloured sweets, breads, pawpaws, hands of ripe bananas, bunches of coconuts, yams, honey – everything the land had either yielded or the villagers had made – a tangible defiance of the ongoing destruction of the land.

A man I had never seen before joined them. His head was clean shaven and he looked smart in his tanned cotton pants and matching shirt. Franco spoke a few words to him. Sam rose and he patted her on the shoulder. Lennox, though, cleared his throat and grumbled.

– De Valremy brave to show he face in here.
– Is that Thomas?
– Yep – one-an-only.
– How come he's at the service?
– I hear he give money for Sam plane ticket, so maybe he is godfather.

I didn't know what to say. Maybe Lennox was joking. Neville tooted. Time was running out. Franco walked up the centre aisle, nodded stiffly at me before he moved out into the open yard. I didn't bother to figure his mood. De Valremy said something to Sam before leaving the tent. He walked past our group without so much as a nod to stand with Franco. I continued to Sam's seat.

– I've come to say goodbye.

She hung her head.

– Sorry I can't stay for the service.

– Is okay.

Her response was abrupt, curt. Her mind was elsewhere.

– Granny in hospital two days now.

She dropped her chin deeper onto her chest.

– I'm sorry, Sam. I didn't know. She'll be better soon, I'm sure.

Her entire demeanour was disconsolate.

– I have to go, but here's my address. Write and let me know how you're doing over there. I would love to hear from you.

Her eyes brightened.

– Thanks, Miss Anna. I glad for it.

– You'll do great, Sam. You're strong.

Her brows knitted a little incredulously. Neville honked again.

– Write me, okay?

She nodded and formed her arms into a muscled pose that drew a smile from me. A woman came up, maybe an elder of the church, and indicated to Sam to come with her.

– I have to go now. Take good care of yourself.

She was led away by two women to a curtained area behind the altar. I watched the sky-blue drapes settle to an undisturbed stillness, like a closed door.

Franco was waiting for me to emerge from the tent. I had not spoken to him for weeks. He held himself aloof, his hands thrust into his pockets, intensifying the feeling in me that he had become once again a stranger.

– So Miss Bri, yuh leaving Macaima for good?

– I wouldn't exactly put it that way.

He cleared his throat and sank his weight onto the back of his heels.

– I glad I see you today. I have something I want you to pass on to Roland.

– He's not going to be at Sam's thanksgiving?

– He say his goodbyes already. Mama Gloria holding protest in town tomorrow morning. He gone to make sure she doh get in too much trouble. There was laughter in his voice.

– A protest?

– Yes, she there with her people. They say is time to move Columbus from Port of Spain, so they petitioning for the authorities to meet with dey demands.

– Demands.

– Yes, to put up Mai instead.

– Mai – La Divina?

– Yes, she belong to this whole place. But that is another matter. Just give Roland this for me. I know he will find you when he ready.

He handed over the instrument.

– His flute! Where did you find it?

The flute was cool and smooth in my hand. Made from the deer's tibia, I remembered.

– He would be glad to know he didn't lose it permanent.

– Yes, he would, but you should return it to him yourself, since you found it,

– Maybe the man looking for a reason to meet up with you.

He eyed me, I thought, a little teasingly. I did not quite buy his suggestion, given all that had passed between us, but it was odd that Roland had tried to give me the knife, and now this. I thought it best to brush it all aside as Macaima banter. With Corporal Luke dead and Mason in remand yard, the whole Mountain Road fiasco, including Marie's death, seemed to have gone underground, and both Roland and Franco being in different ways involved, I didn't want to get further entangled.

– I think it best that you hand it to him in person.

– No problem, Miss Bri. I will do that, but you have to trust somebody.

He dug his heels into the soft earth.

– Anyhow, I glad to see that you take such an interest in how Sam going. No disrespect, but plenty good people looking out for her now.

I supposed that group now included Thomas De Valremy.

– I'm not sure I get your meaning, Franco.

– Is no more meaning than what I say.

He glanced over at the tent.

– Sam going to make Macaima proud.

He drew up his chest.

– I am sure she'll do great, Franco, and I, too, wish her well.

He nodded an affirmation and I felt we were again in a good place until he started up about Danny.

– So you see how Danny stepping up. Elton daughter lucky to catch him. Wedding is Easter.

– Nice to hear.

– Yes, so it should be. So when you reach back Port of Spain, my advice is that you find…

Lucille butted in just then.

– What foolish talk this man hold you in? Franco, Miss Bri car waiting, and since when you turn advisory board to Miss Anna. Doh take he on, lover. He vex with he own self and looking for company. Not so, Mr Executioner?

It was the first time I had heard the nickname, possibly one of the aliases the village had given him. I could guess its origin.

He scoffed and stepped aside.

– You have to learn to handle yuh business.

We hugged for the last time. Lucille was first to break free.

– Okay time to go, Miss Lady. Tell that driver Lucille say drive you safe back home.

She ushered me past Franco and released me to the road with the word *home*. Neville had opened the back door in anticipation of my return. I pushed it shut and settled into the passenger seat.

– I ready now, Neville.

The car eased off. The bucket orchid bobbed in the back seat.

CHAPTER 34: BEGINNING, AGAIN

Before I knew it, 1970 had come. People walked about the streets like trees, their heads touching the sky. Thunder rolled in their throats. Florence, my neighbour, for the past six years, Miss Fas'ness personified, according to Thea, asked the same question whenever she passed by our place: *How yuh story going?* She had somewhere heard that I was writing on the side. I responded the same way every time: *It coming along.* And she would routinely answer, punctuated by her Anancy grin: *Well, move it right along, mih dear, move it along.* In truth, plenty was happening, but I kept developments to myself, only bouncing a few ideas off Thea when I felt I needed another perspective, though she never wanted to meddle too much in my decisions. The story had in fact decided on its own way and I let it go how it wanted to go, beginning from that first Sunday in '63 when I landed up on Macaima junction. All I knew at that moment was that I wasn't there to stay. I was in search of a beginning and discovered that my part in all that happened in those few months was to tell Macaima's story that had somehow ended up being my own. So I start right there on that midday junction. The rest followed from that spot.

There is no wrong in saying that I was the one who had brought the hurricane in my suitcase that September, although I know that is too much responsibility for one person to carry. Macaima was a storm waiting to happen. In that post office, people found a place to put down their pain and talk their concerns. Maybe people trusted that whatever they said there would be sealed up and sent off to a far-far place. Between the purchase of stamps, sealing of envelopes and collecting of mail, news breezes through a post office. Stories want to be told – and they find their way to a hearing, a life, in whatever way they choose. I don't claim anything more than that I've tried to live through to an understanding of what makes a life whole – but that is no claim. People have to find their own way.

I found something in Macaima – my purpose for being in this world, and that was what gave me the strength to let that Henderson yard go and to let my mother have whatever life she chose and is still choosing. Up to this day, she's still *up in England* although Mr Henderson passed, along with the three months she said she was going to stay for. I listen. I hear contentment in her voice and I could only laugh at how quick she make steps to fix up her business and find a way to stay on working as a nanny. What I could say? We have matters to settle but I realise she always chose her life. Now is my turn. That is how I see it. I have this story to tell and it will find its beginning and end. So when she asks what I'm doing, I tell her I am spending Mr Henderson's money on my writing. For some reason that makes her laugh out loud. What I make for myself filing papers in the Government Registry is what I live on, but every page I write on, every ribbon I buy for my typewriter, every pen and pencil is funded by Mr Henderson's money. That means something to me I can't fully explain, only that I believe I am word by word writing my way out of his yard and that 2000 pounds is my due reparations. Thea thinks I have a tyrannical streak, but tyranny is no friend of freedom, and that is what I am working on – my freedom. I can't do that for anyone else, not even my mother who is happy to say she minding English people children and cooking home-food for them. She sounds triumphant. That is not my path. My life is this book that I choose to write, and with every day that passes I am saying goodbye to the shadow that was my father. Everyday I am more willing to laugh with less inhibition at my mother's new exploits – like the cooking classes she tells me she is giving to the mothers of her charges. Maybe that is forgiveness.

I never went back to Macaima but the place stayed with me, and that faithfulness is what I sometimes feel I have most betrayed. I got much more than I had bargained for. Macaima was a beginning and end that I had to face. I was never a talker and people could vouch for that. Centre stage is not my place, but the mysterious woman I had met on Beach Trace put her story in my way. She had chosen me, a stranger, to be the teller of a story that was more than hers. *Dihana.* Someone had bid her farewell; but even when you leave, you return. Goodbye Bay, in a sense, is the story of the one who had stayed, and if her story remains incomplete, like Marie's, perhaps that is why it will not be forgotten and it will carry on past mere survival to where justice resides. I had seen Maria step into her new day at Miss Gomez's ruined grotto. Light, motion – her signature was written that morning on those hills that had broken her. Yes, things have a way of working out, but that is no cure for every wrong. Justice is a necessary action, like making peace. Mama Gloria put a scar on my hand so I would remember my wound and my woundings, and every Maria's. *Dihana.* Is it really a word? Does asking matter as much as the story it carries or is made to carry?

In the meantime, stories arrive on currents that keep their own time. I heard from Lucille that Maria had healed enough to find love and have a daughter that she named Ana, and that Mama Gloria was busy passing on her knowledge before her time came to cross over. Franco, though, withdrew to a remote part of what was left of L'Avenir, somewhere beyond where the road project came to an unceremonious halt and was awaiting the promised second tranche of funding. The story reached me, too, that one day, after drinking at Johnny's, he walked into the police station to inform the officers that he had slit Corporal Luke's throat on his hospital bed. Nobody believed him. Not even Mason who was still awaiting trial. Roland, though, had shared that his father's knife and flute had gone missing the very night of the murder. Who is to say? After his *confession* Franco never came down to the village again, not until his passing, when Danny strapped his body on the back of his own mule and brought him out.

I wasn't able to ever verify, but I heard after the fact, that on *storm day*, the riptide had reversed its flow and the same Waraos that walked into sea way back when, stepped ashore to keep an appointment with something unfinished, a circle left unclosed. Talk said that they had a mission: to give instruction to the Nation to move Columbus right out of Port of Spain. That was the root of the protest Mama Gloria had set out to hold on the same Sunday of Sam's thanksgiving, and that the Nation still holding up to this day, so people will hear and demand that the so-called *Discoverer* be put elsewhere.

Another story made the rounds about a fisherman named Sharky who had gone to Goodbye, the same night that Flora hit Tobago, to make sure his boat, *Serenity*, was safe. That was when he saw something like a colony of caimans riding the waves and when they reached the beach – and this he swore to on his mother's grave – when they landed, they walked upright like people. Well, who didn't laugh said Sharky was dreaming because what he saw was driftwood – nothing more. When the Orinoco was in flood, all manner of things, living and dead, crossed the channel, caimans included. That was how Macaima got its name in the first place. Crocodile, caiman, alligator – every last one is master of the water and a shapeshifter. Who's to legislate on what-an-what really happened. I just gathered up everything like clothes off a line to make my notes into turn and turn pages.

When I think about Beach Trace, I remember first the woman, whoever or whatever she was, that spoke my name. She pointed me to discover that Macaima is who I am and all that I will ever have to tell between here and whatever is eternity. So you could say that my story had reached a manner of end when I left. I remember Goodbye Bay like yesterday. It was the first thing I saw when I woke up on mornings. I would look out at the bay that broke through every space in the trees. That time was my church. I watched the sun wake up from somewhere I couldn't see. I saw morning come to life, slow and easy, taking whatever time it needed to tell that story. I watched the day yawn and stretch out along the full expanse of the sky, for as far as I could see, showing off her colours, like a bale of cloth somebody unfurled to break up the darkness.

Time flies, but what stays is something more enduring. Sometimes the very face that you choose to hide away is the very one that can save you – can make you see that another tomorrow is possible. I call that face *Brite*, and I saw her when I wasn't sure on what side of the grave I was standing. She was a beginning word that I had to face and let go. My mother had said, when she knew that I was with her, there was no turning back. She had no regrets. What I do regret is that I was unready to meet something of my own. You could say that I was unready for myself. Never again – if that is contrition. I would say that was the lesson I carried from my stay in Macaima. For that I have no regrets. Whether or not the lesson really took hold is another matter. And maybe I disappointed the place. Sometimes I feel that way. I gave it back what I could. Maybe someone else could take the story further than I could tell it. Maybe they already have. I do know that I don't want to explain anything or worse explain myself. Explanation only kills a story. I wanted simply to tell what happened – the way I saw it, and lived it, in my time, which is revelation enough.

If there is more to say, *that* I will have to discover. Some things I keep in reserve, like how I took two whole years to answer Thea's postcards. There's really nothing to tell. When I finally wrote, it was two words: *I here.* And she echoed. It took me right back to that white envelope Sam delivered to me, and I have to smile my thanks for the journey that unravelled. It took me years to realise that the empty space in the middle of her letter was mine to fill in. Not just for me, but for Maria, Marie, Ana, Brenda, Eunice, Sam, as far back as they go, and maybe for those that are here with us now. Strange to find that your whole life circles back to a storm that happened some place else.

I had heard from Sam almost every month since her return to the States. Details about the Campbells, school, moments of doubt, her *talks* with counsellors. I figured no news was good news. She had settled in and moved on. Good. In the years that followed, letters, when they began arriving again, did so at sporadic intervals. They were mostly two-pagers that read like bursts of carefree greetings and bullet points jotted in between moments of pause in her full life. I was happy for her. She was past her decision about her surgery, though she never said more. I never asked. It didn't matter. She was busy making friends and going great at school. Then the letters stopped.

1970 came. The streets were shouting *Power!* A fight for life was going on and I found myself on Independence Square, watching the marching and holding Sam's latest letter in my hand like a truth I couldn't believe. After years of no word, she was coming home. In her own words, *a big woman, almost,* and thinking about going to some fancy university to study her music. She was coming home, she and her friend, Alex, an aspiring jazz pianist and singer, who she prattled on so much about, even I had to blush. I held on to her letter because Sam had given me a line that said all that she didn't spell out: *Miss Anna*, she wrote, *you always told me that I'm brave; but I am learning that every real living must be brave*. There was no doubt – she was ready for the world.

And I was there, in the current of this massive force of people, the ground under my feet charged with the presence of marchers pushing back on injustice, pounding the streets, rocking buildings and shattering the sky, and asking me why I was on the pavement just looking. And in the middle of all this, with all this crisscrossing in my brain, and people shouting at the tops of their lungs for a new independence, I heard again Brenda's voice, the one that interrupted the Women's Coalition meeting at Johnny's shop, shouting *No!* And just so, my name arrived to meet me from that sea of bodies.

– Miss Anna, that is you?

Standing in front of me was Lucille and behind her, like a constellation, was Brenda and the same Paul she had left behind in Macaima. Patrick was with them, now grown into a young man. Two friends marched with him. Roland, too, was there, with his new lady, Gail. Lucille, though, was the one who broke the spell of our chance encounter.

– So what is this I hear, Miss Anna – you turn writer?

– You could say that.

The answer came without hesitation.

– So why you on that pavement looking like empty bookshelf? Come here, inside the moment, and live like this fight done win already. We is power today!

Lucille bellowed above the thunder. She didn't wait for me to respond but came up and pulled me into the street, linking my arm with hers.

Roland followed her lead.

– Come on, Miss Anna. Dog Star day – remember. Full exposure!

So I joined the march with the people from Goodbye Bay.

Macaima had come to meet me again. I marched and heard my own voice. I marched and sang: *We shall overcome… one daa-ay-…*

The voice over the megaphone was drawing the marchers on. Thea and her gift for finding herself front and centre of all that needed fighting for – who, I knew, had been working for and waiting for this day. In the midst of the marchers, I realised better that we had understood too narrowly the assertion that the land was ours, which we had made way back at the April march in 1960, and that we had passed too quickly over our anthem's claim of an equal place. Ownership was never the issue. Macaima's story of that runaway tribe who had once lived freely between the island and the continent began what should be the real question: What really was home? We were thinking, and maybe still do, mechanically about flags, constitutions, borders. Even Thea with her admiration for the Federation had never really asked that broader question. There was much more to fight for. Ana, Maria, Marie, Sam, the very land. My singing, all of us singing: *We shall over come one day…* and marching on. And yet in the incompleteness of everything, I felt I was home, with my hair loosed to a dancing planet, the all of who I was in that moving body. And inside me was the beginning of another story that was saying YES to this place and to all its beauty and contradictions. Singing… *I do believe…* like a creed.

That day was joy enough…

ABOUT THE AUTHOR

Jennifer Rahim was an award winning Trinidadian writer of poetry, fiction and literary criticism. Her books of fiction include *Curfew Chronicles: A Fiction* (2017), and *Songster and Other Stories* (2007). She wrote several poetry collections. *Approaching Sabbaths* (2009) was awarded a Casa de las Américas Prize in 2010. *Redemption Rain: Poems* was published in 2011 and *Ground Level: Poems* in 2014. *Sanctuaries of Invention* (2021) was her latest poetry collection.

Jennifer Rahim's poems appeared in several Caribbean and international journals and anthologies, including *The Caribbean Writer*, *Small Axe*, *The Trinidad and Tobago Review*, The *Graham House Review*, *Mangrove*, *The Malahat Review*, *Crossing Water*, *Creation Fire*, *The Sisters of Caliban*, *Crab Orchard Review*, *Atlanta Review* and *The Guardian* (UK). Her short stories have appeared in *The New Voices*, *The Caribbean Writer* and *Caribbean Voices I*.

Awards include The Gulf Insurance Writers Scholarship (1996) to attend the Caribbean Writers Summer Institute, Univ. of Miami; The New Voices Award of Merit (1993) for outstanding contributions to *The New Voices* journal; The Writers Union of Trinidad and Tobago Writer of the Year Award (1992) for the publication, *Mothers Are Not The Only Linguists*; the Casa de las Américas Prize 2010, where the jury said *Approaching Sabbaths* "captures a sense of the complexities of historical, social and cultural aspects of contemporary Caribbean"; and the 2018 OCM BOCAS prize for Caribbean Literature for *Curfew Chronicles*, which Lorna Goodison described as "one of the most ambitious books ever attempted by a Caribbean writer. The philosophical, moral and religious themes and ideas put forward about community in all its many manifestations are lightly, deftly handled… Readers are rewarded by moments of sheer grace; and numinous revelations at every turn".

Jennifer Rahim died suddenly and unexpectedly on March 13 2023 at the too young age of sixty.

ALSO BY JENNIFER RAHIM

Songster and Other Stories
ISBN: 9781845230487; pp. 145; pub. 2007; £8.99

Rahim's stories move between the present and the past to make sense of the tensions between image and reality in contemporary Trinidad. The contemporary stories show the traditional, communal world in retreat before the forces of local and global capitalism.

A popular local fisherman is gunned down when he challenges the closure of the beach for a private club catering to white visitors and the new elite; the internet becomes a rare safe place for an AIDS sufferer to articulate her pain; cocaine has become the scourge even of the rural communities. But the stories set thirty years earlier in the narrating 'I's' childhood reveal that the 'old-time' Trinidad was already breaking up. The old pieties about nature symbolised by belief in the presence of the folk-figure of 'Papa Bois' are powerless to prevent the ruthless plunder of the forests; communal stability has already been uprooted by the pulls towards emigration, and any sense that Trinidad was ever edenic is undermined by images of the destructive power of alcohol and the casual presence of paedophilic sexual abuse.

Rahim's Trinidad, is though, as her final story makes clear, the creation of a writer who has chosen to stay, and she is highly conscious that her perspective is very different from those who have taken home away in a suitcase, or who visit once a year. Her Trinidad is 'not a world in my head like a fantasy', but the island that 'lives and moves in the bloodstream'. Her reflection on the nature of small island life is as fierce and perceptive as Jamaica Kincaid's *A Small Place*, but comes from and arrives at a quite opposite place. What Rahim finds in her island is a certain existential insouciance and the capacity of its people, whatever their material circumstance, to commit to life in the knowledge of its bitter-sweetness.

Curfew Chronicles
ISBN: 9781845233624; pp. 208; pub. 2017; £9.99
Winner of the 2018 OCM Bocas Prize

In 2011, the Trinidad government declared a state of emergency and an overnight curfew. The SoE, brought in to combat the crime and killings associated with the drugs trade, was meant to last 15 days but lasted four months. This is the background to these chronicles, but not their substance. They are an imaginative response to the undertones of those days. Taking place over 24 hours, *Curfew Chronicles* brings together, like a Joyce's *Ulysses* in miniature, the lives of two dozen characters (including a father and son searching for each other) whose lives intersect in mostly fortuitous but sometimes quite deliberate ways.

From the Minister and his wife, to those targeted by the state; from those in regular jobs, to those who scuffle for a living on or over the edge of the law; from those who speak out, to the hidden hands prepared to silence them: no one is unaffected by the SoE. What makes these stories individually rich (as well as collectively ingenious) is the depth of characterisation. There is Scholar the streetcorner prophet, Ragga with his vision of better days, Keeper tempted into crime to the distress of his redoubtable partner Maureen, Sumintra, the Pentecostal convert struck dumb in prayer, Marcus the assassin whose life is a movie, Amber the security guard and poet and her policeman lover Calvin, eager to retire from clearing up little matters like the "weed" found in the PM's residence, and many more. Each has a resonant backstory; each is caught at a moment of decision or revelation. As these characters criss-cross Trinidad, Rahim builds an unforgettable world of people in a vividly realised landscape.

"This must surely rank as one of the most ambitious books ever attempted by a Caribbean writer. The philosophical, moral and religious themes and ideas put forward about community in all its many manifestations are lightly, deftly handled... Readers are rewarded by moments of sheer grace; and numinous revelations at every turn," Lorna Goodison, chief judge of the 2018 OCM Bocas Prize For Caribbean Literature.

Between the Fence and the Forest
ISBN: 9781900715270; pp. 88; pub. 2007; £7.99

Comparing herself to a douen, a mythical being from the Trinidadian forests whose head and feet face in different directions, Jennifer Rahim's poems explore states of uncertainty both as sources of discomfort and of creative possibility.

The poems explore a Trinidad finely balanced between the forces of rapid urbanisation and the constantly encroaching green chaos of tropical bush, whose turbulence regularly threatens a fragile social order, and whose people, as the descendants of slaves and indentured labourers, are acutely resistant to any threat to clip their wings and fence them in.

In her own life, Rahim explores the contrary urges to a neat security and to an unfettered sense of freedom and her attraction to the forest 'where tallness is not the neighbour's fences/ and bigness is not the swollen houses/ that swallow us all'. It is, though, a place where the bushplanter 'seeing me grow branches/ draws out his cutting steel and slashes my feet/ since girls can never become trees'.

Approaching Sabbaths
9781845231156; pp. 132; pub. 2009; £8.99

Jennifer Rahim's poems move seamlessly between the inwardly confessional, an acute sensitivity to the distinctive subjectivities of an immediate circle of family, friends and neighbours, and a powerful sense of Trinidadian place and history. Few have written more movingly or perceptively of what can vex the relationship between daughters and mothers, or with such a mixture of compassion and baffled rage about a daughter's relationship to her father. If Sylvia Plath comes to mind, acknowledged in the poem 'Lady Lazarus in the Sun', the comparison does Rahim no disfavours; Rahim's voice and world is entirely her own. There is in her work a near perfect balance between the disciplined craft of the poems, and their capacity to deal with the most traumatic of experiences in a cool, reflective way. Equally, she has the capacity to make of the ordinary something special and memorable.

Here is no self-indulgent misery memoir, not least in its compassion for and involvement with other lives. The threat and reality of fragmentation – of psyche's, of lives, of a nation – is ever present, but the shape and order of the poems provide a saving frame of wholeness. Poem after poem offers phrases of a satisfying weight and appositeness, like the description of the killers of a boy as 'mere children,/ but twisted like neglected fields of cane'.

Winner of a Casa de las Américas Prize 2010 – one of Latin America's oldest and most prestigious literary awards. The jury said the collection "captures a sense of the complexities of historical, social and cultural aspects of contemporary Caribbean".

Ground Level
ISBN: 9781845232054; pp. 100; pub. 2014; £8.99

In 2011 the Government of Trinidad & Tobago declared a state of emergency to counter the violent crime associated with the drugs trade. *Ground Level* confronts the roots of the madness and chaos seething under the surface of this "crude season of curfew from ourselves" when the state becomes a jail. For Rahim, her country is a place where "No-one hears the measure of shadow in any rhythm", a place where "poets hurt enough to die".

In this dread season, Rahim finds hope and consolation in the word and in those places where it is possible to find salvation in "this landscape of ever-opening doorways", such as Grand Riviere, the subject of a long, twelve-part reflection on the values that can still be found in rural Trinidad. Elsewhere she engages in dialogue with those writers who confronted the Janus face of Caribbean creativity and nihilism: writers such as Earl Lovelace, Eric Roach, Victor Questel, Derek Walcott, Kamau Brathwaite and Martin Carter, praying of the last "let his words drop on the conscience of a nation". Alluding to the late Jamaican poet Anthony McNeill, she confides that "The Ungod of things has not changed".

This is an ambitious collection that speaks in both a prophetic and a literary, intertextual voice, which combines the personal and the public in mutually enriching ways; it shows the assurance of a poet who has constantly worked at her craft, but who also takes formal risks to capture the reality of desperate times.

Sanctuaries of Invention
ISBN: 9781845234539; pp. 80; pub. 2021; £9.99

In her sixth collection of poems, Jennifer Rahim explores the power of the imagination to confront the restrictions of the year of the pandemic through reflections on history and the capacity of language to give immediacy and presence to absent place.

In the year of Covid-19, lockdowns, and in Trinidad a state of emergency, it's not surprising that thoughts turn to the nature of time, place and the not quite accidental arrival of pandemics of mass death. For Jennifer Rahim, time is both the history that has shaped the present and the now of social and geographic constriction. At the beginning of the collection, "A Tale of the Orbis Spike, 1610" (the recorded dip in carbon dioxide levels when around fifty million native peoples of the New World were exterminated as the result of European settler invasion), reminds that pandemics have their own history, though never without human triggers. At the end of the collection, "No /Language is a Virus" records the viral power of language for both good and ill, the latter not least in the era of Trump and the resurgence of racist white nationalism in Trinidad's big neighbour to the north. But Rahim also reminds us how much solace we have derived from poetry this last year, because "Words fly the grave, steal/ the only thunder a virus can claim,/ and, alive,/ witness to goodness that quietly thrives."

Between those two points, the collection expands out of the restrictions of home, that place where "We're strategizing for survival/ strip-searching every sneeze/ for an invisible assassin suited in capsid" – though sanctuaries of invention can be found in the smallest spaces – to map the wider worlds of memory and desire – in a vivid series of poems ("mapping home") that chart journeys from Valencia, through Salybia, Balandra, Rampanalgas, Cumana, Toco and L'Anse Noir – places that Rahim's poems bring to sensuous geographic, human and historical life that make you want to visit, but hold back in case you might spoil them.

With the celebration of heroes who range from the fighting women of Greek myth, to poetic inspirations from Marianne Moore to Eric Roach, Jennifer Rahim urges that "Hope/ must always be bold/ and sharpened for tomorrows".